THE OLD TICKET OFFICE DARLING ISLAND

POLLY BABBINGTON

POLLY

PollyBabbington.com

Want more from Polly's world?

For sneak peeks into new settings, early chapters, downloadable Pretty Beach and Darling Island freebies and bits and bobs from Polly's writing days sign up for Babbington Letters.

1

It had been an early start for Emmy Bardot. She'd arrived for work at the port before sunrise, and it had taken her a couple of cups of coffee before she was on the ball. Standing in the middle of the concourse, she was now very much on the ball, overseeing the safe and swift cruise ship check-in area. As she stood in her uniform, observing what had been her place of work for many years, she twiddled her Grandma Emily's ring on the pinkie finger of her right hand and analysed the reams of people getting ready to board the liner that would take them off to lovely climes. Even after years of working and watching, she was always amazed by people's behaviour; how they dressed, how they conducted themselves, how they spoke, and how they navigated their way through travelling the globe.

People were all part of Emmy's day, and over the years, she'd become well-versed in what people would present which problems. She could sum up a person by their exterior presentation to the world to a tee. She was an expert in evaluating people in a split second as they travelled through the waiting area to board. In her little world, these people fell into different categories. There were those with so much money that they seemed aloof, as if they inhabited a different planet from everyone else. These people didn't care how they looked. They would turn up with too much luggage, appearing as if they'd hurriedly got dressed from a bin – a creased linen blazer over stained pink trousers – and the cases they pulled would be worth more than other people's cars. They'd be on a cruise because it had been gifted to them, and more often than not, they really would like to be somewhere else.

In stark contrast were those who flaunted diamonds and gadgets, and whose shoe labels told you where they liked to shop. These people would be coiffed and primped and would not have a hair out of place. You would be able to smell these people at twenty paces. Their passport covers would coordinate with their shiny, top-of-the-range bags. They'd have very good jobs, a couple of nicely educated but usually sulky teenagers in tow, and live in a four-bedroom house with a detached electric-door two-car garage. Most of the time, these people knew how to behave.

Sitting underneath those with the labelled trainers were those with the pre-holiday spray tans and bright pink florals. Too-tight, too-short shorts, flip-flops, and boob tubes were at the fore, and they were normally surrounded by a fair bit of noise. These people would have supermarket bags stuffed to the brim, prohibited oversized bottles of alcohol, and gigantic, slightly grubby, brightly coloured luggage. Perhaps the odd toddler in a pram. They thought nothing of dirty shoes on seats, pillows around their necks, saggy jeans, eating whilst waiting to board, and slouching in a slop.

All of this swirled around Emmy as she circled the waiting area, trying to pre-empt problems. From her left shoulder, her radio beeped. She listened as Ian in the control room informed her a woman had left her phone in the toilet, a child had fallen out of a buggy, and the mother was worried about the child's head. Emmy tapped her work mobile and sent a text to Kelly, head of cleaning, to retrieve the phone. She then adopted her usual work pose as she spied a woman making a beeline for her. Emmy's stance had developed slowly but surely over the years and was initially learnt from her boss, Judy, who herself had honed it over time. Emmy's pose was just right; it suggested, 'I'm friendly enough to help you should you need it, but I'm important enough for you not to be rude.' Her feet were clad in low leather heels and placed tightly together, her legs ensconced in very fine support denier with a subtle sheen, her uniform pressed to within an inch of its life, her head – with its perfectly neat French pleat – was straight, and her hands were clasped together in front of her. A friendly yet professional smile was permanently etched on the front of her face.

'Excuse me!' a woman in skin-tight leopard-print workout leggings shrieked. 'I'm in a premium-budget stateroom! I shouldn't have to queue. This is ridiculous! Absolutely ridiculous!' The woman gestured wildly at another check-in area. 'How come they get to stroll straight in? I paid extra for this. Can't you people get anything right? If I did my job like this, I'd be sacked.' The woman's eyebrows were very thin and very high, her lips pursed, and she looked at Emmy as if she was stupid. 'As I said, ridiculous! I ask you!'

Emmy shuddered inside and touched the daisy bracelet on her left arm, unseen under her jacket. She'd seen it all before. It was all just so predictable. The leggings, the on-trend trainers with the obnoxious cheap gold logo, and the slight spot of lipstick on the teeth. 'Good morning, madam. Just join line three over there,' Emmy said in a friendly, confident, but tightly closed manner. 'It shouldn't be too long.'

The woman shook her head. Her long, dangly, gaudy earrings jangling. If there was one thing Emmy knew, it was jewellery. The earrings were not nice. 'No, no, as I said. I'm in premium. Did you not hear me?'

Emmy stopped herself from rolling her eyes to the back of

her head. The whole of the boarding area was in no doubt that the woman wasn't happy about having to queue or that she was in premium. Emmy also knew precisely what ticket the woman held just by the way the woman was dressed. But she'd learnt very early on, just as she'd learnt how to stand, that this woman wanted to be in the royal suite queue without actually paying royal suite prices. Emmy and her boss, Judy, had a well-practised scenario for this type of customer. It was quick, easy, and usually worked like a dream. If you pretended to check the ticket for one prompt second, the customer would be placated. Emmy engaged her best customer service face and topped it with a beam. 'Could I just check your ticket, please? Thanks.'

The woman looked exceptionally pleased with herself, as if she knew she was right all along. She turned her phone around, holding it way too close to Emmy's face. 'See. Budget. Premium. Stateroom. How hard is it to get that wrong?'

Emmy pretended to look closely at the phone for clarification. She then pointed to the overhead sign. 'Yes, you're just over there in that queue. It shouldn't take too long.'

'You're joking, aren't you?' The woman almost spat. The earrings took on a life of their own.

Emmy proffered her well-practised, patient smile. 'No, I'm not.' She pointed up at the sign again. 'You see the triangle? Just follow that. It makes it quite easy. It will be the same when you board, too, and for most things on board.'

The woman frowned and jerked her thumb towards a roped-off area and a gate with no queue. 'What are they doing there, then?'

Emmy pretended she didn't know what the woman meant. 'Sorry?'

The woman was exasperated. 'What part of that don't you understand? What sign do *they* follow?'

Emmy took a long inhale through her nose. She really wasn't in the mood for a champagne-taste-beer-money customer, as

Judy called them, but she didn't show it. She'd been doing the job for a long time. She was always the epitome of professionalism. She ignored the woman's question and instead gestured to the queue and told a little white lie. 'The premium stateroom area has extra staff at that check-in desk.' She smiled widely. 'And, of course, bubbles when you get through.' Emmy knew the mention of free alcohol would placate the woman. She didn't add that the bubbles were actually sparkling budget white wine shipped in from a gigantic warehouse in bulk.

The animal-print-clad woman looked appeased at the mention of the bubbles, but she still tutted and shook her head so that her earrings danced around manically on either side of her head. 'It's still not really good enough. At the price I've paid, I don't expect to have to line up anywhere at all. You know? I mean, the word premium itself surely explains it. Does it not?'

Emmy chuckled to herself. The woman had basically paid for a few more centimetres in her room, a glass of sparkling wine on check-in, a tiny table on her balcony, and complimentary water in the fridge. 'You'll be checked in and settled with a drink in no time.'

As she watched the woman with her slightly stained, bright pink gigantic suitcase huff over to the queue, Emmy counted down the hours until her shift would finish. She had a lot to do for the rest of the day, including driving over to Darling Island to collect a birthday cake for her son, Callum, cleaning the house from top to bottom because it wasn't going to clean itself, and dropping her car in for a service before the garage closed. She watched as the woman stood in animated conversation with another identically dressed woman behind her in the queue, where they shook their heads in disgust at the roped-off area. Emmy looked over towards the doors and hoped that everyone would board quickly. The fewer customer problems she had that morning, the better.

Four or so hours later, Emmy was in her car, pulling out of the staff car park and indicating to go around the roundabout and get onto the dual-carriageway to go and collect a birthday cake for her son from Darling Island – a little island just off the coast. Just about half an hour or so after that, she was making her way to the Darling Island floating bridge. Arriving at the car park by the estuary, she navigated through a sea of vehicles until she finally spotted a space, parked, killed the engine, closed her eyes for a second and let out a sigh, and headed over to the pay machine. Stunned by the price to park her car, she wondered if it would be easier to drive onto the ferry. But everything she'd read about the ferry mentioned it was less hassle for non-residents to leave their vehicles behind, as the tram service was frequent and parking was notoriously difficult on Darling Island. Looking out at the water, she shrugged. Emmy had been to Darling Island a few times in the past, and the parking situation had been bad enough then, so who knew what it would be like now? She decided to just stump up the cash and walk on as a foot passenger.

She collected the parking ticket from the machine, returned to her car to place the ticket on the dashboard, and then gathered her handbag and phone. She then joined the throng of pedestrians heading towards the floating bridge and gazed out over the hazy blue of the Darling estuary. Emmy Bardot sighed to herself and hoped her jaunt over to Darling Island was going to be worth it. Her son, Callum, loved the cinnamon buns from the bakery he'd tried via a friend, so she'd had a special cake made incorporating cinnamon buns. It had cost her an arm and a leg, and now this journey to collect it had added a few hours onto her already packed day. It had better be worth the effort.

She inhaled the sea air and imagined it travelling down her neck into her lungs and filling her whole upper body with goodness. She told herself that breathing helped with everything in life. With tiredness, with single parenting, with life, with pressure. Especially with pressure. A pressure valve had been tightly screwed shut on top of her head ever since the day she'd found out the person she'd thought had had her back, her ex-husband, hadn't. The ex-husband she'd believed she loved. There was one problem with the ex-husband – he hadn't been who she'd thought he was. The man she'd been married to had spent secret time gambling away their money. The man who had squashed all her dreams and left her and Callum on their own. And here she was, fourteen years later, doing shift work at the port, running a side hustle Etsy store in her spare time, and having to keep all the balls in the air all of the time. Stuff that for a game of soldiers, but there it was, her reality every single day.

Not that you'd know *any* of that stuff with the pressure valve from the outside because, from the outside, Emmy Bardot looked good. It was amazing what you could achieve with supermarket finds, and years of people-watching at the port had taught her like a pro. Fewer nice things, where it mattered, was Emmy's mantra in everything in life, and it had served her well. A good bag. Decent shoes. Neat, clean hair. The internet helped. It was astounding what the University of YouTube offered for how to do just about anything in life. That same university hadn't quite had the answer to gambling husbands, but on everything else, it wasn't too bad.

And so, because of the above, it was always Emmy who'd had to do everything on her own, and here she was, on her afternoon off, standing waiting for the ferry to arrive to get a cake for Callum's sixteenth birthday. He'd wanted a cinnamon bun tower, the only thing he'd ever really asked for. He'd known the deal with budget restrictions for a very long time. Not that you'd know it with him, either. Granny and Grandpa made sure Cal was okay. Private school. Lovely phones. All the things.

Anything related to his education was very much sorted. Everything else, though, was up to her.

Emmy looked around her at the typical spring day – a slight chill still in the air, a mix of sunlight peeking through fluffs of white clouds hinting at warmer days. Her gaze followed along the line of the coast, and she watched as a trail of passengers traipsed towards the ferry gate. She'd been to Darling a few times over the years on day trips with Callum when he was little. They'd just ambled over on the ferry and not done much at all; they'd taken a ride on the old tram up and down Darling Street, gone to the far side of the island and walked by the sea, treated themselves to ice cream, and in the summer, spent whole days just messing about on the beach. Nowadays, Callum wasn't quite as interested in day trips and playing sandcastles. With Emmy working all the hours God sent, it had been a while since she had crossed over the Darling haze to the little island surrounded by the sea. As she looked out and the sea breeze whipped her hair around, she kicked herself for not planning better and spending the day on Darling. Having to work for a living put paid to things like that.

She watched a man in a polo shirt with a blue badge on the breast and navy-blue trousers with a double reflective strip just past the knee call out. 'Foot passengers to the left! Darling Bay! Darling Bay for the bay area! Wait for the gate!'

Approaching the waiting area, Emmy peered up at the Darling Floating Bridge information sign and slowly read through it.

Darling Floating Bridge is a vehicular chain ferry crossing over to Darling Island, nestled just off the dazzling blue waters of the south coast.

Family-owned, wholly operated, and still privately run by The Darling Floating Bridge Company, it is one of the few remaining chain ferries in operation today.

THE OLD TICKET OFFICE DARLING ISLAND

First established in 1871, some of the original ferries can still be seen at our boatyard. The Darling floating bridges remain the only way to cross to Darling Island. The Pride of Darling crosses the narrowest point to Darling Bay.
7 days a week. 365 days a year.
First ferry runs continuously from Darling Bay, leaving at 5.30 a.m.

Once she got to the gate, she watched as the old ferry clanged and banged towards the shore. A man with weathered skin, a peaked cap, and an old leather satchel slung across a white uniform shirt stood on the end of the ferry and waited for it to slide into land. As it did so, he pushed a button and directed the flow of foot passengers off the bridge. Emmy watched as he said goodbye to people and then began to direct the passengers going the other way.

'Hello,' he greeted people with a wide smile.

'Hi,' Emmy replied, reaching into her pocket for her phone to pay.

'Foot passenger?' he enquired.

'Yes, thanks.'

The man squinted up. 'You a resident of the island, duck?' he asked and then chuckled. 'I know, I know. You're not, and so why am I asking? I 'ave to ask by law, you see. If you're a resident, you don't pay. I'm pretty sure you're not, but I must clarify every single trip.' He raised his eyes upwards. 'How many times do you think I ask that question in a day?'

'I *wish* I was a resident,' Emmy confessed, flicking her eyes out to the water. *No such luck.* 'Just here for a cinnamon bun cake.'

The man smiled, the skin at the corners of his eyes deeply crinkling. 'Ah, from the bakery then. Good choice,' he commended, holding out a payment device in front of him and wiggling it in front of Emmy's phone.

Emmy tapped her phone against it, the beep confirming her

payment. The man shook his head. 'I didn't know they made cinnamon bun cakes now.'

Emmy nodded. 'They do, yes. It's special order only, though. Miniature buns on a semi-naked tower and dripped with icing. That's what I've ordered. It's for my son's sixteenth birthday.'

The man chuckled. 'Sounds delicious. I'll be putting an order in. I can tell you I'm a few years off sixteen, though.'

'You don't look a day over it,' Emmy bantered.

The man went to move forward to the next passenger. 'Have a nice visit to our Darling. I hope the cake is nice.'

With a nod of gratitude, Emmy stood by the barrier as cars loaded onto the ferry, and it swayed back and forth underneath her feet. To her right, another man was standing on the back edge of the ferry, directing cars until they were all tightly packed bumper-to-bumper in a line. Looking around at the other passengers, Emmy noted the gorgeous surroundings as the swaying bridge moved away from shore and slowly navigated to the other side. She found herself absorbed in contemplation as she looked out over the sea. The calming, hazy blue was in stark contrast to the hustle and bustle of her early shift at work and her upcoming weekend. She mused it all as she stood there looking at the sea.

She couldn't believe Callum was going to be sixteen. It had flown by in a flash. She remembered the day she'd brought him home from the hospital, a tiny little bundle wrapped up in a blanket and strapped into a car seat. As she looked back, she recalled Callum's newborn days. The days before Callum's dad, her ex-husband, had suddenly, without warning, lost his job, and the injection of stress in his life had started an addiction to gambling. As she looked out across to the island, it was almost as if those days when Callum was a newborn were now memories that belonged to someone else. Since then, the years had passed in a bit of a blur. A jumble of keeping her head above water, working, caring, juggling, and doing. Days filled with routine and predictability swirled in her mind. Each day, a mirror of the one before – same chores, same meals, same conversations. Even her job, save the odd legging-clad complaining customer showing too much skin, was more or less the same every day. Same old, same old.

Emmy tutted. Part of her felt as if she was stagnant. Stuck in a long tunnel, every step leading only to more of the same. The days seemed to blend into each other, a continuous, monotonous loop of familiar scenes and faces all doing the same thing.

She tapped on the barrier and mused about Callum growing up and thought about her plans. Even those felt stuck and the same. For years, the plan had been to get Callum through school, save as much as she could, and buy a flat, business premises, or possibly a little house. The plan had always been in the future, and she'd saved a fair amount of money by watching every penny in every area of her life. Then when her beloved grandma had died and she'd received some money from the sale of the house, she'd realised she would finally be able to action her plan.

Her dream had been to not only have somewhere to live to call her own but to expand her little online business selling jewellery into an actual shop. But that hadn't proven to be easy. She'd been looking for a business property for the few years since her grandma had passed away, but commercial property was a whole different ball game to looking for a flat. She'd never even remotely found anything in her price bracket or even close to the vision she had in her head.

She mulled it over as the waves bobbed around her. She yearned for a change, a break from the sameness that had cloaked her life. The prospect of expanding her little jewellery business, being her own boss, and having her own flat was still only a dream, but one she clung to on long monotonous, boring days. She sighed as she glanced towards the island. As the estuary stretched away from her and she inhaled the fresh sea air, it seemed to somehow ease her load a little bit. She shook her head in irritation. A ridiculous thought that the sea air could do such a thing. She worked at the port every day, and it didn't do that for her there. Her load was full, heavy and strapped to her back, air wasn't going to do much for it.

As the floating bridge reached the island, the weathered man who had spoken to her as she'd got on began to go through the same process he'd done on the other side. As she made to disembark, he raised his hand and called out, his voice carried by the breeze. 'Cheerio. Enjoy Darling. Be careful, she doesn't let you go.'

Emmy gave him a little wave and replied, 'Cheerio.'

As she strolled along towards the Darling Island trams, she was lost in a world of her own, and her mind moved from getting out of the rental trap to her job working at the port. She'd started there not long after Callum had started at preschool. She hadn't realised then how important her job would be in her life, but it had, at one point, been the only thing that had kept her afloat. Once her ex-husband Kevin's mental health had started to really go downhill, the money had too, and Emmy's job had been crucial to saving a sinking ship.

She mulled it over as she followed the stream of passengers walking towards the trams, then stood in an old timber tram shelter and peered up at a small digital sign telling her by way of orange letters that a Bay tram would arrive in a few minutes. She watched as a tram hissed down the tracks on the far side, came to a stop at the end, and the sign on its front flickered to a change in destination. A few minutes later, it moved forward and trundled over to where she was standing in the queue. A woman in the same navy-blue trousers and a white polo shirt with aqua-blue epaulettes as the man on the ferry called out, 'Darling Main. All stops on Darling to Darling Main!'

Emmy bundled onto the tram behind the rest of the passengers and watched as the conductor chatted as people filed on. The woman raised her chin in question when she set eyes on Emmy. 'Hey, love. Where are you off to this fine day? Spring has arrived!'

Emmy was slightly taken aback at the friendliness. She hid it well. 'Umm, I want to go to the bakery on Darling Street. Could you tell me what stop that is, please? I think I can remember, but I'm not totally sure.'

The woman beamed. 'I certainly can. You're off to Holly's, are you? Yep, I'll holler when you need to hop off.'

'Thanks.'

'Not a resident?'

Emmy frowned. The man on the ferry had asked the same. She didn't remember being asked these questions when she'd come for day trips with Callum. It was the second time she'd been asked if she was a resident. 'Nope, if only,' Emmy joked. 'I don't have Darling Island money.'

'Sorry, it's a Darling bylaw. I have to ask. Tap your didgeridoo right there, love.'

Emmy tapped her phone, and the woman smiled. 'First visit to Darling for a while?'

'Yep.'

The woman pointed to the front of the tram. 'Have a seat up the front there. Best view by far and free at half the price.'

Emmy looked at the gleaming timber seats, the brass fittings, the long plaited rope from a huge bell, and the old-fashioned sliding pane windows. It all looked lovely. 'Thanks, will do.'

The woman called out as she walked away. 'First stop, Darling Fire Station. Then all stops, Darling Main!'

As Emmy made herself comfortable and looked out the window, she loved the sight of the vintage trams on the other side. They stirred some sort of sense of nostalgia within her in their blue and white livery, standing proud against the backdrop of the island. Their polished bodies gleamed, blue paint shimmered, and the clanging of their tram bells filled the air. She was lost in thought as the tram jerked into life and trundled along, cruising past rows of white houses, an ivy-covered café, and an old church surrounded by shrubs. Every so often, the blue of the estuary flicked in and out of view between the buildings.

Emmy ran her finger along the polished wood and took a deep breath, absorbing her surroundings as her mind decompressed from her early start. A low chatter of conversation and an occasional chuckle of laughter filled the tram as she found herself soaking in the sounds as they trundled down Darling Street. She leaned back in her seat, taking it all in; the buildings painted in a distinctive palette of blue and white and island life unfolding outside the window. What seemed like seconds later, the conductor tapped the back of her chair. 'You'll be wanting this stop, Cherry Trees, for the bakery.'

'Oh, right, thank you,' Emmy replied with a smile as she got up and inched her way towards the back of the tram.

As the tram came to a slow stop, the woman called out, 'Cherry Trees, alight here for the bakery and southern Darling shops.'

Emmy bundled off the tram behind an elderly man wearing polished business shoes who was pulling a small trolley behind him. With passengers disembarking behind her, she stood looking down the street in the direction of the bakery as the tram took off, its bell dinging.

'Need directions?' the man asked.

Emmy squinted towards the bakery. 'No, thanks. I think I'm okay.'

'What are you up to on this lovely day?' the man asked.

Emmy smiled, not really used to how people seemed to just openly address you in a friendly way, as if they'd known you for years. 'I'm collecting a birthday cake from the bakery.'

The man nodded and gestured over towards a long row of

shops. 'Lovely. I had one recently for *my* birthday, actually. You won't be disappointed. Come far, have you?'

'Ahh, not really,' Emmy said as she looked along Darling Street in the opposite direction and up at the blue and white bunting fluttering overhead. 'It's so lovely here. I should visit more often. I never seem to find the time, you know?'

'Yep, it's not a bad spot to call home. I'm Mr Cooke. I've lived here all my life.'

'I'm Emmy, and I'm off to buy a cake,' Emmy joked. 'Pleasure to meet you, Mr Cooke.'

Mr Cooke touched his finger to his forehead. 'Good day to you. Enjoy Darling, lovely day for it and have a bit of cake for me.'

'Will do.'

'Oh, and be careful with yourself. Take it from me, if Darling likes the look of you, she won't be letting you go.'

As Emmy watched him shuffle away along the pavement, she shook her head. There was a fat chance of that in Emmy's same old same old world.

2

A couple of minutes later, after crossing over the tramlines, Emmy made her way towards the bakery. The scent of fresh bread, cinnamon, and coffee grew stronger as she approached, the aroma wafting from the open door. Stepping in, she was greeted by old-fashioned glass cases filled with treats, fishing baskets wedged to the walls teeming with bread, and cinnamon buns piled high on timber counters. Waiting in the queue, Emmy watched in fascination as the staff behind the counter whizzed through the customers. Just as she got to the front and she'd mentioned that she'd ordered a cake, a small woman with glossy hair appeared, almost as if by magic, beside her.

'Greetings. I'm Holly,' the woman said with a huge smile.

'Emmy Bardot. I'm here for a birthday cake. Was it you I spoke to?' Emmy greeted as she fumbled in her bag to get out her phone.

The woman shooed away Emmy's phone. 'Yep. Two-layer, semi-naked tower topped with miniature buns and our secret icing.'

Emmy flicked her eyes in surprise. 'Yes, that's me.'

'You're the last special cake order to be collected for the day. I've been waiting for you. We like the personal touch when we hand over a cake. I flit between our branches, and this afternoon I'm here on Darling, so you have the pleasure of me at your service.' The woman winked and laughed.

Emmy noted the perfection of the woman's skin and how despite laughing, her face didn't move. Emmy smiled. 'Oh, okay. Right, yes, thanks.'

Holly gestured for Emmy to follow her over to the other side of the shop, where a tall white box sat on a table. Holly carefully opened the box, and Emmy gasped and said a silent thank you. The cake had been vastly over her budget, but she'd decided by the reviews that it would be worth it for Callum's sixteenth birthday. If it tasted as good as it looked, it would be money well spent. She was much more pleased than she thought she was going to be. She knew Callum would love it.

Holly looked at Emmy expectantly. 'Happy?'

Emmy nodded enthusiastically. 'Oh yes, more than. Thank you. Yes, that is amazing!'

'Trust me, it will also deliver on taste.' Holly lowered her voice. 'Much tested and very secret recipe. You'd have to kill me before I divulged what goes into the icing, but I can tell you as I stand here before you now, it is delicious. Not like that rubbish in the supermarket that tastes like chemicals. Looks good, tastes good.'

Emmy gasped. 'It's gorgeous. Thank you.'

Holly nodded to herself. 'We never, and I mean never, *ever* disappoint. And if by some chance we do, we'll do everything in our power to put it right. So if you are not completely and utterly happy, get in touch.'

Emmy's eyes widened. The woman was bordering on scary. 'Excellent.'

Holly beamed, clearly proud of her creation. 'Nothing like a semi-naked tower topped with cinnamon buns.'

Emmy chuckled, appreciating Holly's enthusiasm, and watched as Holly carefully flicked out a white paper bag. 'It's for my son's birthday. He's sixteen.'

'He has good taste.' Holly laughed as she pulled a thick blue grosgrain ribbon from a dispensing roll attached to the wall. 'I'll wrap the box and then double-bag it to keep it secure. How are you getting off the island?'

Emmy screwed up her face. 'Ahh, I didn't think about carrying it. I'm on foot.'

'You should be fine with this box. Just be careful. Take it from me, keep it in your arms, and don't let it dangle. Be careful not to knock it. I've put a stabiliser in the bottom, so you should be fine.'

A few minutes later, Emmy was out on the pavement with the cake box in the bag carefully tucked in her arms. She looked down Darling Street and tried to see if there was a tram, and then gingerly walked along as if she was carrying the Crown jewels. Arriving at the next stop, she peered up at the destination board, and with the next tram in six minutes' time, she decided to stroll along past the delightful shops and indulge in a spot of window shopping.

Just as Emmy was approaching the next tram stop, a door jingled behind her, and a man rushing past bumped into her as he hurried along the pavement. The collision nearly sent the cake box flying out of her arms. She stumbled, stepped back, blinked, and swore. She was not happy. 'Oi!' Her heart pounded as she juggled to steady the box, and it teetered precariously. Pulling the box closer to her body to secure it, she tutted. 'Oi! Idiot!'

'Sorry about that,' the man who'd bumped into her apologised, looking apologetic but not overly bothered. His rush had momentarily subsided, but he didn't look as if he was too concerned.

Emmy struggled with the box and peeked inside. She closed

her eyes for a second as she saw that the edge of the cake was squashed into the box. She swore again. 'I don't believe it,' she tutted at the same time as noting the man was rather, no not rather, excruciatingly good-looking. Not that she gave a stuff about that. She was more or less seething. 'Just be careful next time,' she hissed. 'You really need to watch where you're going.'

The man shook his head and tried to peer into the box. 'Me! You need to look where *you're* going. You were dawdling along, taking up the whole pavement. Just stand right in the middle of the pavement, why don't you?'

Emmy went to blast him, but he looked down Darling Street in the direction of the ferry, and before she could say anything, he'd rushed off. Rather than telling him exactly what she thought of him, Emmy was left gawping.

Just as she was cursing, she looked around to see the back of a tram slowly easing away from the stop. She shook her head and tutted, took a moment to collect herself, held the cake box a little tighter, and sighed. Now not only was the top of the cake a bit squashed, but she'd also missed the tram. She took a few steps nearer to the timber tram shelter and looked up at the board. The next tram going in the direction of the ferry was in twelve minutes. Emmy decided to take a moment to regroup, and spotting a bench nearby, she took a few steps towards it, carefully balancing the cake box in her arms.

A few seconds later, she was on the bench with her back to the trams and looking up at a row of shops. Each shop was painted either pale blue or white, all of them wearing the same regulation stripy awning to the front. She squinted at an old nameplate on one of the shops, just barely able to be made out above the awning.

The Old Ticket Office

The whole row of shops looked as if it had been made for a

movie set with its quaint structure, pretty colours, and turquoise panes in the windows. Emmy sat looking up at the white building, wondering what The Old Ticket Office would have been used for. She sat lost in thought and could almost see a queue of people waiting to buy tram tickets, friendly banter between the residents, and maybe a few tourists here and there. She traced the contours of the building with her eyes and squinted. When you looked closely, it didn't look quite as well kept on the inside as the others. In fact, it could quite possibly be empty. She looked upwards past the canopy and the blue and white bunting. It had a second and third floor, by the looks of it, and dormer windows in a rickety slate roof.

With her hand securely holding the cake box, she got up from the bench and stood looking up at the shop. Lost in a world of her own, she nearly jumped out of her skin when a well-dressed woman and a man came out of the shop door. She earwigged at their conversation.

'Okay, then. Well, thanks so much for showing me around. But I don't think it's going to be quite what I'm looking for,' she heard the woman say. 'I wanted something a bit more modern, and it's nowhere near ready to go.'

The handsome man held out his hand. 'No worries at all. As I said, the likelihood of it being zoned for what you want is slim, bordering on non-existent. Darling beats to its own drum. You have to apply to the council to put a poster in your window.'

'It's a beautiful building, though, if you look past the mess. For someone, this is going to be one very nice place to do business. Have you had much interest?'

'A fair bit, but there's a lot of work to do, and to really make it work, you'd have to do something with the flat, which, as you could see, is in a bit of a state.'

'Yeah, agree.'

'See you then. I'll contact you if we get anything else on.' The man made a little grimacing face. 'As I said, though, things come up very few and far between on Darling. It's so tightly held, I'm lucky I have a job.'

'That won't be likely, will it?' The woman chuckled. 'These shops on Darling Street come up once in a blue moon, don't they?'

'They do indeed.'

Emmy watched the well-dressed woman walk away and smiled as the man turned around. Not really knowing what she was doing, she heard herself address him. 'Sorry to butt in. I couldn't help but overhear. Was this place a ticket office in a former life?'

The man sucked air in through his teeth. 'Many moons ago, it was, yes. It was the old ticket office for the trams back in the day.'

'Right, I thought it might be,' Emmy said, pointing up to the writing on the wall above the canopy.

'I can just about remember it when I was a lad. Then it was an insurance office.'

'And it's up for sale, is it?'

The man's eyes widened, and he laughed. 'Why, are you looking to buy it?'

Emmy heard herself say something positive, and then the man spoke again. 'I can show you around if you like. It's not great inside. The outside looks as it does because it's kept by the Municipality of Darling, but the rest of it needs some work.'

Emmy nodded. 'I'd love to have a look around if you've got time.'

'It's a commercial building with a two-bed plus flat above and a small yard cum garden out the back. Very small.'

'It sounds like what I'm looking for,' Emmy noted.

'As you can see, it's double-fronted with the Dutch canopy outside. Original ceilings, the original sales counter, a stock-room, toilet with wash-hand basin,' the man rattled off. He turned to Emmy as he unlocked the door. 'But that's about it.

No EPOS fittings, modern shop shelving, or the like. It doesn't even have a CCTV system. The water's a bit dodgy too. The pipes and all that. Plus, the heating is decrepit, ditto the wiring.'

Emmy liked the sound of it *very* much. She followed behind him and stepped into a dark room with high ceilings and an old fireplace on the left-hand wall. Dust and time hung in the air. The estate agent took a few steps back and smiled. 'Here we are. I'm Dan, by the way.'

Emmy smiled, put the cake down in a little alcove by the door and held her hand out to Dan. Dan was not too shabby. He smelt expensive and looked put together. She wondered what category she'd put him into if he was queuing up to board a cruise. She chuckled to herself inside. He'd go in the *Very Nice* category. 'I'm Emmy, nice to meet you,' Emmy said as her heels sank into a grubby carpet as she walked to the far side and squinted at the walls.

'You're looking for a shop, are you?' Dan asked with kind sparkly eyes and what appeared to be genuine interest.

'Umm, yes. Well, some sort of commercial premises with accommodation. I've been looking for ages.'

'What line of business are you in?'

Emmy smiled. 'I have a side-line jewellery business online. I've been doing it for years, and I'm looking for a shop. Mostly I'm a digital business, so I'm looking for a property to fill many roles.'

Dan whooshed air in through pursed lips and added a low whistle. 'Right you are. Not sure how well that would do on Darling. Not sure of the foot traffic on that. There was a branch of Jiney Jewellers here many moons ago that I do know.'

Emmy waved her hand and grimaced. 'Oh, gosh, no. No, no, no. Not that sort of jeweller. Nothing like that at all.'

Dan frowned. 'What sort of jeweller are we talking?'

'Think the opposite to Jiney Jewellers. Lovely but simple things for special occasions.'

Dan didn't look too interested but pretended he was. 'Right.'

Emmy laughed. 'Probably not your area of expertise or cup of tea.'

Dan chuckled. 'No. So, yeah, this needs some tidying up.' He looked up towards the high ceilings. 'I mean, you could put a drop ceiling on there and downlights, brighten it up a bit.'

Emmy peered up at the high ceiling dwarfing them. It was just what she was looking for. It gave the space an airy, olde-worlde feel, hinting at the building's former glory days. She glanced over to the fireplace; its mantle displayed a forgotten glass trophy of some sort and a forlorn-looking framed certificate. Dan took a few steps into the corner and tapped a melamine counter at the far end of the room. 'This is the old ticket counter, under here. Someone who should remain nameless boxed it in.' He led Emmy behind it, bobbed down, and pulled some of the board away. 'Oak, if I'm not mistaken.'

Emmy squatted beside him, peered, and ran her fingers along the edge of an old, beautifully carved counter. 'Wow, it's gorgeous.'

Dan stood up. 'The whole place is. Depending on the look you're going for. It could work. If you peer past the dust and look at it with different eyes.'

'Yes, you're right,' Emmy agreed.

'Even that,' Dan said, pointing overhead to an antique chandelier hanging from a weathered chain, its glass prisms catching the light and casting rainbows around the room. 'It's a miracle it survived. Doesn't really go with an insurance office.'

Emmy followed his gaze. 'It's beautiful.'

'You wait until you see upstairs. There's a lot of dust and a lot of potential.'

Emmy took in the walls, lined with deep-set skirting boards, faded with a patina of age, their paint peeling to reveal layers of colours from the past.

'It's got a lot going for it if you have the right eye. Not many do.' Dan chuckled, his voice echoing slightly in the empty room. 'The insurance company that owned this place for the last forty or so years didn't do much. I guess you could say they were more into insurance.' Dan laughed at his own joke.

As Emmy listened as Dan told her about the frequency of the trams and the foot traffic on Darling Street, she absorbed every detail of the lovely room and could almost hear the sound of people shuffling up to the counter, the rustling of paper tickets. She sighed wistfully. There was no way she'd be able to afford it. She shouldn't have even agreed to look around. She would now end up despondent, as she had many times when looking for somewhere to house her dreams and plans.

As they walked through to a back room, the uneven texture of old nylon carpet, worn thin with age and traffic, crunched under their feet. A series of old grey filing cabinets, their surfaces marred with rust spots and the occasional dent, lined the periphery of the room. On the filing cabinet fronts, faded labels with curling corners held the names of countless policies and clients organised meticulously in order. Against one wall, a large cork noticeboard, its surface littered with old memos, faded photographs, and a handful of dusty letters, was skew-whiff on the wall.

Emmy moved slowly through the room, drinking in every tiny detail. It was an outdated office, suspended in the eighties, that was true. But the bones of the place were the allure. It was almost as if the old building was whispering to her, inviting her in. Her heart pounded as Dan led her to a small, narrow door in the far wall of the back room. 'Upstairs here, we have a two-bedroom flat.' Dan shook his head and lowered his voice. 'I say two bedrooms, but with the box room, it could be three, and then there's the top room too.'

Emmy held onto a timber handrail and stepped up steep, creaky wooden stairs. The upstairs held more of the same. A small kitchen, a sitting room looking over Darling Street, and a fireplace in the middle of a wall. Two bedrooms, one with a funny little bathroom down a step. A box room just about big enough to swing a cat. The same nylon carpet crunched under-foot, dusty old bare light bulbs gave off light. Remnants of office paraphernalia were dumped here and there. Old metal Venetian blinds were at the windows, and the walls wore a lovely shade of nicotine yellow.

Dan smiled as he flourished his hand around. 'Not too bad, eh?'

Emmy nodded. 'No, not bad at all.'

Dan led her through to the back to a large window over-looking the yard, where another set of steep stairs ran up the side of the building. 'Annexe, loft or attic room, whatever you want to call it, is up here. Now, let me tell you, get ready for the view.'

Emmy swallowed as she got a whiff of Dan again. She may also have taken in his broad shoulders in the suit and his sparkly green eyes. As they got to a tiny landing at the top, she followed him to a large attic room with windows at either end. As she walked over and saw the sea in the distance, she gasped. 'Oh, my goodness.'

'I know, right? How good is that? Sort of a secret view.'

'Amazing.'

'If this was a house, this place would be worth a lot of money.' Dan nodded. 'A lot.'

Emmy felt her heart sink to her boots. 'I see.'

'If it was me,' Dan noted, almost as if he was talking to himself, 'I'd be making the most of this view.' He pointed to a door in the corner. 'I'd be renovating that bathroom, and I'd be waking up to that view,' he said, gesticulating back to the window.

Emmy nodded. It was so obvious it was staring both of them in the face. Emmy squinted, shook her head, and looked around the room. 'So what was this used for?'

'Nothing for the past few years, according to Mr Bell, the owner. There was a lodger up here once upon a time. As you can see, it's more the size of a studio, so I can see how someone lived here back in the day. Yeah, anyway, no one had been up here for ages. Criminal, if you ask me.'

'I should say so.'

'He said they emptied it out once the lodger moved on and pretty much shut the door. Never came up here again much.' Dan ran his finger along the wide window ledge. 'As you can see by the dust.'

Emmy followed him back down the stairs, across the flat, down the next set of stairs, and headed to the back garden. She asked him the price, and as he answered, her mind went at four hundred miles an hour, trying to calculate things quickly. With the money from her grandma, her savings, and the money she had in an insurance policy, she'd just be able to make it. She couldn't believe it. She had to stop herself from asking if he was sure.

Dan turned to her as he unlocked a back door to a small narrow courtyard with a tiny half-shed at the bottom, discarded filing cabinets, and not a lot else. Dan made a wincing face and turned his head to the side. 'This bit isn't great, I have to admit. On the plus side, there is nothing to get rid of, really.' He pointed to a block-paved patio outside the door and a row of window boxes. 'Spruce this lot up, and it could be quite nice with a bit of work. I meant to point out the other gardens all along the back here from the top window.'

Emmy agreed with him. It wasn't too bad at all. She'd seen a lot worse in her exhaustive commercial property hunting. 'Yeah, it's fine. Or it could be.'

Dan stepped back into the little kitchen area at the back. 'So, there you have it.'

'Have you had a lot of people looking at it?' Emmy asked with her heart pounding.

Dan nodded enthusiastically. 'Oh yes. Especially in the first few days it went up on the internet. The trouble is, there are all sorts of things to think about on Darling. Some folk aren't too keen…' He let his sentence dangle.

'Like what?'

'The council has to more or less approve you to breathe, umm, you have to agree to the upkeep of the outside and to keep the regulation colours, the rates are not low, and add in a million other things. The access is tight, what else? Yeah, you have to be the right sort of person to get on here, put it that way.'

Emmy felt mildly alarmed at the same time as intrigued by what he was saying. It was just the sort of thing she'd like to be part of. She followed him back to the front room and repeated the price back to him. She thought about how she could just meet the price but would be left with little else. 'Is it negotiable?'

Dan made a funny clucking sound. 'Depends. I think it *might* be. The owner, Mr Bell, wants shot of it now. I've had a few people get close, but too many tyre kickers, if you know what I mean. Mr Bell is over it. He's had a change of circumstance, as it were. Are your finances sorted?'

Emmy nodded. She would just about have enough. It would mean she wouldn't have any money left over at all, but she would be able to cover it. She'd have to ask her mum and dad for help. 'They are.'

Dan's eyebrows shot to the top of his head. 'Okay. Look, you know what, I might give the owner a quick call on the price now, if you're serious.'

Before Emmy knew what she was saying, she heard herself reply, 'I'm serious.'

Dan nodded, pulling out his phone and scrolling through his contacts. 'Alright then, won't be a tick,' he said, hitting the dial button before holding the phone up to his ear.

Emmy watched as Dan wandered towards the back of the

room, his voice dropping to a murmur as he spoke to the owner. She used the time to take another look around, her mind racing with possibilities.

Dan returned after a few minutes, a pleased look on his face. 'Well, it looks like you might be in luck. Before we get into anything, are you in a chain?'

Emmy shook her head. 'No, not at all. I'm not selling anything.'

Dan looked very surprised. 'Oh, okay.'

'I'm renting at the moment,' Emmy said by way of explanation.

'I see. Great,' Dan replied with a smile. 'Mr Bell, the owner, wants rid of it and fast. He's prepared to take less if you can move quickly, and you are definitely not in a chain. If not, the price is firm.'

'I'm ready to go right away. As I said, I have no chain at all.'

Dan again looked surprised. 'Okay, he's willing to negotiate then. He's keen to have someone in quickly,' Dan said, and then started talking figures and settled on a price lower than the original one he'd said earlier.

Emmy had to stop herself from shrieking or doing an Irish jig. She pretended that she was thinking about the price. She wasn't at all. 'That's umm, yeah, I think that would be great,' she said, trying to keep her excitement in check. 'I can go to that.'

Dan started explaining the process of what would happen if they went ahead. There would be a slew of other things to get in order. But despite what she heard Dan saying, Emmy felt full of it. This could be it – her new beginning, a chance to work on her business and get out of the rental trap cycle she'd been in for so long.

As Dan continued to chat, she collected the cake from the front room and followed him outside; her brain was buzzing. Her mind whirred as she listened as Dan went through the next steps. She would need to call her solicitor and get a survey done.

It all seemed to whizz around her in a blur as they stood under the canopy, and Dan took her number.

About ten minutes later, she watched Dan walk away. She gulped and looked up at the bunting fluttering overhead on the other side of the street. She'd not only just found the shop of her dreams, but she had also negotiated a hefty sum off a property on a little island accessed mainly by a floating bridge. She really had no idea what she was doing, and she hadn't even told Callum.

With the cake box in her arms, a blue-and-white tram came into sight, hissed and trundled up to the stop, and in a bit of a daze, she got on. As she took a seat, she looked out at the building with its stripy canopy and old-fashioned turquoise stained-glass windows. Emmy Bardot and The Old Ticket Office had just made friends.

By the time Emmy had disembarked the tram and stood waiting for the floating bridge, she'd taken her phone out of her bag and tapped the calculator app many times. With the huge, awkward cake box balanced in her arms, she kept adding the money from her grandma to her savings. She somehow had enough money to buy The Old Ticket Office, and because of the negotiation, she'd have a bit left.

She kept shaking her head and not believing that the whole episode was true. First of all, the building itself – it ticked each and every one of her non-negotiables. It was a lovely street frontage shop that had big enough on-site accommodation. It didn't need too much deep work. It was a beautiful old building. It had a tiny outdoor area, and it was near public transport, so Callum would be able to get to school. On top of that, it had fantastic views thrown in for good measure.

All of it felt like a dream Emmy had long envisioned for herself but never really believed would become a reality. She gazed across the hazy blue water, her mind abuzz about what she had just done. She'd only made an offer, nothing was firm or in writing, but it all felt really real. As she watched the chains of the floating bridge go taut and the waves fall over them, she thought about the few years she'd been looking for a shop, and nothing had ever been right. Most things that had ticked anywhere near close to all her boxes had always been way out of her budget.

Her mind flicked in a split second from the old building to Callum. Darling Island was just on the edge of the circle she'd drawn from his school and her work. It would mean a good forty-five minutes for him on the bus, but they'd already discussed it when she'd first started looking. She mentally went down the list in her head and added his journey to school as another tick in a list of positives that seemed to grow with each passing minute.

A smile spread across Emmy's face as she continued to grasp the cake box and watch the ferry clang and bang into place. Had she really found her dream place for her little jewellery business? She let her mind wander to a new beginning. She hugged the cake to her chest as she boarded the ferry and gazed across the expanse of the Darling Estuary. The waters ebbed and flowed as her emotions about her dream business kept popping into her mind. She pictured The Old Ticket Office transformed into the jewellery boutique in her head, the building acting as a backdrop for her jewellery, piercing bar, and all her treasures.

Emmy had dreamt of the jewellery shop for a long time, ever since the days when she'd rifled through her grandma's jewellery box and ran Grandma Emily's gorgeous gold locket through her fingers. Emmy touched the locket at her neck and fiddled with the clasp on the side. She could see the inside of the shop in her mind, a dreamy boutique that pulled at heartstrings and made special moments happen. So far away from the chain store jewellers Dan had mentioned. Nothing like the horrid, brightly lit high street shops with dated purple velvet every which way, staff dressed in cheap black, CCTV screens by the dozen, garish sale signs, and gigantic pull-up screens proclaiming Gold for Cash.

Emmy's little shop would be the polar opposite of that. It would embody the delving-into-the-jewellery-box experience she'd had when she was a little girl. It would be an offering, an intimate, magical shopping experience so far from the cheap signs and windows filled with line upon line of purple velvet and super bright lights. There would be little lamps and soft music, cosy chairs, and pretty things. A beautiful space where anyone could come in and stop for a while, have a mooch, maybe a cup of tea, and discover a piece of jewellery to be treasured forever. A magical boutique experience where, on entering, you didn't quite know where to look first.

Emmy thought about the little website she'd been designing and tweaking for the past few years. How she'd slowly but surely put her vision to life online. How she had a few loyal customers, and how her social media following was small but very niche. She'd already put into place a lot of the digital stuff; interactive elements, virtual try-ons, detailed descriptions of each piece, and personal online consultations were just a few of the ideas Emmy had already started to create.

Looking out over the Darling estuary, Emmy felt excited and nervous, both at the same time. If The Old Ticket Office came off, it would zoom her out of her comfort zone. It would be a massive step, a leap into the unknown, but it was better than living the rest of her life doing the same old same old every single day. She was finally going to *do* something. It was as if a light had gone on and she was at long last saying to herself that she was going to take the risk. Emmy Bardot felt as if something about Darling Island just felt right. Her heart was telling her to go for it. Above that, though, it was about doing something for her. As the ferry made its way over the water, Emmy smiled. She was ready for a new chapter, and it looked like Darling Island might just be the place that was going to provide it.

3

It was the day after Emmy's trip to Darling, and she was sitting in the tiny lean-to conservatory off the kitchen of her rented cottage. Opening her laptop, she clicked the browser button, opened a tab, and navigated her way to her online jewellery shop. She said a silent thank you to Google for remembering her passwords and navigated her way around the dashboard. It all looked lovely online, and from a very slow start, she had a core group of customers who followed her on Instagram from the days when she'd only had an Etsy shop. She clicked on the Contact page and thought about how it was looking likely she'd soon have a brick-and-mortar shop too. She would actually have an address and a shop of her own. She gulped and closed her eyes for a second. It all felt very scary indeed.

She frowned at the sound of the doorbell, got up from the chair, and then peered out the little window beside the door onto the front step. Her sister, Amy, waved. Emmy smiled, slid the bolt back, and opened the door.

'I made a detour because of the traffic, but it didn't work. So, I thought I'd stop and see if the jam clears. What's with those traffic lights up near the interchange there? There are about three sets of them now all in a row. You finally get through one set and then start queuing for the next. '

'Awful! Who even thought about digging up the road at this time of year? Someone who clearly doesn't use the roads,' Emmy said with a sigh.

'The queues are a joke. How was work?' Amy asked as she traipsed in behind Emmy.

'The usual. Tea?'

'I need a bucket of it.' Amy laughed.

'I'll put the kettle on,' Emmy said as Amy stood by the back door and leaned on the architrave.

'What are you up to?' Amy said, pointing to Emmy's open laptop.

Emmy raised her eyebrows. 'Right, well, you're not quite going to believe this.'

Amy side-eyed. 'What?'

'I've seen a property.'

Amy shook her head. 'What? Really! Where? I didn't know you were going to look at one.'

'I wasn't. Darling Island.'

'Oh wow!' Amy said with a surprised tone to her voice. 'That's not cheap.'

'I know. It's not.'

'When did this happen?'

'When I went to collect the cake yesterday.'

'Right. Yeah, sorry, I meant to message you to see how that went.'

'Umm, so I might have bought it,' Emmy stated as she shook her head.

'What the?'

Emmy laughed a strange sort of panicked laugh. 'Well, obviously I've not bought it, but I'm in the throes of it. I mean, at least, I will be. I am. I think.'

'Isn't Darling super expensive? Like majorly high-end?' Amy frowned.

'It usually is, but this is just in my budget. I negotiated. Plus it's a bit, well, a bit old and I dunno, niche.'

'Wait. Hang on. You did all this yesterday? What when you went to collect the cake? You need to back up a bit, Ems.'

Emmy could hear herself garbling. 'Yep. It was all very spontaneous. This bloke bumped into me and knocked the cake, so I sat down on a bench. An estate agent was showing someone around the building in front of me, and I sort of found myself in there too. It's got everything I want. You know how long I've been looking. I knew it straight away. Like as soon as I stepped in the door. It blew me away right from the get-go.'

'Wow. I don't know what to say,' Amy said as she shook her head.

'The only catch is the ferry. Getting on and off the island could be a pain.'

'Well, I do know one thing – it's nearer to me if you live there, even with the ferry in the equation.'

'I know.'

'What about Cal?'

'He's fine.'

'You think it will work there?' Amy pointed to the laptop. 'I mean the shop. Is it the right sort of place?'

'It's got great foot traffic, and the streetscape is amazing. If it's going to work anywhere. Anyway, if the plan goes well, it's mainly about the digital presence with the store as the add-on.' Emmy held her hands up. 'I can't really predict that side of it.'

Amy winced a little bit and raised her eyes to the ceiling. 'It's a big risk, isn't it?'

'Is it? With Grandma's money, it really isn't too bad. Oh, dear, I don't know. I've been looking for so long…' Emmy trailed off. 'I feel like someone is telling me to go for it.'

'Plus all the money you've saved,' Amy noted.

'It means I will be out of the rental trap. Finally, I'm so over it.'

'You will,' Amy agreed. 'So what's the accommodation like?'

'A three-bed flat with an attic room with views,' Emmy said, slipping her phone out of her pocket, tapping on her photos and passing the phone to her sister.

Amy was quiet for a bit as she flicked through. She looked up with wide eyes. 'It's great. I can tell that from the photos. After all the properties we've looked at over the past few years.'

'I know. As soon as I stepped in, I felt it. I know that sounds weird. I meant to message you yesterday about all this and then time ran away with me, and you said you were having an early night.'

'Wow,' Amy said. 'So you've finally found it.'

'Yep.'

'You go to collect a birthday cake and come back with a shop.' Amy laughed.

'It's looking that way. It's early days, but I've already been on the phone with the agent, and I've emailed him. Plus, I've spoken to the solicitor this morning. You know, the one you used when you moved. She was great.'

'Well, what a turn-up for the books. Exciting!'

'I'll set up another viewing so you can come and see.'

'Great. Wow.'

'Yes, I know. Wow indeed!'

'Mum will have kittens. Have you told her?'

'No. I thought I'd wait and see what happens today.'

'Right. Anyway, after all that, how's the cake?'

Emmy opened the fridge and pulled out the cake box. She tutted and shook her head as she opened it and pointed to the squashed section at the top. 'Some idiot bumped into me right in the middle of the pavement, and the whole lot knocked on the side. I nearly lost the lot.'

Amy screwed up her nose as she peered at the section of

squashed cake. 'Oh, not good. You'll have to turn that bit to the back.'

'Yeah, thank goodness I didn't lose it all. I could have murdered the bloke. He wasn't looking where he was going, but then again, if that hadn't happened, I would have been on the tram, and I wouldn't have seen the estate agent coming out of the shop.'

Amy peered at the cake. 'My, that is some cake. Miniature cinnamon buns and that icing. What's not to love? Cal's going to be well happy with that.'

'Yep. It *should* be nice, the amount it cost me!'

'It looks gorgeous, I'll give it that.'

'I know, right? The woman in the bakery insisted that it would taste fabulous too. In fact, she guaranteed it.'

'Can't argue with that.'

'And if all this goes to plan, I will be living down the road from the bakery.' Emmy closed the box and tapped the top. 'So plenty more of these, or at least the buns.'

Amy shook her head. 'I can't believe you've finally found somewhere. It's been a long time coming.'

Emmy shook her head. 'Neither can I. It's not a given yet. We'll have to wait and see, but if the stars align, I have a shop and a flat.'

'I don't really know what to think,' Amy said.

'You and me both.'

Amy's eyes were wide. She held up her right hand. 'My fingers are crossed.'

'Nowhere near as tightly as mine.'

4

The following week, Emmy smiled at Rachael, the woman who ran the staff coffee shop in a portable cabin in the industrial area behind the car park at the port. 'Morning, Rach. How are you?'

Rachael smiled. 'Morning. I'm good. How are you? How was the birthday party of the decade?'

'It was good. The cake made it,' Emmy replied. 'Cal was happy, so I was happy.'

'Great. Everything go well?'

'Yes, very well. I let out a huge sigh of relief once it was over.' Emmy laughed. 'I don't want to be in charge of a sixteenth birthday party ever again.'

'Usual?'

'Yes, please.'

'I'll bring it over.'

Emmy sat down at her usual table by the window in the corner. At the next table, Emmy's colleague Jessie was sitting with her phone propped up and earphones in. On spying Emmy, Jessie smiled and took out her earphones, letting them drop to the table. Jessie and Emmy worked for the same company but in different departments, and were nearly always on their breaks at the same time. Emmy had been sitting at the next table to Jessie for what felt like years.

'Morning. How are you?' Emmy asked.

'Morning, Ems. Yes, good. Busy! How are you? How was the birthday party and the cake?'

'It went well, thanks.'

'Good. How's the sixteen-year-old?'

'Being a sixteen-year-old,' Emmy joked.

Jessie seemed to get the message that Emmy didn't really want to speak, and a few minutes later, after a bit of chitchat back and forth and once a large mug of tea and a bacon sandwich had arrived, Emmy pulled her iPad out of her bag and read through her emails. A few minutes after that, she was perusing business success stories on a podcast she subscribed to. She scrolled to her saved items and read through the very familiar stories of independent jewellers who had done well. She also reread, for what felt like the trillionth time, an article detailing how a little shop in London selling fabric back in the nineties had turned into a worldwide brand with stores in many major cities. The article gave her hope that it could be done. She scrolled further down through articles and stories, reread things, and made a few notes on her phone. Then, with her chin resting on her hand, she gazed out of the door, trying to think about how she was going to turn all of the inspiration she'd been consuming for years, all the visions in her head and all her ideas, into reality by way of a little shop with a stripy canopy out the front on Darling Island.

The idea for a little jewellery boutique had first come to her years and years before when she'd been looking for a present for her sister. She'd traipsed around an indoor shopping centre, going from one regular old high street jewellery shop to another, totally uninspired. Rather than a feeling of excitement for the special occasion, she'd felt rather glum as she'd stood staring into the identical windows; horrid gaudy purple packaging, cheap-looking boxes, and way too bright artificial lights. Inside, she'd received less than mediocre, bored, I-don't-care service and cheap plastic carpets. All of it had been a bit cringe, and she'd walked to her car with a too-shiny purple bag in her hand, a bad taste in her mouth, and a gloomy look on her face.

The shopping experience had been a mediocre one, to say the least, and it had sparked an idea for a lovely little shop Emmy would like to go into to buy a special piece of memento jewellery. And there it had stayed parked in the back of her head while she got on with other things. Not long after that, she'd started to look for a heart locket online. She'd had a similar sort of experience where, instead of shiny purple bags, ugly websites offered too much bling. Despondent, she'd found the exact locket she wanted via a supplier on a wholesaler distributor. In the end, she'd bought ten of the things, put nine of them up for sale in an online auction, and from that, her Etsy shop, Love Emmy x, was born.

And from that day on, her little side hustle had grown like a slowly lumbering snail. As the snail had crawled along, so had Emmy's vision for her boutique. All of it was in her head – how customers would come into the shop looking for something for a loved one, how they would be taken on a delightful journey to find a special item. There might be a cup of tea and a chat. It would be so far from her initial experience in the indoor shopping centre to get Amy's present that the two wouldn't even compare. That experience, whereby a bored woman dressed head to foot in black had shoved cheap trays of velvet in her face and could barely wait to get her out the door, would not even be on the radar. It would, in fact, be in the how-not-to-do-it manual.

Emmy's mind continued to whirl around the topic as she sat in the staff canteen. It all sounded quite good in her head. But in reality, she had no actual inkling of what running a shop entailed. She had zero experience in retail. Yes, she had numerous suppliers at her disposal and a handful of devoted customers, but that was about the extent of it. How many lockets would she need to sell to cover the bills? Was she deluding herself into believing she could make it work? Opening the calculator app on her phone, she began to crunch some numbers. She swallowed hard. It wasn't going to be a walk in the park.

Yet, the desire to be her own boss and control her destiny was so immense and so insistent, sometimes she could barely think about anything else. No matter how often she shook her head, convincing herself this wasn't one of her better ideas, she knew that if she didn't attempt it, she would spend the rest of her life wondering. And there was no way she was going to end up like that. When her grandma had died, she'd grasped Emmy's hand hard and said to always try new things.

Love Emmy x – carefully curated, specially selected jewellery for those special occasions in your life. A beautiful, old-fashioned shopping experience provided with a smile. Love Emmy x is a jewellery shop with a difference – the prettiest jewellery you'll find anywhere and lovely items carefully put together with love. A destination boutique you'll not only adore but will make your jewellery purchase so very special. Love Emmy x.

Emmy nodded. It didn't sound too bad when you put it like that. But what would reality be like? Every other time she read the news, another retailer had gone under. Not small little boutiques on tiny little islands. Huge worldwide retailers and big British brands who couldn't make retail work in the digital world. What, in fact, was she doing?

Trying to convince herself that her idea was a good one, she navigated to a high street jewellery shop's website on her phone and recoiled as a glaring sale sign flashed on the homepage.

"Sale, sale, sale!" it told her over and over again. Intrusive pop-ups touted interest-free payment terms at the same time as making it known that all items excluded postage. Keeping the vision of The Old Ticket Office in her head, she navigated to the lockets section, where her idea had initially taken root. Precisely two hundred and thirty-seven lockets, displayed against purple velveteen backgrounds, glared back at her. Factory-made jewellery for the masses – a far cry from anything Emmy had in mind.

No, Emmy's store would be different. She would offer unique, personal pieces of jewellery that told a story and held meaning. Not items mass-produced and soullessly sold. Love Emmy x was about connections – to jewellery, to purchases, and to the store itself.

Emmy started scrolling through her list of suppliers, considering the pieces that would align with her vision for the store. Her mind wandered to delicate earrings, handcrafted bracelets, and necklaces, each carefully selected and curated by her. The Old Ticket Office would be a place where customers could find items that spoke to their hearts, evoked memories, and created new ones. The experience would be so very different from the one Emmy had had in the shopping centre all that time ago.

Emmy sat with her fingers wrapped around a cup of tea, her mind a tangle of ideas and possibilities. She closed her eyes and imagined the boutique she had always dreamt about owning. She could see it in her mind's eye – the layout and decor, the old counter as the cornerstone of the whole thing. There would be a quaint, pretty, vintage aesthetic: antique display cases, floral wallpapers, and soft lighting. It would be a haven of loveliness. A place where customers would feel welcomed and cherished, and so very different from the conveyor belt of jewellery nothingness she'd had been on in the high street chain stores.

Emmy imagined her customers leaving the store, clutching small, ribbon-wrapped boxes, feeling satisfied. They would be excited not just about their purchase, but about the whole experience: the conversation, the personalised service, and the beautiful environment. She wanted her boutique to offer and be more than just a jewellery shop. Since owning her online shop, she understood the significance jewellery held for people. It was often a tangible representation of important milestones – a wedding, a birth, a goodbye, or even a hard-fought divorce. Every jewellery purchase normally held a story and was rarely bought just on a whim.

Emmy wanted to create something that when the old door opened, her customers' breath would hitch, their eyes widen, and 'wow' would escape from their lips. She imagined the jewellery displayed under beautiful bell jars, draped over antique books, and mingled in among fresh flowers. A dream where cheap purple velveteen most definitely didn't have a place. Every nook and cranny would delight; a beautiful old gramophone here, an old typewriter there, diffused light from a Tiffany lamp, old-fashioned display cabinets, and fairy lights strung around the edges of the room. Thick Persian rugs would be on the floor, soft, old jazz tunes or instrumental pieces would play. It would be an experience, a joy of unhurried shopping. Love Emmy x would be a place where every visit felt like coming home.

Emmy sat there, sipping her tea, her mind projecting into the future. She imagined the shop that had been in her head for years actually existing in real life on Darling Island. She nodded as she mulled it over and saw the little shop with its blue canopy in her mind's eye. The setting couldn't really have been better. The island itself would be part of her dream shopping experience. With its iconic floating bridge surrounded by the soft, hazy blue mist, the journey alone would set the tone. Love Emmy x, the actual shop, would fit in perfectly on Darling Street with its jumble of little independent boutiques, quaint cafés, the lovely bakery, and tiny shops here and there. Trams would trundle on by to the sea, and blue and white bunting would flutter overhead. All of it was not far from perfect in the scenario she was painting in her head.

With her head flitting from one thing to the next, Emmy felt terrified but excited for the future. She'd spent too many years with her head down, bum up, getting on with the realities of what life had thrown at her, but now it was time to crawl out of the trenches and take a leap. The Old Ticket Office was no longer a dream but a walking talking reality with its own business plan and registered business name. All sorts of scarily real.

Emmy watched as Jessie pushed her chair out and picked up her phone. Jessie balanced her empty plate in one hand and her bag in the other. 'See you tomorrow for more of the same,' Jessie said with a smile. 'Back to the grindstone then.'

Emmy chuckled. It was a standing joke between the two of them and a line they'd exchanged countless times before. They'd chatted about all sorts over the years as they'd each enjoyed their tea breaks, settling into their favourite spots in the small staff café, ensconced amidst a hustle of workers with more or less the exact same routine. They'd spent many a morning chatting, watching as familiar faces flitted in and out, their conversations veering from what was going on in the world to the latest scandal in Jessie's family.

Emmy responded with a nod, tipping her chin up. 'Yep, see you. Have a good day. Be good.'

Jessie finished as she always did. 'And if you can't be good, be careful.'

Emmy watched as Jessie made her way to the counter, popping her plate on the side and waved to Rachael. Her mind fizzed with Jessie's words, and she found herself thinking how things were changing. She had something new on the horizon, and it definitely felt good.

As she finished the last of her bacon sandwich, she was suddenly acutely aware of the sameness that had crept into her life; the same monotony to her week, the same conversations, the same observations, the same people, and the same work buildings looming in the distance. More or less, since Kevin, her ex, had started gambling, it was as if she'd been stuck in a loop of same old, same old. Each day just another one on the conveyor belt of work and life. She had unwittingly done the complete opposite of what Grandma Emily had said. But with the enormous undertaking of the purchase of The Old Ticket Office, things felt different, thrilling somehow, as she pondered having jumped off the conveyor belt and stood observing from the side. Emmy Bardot was shaking things up – pushing boundaries, stepping out of her comfort zone. It all felt scarily, deliciously good.

She let her gaze wander back to the table opposite her as a man from the accounts department smiled, raised his eyebrows, pulled out a chair, and sat down. Jessie's words and laughter rang in Emmy's ears as she watched the man tuck into beans on toast. She felt strange, almost as if she was observing the goings-on around her from above. From her side of the table, the monotony felt different. Things were about to change. Time for a new chapter. She gulped as she put her mug on top of her plate and stood up, and the familiarity of the café suddenly felt nice. What was she doing even thinking about some harebrained scheme to change her life? As she put her plate on the counter in the dirty section, she shook her head to herself and hoped that she'd not made a ginormous mistake.

5

Emmy gripped the steering wheel tightly as the car bumped on the road on the approach to the Darling Island floating bridge. The anticipation of showing her family The Old Ticket Office filled her with a mix of excitement and nervousness. She'd been trying to find a commercial property that suited her needs for so long, but now one had arrived, she wasn't sure what to think. She wasn't sure if she was ready or, more importantly, *able* to take on something like The Old Ticket Office. It now felt all sorts of scarily real.

In the backseat, her dad Bob was chatting away with her sister Amy, and Emmy's mum, Cherry, sat beside her in the front seat, holding onto the grab handle above her head as if it was a lifeline. As they sat in the short queue for the Darling Island ferry, Emmy's heart fluttered with nerves. Bob leaned forward from the back seat, pointing at the Pride of Darling ferry sign with a grin. 'Looking good so far,' he said cheerfully. 'Not a bad way to arrive, Ems. You have to give it that.'

Emmy nodded, her eyes scanning the surroundings. 'It looks nice today. The ferry is both a positive and a negative, though, according to my list. It makes it all very idyllic, but on the other hand, I think this could be a bit of a pain. Commuting and stuff could get very long-winded with this thrown into the mix.'

Cherry chimed in. 'I can't see how you can go wrong with it myself. It makes it all the more lovely. Just imagine getting home to this after a long day at work. Fabulous.'

They watched as the ferry slid into place before them, and the car seemed to be surrounded by the hazy Darling blue. 'It's a lovely blue, isn't it?' Cherry commented as she peered out the passenger window and wrinkled up her nose. 'Sort of hard to put your finger on what shade of blue it is. What would you even call it?'

'Not sure. It really is a unique blue,' Emmy agreed.

'I wonder what it's like in the winter? I bet it's freezing when there's a cold wind blowing along the coast,' Amy mused.

Bob chuckled from the back seat. 'Definitely a bit chilly in winter here, I should say so. Nice though. I do love a nice cold clear day at the seaside, as you girls know.'

As Emmy guided the car onto the ferry, it clanged and banged underneath them, and then it seemed they were quickly leaving and heading for the other side. As the ferry pulled away, the wind breezed in the windows, and salty sea air filled their lungs. Emmy watched behind her as the mainland slowly drifted away, and Darling Island loomed larger ahead. As the ferry glided through the water, she wondered if she'd made the right decision about The Old Ticket Office.

'Look, all along there. I bet that's a nice walk,' Amy noted, pointing out the window to a path along the shoreline.

'Yes, it's all so pretty,' Emmy agreed.

'It is,' Cherry said. 'If the building is anything like the setting, you'll be fine.'

Emmy smiled, feeling grateful for her family, and as the ferry reached the other side and she pulled off, they commented on the trams, the old white four-storey houses and the cobbled streets. Just as it had done with her, the island's charm captured them as they took in the sights of Darling. Emmy slowly pulled off Darling Street and parked on a side road. A few minutes later, all four of them were standing outside The Old Ticket Office, looking up at the roof and windows, waiting for Dan, the estate agent, to arrive. The sound of seagulls circling overhead and the occasional ding of trams passing by filled the air. Emmy's heart raced with excitement, nervousness and somewhere in the back of her mind, a little bit of dread at the enormity of what she was taking on.

'Well, so far, so good,' Cherry said, breaking the silence. 'First rule is the location.' She looked down Darling Street as a tram eased away. 'And this is like something out of a children's book. Dare I say it, but it's perfect.'

Emmy nodded, her eyes fixed on the building. 'Yep, I thought that too. The trams just make it, don't they?'

'Agree. It's such a lovely place,' Bob commented. 'I can see why you fell in love with the building too.'

Cherry smiled. 'Yes, there's something about it.'

Just then, Dan arrived. 'Hello. So glad to see you again, Emmy. And you must be her lovely family. I'm Dan, the estate agent. I bet you've heard all sorts about me.'

Bob laughed and held out his hand as Emmy introduced her family to Dan. They exchanged pleasantries before stepping inside The Old Ticket Office. Emmy gulped. There was certainly a lot of dust, and it was very sad and in need of love. Bob looked up at the high ceilings, the coving, and ran his hand along the walls.

'Right, yes,' Cherry said as she walked over the industrial carpet. 'I can see the potential. Quite a bit of work, Ems. Hmm, yes, lots of work.'

Bob nodded in agreement. 'So much potential, though.'

As they explored the different rooms, Dan filled them in further, providing them with more details about the property. Emmy's mind raced at the prospect of turning The Old Ticket

Office into a shop. Once they'd looked around the flat upstairs, traipsed through the back storage room and looked at the lane behind the building, Cherry sucked air in through her teeth and shook her head. 'Very good. A lot of work but more or less just what you've been looking for for the past few years.'

'I know,' Emmy agreed.

Bob nodded. 'You've found a real gem here. We'll all need to roll our sleeves up, though.'

Emmy's heart was a whirl of contrasting emotions as she took in the old building. Somehow it was as if it was speaking directly to her, saying it had everything she had been looking for. But despite the realisation of that, a tiny voice of apprehension echoed in the back of her mind, questioning the monumental decision she was making. A monumental decision that she was mostly taking on her own.

They went back in, her eyes roamed around, and her brain mentally ticked things off; the creaking wooden floorboards underneath the carpet, the old-fashioned fittings that lent an air of grandeur, and the old ticket booth underneath its horrible melamine casing. Right at the back of her mind, though, Emmy really had no idea whether or not she was doing the right thing. Transforming the place would be no small feat. It would require more than just money, and at the end of the day, the buck would stop with her. Her mind raced as she walked around, weighing the pros and cons, asking herself if she was ready to take the plunge.

As she stood watching her mum and dad and listening to Amy speak to Dan, she tried to gauge what they thought. It seemed as if all three of them were genuinely just as taken by the place as she'd initially been. She listened to Amy's enthusiasm as she conversed with Dan telling him what a great opportunity she thought it was and how the old building had so much potential for someone with the right business in mind and the right eye.

Standing and looking into the back store room, Emmy nodded to herself. It really was now or never, and if she was going to do it, she had to pour her heart and soul into it and not look back.

Emmy climbed the stairs with Cherry, and once they'd looked around, Cherry gave Emmy's hand a squeeze. 'I really like it, Ems. It's just what you've been looking for.'

Emmy let out an inner sigh of relief. She'd wondered what her mum would think, and the reassuring words felt good. 'I know. I thought the same when I first stepped in.'

'I think this place is a really good choice,' Cherry continued, her gaze roaming around the room. 'The flat could be lovely for you and Callum. The kitchen's a bit small, and the whole place needs work, but nothing that can't be fixed. Nothing I can't get my teeth into either.'

Emmy was so pleased her mum was reiterating all her own thoughts. It was one thing to trust her own instincts, but to have Cherry back her up was great. As they wandered through the rooms, Cherry kept nodding in approval, standing with her head to the side, lost in thought.

Bob followed up the stairs behind Dan and stood beside Emmy in the sitting room. Bob had remained largely silent as they'd looked around as he'd absorbed the details. He'd not said too much at all initially, just the occasional nod or hum of approval here and there. 'I think you've found it. If you're ready to put in the graft, I believe you can turn this into something great. It has everything on the list.'

'You really think so?'

'I do. It's the best we've seen so far, and we've sure seen a few,' Bob joked.

'But what if I'm doing the wrong thing?' Emmy said with her voice lowered, her eyes filled with uncertainty.

Cherry, ever the voice of reason, butted in. 'At some point, you just have to take the bull by the horns and do something.'

Bob nodded thoughtfully. 'If you spend too much time thinking about this and making sure everything is perfect, you're just not going to do it. It's not like you haven't looked at a lot of other properties.'

Emmy nodded, her mum and dad's words sinking in. They were right. There would always be doubts, and there would always be risks. She tried not to let them paralyse her.

'I think you're right,' Emmy agreed, the words coming out as a whisper, more to herself than anyone else. Not only did she think they were right, but the place itself felt right.

Amy, who had been standing looking down at the trams, joined in. 'It's time to bite the bullet,' Amy declared. 'This place has everything. It's the best out of all of them we've seen.'

Emmy nodded. She knew they were all correct, and despite her nerves, she felt a shift. It was subtle, barely discernible, but it was there. She was ready to go for it and not look back. She felt tears welling up in her eyes, overwhelmed by both the potential of the building and her family's support. 'Thank you. What do you think Grandma would say?'

Cherry put her arm around Emmy. 'She would be very proud of you, sweetie.'

Emmy nodded and wiped the corner of her right eye. 'You really think she would? You think this is a good way to use her money?'

Cherry smiled. 'Absolutely. She'd tell you to go for your life.'

6

A few weeks or so later, things with The Old Ticket Office had moved on in leaps and bounds, and Emmy was driving home from the port after a very early start. Her feet ached from standing, her cheeks ached from plastering the customer service smile on her face, and her brain ached from complaining passengers. She tapped her fingers on the steering wheel as she sat at a set of lights in a long queue of slow-moving traffic. Thinking about The Old Ticket Office, she shook her head in disbelief as she watched the blink of an indicator light in front of her. She was actually doing it. Her long-held dream was coming true. She was going to take a huge risk and start a new life on a little island off the sea. Unbelievable.

After finally reaching the front of the queue, Emmy sat at the red light, her heart pulsating with a mix of anticipation, uncertainty, and fear. She was really stepping away from the safe harbour of familiarity and sailing towards uncharted waters. The traffic light blinked to green, snapping her out of her thoughts, and her hands tightened around the steering wheel as she navigated her way home. Her brain whizzed as it went over the reality of her situation and how much she had to do. Part of her doubted. Part of her felt irresponsible. Was she just as bad as Kevin, her ex, and his gambling addiction? Was she gambling with the money from her grandma and her savings? As she inched along to the next set of traffic lights, her journey blurred into nothingness as she thought about The Old Ticket Office purchase and the consequences it had not just for her but also for Callum's life.

Her on-a-whim decision meant more than just different scenery or a new business venture. It came loaded with years of thought and struggle. Moving to Darling Island was about change. Taking a leap of faith and shaking off the shackles of when Kevin had started gambling and turned her world upside down. Emmy gritted her teeth together and felt the little muscles at the side of her jaw tighten. She was determined to make it work.

As she continued to sit in traffic piled up to get to the other side of town, her dashboard flickered to life with an incoming call. She pressed the steering wheel's button, and her sister's voice came through the speakers.

'Hey. How are you? You were on the early shift, weren't you?' Amy asked.

'Hi. Yep. Oh, the joys.'

'How was it?'

'Long. Loads of problems. Need I say more? How are you?'

'Good,' Amy replied. Emmy smiled as she heard the familiar hum of Amy's bustling household in the background – children squealing, a TV babbling away. 'So, how is everything going with the move?'

Emmy smiled. 'I've had a chat with the estate agents today, and the solicitors are on it. What else? Oh, yep, the building survey has been done.'

'Wow, you've been busy! So, it's really happening. We're close.'

'Yep, it's really happening,' Emmy said with a laugh, still half incredulous herself. 'It's all coming together.'

'Amazing! I'm so excited,' Amy gushed.

'It's going to be a lot of work.'

'Yeah, think about how amazing it'll be once everything is set up. Think about how long you've been looking for the right place.'

Emmy nodded. 'I know. I am ready for this. I think.'

The conversation continued as Emmy navigated through the traffic.

'So, what has work said about you doing less hours?' Amy asked.

'Actually, they were quite supportive. They agreed right away,' Emmy said.

Amy let out a low whistle. 'Really? I'm not surprised, though, to be quite honest.'

'I know. I thought they'd be okay, but you never really know. Trying to get good staff is a nightmare, as you well know, so I guess that was on my side.'

'Never a truer word.'

'Yes, and not just that,' Emmy continued. 'They've said I can do double shifts if I want. So basically, I'll be able to dedicate the rest of the week to the boutique.'

'That's a really good deal, Ems. It's like everything is falling into place. I'm so happy for you.'

'Imagine me after a double shift. I won't be able to walk.'

'Ha ha. It's good, though.'

'It was Judy who suggested it, actually. She said it made sense because of the commuting.'

'No flies on her, as we've said before.'

'She understands, I guess. I've been talking about it for long enough! I mean, she's been part of the journey all along.'

'I can't believe you're really doing it, Ems. Opening your own shop. It's incredible, really.'

Emmy chuckled. 'Yeah, it feels unreal. Thank goodness for Grandma's money, eh?'

'Yep. Mine went straight into the house – nowhere near as exciting as this. Once we get the date, I'll book a few days off work so I can help. Have you spoken to Mum?'

Emmy sighed. 'I did. She's a bit hyper about the whole thing. You know how she is.'

'Yeah. She's also been watching DIY shows even more than usual in preparation. There'll be no stopping her.'

Emmy replied, 'There won't.'

'What about Callum? Has he said much else? He seemed into it when I spoke to him at the party the other week.'

'He's excited about it for the most part,' Emmy began, her mind shifting to Callum. 'You know what he's like. Water off a duck's back. It's not like he's got a new school or new friends or anything. It mainly just means he'll have to get the ferry and then the bus.'

'You lucked out with him. He's always so laid back.'

Emmy sighed. 'I know.'

'Unlike his father,' Amy noted.

'Don't even go there.'

'Have you told him?'

'Yep.'

'What's he up to?'

'Nothing much. I didn't talk to him a lot at the party, did you?'

'Not really. He seemed okay.'

'Yeah, he *is* okay when he's not gambling.'

'He's happy for you, though.'

'Of course.' Emmy sighed again. 'I don't need his validation, though.'

'I know. I'm just saying. Anything else on the ex-husband front?'

'Nah, I think that covers it.'

Amy chuckled. 'If in doubt, what do we do?'

Emmy laughed. 'Just blame Kevin.'

'Good girl. Ems, we're going to make a lot of money out of that saying one day. We'll be millionaires.'

'I hope so. Now, onto more important topics. Like, how much chocolate I'm going to need to get through the rest of this packing.'

'Wine, more like.' Amy's laughter echoed through the car speakers. 'Alright, I'll let you go. Text me if they let you know a date today. Speak to you tomorrow.'

Emmy smiled as the traffic finally started to move, and she turned onto a side road. It really was happening. She was moving to Darling Island. Amy was right; for the first time in what felt like a very long time, everything really was falling into place. All the pieces of her plan were fitting together, just as she'd hoped. Her dream to have her own home and a small business and a new start was becoming a reality. It felt all sorts of strange on one hand and on the other, as if something around the corner was hanging around waiting to trip her up. She wasn't sure if she wanted to find out.

7

Emmy opened the door to the box room in the small rental cottage. It was a tiny space but one which had served her well when she had first started Love Emmy x. Just about big enough for a cot or single bed, it had been the space where her small but growing business had started in earnest. It was filled with tonnes of hard work, a lot of thought, and big dreams. The room was organised to the max, lined with large plastic storage tubs with snap-on lids, all categorised into sections of jewellery styles and types. Each section was further clarified; vintage style, antique pieces from Emmy's vast collection, pearls, floral, charms, bracelets, and many more.

To the right side of the room, a small table held Emmy's packaging supplies – rolls of beautiful grosgrain ribbon, stunning cream jewellery boxes, pretty padded envelopes, and lovely gift bags. All of it thought through to the ninth degree. All of it delightful. All the start of the Love Emmy x dream. Emmy sighed happily as she looked around, checking that everything was in order for the move to Darling Island and marvelling at how far she'd come. It had all started with a simple love of a locket her grandma had given her when she was a little girl and grew steadily from there.

Emmy had been collecting jewellery for years, fuelled many moons before by sweet little shopping trips with her Grandma Emily. In those days, they would trundle off to charity shops and independent jewellers, and spend hours wrapped up in a world of sparkle and beautiful trinkets, topped up with a stop in a tea shop for a bit of a sit-down. Emmy cherished those days now that her Grandma Emily was no longer around, and couldn't quite believe that now, with the help of Emily's money, Emmy was somehow able to capture those days. She not only had her own online store, but an actual commercial business premises to call her own. She could barely get her head around it; it felt so unreal. She did know that she felt as if a little bit of Grandma Emily was a part of it all.

She glanced over to a small shelf above the wrapping table where it had all begun. Grandma Emily's antique jewellery box, with its layers of tiny drawers, took pride of place and reminded Emmy of so many things from the past. Beside it, Emmy's first jewellery box of her own from when she was a child. She ran her finger over her name, painted in a soft pink by her dad on the top, then she turned the gold key with its old frayed tassel on the end, opened the lid, and watched as the ballerina inside twirled in her tutu on her toes. The familiar Swan Lake tune filled the room, and Emmy smiled to herself as goosebumps ran up and down her arms as her mind filled with memories. Suddenly she was back in her bedroom at the top of her mum and dad's house, tucked up against the radiator on a cold day. There she would open and close the lid over and over again, wind up the key at the back, losing herself in charm bracelets and necklaces, her mind whirling to the tune of Swan Lake. As Tchaikovsky filled the room, Emmy would sit and sigh and dream. Now, here she was all these years later, older, grumpier, not quite as rose-tinted, tainted by the realities of real life but more or less doing the same.

Looking around the box room with her mind flooded with memories of Grandma Emily, she wondered if this next move she was undertaking really was her living the dream. It had certainly felt like it at the beginning. When she had been on Darling Island to collect Callum's birthday cake, just after the man had knocked into her when she'd first seen The Old Ticket Office, she'd felt as if it had been meant to be. Emmy's mind went back and flicked over the day that she'd followed Dan, the estate agent, inside the building. She'd been clutching the huge cake box with wide eyes when a feeling in her bones had whooshed in and taken her by surprise. The building, the estate agent, the trip – it was all somehow as if it had been meant to be. And now somehow, she felt as if Grandma Emily had been looking down on her all along.

Emmy stood by the window, peering down onto the street outside, contemplating her dream's progression. She tried to envision The Old Ticket Office without its nicotine yellow paint, without the dust, and with a new lease of life. She closed her eyes and thought about the front of the shop and how, once she'd got her hands on it, it would look. Plonking herself down on a cardboard moving box, Emmy slid her iPad over and clicked on her Pinterest board, where she'd noted hundreds of shop decor ideas. As she scrolled down, her mind filled with how The Old Ticket Office was going to look dressed in a cascade of flowers out the front. The dream in her head was lovely – a gigantic garland of flowers going over the front door, trailing across the windows and falling down the sides.

She flicked to her spreadsheet and the quotes she'd had for an artificial flower installation and shook her head. The price hadn't been part of the dream and had made her eyes water. She'd quickly realised that in the Love Emmy x shop story, there would be less professional florists at work and more Emmy Bardot DIY.

Once Emmy had worked out that if she wanted the artificial floral display outside the shop, she'd have to do it on her own, she'd got her dad, Bob, on the case, and together they had spent hours forging a plan. The two of them had watched many a video on installing flowers on a building – from a flower shop in Tokyo showing tips on Hanging An Artificial Flower Installation, to How to Create a Wedding Canopy Installation. They'd become well-versed in how to create a shop window floral installation on a budget. Bob had overnight become a 'mono floral groupings' expert and savvy in the intricacies of putting one up.

Emmy laughed to herself at the thought of Bob surrounded by flowers as she flicked onto her emails and checked the artificial flower vines she'd ordered. She gulped – hundreds of the things were on their way to Darling Island, and she needed to make it work. It had taken a substantial part of her budget, and she'd probably tried to run before she could walk, but the vision in her head was what had spurred her on with her dream in the first place, and so she'd let the dream run as fast as it liked. She laughed as she imagined Bob, her dad, knee-deep in flower garlands, grinning from ear to ear as he tried to tack flowers to The Old Ticket Office's exterior walls.

Emmy closed her eyes and tried to skip past the before shot of The Old Ticket Office and move swiftly to the after. She imagined sunlight streaming through the shop's windows and the light twinkling on the vintage display cases that would house her jewellery bits and bobs. She scrolled through her emails, confirming delivery times and checking through the order receipts. Her finger brushed over the little icon of her online shop, and for a moment, she allowed herself to take in the reality of it all. Love Emmy x was about to go from the virtual world to a tangible, physical place where customers could walk in, talk, and touch the items they were buying. She thought about the front step, which would welcome customers as they arrived. There would be hexagonal tiles inlaid with Love Emmy x at the entrance. On stepping inside, beautiful old display cases would be filled with the jewellery currently stored all around her in gigantic tubs. Emmy opened the eBay app and studied the images of a lovely old vintage timber twelve-glass drawer unit she'd bought, which had been going for a song. She'd found it almost by chance with a low starting bid and had promptly put it on her watch list. A week later, as the listing was coming to an end, she'd bid on it and, to her surprise, successfully won – another thing that had been meant to be.

For a few minutes, she just sat where she was, lost in a world of her own, thinking about her new shop. She imagined the chime of the shop bell over the door as customers entered, the smell of fresh flowers wafting in from huge jugs of pretty roses scattered here and there. She could hear soft chatting, a happy hello, maybe cups of tea. She imagined Love Emmy x with its gorgeous floral display out the front being an integral part of everything Darling Island. She imagined the fresh sea air, the sound of seagulls in the distance, and the bustle of island life, all combining into one happy little jewellery shop place.

Yes, this was the dream, one that had started many moons ago on Saturdays out shopping with Grandma Emily. Emmy Bardot was more than just opening a shop; she would be connecting people to memories, to emotions, and to dreams. Most of all, though, she was doing something for her.

Emmy glanced at her watch and stood up from the cardboard box. There was still a lot of work to be done. But as she stepped out of the box room, closing the door behind her, she was heading towards the realisation of her dream. And she couldn't wait to see it come to life. Love Emmy x was no longer something on a laptop screen and in her head; it was, indeed, on its way to becoming a beautiful reality on its very own little island surrounded by a hazy blue English sea.

8

Emmy had been securing tape to the tops of cardboard moving boxes all morning. Her eyes lit up as she watched a delivery van reverse park in a spot outside, and a woman emerged from the driver's seat, slid the van door open, and began to extract a sizable parcel from the back. Among a multitude of deliveries that had been arriving in preparation for her new endeavour with her shop on Darling Island, there was one in particular that Emmy had been eagerly awaiting – the decal to go on the front door. As per the advice of just about everything she'd read about small business, she had significantly upgraded her branding. Her old Etsy shop feel, though functional, was being replaced with a premium, pretty, very Darling-esque look. She scooted through to the hallway and opened the front door.

'Hello, love. Parcel for E Bardot?' the delivery woman called out as she looked over the stumpy cottage wall by the pavement. 'Would that be you?'

'That's me,' Emmy affirmed, making her way to the end of the path, watching as the woman put the large box down and busied herself with the delivery gadget.

'I've got a couple more in the back,' the woman commented, gesturing towards the logo emblazoned on the parcel. 'What have we got here then?' she asked, passing the time of day.

'New branding for my new shop.'

'Setting up in town, are you?' the woman said as she tapped into the gadget without looking up.

'No, not here. I'm moving to Darling Island. Down on the coast. Do you know it?'

The woman stopped tapping, looked up, pursed her lips and raised her eyebrows. 'Pricey! My nan lives on Darling. A lovely part of the world.'

'Yes, I hope so.'

'On the main drag there, are you? On Darling Street?'

'I am, actually, yes.'

'Nan lives on the other side. Ahh, you can't go wrong on Darling if you ask me, not that you were,' the woman said as she clanged the gate and continued to chat as she pulled a couple more parcels from the back of the van. 'My nan loves it. The trams were the clincher. Best thing she's ever done retiring down there. The people are lovely. Most of them, anyway.'

Emmy grinned. 'You think so? That's reassuring to hear. I've been having kittens whilst I've been packing boxes all morning.'

The postwoman chuckled. 'Absolutely. You'll do well on Darling from what I've seen.'

'That's the hope.' Emmy beamed as she signed for the parcels. 'I'm opening a jewellery boutique.'

The postwoman's eyes widened. 'A jewellery shop, eh? How exciting!'

'I hope so.'

With a wink, the postwoman added, 'Just make sure you suck up to the residents. They are funny like that. That's your winning formula.'

'Thanks for the advice. I'll bear it in mind,' Emmy said as she picked up one of the boxes.

'All the best with your new shop, love,' the postwoman called out through the window as she settled back into her van.

With a box in her arms, Emmy walked back into the cottage. She smiled as she slit open the packaging and then held up a decal she'd had printed for the front door. She smiled as she examined it – a beautifully crafted logo to go on the glass door. Handwritten calligraphy writing in matte gold looked back at her. She felt a little sigh of relief inside; alongside loads of other things in the previous few weeks, the branding had been a gamble and an expensive one at that. But as she held the decal up to the light, she was more than pleased. It looked just as she'd hoped, possibly better. Just right for an old ticket office with a beautiful shop counter waiting for a new owner and a transformation.

After marvelling at the decal a bit more though and thinking she'd started to run before she could walk, Emmy carefully rolled it back up and tucked it next to the pile of boxes with essentials that would be travelling to Darling Island with her in the car. She then shimmied around a stack of boxes by the kitchen doorway, filled the kettle, and then walked out into the garden to see if the washing was dry. Just as she was standing unpegging it from the line, her neighbour Marcel appeared over the fence.

'A drying day if ever I saw one,' Marcel said cheerily, pointing up to the sky. 'One of your last ones in this house.'

'Yes, yes, I only put this out a few hours ago,' Emmy agreed, also looking up at the sky.

'How are you getting on with the packing?' Marcel asked.

'I'm about all done. It's getting very real,' Emmy said with a little shudder.

'All going well?'

Emmy sighed lightly. 'Good, I think. It's just… suddenly, I'm having a few wobbles. I mean, why would I do this? Callum is happy here, and my job is a bit same old, but it's fine. We're settled and happy enough. I'm just doubting myself, actually. I just said the same to my sister on the phone earlier.'

Marcel studied Emmy for a moment before responding, 'I get you. It must be quite nerve-wracking. The thing is, you won't know unless you try. Better than not knowing, even if it turns out to be a mistake.'

'You think so?' Emmy said with her face wrinkled into a frown. 'It's not feeling like that at the moment.' She looked around at the garden. 'It's so safe here. I know what I'm doing.'

Marcel nodded. 'Absolutely. Look at me. Oh, if only I could turn back the clock. I wanted to set up a little tea shop down in Cornwall for as long as I can remember. It was always a little daydream of mine. Back in the day, it was cheap as chips down there. Now it's drowning in millionaires from London who don't even live there.' Marcel sighed wistfully and then tutted at herself. 'I even looked at a little place down there in Padstow. Worth a fortune now. And here I am still in the same house I got married in. I'll always regret that decision. It is what it is.'

'Oh, yes, I remember you told me about that little tea shop idea you had for Cornwall.'

'Don't remind me about the regret.' Marcel shook her head. 'What I'm saying is, if you're feeling the pull, go for it. You never know what's around the corner. Life's too short for regrets. Learn from my mistakes.'

Emmy found herself agreeing. 'You're right. I'll never know if I don't do it. On the other hand, it's all good in theory, but now the reality of the move is kicking in, I'm wondering if I'm crazy to be doing this. You know?'

Marcel widened her eyes and shook her head. 'Nothing is irreversible, I reckon.'

'You really think so? Callum has to make local friends, I put all my savings into this shop, and what if it fails?' Emmy countered.

'You won't lose money down there from the little I know, so

there's that,' Marcel noted. 'As for Callum, that lovely boy will do well. So there you go, nothing to worry about.'

Emmy laughed. 'When you put it like that.'

'Trust me on this. Grab the chance while you can. I don't think you'll look back. Even though I'm going to really miss you.'

Emmy mulled over Marcel's words for a second. 'I guess so.'

'And another thing,' Marcel added. 'You won't be paying someone else's mortgage for the rest of your life. How long have you been saving so that you can do that?'

'Yes, true. A long time!'

'We've chatted right here over this fence about it many a time.'

'We have. Thanks for the wisdom. I needed someone to boost me a bit.'

'Happy to help,' Marcel said. 'Listen to that inner voice, my love. Do what you really want to do. Plus, you have your lovely mum and dad and Amy to support you. Not many have that.'

'Thanks, Marcel. That's really great advice, I will,' Emmy said as she picked up the washing basket.

As Emmy stepped back into the house, she felt a little less pressure. Marcel's words had given her a fresh perspective. The doubts had definitely arrived, and despite her mum and dad and Amy's help, she was nervous and wondering if she was doing the right thing. But if nothing else, she was ready to give it a go. Darling Island was the start of a new chapter in her life.

Two hours later, after lugging around more packing boxes and making Callum a cheese omelette after he'd come in from school ready to eat a horse, she found herself squeezed between boxes in the sitting room with her laptop open in front of her. She was mindlessly perusing the inspiring stories on the entrepreneur website she subscribed to. She let herself get lost in other people's success as she clicked over to watch videos and dove into the addictive world of independent jewellery boutique owners. As she watched a woman from Manchester with a beautiful boutique, and one in New York who had started off selling vintage jewellery and was now turning over half a million dollars a year, she felt inspired. Right in front of her were the goals for her new life. Emmy found herself bobbing her head affirmatively as if she could convince herself this dream was within her grasp. She tried to hold onto the thought that she, too, could join the ranks of those in charge of their own destiny. Those without a boss and thriving in a lovely small business.

With towers of cardboard boxes beside her, Emmy voraciously consumed video after video. She then went down a rabbit hole of related social media hashtags and found herself lost in a world of sparkly nice things, at the same time as exploring how to make a female-led business work in the real world. It was not for the faint of heart. She absorbed insights about everything from maximising profits without compromising integrity to budget-friendly ways to set up a productive workspace. The more she learned, the more she realised she knew more or less *nothing*. So far, the only experience she had was a fairly vast personal collection of jewellery she loved, wholesale orders which she photographed and put on Etsy and a small fairly busy business website. She realised with a sense of doom that her upcoming endeavour would be no little role play in pretend shopkeeping. She also realised she had her work cut out for her.

Emmy gulped and tried to convince herself she would be able to do the whole thing on her own whilst working double shifts a few days a week and looking after Callum. She'd thought she'd known what she was doing because she had a few suppliers she regularly bought from, a very healthy second-hand jewellery buying habit, and an Etsy profile which ticked over not too badly. Now she could see that everything was a steep learning curve, and she had so much to do. From business processes in retail to insurance to the whole area of logistics – all of which she had not much of a clue.

Squeezing her eyes together at the enormity of what she'd taken on, she tried to remain calm and convince herself that what Marcel said was true. She had to do it, or she would never know. Navigating to her online banking, she reassured herself that she still had a small pot of savings for all the things she needed to do. She attempted to cling to the notion that she would finally be out of the rental trap she'd been drowning in the centre of for years. But all the positive talk in the world couldn't stop the nagging question of whether or not she was making the right decision. A voice inside was yelling that she so was not.

Emmy thought about her job at the port and how, over the years, it had thrown up all sorts of problems and conundrums. If there was one thing it had taught her, it was that she was good at getting over hurdles, whatever they might be. While she, of course, had no formal qualifications in how to solve a problem, she was highly skilled in Problem Solving 101. But this conundrum she now found herself in the middle of was a bit different. It wasn't a person who had left their passport at home or someone complaining about being in the wrong queue. This was more or less a complete life change, a venture into the uncharted waters of entrepreneurship. The stakes seemed dauntingly high as she sat surrounded by brown paper boxes in her tiny rented cottage. And as much as she loved jewellery and her little dabbling with Etsy, owning and running a real jewellery store was an entirely different ball game altogether. Was she, in fact, just as much a gambler as Kevin? The daunting realisation made a little bit of sick come up at the back of her throat.

After sitting just staring out the window for a bit, Emmy navigated to Darling Island's community page Dan the estate agent had told her about. She'd have a look to get a feel for what was what. As Dan had said, it was full of all sorts. A real smorgasbord of all things Darling. Lost pets, locals who ran walking expeditions, the goings-on at the sailing club, and early tomato seedlings for sale outside the local coffee shop. She chuckled at the adverts – a weekend cleaning position at a local fish and chip shop, someone trying to sell a boat, and the football team was looking for a goalkeeper. Emmy wondered how a post from the new owner of The Old Ticket Office would go down.

She smiled to herself as she scrolled. If nothing else, it seemed as though there was a real sense of close-knit community on Darling. As she mindlessly scrolled, telling herself she had little time to waste wading through social media, she wondered how Callum would settle on Darling Island. She thought about him having to go to school via the floating bridge every day. First-world problems. She nodded her head that he would be fine. He had been into the idea of a commercial property right from the outset. When Emmy had first voiced her ambitions about the jewellery boutique, she'd resolved that if Callum wasn't on board and enthusiastic, she'd reconsider the whole plan. Callum, though, had been fine. He'd merely shrugged his shoulders nonchalantly, as only a teenage boy could. He'd expressed mild interest about the prospect of taking up surfing and living right on the sea and continued playing FIFA without really a care in the world.

As Emmy contemplated the huge leap she was about to make, she felt a pang of outright pure and simple fear. The uncertainty was almost suffocating. She swallowed as her stomach swirled. She suddenly got it about the gambling thing she'd never understood for years. She had a realisation about gambling and its high that had taken Kevin by the scruff of his neck – only hers was a gambling low. Very, very low. She kept berating herself that she was just like Kevin. She was gambling with her future, and as she was almost engulfed in brown cardboard, she felt as if she'd made a gigantic, no going back mistake.

9

Emmy was just about to head back in from the garden when the familiar ringtone of her phone broke the air. Pulling it out, she saw Kevin's name flash on the screen. Her stomach tightened, and she shook her head slightly. Their relationship had remained, from the outside, mostly amicable since the divorce. On her side of the bargain, though she never let it show, the relationship was strained. Because of Emmy's commitment to Callum, it *appeared* that she was friendly and happy towards Kevin, but underneath, everything about what had happened was raw and, even years later, still hurt. A lot. Kevin's gambling habit, which had torn their marriage apart, still lingered inside for Emmy every which way she turned. She sometimes wondered if she would ever be able to let it go. It would linger in the wings on her deathbed, waving its ugly acerbic self in glee. Although it appeared as if she and Kevin were friends to almost everyone, apart from Amy, who knew the real truth, underneath, Emmy had never quite been able to forgive. She had certainly not been able to forget. She was oh-so-bitter, and didn't she know it.

She felt a twinge of unease as she looked at her phone, her

thumb hovering over the slider. She knew Kevin's calls were sometimes unpredictable, depending on what was happening in *his* life. Outwardly, it was all friendly enough, but inside she often found speaking to him disruptive, and the last thing she needed just as she was about to embark on moving to Darling Island was anything that might potentially unsettle the precarious balance of her current life. Just seeing his name sometimes on her phone made her feel a strange mix of sadness, disappointment, bitterness, and loss for the life that she thought she was going to have. With him, she couldn't help herself but to lay masses of blame at his door. It was an in-joke with Amy and her mum and dad to 'just blame Kevin.' However, all joking aside, Emmy really did.

The phone continued to vibrate in her hand. Was she up for a Kevin call? She was tempted to let it go to voicemail and deal with whatever he wanted later. On the other hand, she wondered if it was about Callum. Despite their past and Kevin's flaws, they were both still parents, and that, if nothing else, required Emmy to swallow her feelings and continue with the pretence that she and Kevin were good friends. That they had an 'amicable' divorce. ******** to that. Drawing a breath, she slid the button and brought the phone to her ear.

'Hey, Kev. How are you?' Emmy greeted, her voice steady and friendly. An uneasy feeling churned in her stomach – calls from Kevin often meant trouble and that he was needing money or help.

'Hi, Em.'

Emmy let out a sigh of relief. She knew this voice. He was fine. She could almost see his broad grin, the same one that had once charmed her.

'Just calling to see how you're getting on with the packing.'

Emmy glanced around the cottage, her gaze landing on the new decal propped up in its box in the corner. 'I'm actually doing okay. Everything is sorted. Yeah, I'm fairly organised.'

Kevin, as usual, didn't really listen to her answer. She tutted inside as he made the call about himself and launched into a rambling anecdote about his latest exploits and how with Callum on Darling they would be able to take up boating. Emmy listened, half-distracted, one hand toying with the edge of the decal. Kevin had always been full of grand stories and wild dreams. It was one of the things that had initially drawn her to him – his unabashed enthusiasm for life. But over time, she had learnt the hard way that not all that glitters is gold. As he chuckled at his own joke, Emmy felt a bit sad. Here she was on her own, heading on a new adventure. When she'd married Kevin, she'd thought her adventures would be with him. Once, they had shared everything. They would scheme and plan and chat late into the night. Now, they were supposedly friends who had once been married, united by a shared history and Callum. Even years later, it was a strange reality to grapple with, and though they had been divorced a long time, she still hadn't ever really liked how it made her feel.

Kevin's voice broke through her thoughts. 'Callum was telling me all about the shop. It sounds great, Em.' There was genuine warmth in his voice. 'I was surprised you didn't ask me to have a look.'

'Thanks.' Emmy found herself softening. No matter his faults, there was one thing she could say about Kevin; he had always been her cheerleader. Especially when he was spending her money on gambling or when he'd been suffering from the subsequent post-gambling binge depression. He'd raised his glittery pompoms doing that many a time. She shoved that old bitter thought to the back of her mind. 'It's been a lot of work, but I'm excited to get on with it now.'

'I bet,' Kevin replied. 'You know, I always knew you'd do something amazing.'

Emmy's heart squeezed. Despite the messy divorce, the

heartbreak, and the countless let downs, she couldn't ignore the past.

Kevin's voice took on a serious tone. 'I'm really happy for you, Em.'

Emmy hesitated, the silence heavy with unspoken words. 'Thanks,' she managed finally. His words and being surrounded by moving boxes and everything that was on her plate, reminded her of their past dreams. All of that, though, was long gone. Kevin had had enough chances, and he'd never come up trumps. What they'd had together had been replaced by new hopes, new aspirations, and a new life that she was building for herself and Callum. Top of that was the fact that she would finally be getting out of the rental trap – the place Kevin's actions had ceremoniously dumped her in and left her for dead whilst he'd indulged in the joys of shiny, happy slot machines going around and around.

'If you ever need any help, the offer is there. You know how much I, well, you know all that.'

Emmy wasn't even going to go there. She couldn't be doing with Kevin and his grand proclamations. 'I'd better go,' Emmy said. 'I've still got loads to do.'

'Take care. I hope it goes well.'

'You too.'

As she put her phone down on top of a box, Emmy took a deep breath. The combination of the conversation and her current situation had zoomed her backwards to a place and thoughts she'd buried for a long time. She felt strangely nostalgic, memories of how she thought her life with Kevin was going to turn out. Scenes from the past when Callum was a baby came rushing back. But as she looked around at the boxes, the struggles when Kevin had finally moved out came crashing back. She remembered how much she'd relied on her mum and Amy when his gambling addiction was at its peak. How her dad had been on the end of many a call for help. Emmy stared at the idle screen of her phone, Kevin's words echoing in her mind. He was not a bad man when he wasn't wrapped up in gambling debt. His laughter had a way of spreading, and his heart was mostly in the right place. These were the qualities that had drawn her to him in the first place, and the reasons they had remained on mostly friendly terms even after their split.

Her mind wandered to Kevin's offer of help, and she imagined him helping her with The Old Ticket Office. How nice it would be for him to help out and be around more for Callum. Reality didn't take long to vigorously shake her out of *that* daydream. There was a shadow that loomed in the background of the scene where Kevin was there for her and Callum. A big dark phantom shadow of his gambling addiction that had strained their relationship, leaving scars so deep they sometimes felt to Emmy as if they physically ached.

She looked out the window, her gaze unfocused as she played with the idea of Kevin being involved with her new venture. Maybe he had changed, maybe he was more responsible now, maybe he could be a part of her life without causing upheaval. Maybe *not*. Kevin's cheerful offers over the phone were eerily reminiscent of the past. She had been down that road before. One that led to sore and rabid disappointment. In a flash, Emmy remembered the times she'd opened the post to find unpaid bills and final notices, the result of Kevin's gambling habit that had drained their savings. She remembered the countless therapy sessions, the hollow apologies, and the eventual realisation Kevin's promises never really lasted long. She remembered moving into a dark and dingy rented flat not long before Callum had started school. She thought about how hard her dad had worked to help her make the best of the crummy little place.

She shook her head and pulled a face. There was no way on earth Kevin was going to get even close to her dream. She squeezed her eyes together and shook her head quickly. Her relationship with Kevin was part of her past, a chapter that had ended. She didn't have time to even think about it, let alone allow it to fester in her head. Emmy Bardot was looking forward, not back. It was time for a new start and to think about herself. Yes, she was always going to have Callum front and centre of her mind, but The Old Ticket Office and Darling Island were going to be central in the next part of the story – the chapter where Emmy was the lead in her own life.

As she sat beside skyscrapers of cardboard boxes, she turned her attention back to her plans and let thoughts of Kevin, of Callum as a baby, of the rental trap and the gambling, slowly drift away. She nodded. She had a shop to set up, a life to start, and no room for ghosts of the past. If there was any betting going on in her life, she was going to be the one doing it. This time, she was betting on herself, on The Old Ticket Office, and on Darling Island. And as far as she was concerned, she was the odds-on favourite by a long shot.

10

Emmy fiddled with Grandma Emily's beaded pearl earrings in her ears, placed glasses on her nose and carefully scanned the list displayed on her iPad. She couldn't shake off the feeling that something was missing. She had packed everything neatly into boxes, dealt with the utilities, prepared a separate box with arrival things, and emptied the fridge. On paper, or as it actually was, on screen, it appeared as if her new life was about to start.

She paused in Callum's room, staring out onto the street outside, and watched as Marcel from next door clicked her car remote and got into her little blue car. Emmy gazed at the busy street scene and grimaced at what she was doing. She hated more than anything being in the rental trap, but she'd been in the little cottage for a while. The landlord was lovely, and although it was expensive and tiny, overall, the cottage had served her and Callum well. She felt safe and sound and knew what was what. As she watched Marcel's car drive away, her stomach churned. This was it. It was really happening.

She had willingly spent all her grandma's money on a dream. She was just like Kevin. She'd gambled on a somewhat neglected property on Darling Island she knew more or less nothing about. She would be plonking herself in an area where she knew not a single soul and had no idea if it was going to work out. Uncertainty fluttered in her chest, intensifying the unease that had been hitting her in spades as the moving date approached. The doubts had dug in deep when she'd started to finalise all the last-minute details of packing up her and Callum's life.

Now, as she watched the little familiar movements on the street outside Callum's bedroom window, the worry here and there had grown into full-on tremors of anxiety. Inside, she questioned not only whether the leap of faith was the right thing to do but her sanity too. She'd been floating along quite nicely with everything in her life not too bad. She'd willingly taken a gamble on all of that.

She tried to reassure herself of the positives. She had the support of her mum, dad, and her sister, she was out of the rental trap, and she had the luxury of working part-time and building a business. She needed to be more grateful and try and think how it was all going to turn out for the best.

Glancing around Callum's room, where his boxed-up things were stacked neatly in the corner, Emmy swallowed hard. It might not be hers and could have been taken away at any time, but she loved the room where Callum had done his growing up. Now they'd be going somewhere else. Somewhere strange and unknown and what felt like a long way away.

She walked down the stairs and did one final sweep around. It was a rental place, but it was filled with memories, and it had been their home. When she'd moved out of the flat, the cottage had been like a palace, the place her heart had healed from Kevin, and she'd settled into life on her own. There had been a few nice relationships too. There'd been the dad she'd met at Callum's school. He'd been kind and sweet, good-looking, and nice to boot. But even though they'd stayed together a while,

Emmy had always known inside he wasn't quite the one. Then there'd been Amy's neighbour. That had been quite the ride, but when he'd started to talk about babies and all that jazz, Emmy hadn't been seen for dust.

Picking up a box and taking it out to her car, Emmy thought about The Old Ticket Office. She mused about how as soon as she'd stepped in, she'd known it was the place she'd been looking for for years. The building, with its street frontage and charm, had spoken to her. It wasn't absolutely perfect, but it ticked so many of her boxes it was untrue. And it came with complimentary extras; a place to actually call her own, a space for her business, and a chance to live by the sea. Surely, there could be nothing wrong with that?

Emmy's stomach knotted at the thought of the shop as she pushed a box across the back seat of the car. She could see the finished space in her head as clear as day: beautifully hand-crafted pieces of jewellery displayed in antique glass cases, twinkling lights, piles of old books, quaint old things. She could almost hear the chime of the bell as customers entered. Little candles would flicker, the air would smell of aromatherapy oils, jugs of flowers would be dotted here and there, and piles of old books would display pretty unique necklaces and rings. A shop full of stories ready to please. This was a chance for her to finally turn her dream into a reality, but what she hadn't bargained for was the fear.

'I can do this,' she affirmed out loud, giving herself a nod in the reflection of the hallway door. Then, with a deep breath, she closed the door to the cottage. As she walked down the path heading for her car, she tried not to feel sad. A new chapter was about to begin.

11

By the time Emmy found herself in the queue waiting for the ferry to Darling Island, she wasn't feeling positive. Nowhere near it. In fact, she was engulfed in a tidal wave of regret. Her car was so crammed full to the roof with boxes and bags that her knees touching the steering wheel felt strange and unfamiliar. It was as if the past ten years were bundled up beside her, and the remainder was somewhere in a removal van. As the ferry swallowed the cars ahead of her in the queue, she looked in the rearview mirror at the mainland. It was almost as if she was leaving her old life behind. Her old life that wasn't too bad.

Casting a sidelong look at the empty passenger seat, she pondered over what Callum would make of his first commute home from school on the ferry. Knowing him, he wouldn't be phased in the least. When they'd come for a third look at the flat, he'd shrugged and remarked he thought it was alright. As she inched the car closer to the one ahead, nearly touching the bumper, Emmy's gaze flicked to the console and landed on the bulky envelope from the solicitors. It housed not only crucial documents but also a rough draft of her business plan, and the letter her grandma had sent her when Callum was born.

She watched from the driver's seat with a tightened chest as the ferry descended into the water, the hazy blue seemingly wrapping itself around the entire vessel. As Darling Island loomed closer, she fought back the urge to burst into tears. She was embarking on what now appeared to be a hare-brained scheme that looked and felt absurd. Jewellery boutique? Okay then. The unknown felt disgustingly daunting. Suddenly, the small ferry didn't appear quite as quaint or sweet. It banged noisily, swayed haphazardly and juddered not happily at all. Right at that second she hated everything about the ferry, its tower and the crew dressed in blue.

On the other side, Darling Island was shrouded in its usual haze, and it seemed like a whole new world. Emmy shook her head and closed her eyes. She wasn't sure why, but as its newest resident, Darling Island was definitely not seeming quite as friendly or welcoming as before. Her phone buzzed, breaking her from her thoughts and jumbled stomach. A text message from Amy.

Amy: *Good luck for today. Sorry I couldn't get the day off. See you tomorrow.*

Emmy smiled. Thank goodness for Amy.

Emmy: *Thanks. I'm having MAJOR second thoughts.*

Amy: *Oh.*

Emmy: *I must be nuts to be doing this.*

Amy: *Just blame Kevin.*

Emmy: *Ha!*

Amy: *You'll be fine.*

Emmy: *I hope so.*

Amy: *Wait until I get there. We'll get it shipshape in no time.*

Emmy: *I'll hold you to that.*

Amy's text made it feel all the more real. The weight of the decision hit Emmy like a tonne of bricks. She really was doing it.

As she gripped the steering wheel like a vice and steered her car off the ferry, the place *looked* good, she'd give it that. As she looked to her left, it was straight out of a coastal postcard, bathed in morning sun, the hazy blue sea stretching out infinitely into the distance. Boats dotted on the water gently bobbed, and the sea air, laced with a tang of salt, filled her lungs as she took in a deep breath. At least the air was good. In the distance, she could see the trams trundling along together with the faint sound of clanging bells.

Driving along with her heart in her mouth, she took in neat rows of white townhouses snaking away down Darling Street. People chatted outside small cafés, others strolled along the pavement, and no one seemed to be too much in a rush. Halfway along Darling Street, just past the doctor's and the church, she saw the parade of shops and The Old Ticket Office. The row of identical shops was unmissable, with hers sitting just about in the middle. She shook her head as she got closer. There it was, The Old Ticket Office with its double frontage, lovely old turquoise glass, and Dutch canopy in stripy blue and white stretched over the front. Emmy felt a flurry of butterflies at the sight of the shop. It was actually hers. She had somewhere to call her own. She still couldn't quite believe it was actually true. Bunting danced above the shop and swayed in the breeze. Her stomach followed suit.

A few minutes later, with the keys in her hand, she walked up to the entrance, her hands trembling, and her legs felt oddly shaky. As she turned the key, her breath was coming in rapid gulps, and as she stepped in, she winced as the dusty old former insurance office looked back at her. Standing in the musty old room, Emmy suddenly felt very alone. Callum was at school, her sister wouldn't be coming over until the next day, and her dad had a long-awaited appointment at the hospital, meaning neither her mum nor dad had been able to help on moving day. On top of being on her own, instead of what she'd anticipated happening when she walked in, she felt her heart sink. When she'd first viewed the place, she'd clung to some romantic notion that the building and she were a match made in heaven and that it had all been meant to be. She'd even stupidly and secretly told herself that Grandma Emily had somehow orchestrated it from above. However, with the keys in her hands, none of those former romantic notions were at the fore. Instead, there wasn't a whole lot of romance going on. What presented to her was precisely what it was; an old insurance office complete with yellowing walls, a lot of dust, and a sad, boxed-in counter in the corner. Inspiring it was not.

Emmy tried not to get disheartened. Dan, the estate agent's words about the potential rang in her ears, and she tried to focus on those instead of the reality all around her; a grubby old insurance office with not a lot of glam. She took a step back towards the door and stood on the step, looking down the street. A tram trundled away in the distance. The combination of quaint homes, bustling shops, and glimpses of the sea stretching beyond the horizon looked back at her. Outside the office, the things she couldn't change were more than lovely. At least there was that. She'd have to cling to them for dear life. She tried to convince herself that she'd known that and taken into consideration the thing they always said on the house-buying shows; location, location, location. The street had that in spades. Darling Street was nothing short of gorgeous.

Inside, though, not so much. Emmy could now see as clear as day that the place left a lot to be desired. She'd obviously been swept up in the fantasy of it all. She breathed in and out and tried to stop her heart from racing, and endeavoured to remember the feeling she'd had when she'd first viewed the building. How she'd somehow felt a sense of connection to not just The Old Ticket Office, but to Darling Street.

She peered down the street, wondering why she'd felt that in the first place. She tried to work out how and why the street, with its trams and bunting, had pulled her in. It was all a bit of an odd mix – a seemingly tranquil feel from the nearby sea and surrounding hazy blue, juxtaposed with the energy from the bustle of locals and the livery of the blue and white trams. Emmy just stood there for a while, watching and procrastinating about going back in. The bunting overhead fluttered, a man on a bike rang his bell as he cycled by, and a woman with a basket over her arm pushing a pram raised her eyebrows in greeting. Emmy tried to remain positive and thought about how this lovely little place was going to be her new home.

On walking back in, Emmy didn't know what to think. The Old Ticket Office now looked exactly as it was and quite grim. She was standing in an insurance office housed in an old building with a three-bed flat above and an odd in the eaves room on top of that. She didn't know whether she was over the moon or terrified as she gazed at what suddenly seemed to be a gargantuan amount of work. It had all looked so good on paper and with the inspiring stories of other jewellery shop owners in her head. Now the rose-tinted edges were a different colour; a sad, yellowed magnolia cream with a dollop of dust-induced depression on top. The only positive thing Emmy could think as she stood on the horrid nylon office carpet was that things could only go up.

12

Once the removal men had done their job and Emmy had spent most of the day lugging boxes around, it wasn't just the shabbiness of the shop that was front and centre. Together with that, the initial thrill of her actual new business wasn't quite in the room either. Love Emmy x had most certainly been left in the rental cottage. Everything was looking dismal. Plus, she felt really, really stupid about the decal for the door and the display unit she'd bid on; the building was nowhere near ready for anything even remotely like that. The almost overwhelming spaciousness compared to the tight little homely feel of the rented cottage, the dreariness of the back rooms, and the dust had meant that the whole dreamy, sparkly vision in Emmy's head had very much lost its lustre. Just blame Kevin.

As she stared at the water running from the tap for ages to make sure that it ran clean so that she could fill the kettle for tea, everything appeared more or less rubbish. As the sun moved and the building was partially in the shade, it got worse. Any scrap of loveliness streaming in with the sun coming through the window was diluted by shadows. As she sat on a cardboard box peering out the window on the first floor, looking down at the trams below, there was no denying that there was very much a sombre tone to the atmosphere. Not what she had envisioned at all. Emmy Bardot was having a major case of buyer's regret.

Later that day, after Callum had come home from school and attempted to help with the contents of her kitchen in boxes, Emmy and Callum had walked down Darling Street for fish and chips. After that, they'd spent ages trying to get some order to the moving boxes but had mostly just moved things from one space to another. What felt like organised chaos surrounded Emmy as she made up the beds. However, even with her and Callum's beds put together and made so at least they could comfortably go to sleep, Emmy found herself questioning not just her decision about buying the property but just about everything about the previous ten years. It did not feel like a fairy tale in *any* shape or form. The reality of her situation hit her with stark clarity – alone in a dusty old building, surrounded by a sea of boxes waiting to be unpacked, preparing to make sure Callum settled okay, and with the regularity of her normal work weeks completely out the window.

Once Callum had gone off to bed, Emmy felt the brave face she'd been wearing since he'd come home from school slip to the floor and land in a heap on the dusty nylon carpet. After making herself a hot chocolate from a sachet, she was sitting up in bed, forcing herself not to cry. Every now and then, she heard a tram go past, and the faint sound of the sea rumbled in the distance. An orange glow from a streetlight filtered onto the floor, and she could just see the moon hanging in the sky outside the window. The streetscape and moon made her think of the little rented cottage, which hadn't been her own, but *had* been home. She sighed as she sat alone, everything around her musty, shabby, a bit creepy, and she didn't feel that secure. Not only that, there was so very much to do. She stared at the rusty past-their-best metal blinds at the window and cast her eyes to the outdated bathroom in the corner. She shivered at the thought of the place in winter and absent-mindedly wondered if the heating worked.

With her mug of chocolate in one hand and phone in the other open at the notes app, she went down one of the gigantic lists of things that she had to do. It was all a startling wake-up call compared to the little dream she had of a lovely shop inspired by the opening of her grandma's jewellery box.

Emmy told herself her situation could be much worse. She lectured herself that she should be grateful for her inheritance from her grandma. However, reality was a startling wake-up call and not a very nice one at that. The daunting to-do list seemed endless. The enormity of it all made her heart race and her stomach churn. She and Callum had always managed okay, just the two of them. But now, alone in the dingy little flat with just her phone for company, she felt horribly down. Worry and concern flooded her mind. She sighed as another tram trundled past, and she rubbed her temples around and around, over and over again. Everything around her, from the horrid nylon carpet to the unfamiliar sounds, was telling her that she wasn't going to be living the dream for a very long time. This place was no dream. As she took another sip of her chocolate, thoughts crept into her mind that she had made a terrible mistake. But as had been the case since the day Kevin had started gambling, she didn't really have a lot of choice. Emmy Bardot had made her bed – it was time to lie in it.

Emmy jolted awake, the taste of the fish and chips and her misgivings about her decisions still lingering around her like a bad smell. She sat up for a second, wondering what had woken her as she took in the rusty metal Venetian blinds at the window. Hearing only silence, she told herself it was nothing, laid back down, and closed her eyes. Just as she turned over, she definitely heard something. A noise, like a rustle. It echoed through the empty flat. She lay still for a moment, straining her ears further and then, it came again – a tiny scratching sound, coupled this time with an unnerving scurrying. Then there was silence. Then it came again. There was no doubt about it; something was in the flat with her. She shuddered and shook her head. Things had, it seemed, got worse. Dust and disappointment weren't enough.

Levering herself up from the bed, she crept quietly into the sitting room, squinting her eyes as they adjusted to the light. Every creak of the aged floorboards tripled her apprehension as she screwed her face up into a wince. Flicking the light switch by the door, she scanned the room warily and listened again. Her eyes landed on a tower of moving boxes stacked up in the corner, and she froze as the sound came again. The rustling was coming from behind the boxes. And unless she was imagining it, there was also something coming from the direction of the kitchen.

In the harsh light from the bare bulb overhead, she moved closer to the pile of boxes, as her gut was telling her to do the opposite and run. As she approached the boxes, a tiny, sleek, dark creature darted out from the base and scurried into a crack in the faded skirting board. Another one then decided it might follow suit. Emmy jumped back, a scream catching in her throat. Mice. She shuddered. She'd not seen this coming. The Old Ticket Office was alive with moving things that were not her friends.

As she heard more rustling from what felt like everywhere, reality sunk in, and Emmy's heart thumped in her chest. A huge wave of regret washed over her as she stood in her pyjamas rooted to the spot with her hand clamped over her mouth, unable to do anything at all. With the horrible light from the nasty bulb, buyer's remorse clung on for dear life. She questioned every decision that had led her to this point, along with just about everything in her life. Her mind filled with thoughts of what she'd left behind – her familiar setup, the safety of her well-worn routine, Callum doing well at school. She'd chucked it all in and lusted after a shopkeeper's dream.

After not seeing any further scurrying animals, Emmy went back to bed. As she lay on her back staring up at the ceiling, listening to the intermittent trundle of the night trams and straining to hear scurrying noises, she felt isolated and alone. Things were not good. Just blame Kevin.

A few hours or so later, with the morning light filtering through the old blinds, Emmy heard Callum in the bathroom. She'd barely slept a wink, tossing and turning, her mind full of furry intruders. Even with the safety of daylight, the thought of what she had seen behind the boxes in the front room sent a shiver down her spine. Deciding not to tell Callum, she put on a brave face as she emerged from her room. Bare, yellowing walls and stacks of unpacked boxes greeted her as she plodded to the kitchen. Things were not looking any better in the morning light. The whole sorry flat was a far cry from the warm, welcoming space she'd left behind. She heard Callum turning on the shower and the sound of the old pipes creaking around the building and hoped that at least they would be able to have a hot shower before the day started. After she'd made a cup of tea, Callum emerged from the bathroom rubbing a towel on his hair.

'Morning, Mum. Alright?'

Emmy knew instantly by the tone of Callum's voice alone that he hadn't slept well either. 'Morning. Yep, fine. You?'

'Yeah, err, look, I think I saw a mouse last night.' Callum

winced. 'Or something at least. A noise woke me up and I came out here.'

Emmy sighed, her brave front crumbling a bit. 'Yep. Same. I know. I did the same.'

Callum's eyes widened in surprise. 'Oh right, okay.'

They stood in the middle of the less-than-homely flat with mugs of tea and stared into the room at the front. 'I'll get someone in to sort it,' Emmy breezed as if it was all fine. It so wasn't fine. However, there was no way she was going to let either her regret or her fear show. She wasn't about to let Callum see that she was wishing she could turn back the clock.

'Don't worry,' she assured. 'I'll call a pest service. It won't be too hard. Remember when Marcel had them next door?'

Callum nodded. 'Yeah.'

'At least they're not rats, from what I saw. Marcel had rats gnawing through the electricity cables, remember? Thank goodness for small mercies.'

'Yep.'

Emmy busied herself with making breakfast, pretending that the mouse problem wasn't a problem at all. It was *so* much a problem. As she delved into a cardboard box for a cereal bowl, she shuddered at the thought of the mice getting into their food. Things in The Old Ticket Office were not looking fantastic at all.

Once Callum had headed off to school, the flat seemed really empty and really grotty. It felt worse with Callum gone. Emmy found herself questioning more or less her whole existence. She must have been barmy to have even contemplated such a place.

After phoning a pest control company who were not only friendly but said they'd pop in that week, Emmy felt slightly brighter. Gathering her resolve, she went down the stairs, through the shop's back rooms, out via the tiny dated kitchen area, and opened the back door. The pest woman on the phone seemed to know about The Old Ticket Office and said someone would come by and would sort out the back area too. She'd said she'd thought they'd probably be outside as well as inside. Emmy went out to look, stepping out onto mossy old pavers, and stared around and down towards the half-shed. Passing old Victorian brick walls on either side, she pulled the rickety shed door towards her. It creaked loudly, revealing a musty interior, a mix of damp earth and something else, something that made her stomach churn. She knew exactly what it was. The same revolting smell from when Marcel next door had discovered rodents. Holding her breath, Emmy looked around the shed, her heart pounding in her chest. The signs were there – tiny droppings and the vile smell. A shudder ran down her spine. She slammed the door shut. Emmy stood there for a moment, staring at the shed, feeling despondent and furious with letting herself dream.

Overwhelmed, Emmy could hear the distant sound of the ferry and the clatter of trams passing along Darling Street. She looked back up at the three-storey structure that was now her home and livelihood. Its paint peeled in places, the windows reflecting an overcast sky. Mostly from the back side, it all looked quite forlorn. The charming double-frontage on the street with its Dutch stripy canopy and fluttering bunting that had caught her eye wasn't quite the same from the back. The dream of a new beginning, her floating around with a picture-perfect jewellery shop and a thriving business in a quaint island town, was replaced by the smack of reality. The vision in her head of fairy lights and pretty jewellery had been replaced by chats with people from pest control and dust. Regret washed over Emmy in waves as she closed her eyes and shook her head.

The worst thing about all of it was that Emmy felt totally

and utterly stupid. What had she been thinking? She gulped and shook her head over and over again. She was just like Kevin. She'd gambled her future and her grandma's money on something that was a silly, futile pipe dream that was going nowhere at all.

After going back upstairs to the flat, making her bed and having a shower, Emmy tried to focus on getting the flat sorted and deal with that first. With a mug of tea, she walked around assessing and reiterating her plan on what to do when. It had all looked so simple and easy from the comfort of the little rented cottage or the warm coffee shop at work. In the dreary light of an overcast day, it wasn't anywhere near as straightforward.

She definitely wasn't feeling very positive. With little choice but to put up and shut up, she picked up her keys to go and take her car to the petrol station so that it was full, get out of the place, and get some milk. In jeans, a big jumper, and with her hands full with her mahoosive handbag, a couple of letters from the utility companies, and her water bottle, she tried not to think about the shed and its droppings as she walked past.

Struggling with her full hands to yank the rusty old bolt across on the back gate and having to shove it as it stuck, she stepped out and frowned at a glossy black 4x4 Mercedes bumped up on the verge right outside the gate. Not only was the car parked haphazardly, it was obstructing both the lane and the access to her yard. By the looks of it, it had also blocked her in. Emmy tutted at the shiny, sleek car, which looked as though it had just rolled out of a showroom. She looked at her little car to the right, an old but reliable hatchback which had previously been her mum's, and the space the Mercedes owner had left for her. It would be touch and go with her parking skills as to whether or not she'd be able to easily get out.

Just as she was tutting, shaking her head in irritation, attempting to shimmy and sideways step between the cars, her bag toppled from her arms, its contents spilling over the lane. Swearing as she watched a lip gloss roll under her car, she bobbed down onto the ground and reached for it with her right hand. Just as she was gathering all manner of things all around her, she stopped as she came across a pair of brown leather boots on the end of jeans. On her hands and knees, she looked up to see the owner of the boots frowning down at her. The boots' owner had twinkly blue eyes, dark hair, and a strangely familiar look about him. He was clearly in a rush, and she could tell right away that there was an air of arrogance about him she found instantly grating. She watched as he slid a pair of sunglasses onto his face and stepped towards what was clearly his car with a confident stride.

'Excuse me!' Emmy said as she scrambled to get up, not bothering to hide the irritation in her voice. She inclined her chin towards the Mercedes as she lugged her bag onto her shoulder and brushed herself off. 'Is this your car?'

The man turned and looked at her, surprise raising his eyebrows. 'It is,' he said, a slight smile on his lips as he looked her up and down. 'Sorry, is that a problem?'

Emmy squared her shoulders, trying not to feel flustered by his good looks or his annoying attitude. 'You blocked me in,' Emmy said, flicking her eyes back to her little car.

The man pointed to a parking sign. 'As it says. Residents only. If you don't want to get blocked in, don't park here, even though there's still plenty of space to get out. It's not hard to work it out.'

Emmy followed his gaze to the parking sign as her blood boiled. She went to say something, but the man held his hand up and clicked the remote on his car. She started to explain, but he pulled open his door. 'Sorry, but I've heard every excuse in the book. If you're not a resident, don't be leaving your car parked where it shouldn't be,' he said dismissively as he looked Emmy up and down. 'It really isn't that hard to understand. Read the signs.' He pointed. 'Right there in front of you in black and white.'

Emmy spluttered and then, to her annoyance, heard herself squeak. 'I *am* a resident.'

The man frowned and flicked his eyes upwards. 'Course you are. Yeah, heard that one before, too. Whatever. Not interested.'

Emmy struggled with her water bottle and held up an envelope. 'My parking permit is in here.' She wiggled the envelope and the crinkly paper in front of her.

The man didn't look convinced. 'Sorry, but you need to be in the Darling Street Ticket Office Zone to park here.'

Emmy fiddled with the paper and squinted. 'Yeah, well, that's right. I am. That's what this says.'

The man just looked at her. 'You're in this zone?'

'Yes. I'm the new owner of The Old Ticket Office,' Emmy said quickly and flicked her hand towards the back of the building beside them.

The man's eyebrows raised in surprise. 'Ahh, the elusive new owner.' He looked at Emmy's car and then back at her. 'Okay, so that *would* make you a resident. Tom Carter. Nice to meet you.'

Despite herself and this Tom person's most definite superior attitude, Emmy felt a flutter of attraction. She attempted to scowl. 'Likewise, Tom. Not being funny, but would you mind not parking quite as closely in future?' she said, moving the water bottle and the envelopes into the crook of her left arm and then crossing her arms in front of her.

Tom laughed, a sound that made Emmy's insides turn over. He was annoyingly attractive. She couldn't be doing with that. She had no time for attraction in her life.

'Sorry about that.' Tom then mimicked what she'd said back to her. 'Not being funny, but you have plenty of room to get out there. Anyway, welcome to the island. I'm sure I'll see you around.'

Emmy watched, a bit dumbstruck, as Tom slid into the

driver's seat of his car, and in a quick flash, he was pulling onto the lane. She stood there with her arms full, a bit bewildered as she watched his car proceed to the end of the lane and indicate left. As the Mercedes disappeared from view, Emmy sighed and peered up and down the lane, then turned back towards the gate. She was simmering with irritation, with a dash of indignation thrown in for good measure. Underneath, there was an undercurrent of something else she couldn't quite fathom. A most definite flicker of attraction. It was unsettling and strange but sort of nice at the same time.

Emmy frowned as she walked to the driver's side of her car and fumbled with the door handle. She recognised this Tom from somewhere but couldn't quite place him. As she slowly manoeuvred her way down the road heading to the petrol station, her mind went over the previous twenty-four hours. It had all been stressful, and things hadn't gone quite to plan. The flat was a mess, the shop was a far cry from the vision in her head, and she had an uninvited mouse problem. One thing was looking up, though. The calibre of the neighbours on Darling Island wasn't too bad at all.

Emmy paused on the forecourt of the petrol station, the overcast morning matching her mood. She sighed as she looked at her car, still strewn with a few boxes. Closing her car's fuel cap with a click, she made her way across the concrete, and as she walked through the automatic doors, a whoosh of warm air hit her as she hurried in. She reached in to take a pint of milk from the fridge, picked up a packet of biscuits, and waited behind a man who was catching up with the woman behind the counter. Once it was her turn to be served, the woman smiled and tapped the computer to her right.

'Morning. Bit overcast out there, isn't it? No sunshine for us today. No such luck.'

Emmy smiled. It was nice to hear a friendly voice. 'Yes.'

'No fog, though. Not yet.'

'Are you expecting fog?' Emmy asked.

'Ahh, we always expect fog on Darling. It doesn't announce its arrival. That's what the foghorn is for.'

'Right. I see, yes, of course.'

'Here for the day, are you?'

'Err, no, I've just moved here, actually.'

The woman's head flicked back from the computer to Emmy's. 'Oh, sorry.'

Emmy frowned as she tapped her card against the payment machine. She hadn't expected the woman to know who she was anyway and wondered why she was apologising. 'All good.'

'Sorry, where have you moved to?'

Emmy put her card back into the slot on her phone cover. 'Darling Street.'

There was an understanding nod. 'Right you are. I'm Molly.'

'Emmy.'

'Whereabouts would that be on Darling Street then?'

Emmy wasn't sure if she liked the nosy nature of the woman's question. 'South Darling, at the bottom end.'

The woman's face wrinkled in confusion. 'Sorry, where? Where do you mean?'

Emmy felt a bit irritated, but she didn't let it show as she picked up the milk. 'What was the insurance office on the main road there.'

'Ahh, The Old Ticket Office! Yes, of course. So you're the new owner. Right, yes, nice. You'll fit in well by the looks of you, duck.'

'Thanks. Well, that's good to hear. Nice to meet you, Molly.'

'How are you getting on with it?' Molly queried. 'When did you move in?'

'Yeah, I've err got my work cut out for me, put it that way. We moved in yesterday.'

'Stressful, huh?' Molly asked with a sympathetic look.

Emmy lifted an eyebrow. She wasn't going to start telling this stranger that she felt as if she'd made a huge mistake and that she'd left what was a perfectly nice life on the mainland. 'Not too bad, it's just been a whirlwind of activity and well, there's a lot to do.'

'Ahh, well, you'll be fine once you're in. Welcome to Darling.'

'Thank you.'

'Jewellery boutique, isn't it?'

Emmy hid her surprise that the woman knew about her. 'Yes, that's right.'

'Well, if there's anywhere that will work, it's on Darling Street. Especially in that spot, not far from the homewares emporium and the deli.' Molly nodded and sniffed. 'Yeah, good choice, if you ask me.'

'Thanks.' Emmy didn't feel as if it was a good choice at that moment in time.

'Not at all. You'll do a roaring trade there if you ask my humble opinion. If there is one thing Darling and its visitors love, it's a nice shop, and we haven't had a jeweller on Darling for years and years.'

Emmy took the milk and packet of biscuits and smiled. At least someone was positive because, at that precise moment, Emmy Bardot was many things. Positive, she most definitely was not.

As Emmy got back to the lane, she noted that the Mercedes owned by Tom was nowhere to be seen, so she easily bumped her car up onto the grass verge and popped the boot. As she unloaded a box from the boot, she peered up at the top of the old building in front of her. From the back on the overcast day, it was a far cry from what she'd envisioned. There was one good thing that she needed to keep in mind – it was all *hers*. All hers, and she needed to make it work. She was left with little choice. She had to make the place a success one way or another.

With a big box in her arms, as she started to struggle towards the gate, she wondered who Tom was as she took in the space where his car had been parked earlier. She winced in embarrassment as her mind replayed the situation when she was crawling around on the ground, picking up the possessions from her handbag. Something nagged at her, a prickling sense of familiarity about Tom she couldn't quite place. She recalled the way he'd studied her when she'd stood up. He'd looked at her with a mix of mild interest, and she couldn't decide what, as he'd taken in her frazzled appearance.

She thought about his not-very-friendly smile and the way he'd been so confident it was borderline arrogant, definitely infuriating, but also *kind* of charming. It had stirred something in her, and she racked her brains to try and remember where she knew him from. The set of his jaw, his casual confidence, his mannerisms – she had seen him somewhere before. She went over where she might possibly know him from. Something to do with Callum and his sport, was it? Emmy had been all over the show with Callum's cricket over the years, and perhaps their paths had crossed at some point. Or was it from work? Tom seemed around her age, and the world at the port was a small one. Her brow furrowed as she tried to place him. With a frustrated sigh, she hoisted the box to her other arm and shook Tom out of her head. Now wasn't the time to be thinking about him. She had things to unload, a shop to sort, and a life to start.

As she put the box down, opened the back door, and clambered up the stairs to the flat, she suddenly stopped as she realised exactly where she knew Tom from. It had come to her. The day she'd first viewed the property when she was collecting the birthday cake. Tom was the man in the street who had bumped into her and messed up the cake. She had been too flustered and distracted to notice much about him at the time. Now, as she replayed their recent encounter in her mind, she realised he'd been the man in a rush. She also realised that he'd had the same confident, hurried demeanour then. She also realised she'd quite liked the look of him then, too. She could so manage bumping into him again.

13

Emmy had waved to Callum as he'd got on the tram, and she'd decided before she got stuck into lugging and sorting that she'd have a little exploration around Darling. As she watched the back of the departing tram, she smiled. Callum had settled in fine and had been using the longer journey to school to catch up on assignments. At least, that was what he'd told her. It was more likely he was scrolling through his phone, but as long as he was happy enough, it was good for her. Thank goodness for Callum's ability to take everything in his stride and get on with life.

Thinking about Callum, she remembered the tram from the day trips she'd had to Darling when they'd left the car on the other side. Callum had loved the tram when he was little, and they'd ridden up and down with him gazing out the window, pointing out all sorts. Now, years later and with Callum taller than her, as the tram trundled along with its bell ringing, Emmy loved not only the memories it poked but also how little had changed about the tram itself. It was mostly exactly the same as it had been all those years before.

Standing in the Victorian timber shelter on the other side of the road from The Old Ticket Office, she stood waiting for the next tram and peered up at a small digital sign screwed to the timber of the shelter. The sign changed, telling her a Bay tram would arrive in under a minute, a Castle tram in six, and a Darling Main shortly after that. Once the Bay tram arrived, Emmy watched as passengers got off and a pretty woman in a white polo shirt with blue epaulettes on the shoulders and waistcoat bustled around at the back. The woman called out towards the tram shelter. 'All stops, Darling Bay. For Castle, wait for the next tram. This one is Darling Bay! Darling Bay only!'

Emmy waited patiently as she stepped on behind a woman in a blue dress. The woman in the waistcoat spoke to the woman as she sat down.

'Morning, Mey. How are you on this fine day on Darling?'

'Good thanks, Shelly.'

'What have you been up to?'

The woman named Mey winced. 'I've been to the dentist, unfortunately.'

'Ahh, right you are. Not a fun way to start the day.'

'Nope.'

'What's the weather forecast for later?'

Mey chuckled. 'If you ask me, fog will be rolling in later.'

'Yep. I reckon so.' The woman laughed and then shimmied around a passenger and smiled at Emmy. 'Hello, there. Where are you off to?'

Emmy smiled. 'Hi. Thanks. I was hoping for a recommendation, actually. Somewhere for a cup of really good coffee would do me wonders.'

'You'll want the Bay. There are a few places down there,' the woman said as she waved a dongle in Emmy's direction. 'Tap on here, duck.'

Just as Emmy went to tap her card, the woman looked up. 'You're not a resident?' The end of her sentence lilted up in a question. 'I know you're not, but we have to ask. It's the law on Darling,' the woman said with a dismissive, slightly uninterested smile.

Emmy nodded. The odd resident question she'd now had a few times. 'I am, actually, yes.'

The woman Emmy had heard the other woman call Shelly, who was peering over to the other side of the carriage, snapped her head back to the conversation. 'No, sorry for the confusion. I meant do you *live* here on Darling Island? Do you reside here?'

'I do live here on the island, yes,' Emmy clarified.

Shelly lifted her chin and widened her eyes. There was a hint of a notion in her voice that she didn't believe Emmy. 'Sorry. You have to pay otherwise. Where's that then?'

Emmy was a little bit peeved. She looked to her left and right. She didn't really want to be discussing her address with the whole of the packed tram. Clocking the look on Emmy's face right away, Shelly raised her eyebrows. 'You're all good. So if you're a resident, you don't pay, of course,' Shelly said, with a slight frown. She didn't give up. 'Got a resident's permit, have you?'

Emmy shook her head. 'I've got the parking permit, but not the other one yet.'

Shelly smiled. 'Best you get yourself off down to the town hall, then.'

'I did apply for it online, but apparently, there's a delay,' Emmy replied as she went to sit down.

'Ahh, that's technology for you. It's great when it works.'

Emmy felt a bit mean that she hadn't said where she'd moved to. Shelly appeared to be friendly enough. 'I'm in The Old Ticket Office just down the way here.'

Shelly nodded and instantly seemed more friendly. 'Ahh, I see, right you are. Welcome.' Shelly chuckled. 'Lucky you. That place is a gold mine right there on the main street.'

Emmy didn't like to say that she was having serious doubts. As far as she was concerned, it was not a mine of gold. 'Mmm.'

'Well, have a seat and welcome to Darling.' Shelly gestured to the seats at the front and then moved towards the back of the tram, grabbed a plaited rope on the huge bell and yanked it back and forth. 'Now I know you're *actually* a resident wanting a good cup of coffee, I'll tell you where to go so that you're in the know.' Shelly chuckled and lowered her voice. 'Head on over to Darlings around the back there.'

Emmy repeated, 'Darlings?'

'I'll let you know the stop. It's a bit out of the way, as it were, but if you're a resident, you'll want to pop in and get yourself acquainted. If you want to know anything about Darling, go in there and speak to Evie or Lucie or any of the girls in there.'

'Thanks. Well, as long as the coffee is good, it'll work for me.'

'The coffee is great, but if you live on Darling, you'll need to go there to be part of it. You'll see what I mean. That, the ferry, and this tram are where everything goes on.'

Emmy didn't really understand, but she smiled anyway.

'Take it from me, you'll want a Darling basket. Ask for one. They'll know what that means.'

Emmy nodded, no idea what the woman was talking about. 'Will do.'

'All stops, Darling Bay!' Shelly called out towards the back of the tram.

As the tram trundled towards the bay, Emmy felt a little bit of the regret slip from her shoulders. She glimpsed the Darling hazy blue in between things and stared out at the old buildings as they passed – a fire station to her right, a butcher's, a shop doused in the blue and white bunting, and a bicycle shop. Emmy let it all wash over her, and she nodded. If nothing else, at least the scenery was nice, and the people seemed quite friendly. It did seem to have that going for it, it had to be said.

Once she'd hopped off the tram and walked along, she didn't

know where to look first. Despite her rocky start with the mice, the weather, and her regrets at the job in hand, she'd forgotten how nice Darling actually was. Had everything been as lovely in the days she'd visited as a day tripper? Had the hanging baskets always seemed bountiful? Had the bunting always looked as pretty? Had the cobblestone streets and winding alleyways always seemed so gorgeous? She couldn't really remember, but everything from the tram to the hanging baskets was somehow telling her that things were going to be okay.

She followed Shelly's instructions to walk through an alleyway, along a cobbled road with mews houses, and to turn at the end. She followed her nose until, just as Shelly had said she would, she came to a small café. Emmy squinted down the road at Darlings. It looked like just the sort of place she was after: a squat white bow-fronted shop covered at the front in a tangle of climbing flowers and window boxes full of plants. A sign announced 'Darlings' to customers, a few small café tables and chairs sat in front of the window, and old-fashioned lights hung on either side of the bow-fronted door. Emmy sighed at the scene where a row of bikes was wedged into a bicycle rack to the left, lace café curtains were at the window, and herbs in pots in a little cage hung from the wall by the door. As she got closer, she could see that a glass-fronted timber box held a menu, a black bike was leaned up beside the door, and an old doormat on a half step showed the way in.

A bell sounded overhead as Emmy pushed open the door, and she was surprised at what confronted her inside. The tiny place was both packed with patrons and exquisitely designed. She let out a little sigh. If this was how Darling Island did coffee shops, she'd stay. Small bistro tables were squeezed in on top of each other, the whole place was lined with floor-to-ceiling shelving, blue gingham tablecloths matched the napkins, and pots of plants and flowers were dotted here, there and everywhere. On top of the aesthetically pleasing interior, the air was filled with chattering and the chinking of china. As she stood just gazing around for a second, a small woman with long hair in a glossy ponytail appeared from nowhere and beamed. 'Can I help you?'

'I was after some coffee,' Emmy said as she looked around at the packed tables. The woman's eyes flicked around, and Emmy continued, 'I was sent this way from the tram. I was told to ask for a basket?' Emmy lilted her sentence into a question at the end.

The woman frowned. 'You were sent from the tram?'

'Yes.'

'Hold on a sec.' The woman whizzed down the centre of the café and then came back and pointed to a table in the corner where two old ladies were just getting up from their seats. 'I can squeeze you in there if you like.'

Emmy followed the woman. 'Thanks.'

Emmy sat down on a chair with a blue gingham seat pad and watched as the woman, who'd seated her, chatted to the ladies on their way out the door. Right after that, the woman was back and standing in front of Emmy. 'Coffee, you said?'

'Yes, please. A large one would be good.'

'And a basket? Just to clarify, you're a resident?' the woman said with a frown on her forehead, a question in her voice and a friendly, intrigued tone.

Emmy decided to cut straight to the chase. 'I've just moved into The Old Ticket Office. I should say the flat above it, rather.'

'Ahh, got you. Well, nice to meet you, I'm Evie.'

Emmy looked around. 'It's stunning in here. I would never have known it was here, tucked away.'

'Thanks, yes, it is just the way we like it. I do my best,' Evie joked. 'I hear we have a jewellery boutique coming to Darling.'

Emmy was surprised that Evie knew what was what, but she was beginning to realise that Darling Island locals were clearly clued-up on what was going on around them. 'Yes, that's right. At least, that's the plan.'

The woman smiled at a couple of customers who'd just come in the door and flicked her eyes back to Emmy. 'You have quite a bit of work on your hands there, then.'

That was an understatement, Emmy thought. *Just blame Kevin.* 'I do.'

Evie nodded. 'I'll bring you a basket. You'll need it.'

Emmy frowned to herself, not sure what a basket was and how the funny little place worked. She decided she'd just go with the flow and hoped it wouldn't be too expensive. As she sat back in her chair and took a proper look around, she suddenly realised that she was more or less completely surrounded by hundreds of bowls of all shapes and sizes filling shelves all around. Alongside the bowls, a plethora of teapots and gigantic glass jars filled with bags of coffee. At the back of the shop, shelving over the counter displayed bottles and kitchen paraphernalia, a coffee machine hissed and whirred, and a couple of staff in aprons whizzed around looking all sorts of efficient.

Emmy sat gazing around, lost in a world of her own, as a man in Ugg boots, a wetsuit with the top rolled down, a towel over his shoulders, and wet hair walked in, smiled at the girl behind the counter, took a basket and a coffee, and walked back out again. As Emmy sat staring around, Evie was back and placed a small bowl of coffee in front of her. 'Seeing as you're a resident, I got you a bowl. On the house, of course. It's how we do it on Darling. Yell if you want a mug. Basket is on the way.'

'Thanks.' Emmy smiled. The odd little place was getting more and more strange. Baskets and bowls were clearly a Darling thing. She touched the edge of the bowl, not sure what to do and looked around to see that nearly every person around her sat with a small bowl in front of them. She then noticed that there were little white wicker baskets all over the place too. Thirty seconds later, there was one in front of her. She looked down at it and wondered what to do. A small white basket with a blue and white gingham napkin knotted at the top looked back at her. Trying to act as if she knew exactly what she was doing, she fiddled with the knot and unfolded the fabric. Inside, small slices of French bread sat beside a glass jar with a ceramic lid with what looked like raspberry jam, and a boiled egg. Two mini Florentine biscuits wrapped in greaseproof paper were wedged in the side. As she looked back up, another member of staff was collecting bowls from a nearby table.

'Hi, I'm Lucie. Evie said you've just moved in. Welcome.'

Emmy was surprised at how friendly everyone was. It almost made her want to cry. 'Thanks. I'm Emmy.'

Lucie looked at the basket. 'I bet you're thinking this is all a bit odd, aren't you? Getting a basket plonked in front of you...'

Emmy pretended she wasn't. She so was. 'Not at all.'

'Ha! I did when I first moved here. The basket thing blew my mind. Yeah, so you've got the last of the morning baskets.'

'How does it all work then?'

'Ahh, we do them for all sorts. Every day is a different basket in Darlings, depending on what we have and what is in season.' Lucie pointed to the basket on the table in front of Emmy. 'Today, we had eggs from the farm and homemade Florentines from Hennie around the corner. You can order a breakfast or lunch basket to pick up, and we do them for school and work lunches and all sorts. Anything really, or you can make your own up. Let me know if you need anything else.'

Emmy took a sip from the bowl and looked around the packed coffee shop. The baskets were everywhere, and unless she was imagining it, people seemed to be happy. She picked one of the biscuits out of the basket, took a bite, and closed her eyes. If the rest of Darling was half as good as the food and the coffee, maybe she'd be okay after all.

14

Emmy walked into the front room of the old building, the one that would be the shop, dragged an old garden chair to the window, perched her laptop on the windowsill, and typed 'renovating a shop' into the search bar of Google, hoping to find some inspiration. She then watched in fascination as a woman in Pennsylvania bought a house on her credit card, a man in Cheshire turned an old garage into a yoga studio for his wife's business, and a couple on the coast of Norfolk turned a newsagent into a shop to sell handmade candles. As Emmy ultimately procrastinated and wasted time she didn't have on voyeuristically watching other people via the World Wide Web, she shuddered. She realised that along with the purchase of the building, she'd unknowingly dropped herself into a place she knew nothing about and had few resources to help her learn. Thank goodness, she did have one card to play up her sleeve – her dad. He, along with Amy, was coming to help for the day, and she was so very grateful she had them in her life.

It also dawned on her, as she sat with her chin on her hand and looked around what was still very much an insurance office, that in her job at the port and in the little rental cottage, she'd been in a bubble. At the time, she'd thought the bubble had limited her and hemmed her in at the edges in just about every aspect of her life. Now she realised that the bubble had been nice and safe, cosy even. It had kept all her ducks in a row, and she'd known every little piece of it very well. She'd quite liked her nice neat ducks. Now, with the remnants of the insurance office all around her, the bubble had burst. It was all very well not wanting to be ensconced in humdrum bubbles, that was, until they weren't there anymore. It was also all very well wanting to start anew and hoping to improve one's life. But as the actual logistics of that new life surrounded Emmy, it felt not only unachievable but as if she was destined to fail even before she'd begun. It did not feel nice. What was nice were the high ceilings, the old fireplace and the antique turquoise windows right in front of her eyes. She had good things to work with. She was going to have a go.

She opened her phone, tapped on Instagram, and scrolled to her favourite independent jewellery account. The woman who owned it was skipping along the road in a flower crown, a pink jumper with '1970' splashed across the front, and gigantic winged sunglasses. As the woman walked along a posh Harrogate street with her phone in front of her, she smiled and twirled a necklace in front of the screen.

'Tra la la. Off to the shop this morning, and hubby is coming along later to install the new display cases. Woo! So exciting! Thank goodness for gorgeous husbands and their help always. So blessed. Just *so* blessed. Tra la la.'

Emmy felt a little bit of horrible green envy swirl around the bottom of her stomach. The woman had even jigged. She wasn't feeling bouncy or twirly, and she certainly didn't have a husband to help her, gorgeous or otherwise. She didn't feel blessed either. Far from it. Her mind flicked to what had been her husband, and she let the bitterness she normally kept at bay flood in. Even years later, when she allowed it, she felt so much bitterness towards Kevin it was untrue. He'd had all sorts of hopes and dreams for them. She'd thought she'd loved him when she'd swept up the aisle, swathed from head to toe in white. Now, even though Kevin wasn't all bad, she felt let down on every level. She'd thought she and Kevin would have a nice little house, a nice little family, and a nice little life. What, in fact, had happened was Kevin had gambled most of that away, and Emmy had been left without a nice little anything. She couldn't stop her face from curling into disdain at the thought of how she had thought her life was going to go. Kevin had dreamt and schemed and promised so much, but none of it had come to be. And now, just as when Kevin had finally left after a massive month-long gambling binge, Emmy was the one trying to crawl her way out of a mess. Not that any of her current circumstances were Kevin's fault, but she felt as if somehow they were. Just blame Kevin. She tapped on the stories and watched as the woman continued to bounce along the road.

'Living my best life. Can't wait for hubby to arrive later and put the new cabinets in. So, so, so blessed. Life. Is. Good.'

Emmy looked around at the office and shook her head. Living her best life? Not quite. She had a dusty old insurance office with nylon carpet, unwanted guests, and a teenager to look after on her own. Emmy felt like crying, but as she looked around at the daunting task, she knew she didn't have time for blubbing. Shoving her phone in her pocket and putting her laptop on the stairs to the flat, she peered down at the carpet just as her phone rang.

'Hey, how are you?' Amy asked.

'Fine.'

'Oh! You sound terrible! What's happened?'

'Just about everything.'

'Like what?'

'Like I'm having a massive case of regret.'

'Woah,' Amy said and swore. 'What's happened about the mice?'

'I've got someone coming over.'

'Right, well, at least that will be sorted.'

'Yeah, I guess so.'

'How is Callum?'

'His usual capable self. Unlike his mother.'

'Well, there you go, you have that too.'

'Yeah. Are you on your way?'

'I am. I'll pick us up some coffee, shall I?'

'Yes, sounds good. Search for a place called Darlings. It's just down the road here. I went there yesterday, and it was great. You have to see it.'

'So what's the plan for this morning?'

'The skip is arriving, the carpet is going in that, scrape the walls, and then get the board off the counter, and I think that will be about it.'

'Okay. It sounds like you're in control.'

Emmy shook her head. 'I feel rubbish.'

'I can tell.'

'What have I done?'

'You'll be fine. Once Dad arrives, he'll get stuck into it, and you'll feel better.'

'I hope so. I am questioning everything.'

'Just blame Kevin,' Amy joked.

Emmy chuckled. 'Don't worry, I've already done that. You know me too well.'

'Yeah, I do.'

'Right, I'll crack on. There are so many things to do. See you in a bit.'

'See you soon.'

An hour or so later, Emmy felt as if she was going around in circles and had not got much done at all. Amy had arrived with coffee from Darlings and was attacking the walls with a wire brush, and Emmy was on her way to the back lane for the delivery of a skip.

She moved her car along a spot and stood by the gate, waiting. A few minutes later, a skip lorry inched its way along the lane, put its lights on, and a man jumped out of the cab.

'Morning, love,' the man said, making a wincing face as he looked at the lane. 'Bit tight down here.'

Emmy smiled. 'Yes.' She gestured to the space. 'Will it fit here, do you think?'

'Yep, not a problem.'

'What about the council and everything? It seems I need permits for everything here. I should have asked before.'

'All done, love.' He pointed to the back of the skip lorry. 'That size is fine for here and the permit is sorted. That's the way it works on this island.'

Emmy let out a sigh of relief. 'Great.'

'How long do you reckon you'll need it?'

'Not long, by the looks of what's in there. We've got carpet for the whole place to get rid of and various other odds and sods.'

'Right you are.' The man looked along the line of buildings. 'Don't make them like that these days. Got to love the old Darling buildings.'

Emmy followed his gaze and saw again what she'd first seen in The Old Ticket Office rather than the grotty, depressing look she'd seen since she'd moved in. She suddenly felt a bit more grateful and happy about what she'd done. 'Yes.'

'Got big plans, have you?'

'I have.'

'Ahh, well, best we get on with it, then.'

Just as the man was hopping back into the cab, there was a beeping from behind. Emmy took a few steps and peered around to see the same black 4x4 as the day when she'd dropped her bag. Tom Carter was behind the skip lorry and opening his door. Emmy called out as she got to the back of the lorry. 'Hi.'

'Morning. What's going on here?'

Emmy half-rolled her eyes. It was pretty obvious from her side of the fence. There was a skip being placed on the lane. Tom Carter did not look best pleased. Tom Carter looked exceedingly hot. Tom Carter was divine. Emmy squinted towards Tom, whose expression was a mixture of confusion and irritation, an eyebrow raised in question. She jerked her thumb towards the skip. 'Sorry,' Emmy called over the engine. 'I've got a load of carpet and stuff to get rid of. It won't be here long.'

Tom looked rushed. 'Right, yeah, I need to get through.' He looked at his watch. 'I've got a meeting and time's ticking on.'

Emmy wasn't sure what to make of his brusque manner. He wasn't rude as such, just quite short. Not that neighbourly. She did know it was attractive in a curious way. She was inexplicably drawn to this Tom, but he irritated her at the same time. 'Right, okay,' Emmy said, feeling a tad flustered. She looked towards the other end of the lane. 'Umm, you'll have to go the other way.'

Tom tutted and shook his head. 'Meaning I have to go all the way around the one-way system.'

Emmy raised a hand to gesture at the driver, asking him to pause. The drone of the engine stopped. The driver nodded and began fiddling with his phone. Tom's eyes swept over the expanse of the back of the building and then at the lorry. 'How long before he's out of the way?'

Emmy didn't have a clue. *As if I know that,* she thought to herself. 'Not sure. You'll just have to wait.'

Tom shook his head and looked down the lane the other

way. 'I'll have to leave it down there. It would have been good if you'd given us some notice.'

Emmy screwed her nose up. *Idiot.* 'I didn't think it would be a problem.'

'Yeah, that's obvious.' Their exchange was interrupted by Tom's phone. He pulled it out, glanced at the screen, and his smile faded. 'I've got to take this. Make sure you let us know if you're going to get a skip again.' He stepped back into his car, closing the door behind him. Emmy watched as he put the phone to his ear, his face serious and focused. As she saw him put his phone in the cradle and start to reverse his car, a twinge of disappointment squeezed her. Clearly, this new neighbour of hers thought she was an irritating, inconsequential blip in his day. The lorry's engine roared back to life, the chains on the skip clanged, and Tom poked his head out of his window.

'Hopefully, it won't be here long,' he called over. He gave a small nod, then turned his attention back to the phone call, rolling his window back up.

Emmy was left standing there, the noise of the lorry in her ears and a strange fluttering feeling in her stomach. Tom Carter was irritatingly charming. And for some inexplicable reason, she was looking forward to further altercations over a skip. Or really anything else at all.

15

Emmy walked back into the building to find Amy opening the door to their dad. Emmy felt a sigh of relief as her dad, Bob's, comforting smell and can-do attitude immediately filled the room.

'Morning, girls. How are we?' Bob asked. 'Ready for a bit of hard graft?'

Emmy raised her eyebrows. 'Thank goodness you're here.'

'As good as that?' Bob chuckled.

'Terrible night,' Emmy clarified. 'Absolutely awful.'

'Yeah, Callum called me on his way to school and told me it was another bad one,' Bob said as he looked around. 'We knew it needed some work,' he remarked, clapping a reassuring hand on Emmy's shoulder. 'There's nothing we can't handle, Ems.'

Emmy tried to smile, but her insides churned. 'I don't know, Dad. I'm starting to think I've bitten off more than I can chew. You know?'

Her dad looked at her, an understanding glint in his eyes. 'Regrets?'

'Maybe,' she admitted, looking around the room. 'It's just a lot to take on. I think I was wearing very large rose-tinted glasses when I first viewed this place. Actually, they were not just large, they were enormous.'

Her dad gave her hand a comforting squeeze. 'It'll be fine. Rome wasn't built in a day, as they say.' He looked around. 'As I said when I first looked at it, all it needs is a bit of muscle.'

'Exactly,' Emmy replied with disillusion. 'I don't have a whole lot of muscle in my life, in case you haven't noticed.'

Amy chimed in, full of optimism. 'You've got us. Just think of the potential, Ems. This place will be amazing when you're done with it.'

Emmy sighed and looked around again, this time with a tad more determination. 'I hope so.'

An hour or so later, The Old Ticket Office was in a state of organised chaos. Large rolls of the old nylon carpet stood ready to be banished to the skip outside, and dust hung in the air, sparkling in the streaks of light coming through the old windows.

'Blimey, this carpet's a beast!' Emmy grunted, her arms straining as she rolled a mass of it towards the door, her face flushed and a sheen of sweat on her forehead. 'What on earth is in this underlay?'

'You're not wrong there,' her dad responded, standing by the door, ready to help haul the carpet outside. 'They knew how to make them last in the old days, didn't they?' He was grinning, his eyes gleaming. Emmy wasn't quite sure where he got his energy from. She knew she hadn't inherited it.

Amy was picking up random bits of debris and placing them in a bin bag. She shook her head and joked, 'I can't believe you fell for this place, Ems. It's a nightmare.'

'I told you that on the phone and you talked me up,' Emmy replied, shooting Amy a mock glare.

'Joking,' Amy said, sweeping her arm around. 'Look at the difference already. Just wait until we're done. It's going to be brilliant. I can see it already.'

Emmy raised her eyebrows. 'I'm glad *you* can.'

Emmy's dad chuckled, grabbing the end of one of the rolls of carpet and heaving it out the door. 'That's the spirit! You've got to see the potential in these old buildings. They're not like your modern, throwaway places that spring up in no time. This is going to be special. Take it from an old bloke who knows what he's talking about.'

Emmy stood, panting slightly, and nodded. 'I hope so. It does have a lot of character, I'll give it that.'

Amy coughed. 'Character, charm, and a lot of dust. So much dust.'

After a few more hours, much banter, and a lot of hard work, Emmy felt her doubts recede slightly. It was now clear to her that she had taken on more than she'd anticipated, but with her family helping, she felt more hopeful. If they could pull up a whole building full of carpet and survive, it gave her hope that her dream might still be intact. Just.

Despite the sweat, the dust, and their aching muscles, she felt buoyed at the sight of the floor. 'I'm shattered,' Emmy admitted, brushing her dusty hands together. 'And I thought I was fairly fit.'

'I reckon we've earned ourselves a good break,' her dad suggested, his stomach growling in support.

'You're telling me.' Amy laughed. 'What about that café where I got the coffee?'

'Works for me,' Emmy replied. 'I'd eat a table right now.'

Twenty or so minutes later, they were seated in Darlings with three bowls of milky coffee in front of them.

Amy lowered her voice and looked around. 'This place is gorgeous.'

'I know, right?'

Amy looked at the little coffee bowls everywhere. 'I could live here.'

'Ha.' Emmy laughed.

Amy took a sip from her coffee bowl and joked, 'What a morning. You're a bit nuts, Em, you know that? Taking this on.'

'Tell me about it. Well, you're here too, so what does that make you?' Emmy shot back, chuckling. 'Thank you, though. I really appreciate the help. I'm feeling much better, thank goodness!'

'Well, I believe in your dreams, Em. The shop is going to be amazing,' Amy reassured. 'Hopefully as nice as it is in here.'

Bob looked from one to the other. 'It'll be something special. Just needs some TLC.'

Emmy let out a strange panicky laugh. 'TLC and quite a bit of cash. And probably a few more hands.'

Bob chuckled. 'I guess I'll be assisting with all of the above.'

Emmy smiled as three lunch baskets arrived on the table. 'I'm going to need all the help I can get.'

Later on that afternoon, the carpet not only from the office and back rooms but also from the flat was neatly rolled up and stacked meticulously by Bob in the skip. Bob seemed to have more energy than both his daughters put together, and with his toolbox by his side, made light work of removing both the metal blinds on the front windows and the melamine casing on the old ticket counter.

As he pulled off the last piece, Emmy crouched down at a small timber plaque on the bottom. She traced her fingers over a metal plate on the front, feeling the worn-out texture. It was about the size of her palm and nestled snugly in the centre, almost unnoticeable if you didn't know it was there. The words 'Built by L Darling and Sons, 1901' were engraved on it.

'Look at this,' Emmy called out, beckoning Amy from the back room. 'This must be from when the Ticket Office was first built. Wow. I'll have to look it up. Dan said this whole strip of shops was built at the same time.'

Bob knelt down, squinting at the plate. 'I reckon you're right. History in every nook and cranny. Look at it all. The floors, the high ceilings, the woodwork.'

Amy made a face. 'And possibly a family of mice in the walls. It's all part and parcel of the place.'

Emmy swatted Amy. 'Thanks for that. As if I don't have enough to worry about, you remind me about our little friends.'

'All part of the service.' Amy laughed.

As they all chuckled, Emmy suddenly felt much brighter. There was even a twinge of excitement, which had been sorely missing since reality had taken its place. The sense of history, the years of stories in the walls – it was exactly what she'd been looking for ever since she and Amy had been left the proceeds from their grandma's house and holiday apartment in Spain. 'Things are possibly looking a bit better,' Emmy noted.

'That's our Ems. A fighter,' Bob said with a smile.

By the end of the day, The Old Ticket Office was looking a little less grim than when they'd started, and the progress they'd made was undeniable. The old nylon carpet had been banished to the skip, and the dust had settled, revealing the true bones of the place.

Emmy, Amy, and their dad stood in the doorway, surveying the room. Amy was the first to break the silence. 'Well, I'd say that's a good day's work, wouldn't you?'

'Wait until your mum gets here, too.'

'You're not wrong. I can't believe how much we've done already.'

Bob looked at his watch. 'Yep, we made short work of it. I'd better be off.'

Emmy hugged him. 'Thanks, Dad. You're a lifesaver.'

As he walked off towards his car, Emmy felt a twinge of

loneliness creeping in. Amy seemed to sense it. 'Don't worry. You've got me. And Mum and Dad.'

Emmy nodded, feeling her throat tighten a little. 'I know. I just... I'm starting to realise what a big job this is. Even with four of us here there's so much to do.'

Amy gave her a soft punch in the arm. 'You can handle anything. We all know that.'

But as Emmy laughed, she wasn't sure. It looked like that on the outside, but inside, she was panicking. Massively, hugely panicking. Amy then also left, leaving Emmy alone in the empty building. She looked around at the bare room, the stripped walls, and the old floor. It was all so daunting, but for the first time since she'd moved in, she felt hope rather than just fear. She was possibly ready for the challenge. To be quite frank, she didn't have a whole lot of say in the matter.

16

Much later, Emmy was crawling around on her hands and knees with one of her dad's tools, yanking nails from the gripper rods out of the floor. She was mentally preparing herself for another night, when a few friendly visitors might appear, when there was a sharp knock at the door. It startled her, she hoped it was Tom Carter as she scrambled up and pulled the door open to see a woman standing on the step. The woman was younger than Emmy, with a very pretty face, bright pink lipstick, dark hair tied back in a neat ponytail, and eyes that sparkled.

'Afternoon,' the woman said with a confident smile and a chuckle. 'Jodie. South Darling Pest Control. Sorry, I'm later than we said. I hear you've got a mouse problem on your hands.'

Emmy shook her head, trying to connect her call with the pest control company with the pretty woman standing in front of her. Her voice was full of surprise. 'Oh, right, yes, sorry, yes, come in. I was expecting someone older... and, well, I don't know.'

Jodie laughed. 'You were expecting a man in work boots, yes?'

'Sorry, I didn't mean…' Emmy began, but Jodie waved away her words.

'No worries. Happens all the time. At least three times a day. Apparently, I don't look like I deal with pests, although I can tell you I have dealt with many of the human kind,' Jodie said, laughing at her own joke. 'Especially down the pub. Ha ha.'

'I hear you.'

Jodie passed Emmy a small wicker basket. 'Welcome to Darling. From all of us at South Darling Pest Control.'

Emmy took the basket and smiled at a beautifully wrapped candle inside. 'Wow! Thank you.' She pulled off the paper and inhaled. 'Gorgeous.'

'Right, what have we got here then?' Jodie asked.

Emmy nodded, leading Jodie into the building. She watched as Jodie quickly scanned the room with a professional air as Jodie listened to Emmy detail the extent of the problem from the little she had seen. When Emmy finished, Jodie looked thoughtful. 'Well, it's not an uncommon problem,' Jodie said. 'Especially in these old Darling buildings on this side of the island.'

Emmy looked at her in surprise. 'You're familiar with these buildings?'

Jodie nodded. 'Oh yes, these old places have a knack for attracting all sorts of things. Nothing we can't handle, though. I've seen it all. As long as you keep on top of it, you'll be fine. Now, if we were talking bats, we'd be worried. Those little creatures are protected.'

'That's good to hear.'

Jodie gave her a reassuring smile. 'Trust me, it's not as bad as it feels. We'll get your little invaders sorted. You'll be mouse-free in no time. Though, to be quite frank with you, I'll put money on it that you've got rats too. Have you seen any evidence of them so far?'

Emmy shuddered as she recalled the smell in the shed and

explained it to Jodie. Jodie waved her hand in dismissal. 'By this time in a couple of days, you'll be fine. At least you'll have a solution in place.'

As Jodie went back out the door to go to her van, Emmy felt slightly hopeful. If the pests were a 'Darling problem,' then maybe she could handle them. Maybe she could transform The Old Ticket Office into something wonderful, mice or no mice.

When Jodie came back in with a gigantic bag slung over her shoulder, she smiled. 'So, you just bought this place?' Jodie asked with her eyebrows raised.

Emmy nodded, watching as Jodie began unloading items from the bag. 'Yes, the plan is to turn it into a jewellery boutique. That's a while away, though.'

'Ooh, sounds nice,' Jodie said, straightening up from her bag. 'That's a great idea for around here. These buildings are ideal for quaint shops. This one needed a bit of love. I was interested to see it up for sale. It didn't last long.'

Emmy chuckled. 'That's what I thought. I just wasn't expecting it to be as grubby as it is in reality, and I certainly didn't anticipate the mice.'

Jodie flashed a knowing smile. 'No one ever does. Don't worry, we'll get it sorted. Oh, by the way,' she added, a glint in her eyes. 'Have you met your neighbour yet?'

Emmy frowned. 'Err, I haven't really met anyone yet, no.'

'Oh, okay, you've not met Tom Carter just along from you here?'

Emmy could hardly believe that she felt her heart thump a little faster at the mention of Tom's name, who she'd barely met and knew absolutely nothing about. 'Oh, yes, I have, actually.'

Jodie nodded. 'Yeah. What did you think of him?'

Emmy felt a blush creep up her cheeks. *Blooming gorgeous.* She wasn't sure how to respond. 'Umm, he seemed quite, err, nice.'

Jodie winked at her. 'Ha ha. Gotcha. That's putting it very

politely. This strip of shops comes with dashing neighbours.' Again Jodie laughed at her own joke.

Emmy laughed, too, unsure of what to think but not wanting to sound as if she was interested. She was indeed very interested. It seemed like everyone in town knew something about each other and her. The last thing she was going to do was look even remotely bothered by Tom Carter, though. While she was tempted to sit Jodie down and ask exactly what the go-to with Tom was, she resisted. She had a renovation to undertake, a mouse problem to resolve, and a flat to decorate. She had no time to engage in gossip, let alone dwell on the circumstances of someone like Tom. But she would have loved to have found out exactly what was what with the dashing Tom Carter. 'Ha ha, yes.'

Jodie picked a load of black plastic boxes up and headed out toward the back. 'I'll get going on this.'

'Thanks, Jodie.'

Later that evening, Callum had gone off to cricket training and was staying overnight at Kevin's, and Emmy, who had spent way too long in B & Q, was lugging tins of paint from the boot of her car to the flat ready for her mum and dad to help in the morning. As she pressed the remote to close the boot, she was weighed down with two industrial tins of primer as she struggled to the gate. Failing to nudge the gate open with her foot, she tutted, put the paint tins down and pushed the gate with her shoulder. It stayed exactly where it was. For a second, she stood just staring at the heavy, old gate with a scowl as it had decided to stick stubbornly in its frame. She gave it another shove, and it still didn't budge.

'Right,' she muttered to herself. 'Come on. I do not need this at this stage of the game.' Emmy swore repeatedly as she tried to barge the gate open with her shoulder. Determined, she put one of the paint cans down, yanked the handle down and pushed with all her might. Nothing but a creak. She tried again, groaning with the effort of it as if she were giving birth, pushed, then pulled the handle as hard as she could, then kicked the bottom in frustration. She shouldn't have bothered as it refused to budge. Giving it one last go, she took a few steps back, squared at it with her right shoulder, and with a low, less roar, more weird, sad groan, she threw herself at the gate. As she did so, her shoes skidded on the cobbles, her feet almost slid away from underneath her, and she wobbled precariously, hovering above the ground for a second and just about keeping herself upright.

'Damn it,' she breathed out, resting her forehead against the gate. 'This bloody place. Last thing I need. Ahhhh!'

A low chuckle broke her focus. She turned, heat flooding her cheeks, to find Tom leaning casually against the brick wall of the building next door. His arms were crossed over his chest, his face illuminated by the light from a street lamp overhead. He appeared amused. 'Problem with the gate?' he asked.

Emmy straightened up and pushed her hair out of her eyes. 'No, I'm doing this for fun. It's stuck, and it's the last thing I need at the moment. So over it.'

Tom raised an eyebrow. 'Stuck?'

'Yeah. It's old, you know,' she replied defensively. 'Stuck. As in, it won't open.'

'Right,' Tom said, uncrossing his arms and stepping forward. 'Do you want a hand?'

Emmy stepped back, feeling a twinge of embarrassment. 'I'm fine.'

But Tom was already at the gate, his hand on the handle. With one smooth, effortless push, the gate creaked open. Emmy tried to keep her chin under control as she watched Tom's arm.

Tom Carter clearly worked out. Emmy blinked, staring at the now open gate, then at Tom.

'There you go. It just needed a bit of a nudge. There's a knack. It's the same on all the gates along here,' he said, his smile warm. His eyes sparkled with banter. He seemed a lot happier than the first few times she'd seen him in the lane. She may have just melted.

Emmy felt her cheeks heat up. She muttered a thank you, hoping her embarrassment wasn't as visible as it felt. She busied herself with gathering the gigantic tins of paint. 'Thanks.'

'No problem. If you need any more help with stubborn, old things, you know where to find me.'

Emmy frowned. Was this the same person? Tom Carter had been irritatingly full of his own self-importance before. Now, he was attempting to be friendly. Strange. 'I hope it doesn't happen again. I've got so much to do and loads of things to bring in from the car to get sorted before tomorrow,' Emmy said with a bit of a sigh.

Tom looked at the gate. 'It just needs a bit of oil to loosen it up. They need oiling every now and then.'

'Because I have so much oil at my disposal,' Emmy whispered to herself sarcastically. To Tom, though, she nodded and widened her eyes. 'Yeah, right. Helpful.' She glanced down the lane to her car. 'I have a car full of what feels like most of the contents of B & Q, and I want to get it in this evening so that my dad can get going on it right away in the morning. Plus, his back isn't great these days, so I want it to be inside so he doesn't have to lug it all in.'

'I've got some inside,' Tom said. 'I'll pop back and get it.'

'Thanks. That would really help me out. Thank you.'

'You're lucky I turned up.' Tom winked before heading towards his property. 'I'll be back in a sec.'

While Tom was away, Emmy glanced around. The cobbled lane at the back of the building was quiet except for the distant hum of the trams, and it looked as if it was starting to get foggy. When Tom returned, he was carrying a toolbox and holding a small cylinder of oil in his right hand. 'This should do it.'

Emmy looked grateful. 'Shall I hold the gate steady?'

'Nah.' Tom put the oil on and then pushed the gate. 'See.'

'Wow. Lifesaver. Thanks.'

Tom picked up the two huge tins of paint as if they were as light as a feather. 'I'll give you a hand. Then I have to shoot off.'

'It's fine. You've helped me out loads just by doing that.'

'Thought you said you have a car full of stuff?'

'I do.'

'I'll give you a hand, then.'

Ten or so minutes later, after a multitude of trips back and forth and Emmy trying not to openly swoon at Tom making light work of the heavy stuff, Emmy's car was empty.

'So, why Darling? And why a jewellery boutique?' Tom asked.

Emmy was taken aback by the sudden question, and she wondered how this Tom, like the rest of Darling, knew her business plans. 'I needed a change. Something different. And I've always loved jewellery. Yeah, and a whole load of other reasons that I won't bore you with.'

Tom nodded. 'Well, you're in the right place.'

As they stood by the back door, the conversation from Emmy's side felt a bit awkward and stilted. What did not feel awkward was the delicious swirling of all manner of things in her stomach. Tom was gorgeous. Emmy laughed. 'That's good to hear.'

As Tom stood on the doorstep by the back door and picked up the can of oil from the windowsill, he smiled. 'You'll fit in well here.'

'Thanks. What about you? Do you live here too?' She swallowed, totally wanting to ask him about his circumstances. She attempted to sound casual. 'With your family?'

'Nope. On my tod,' Tom answered quickly. 'Okay, look, I've got to shoot.'

Ahh, you live on your own. Excellent. Fandabbydozy. 'Yep, thanks for the help.'

'Anytime.'

Emmy leaned back against the door, exhaled slowly and let her heart get back to its regular beat. The move to The Old Ticket Office was looking up. Way up. Tom Carter was quite the neighbour, it had to be said.

Once Emmy had shut the inside door to the shop, she sorted through the stuff from B & Q and made her way up the stairs to investigate the room at the top. As per her first viewing with the estate agent Dan, and in all her pre-move planning, the top room was earmarked to eventually be her bedroom. Now she had actually arrived, all of it looked daunting. With aching muscles from spending the day lugging carpet around, she heaved herself up the stairs, flicked on the light, and stood staring around at the room. Overall it wasn't great; old cardboard boxes were strewn about here and there on horrid shelving, dust bunnies claimed every corner, and the grime-coated windows looked as if it had been a long time since they had been cleaned, if ever, but it had so much potential, it was mind-blowing. Emmy squeezed her eyes together and dragged an old fold-up chair over towards the window and sat staring out towards the estuary, just able to make out the lights from the ferry as fog started to roll in.

For a long time, she just sat there staring at the room, thinking about her encounter with Tom, her move to Darling, gazing out the window at the ferry, and listening to the trams go past every now and then. She swore she heard a scurrying in the walls and shivered, but she wasn't quite as worried. Emmy

Bardot was feeling happier as she sat at the top of the building, thinking about what lay ahead and what was in the past. Her old life, where she'd trundled off to work at the port and let someone else deal with the place where she and Callum lived, was waving at her in her head. It had a bit of a smirk on its face, and it was trying to tell her how stupid she was to have given it up. It nodded and sniggered and looked so cosy and warm compared to the bare walls around her and the cataclysmic levels of dust. But that place wasn't hers, and The Old Ticket Office was. The view of the water and ferry was amazing, and it wouldn't be long until she woke up to it every day, plus the quality of the neighbours on Darling was very high. Just as she was thinking about getting up, her phone buzzed.

'Hi, Amy.' She sighed, the exhaustion evident in her voice.

'Hey, just seeing how you got on with the paint,' Amy said. 'All good?'

'Yeah, fine. I got everything on Dad's list and then lugged it all in so his back will be okay.'

'Where are you? It sounds echoey.'

'I'm upstairs in the top room.'

'What, looking at the view?'

'Yeah, I've been watching the ferry go back and forth.'

'Nice.'

'It's not really nice, but it will be,' Emmy said, looking around at the room and the bare lightbulb hanging from the middle. 'Everything is such a mess. I just saw some droppings too. You know, just to really put the icing on the cake, but I know it's going to be lovely up here. I own a property on Darling Island, I have to keep that in mind. There's just so much to do, though.'

'You sound overwhelmed. Do you want me to come back now?' Amy offered. 'The girls are in bed.'

Emmy's heart tightened at her sister's kindness. 'No, no. I'm fine. I'm just tired. I might just go to bed.'

'Have you spoken to Callum?'

'Yeah, he's good. He went from cricket training straight to Kevin's, so at least he won't be having visits from mice tonight,' Emmy joked wryly. 'They should be gone soon now the pest control has been.'

'Seriously, I can come over if you like.'

'I'm fine. I'll be a bit more lively in the morning.'

'Yep. Time to get on a mission, as Mum would say.'

'It's a monumental task.'

'It is one you will face head-on. You've had worse, Ems. Remember that flat when Callum was little?'

'You think that is worse than this? No way! At least that was small. This place is going to take years to get right.'

'Yep, it's not small, but it is all *yours*.'

'Yeah.' Emmy sighed as she looked out towards the ferry. 'I know. How lucky am I? I have all this at my disposal. It must have been fate that day.'

'You've done the right thing for you and Callum.'

'Yep. The island is lovely – the trams, the pubs, the ferry.'

'The ferry is what makes it,' Amy added. 'It's so quaint and gorgeous.'

'I know. I just feel pretty tired already.'

'Blame it on Kevin.' Amy joked.

'Always.'

'What state is the bath in? I didn't look.'

'Filthy.'

'How bad?'

'I don't know. The bath is the least of my worries.'

'Scrub it out, pour yourself a glass of wine, chuck some bubbles in and then go to bed.'

'Good idea, but I don't have any wine.'

'You do. I put a bottle in the fridge earlier. And a load of M&S bits you can heat up in the microwave. Dad unboxed the microwave and plugged it in too.'

'What? I didn't realise you did that!'

'Ahh, I thought you might feel like this tonight…' Amy left her sentence dangling.

'You're so good to me. I don't deserve a sister like you.'

'I am. Don't worry, I'm noting all this stuff down for when I'm in need.'

Emmy rolled her eyes to herself. Just about everything was perfect in Amy's life. Perfect house, a nice perfect, very handsome husband, two perfect girls in a nice perfect school. Perfectly highlighted hair. Perfect first-class degree from perfect red brick. Three perfect holidays a year. Perfect part-time, remote working friendly job. New perfect car. On top of that, Amy always looked perfect too. 'Thanks.'

After she'd got off the phone with Amy, Emmy nodded and tried to remain stoic. It wasn't quite as plain sailing as she'd thought, but she'd survive. Deciding that Amy's advice was normally both correct and well-intended, she walked into the kitchen and surveyed the array of boxes scattered around. Her eyes quickly found a cleaning supplies box, and she pulled open the flap at the top and dragged it over the hallway and into the bathroom. Pulling out a bottle of bleach, a scrubbing brush, a pair of rubber gloves, and a few other essentials, she sighed at the sight of the grimy bathtub trying to keep Amy's words in mind that a glass of wine and a bath and then bed would do her the world of good. Going out to grab her speaker, she put a playlist on Spotify, and to the sound of Adele, she slipped on the rubber gloves and started spraying the tub as if it was the last thing she would ever do. With the sharp, clean smell filling the air, she scrubbed and scoured the tub for all she was worth. As she sang at the top of her lungs, sounding more like a drowning rat than Adele, she vigorously attacked the grime and tidemark as if they alone were responsible for her feelings. With every bad wail and scrub, the grubbiness of the day floated away, and her thoughts meandered. This place was her own. She had her own house! Every bit of effort she put into it would finally rebuild her life. A life that had been teetering since the day she'd discovered Kevin's secret gambling.

Thirty or so minutes after that, she'd zapped and eaten an M&S meal, the bath was full of bubbles, her dressing gown was by her side, and she'd lowered herself down into hot bubbly water. With the glass of wine in her hand, she just lay there thinking, listening to the sound of the trams down on the street below. With her eyes closed and her head leaning on the back of the old bath, a loud sound made her open one eye. At least it wasn't the sound of scurrying feet. She frowned as it went again. The third time it went off, she nodded as she realised what it was. The foghorn had blasted three times which, from what she'd read here and there, meant thick fog was surrounding the island and the estuary.

Emmy spent a long, long time in the bath: the water and the wine had softened her frazzled edges, and she felt better when she finally emerged. Her mind kept going over what her dad had so rightly pointed out that Rome wasn't built in a day. After she'd put her dressing gown and slippers on, she poured herself another small half glass and took it back upstairs to the top room to further assess and dream about where her bed was going to go, so she could wake up to the view. As she walked to the window, she was amazed to see a thick blanket of fog outside. A layer of fluffy white had draped itself over Darling Street, swallowing up the world Emmy had been observing just a few hours earlier. It was as if someone had taken a brush loaded with cloud and swiped it across the night. A thick smudge of dense fuzz had plopped down onto the street, punctuated only by the streetlights and the odd gleam of a tram.

Emmy was startled at quite how thick the fog was. No wonder the foghorn had blared a warning. It was so palpable, it looked almost as if she could reach out and grab a handful. It hung heavy and low, seeping into every nook and cranny of the buildings and the trees, blurring the lines and softening the edges. Emmy just stood staring for ages. She'd heard about the famous Darling hazy blue and the fog, but she hadn't expected to be quite as captivated by it. It was as if it had snowed fog, everything hidden beneath a cloak winding around lamp posts, the old tram shelter, and chimney pots. Everything seemed muffled and like time had slowed down. All very nice and all very odd. And soon enough, she'd be waking up to it. Gorgeous.

She strode over to the other side of the room to peer out into the lane and stood mesmerised as the fog swirled and twirled. The white seemed to dance in front of her eyes and all but enveloped the lane. Suddenly seeing movement through the fog, Emmy stepped back a touch from the window. The lights from Tom Carter's car pulled up outside his property and parked. Emmy had never thought she would turn into a curtain-twitcher, but she remained stock still where she was, the glass of wine still in her hand, and observed. As she watched Tom's car, she felt a ridiculous thrill of anticipation as he climbed out.

'Why are you so fascinated by him?' she muttered to herself, shaking her head as she stepped back further from the window. She had far more important things to concern herself with than spying on hot men. Although it was quite a nice pastime. She was rooted to the spot and wondered what it was about Tom that piqued her curiosity so much. *As if she didn't know.* It might have had something to do with his undeniably handsome good looks. It was something else, though. Yes, this Tom had something more than good looks. A sort of air of mystery hung around him, a sense of confident I-don't-care, borderline arrogance. She liked it. A lot.

It was maddening to Emmy that she was even thinking about it, let alone standing at the window spying. She should be focusing on the mess all around her, and a handsome stranger next door had not been in any of the plans she'd so meticulously detailed prior to moving to Darling Island. She was supposed to be drafting a to-do list of tasks to tackle, not spying on her neighbour. However, who gave a stuff about her stupid lists? Spying was a lot more fun. As were the tingles in places long since dead. She smiled as she found herself watching as Tom unloaded a large box from the back of his car. As his figure, surrounded in fog, disappeared along the path, she sighed. She needed to concentrate. She couldn't afford to waste time gushing, and she looked back into the dusty room. Trying her best to keep her attention off the man in the lane, she attempted to work out how long it would take to paint the walls. Emmy glanced back out and saw Tom again, this time carrying what looked like bags from the supermarket. She sighed. It was no good. She was far too distracted mooning over her neighbour.

'Stop being ridiculous,' she scolded herself. 'You're not a teenager.' Yet as she started noting down the work needed, she couldn't help but wonder what Tom was doing, what his world was like, and whether their paths might cross again. She very much hoped that they would. She couldn't actually wait to bump into him again. Maybe she'd go and buy another cake.

17

As the Darling foghorn sounded and nearly made her jump out of bed in fright, Emmy couldn't remember where she was. Opening her eyes, she turned over and stared at the time on her phone. She'd set her alarm super early so she could get a head start on the day before her mum and dad turned up to help. Walking across the bedroom, she pulled the cord on the grotty old metal blinds whilst thinking that she couldn't wait for them to be in the back of the skip with the carpet. As she looked up at the sky, she was presented with the same thing as the night before and the reason the foghorn had gone off. A thick layer of fog covered everything in a cloud of white.

Padding down the stairs, she thought about the night before, the deep bath, and getting into bed early. Amy had given her good advice, and it seemed it had worked. She'd climbed in bed with a hot chocolate and had turned off the light, thinking how nice the top room would be when it was done, and maybe had a little thought here and there about Tom as she'd drifted off to sleep. What had proceeded was a deep, heavy sleep where she'd not been woken up by anything at all. Thinking about it on the way to the kitchen, Emmy felt remarkably better than she had the night before. Amazing the difference a few hours of uninterrupted sleep could make. She'd made her bed, and not only was she going to lie in it, but she was also going to ply it with fabulous sheets and pretty things.

As she tried not to look at the grotty, depressing kitchen whilst waiting for the kettle to boil, she wondered how her mum, who had been planning to make over the kitchen for weeks, was going to turn it around on a budget and without major work. It couldn't really look a lot worse. She then went down and sat outside the back door with a cup of tea and her laptop open in front of her. With a bit more hope than she'd had the day before, she waited for her mum and dad to arrive and scrolled down through the Darling community page on Facebook. The posts told her one of the tram lines would be running a reduced service because a driver was in hospital, a local author was holding a talk on their new book at the library, and someone with a very nice surname – Le Romancer – was selling what looked to Emmy like a gorgeous sofa. Emmy saved the sofa post and made a mental note to send a message. It looked like just the sort of thing that might make the empty flat look a bit more like home.

She clicked on her emails to see what was new. Fifteen new emails were in her inbox. The usual sales rubbish, telling her that she needed that oh-so-special new dress. An email from the website hosting company to see if she wanted to link her account directly to her social media accounts to advertise Love Emmy x. She mulled it over for a second, and before she'd known what she was doing, one of her posts had miraculously been turned into an advert, and she was signed up to spend a few pounds a day sending sponsored posts out into the world for Love Emmy x. Worth a go.

Making herself her third cup of tea of the day, she mulled over whether or not she really did have the funds to be advertising her little shop yet. Yes and no. Marketing had been part of her plan from day one and she was well aware that Love Emmy x wasn't going to be a success without somehow getting bums on seats, but she was very concerned about cash. But it really was now or never. As she sloshed some milk into the bottom of a mug, she thought about her grandma's jewellery box and how she'd wanted to be something 'in' jewellery for so long. If she wanted it that much, she had to make it happen, and getting adverts out on the socials had to be done.

Sitting back at her laptop with a packet of M&S Rich Teas, courtesy of Amy, at her side, she navigated around the dashboard of her little shop on Etsy. The numbers were there in black and white, telling her that Love Emmy x did have legs. It just needed a lot of work and a fair amount of zhushing to take it to the next level. She was now so up for that.

About ten or so minutes later, she heard a knock on the shop door. Wondering why her mum and dad hadn't come around the back, she walked through the building and opened the door, expecting to see them ready and raring to go. Instead, she was faced with a postman wearing shorts and a big smile standing on the step. He raised his eyebrows and held up both his hands. In one was a parcel, in the other a white wicker basket with a handle. 'Hello. I thought I'd knock, seeing as I've heard on the grapevine you've moved in. Welcome to Darling Island.'

Emmy held her hand out for the parcel. 'Thank you.'

'Paul, don't laugh, Postman Paul.' The man grinned.

Emmy did laugh. 'Emmy.'

'How are you getting on?' Paul enquired.

Emmy looked behind her at the shop. 'Umm, yeah...'

'Had a few friendly visitors, or so I've heard. Jodie,' he added by way of explanation.

'Yep, but I didn't hear anything last night,' Emmy said hopefully. 'So my fingers and toes are crossed that they've got the message.'

'Let's hope you've seen the back of them. They like it down here near the estuary and these old buildings.'

'So I've heard.'

Paul held out the small white basket in front of him. 'This is for you from all of us at Darling Post Office.'

'Thank you so much.' Emmy was getting used to the Darling basket tradition where people arrived and left lovely little welcome gifts. The pest control woman had arrived with a similar thing.

'How do you like the old Darling superstition? It's a good luck thing. People drop them off when a newcomer arrives. I bet you've had loads on the doorstep.'

Emmy wasn't sure about Paul. He seemed a little bit weird to her. She didn't like to be rude but she sort of wanted him to go. She took the basket and looked inside to see a tin of shortbread, a mug, what looked like an invitation, and a packet of posh tea bags. 'Wow, thanks.'

'There's a paper version of an invitation to the regatta. You should have had one of those by email.'

Emmy frowned. 'Oh, I don't think so.'

'Oh, right, you should have one. Maybe look in your spam folder. Anyway, it's a Darling resident's thing. Invite only.' Paul chuckled and pointed to the card. 'That's your invite.'

'Okay. Thank you,' Emmy said, pulling out the invitation and scanning it quickly.

'You're welcome. Just let us know if you're not coming because the tickets are like gold dust. If you don't fancy it, we'll pass it along. Numbers are strictly limited to the beer tent and barbecue. It makes for a lovely afternoon if the sun is out. You'll get to meet a few people too.'

'Lovely, thanks.'

Paul peeked his head around the door frame. 'Looks like you've got your work cut out for you.'

Emmy laughed. 'Just a bit. I, umm, maybe took on more than I could chew. But I'm raring to go now I'm in. It's just going to take a bit longer than I thought.'

Paul nodded and then turned back towards the street. 'Darling has put on the fog for you. I bet you heard the foghorn earlier.'

'I did! That will get you up in the morning.'

'You'll get used to it. Anyway, I'd better get on. Happy painting, if that's what you're doing today.'

'Thanks, Paul. I'm sure I'll see you again.'

'Oh, yes, you can't get away from me, duck. You're stuck with me on Darling, ha ha.'

Emmy chuckled, and after he'd walked on, she shut the door and peered into the basket again. How very odd and very nice.

Adele from the night before had been replaced by Radio 4, which was playing away in the corner of the front room of The Old Ticket Office when Emmy's mum and dad arrived.

'Morning,' Emmy's mum, Cherry, chirped, full of the joys of spring. 'Dad said you were down in the dumps yesterday. What do we say, Ems? No time for being fed up in this family. Am I right or am I right? Come on, let's be having you. I have everything on the plan sorted. That kitchen is going to look like a different place by the end of the day. Onwards and upwards. The Bardots do not have time for sitting around with long faces. Oh no we don't.'

Emmy shook her head and smiled as her mum bustled in

and immediately started to pull on bright pink rubber gloves. 'You really don't mind doing this?'

'Don't be silly. You know me. In for a penny, in for a pound.' Cherry smiled. 'I've been looking forward to this for weeks.'

Cherry loved nothing better than a makeover and a makeover show, and when she and Bob had first come to see the flat, Cherry had volunteered to be in charge of a one-day kitchen makeover. Emmy loved her mum's taste and had happily given her the green light. The two of them had emailed back and forth, and Cherry had been out and bought supplies and was raring to go.

'I can handle anything it throws at me,' Cherry said as she followed Emmy up the stairs and into the kitchen.

When they walked in, Cherry winced and rubbed her gloved hands over the cupboards. 'Well, at least it's got good bones, I'll give it that.' She screwed her face up, opened a cupboard, and sniffed. 'I guess.'

'I didn't seem to notice it was so bad when we viewed it, did you?' Emmy asked with her nose wrinkled at the musty smell. 'It could be a lot worse. I have hope.'

'No. It seems like we were wearing rose-tinted glasses then.' Cherry wiggled the rubber gloves. 'Nothing these can't solve.'

'I'm wondering if it's pointless if the mice haven't left the building.'

Cherry shook her head. 'No time like the present to get on with something like this. I'll get stuck into it and start on the carcasses.' Cherry opened the cupboard under the sink and recoiled. 'Phew, it smells like something might have died in there. Pretty gross.'

'No! Don't say that. It probably has.' Emmy laughed.

Cherry cringed. 'Right, yikes, yes. Look, you go down and join your father and leave this to me.' She flourished her hand around the tiny kitchen. 'I'll have this shipshape by lunch, and by tonight, you're not going to recognise it. Cherry saves the day.'

~

By that evening, all of them had been working non-stop all day. Emmy came in through the back door with fish and chips wrapped in paper. Laying it out on the outdoor table she'd inherited and using a dust sheet as a tablecloth, the three of them, and Callum too, tucked into fish, chips, and gravy.

'Never tasted better.' Emmy sighed, dousing her chips with copious amounts of vinegar and digging in. 'I do love fish and chips after a long day.'

As the food disappeared, Cherry smiled. 'Well, here we are. Look at this place. Grandma would be very proud of you, Ems.'

Emmy stabbed her fork into batter. 'You really think so?'

'Of course. Look at what you're doing. It's going to be fabulous!' Cherry laughed, a twinkle in her eyes. 'It's all a bit nuts taking this on, but that's why she would be proud. The women in this family are strong. They go into battle, take no prisoners and get things done.'

Bob nodded. 'Never a truer word. And they keep the men around them in line.'

'They do,' Cherry shot back. 'Secret to a happy marriage.'

Emmy laughed and seeing as Callum had gone to get the brown sauce, added. 'Yeah, I failed on that with Kevin.'

'True that,' Bob agreed with a wry smile.

'Thank you, you two. I really appreciate the help,' Emmy said.

'Don't be silly!' Cherry exclaimed. 'This place is going to be amazing. It's nothing we can't deal with,' she reassured. 'You've bought a good buy here as we said at the beginning. It's just going to take a bit longer than we thought to get it up to speed.'

Emmy shook her head. 'I really appreciate you guys for helping.' She sighed. It's always blooming well me who needs help.'

Cherry shook her head. 'You need help, we'll be here, no questions asked. That's the way it works in this family. You'd do the same for Callum and so would we.'

'I know, but it's never Amy who asks for help.' Emmy said not mentioning her other sister who was estranged from the family and had been for years.

'Amy doesn't need our help at the moment, that's why,' Cherry stated emphatically.

'What does that mean?'

'It means you never know what's around the corner. Both of us will be here for you three as long as I have breath in my body.'

'I know, thanks,' Emmy noted, ignoring that her mum mentioned her and Amy's sister. None of them had spoken to her for a long time and Emmy wasn't going to open that can of worms.

Just as the last of the chips were disappearing, there was a rap on the back gate. It opened, and suddenly, Tom Carter was standing peering towards the back of the building. He waved, not quite as friendly as before. 'Hi.' He held his hand up to acknowledge Cherry and Bob and then addressed Emmy. 'Just a quick one. Any idea when the skip will be gone?'

Cherry whispered in surprise. 'Oh, my goodness! Who *is* that? Poldark just walked into our lives.'

Emmy swallowed and jumped up out of her seat. 'It should be gone by the end of the week.'

Tom lifted his chin. 'Okay, thanks.'

'Sorry about that.'

Tom seemed to be in a rush. 'Not a drama. Just want to know re: the parking later. I'll have to leave my car out on the road.'

'It should be gone soon.'

'Sooner the better. Sorry, got to rush.' With that, Tom had disappeared as quickly as he'd appeared.

'Who was that?' Bob asked, crumpling up his chip paper and wiping his mouth with a paper napkin.

Cherry chuckled. 'I have the same question. The neighbour isn't too shabby, Ems. Blimey. He wasn't on the estate agent's details,' Cherry joked.

'Mum!'

'Things are looking up on Darling,' Bob bantered.

'That was Tom Carter. He helped me with the gate last night, but overall, he's sort of a bit standoffish from what I've seen so far, no, just always in a rush, it seems.'

'Right. Handsome and standoffish,' Cherry said as she pushed out her chair. 'Looks alright to me. More than.'

Emmy couldn't have agreed more, but she wasn't going to admit it. 'Don't be silly. Just the neighbour.'

Cherry let out a low whistle. 'I've never had a neighbour quite like that and we've lived in a few places.' Cherry laughed.

'Turns out he was the one I bumped into on the pavement.'

Cherry frowned. 'Sorry, what?'

'You know when I first came here to pick up Cal's cake.'

'What, the bloke who nearly knocked you over?'

'Yes. The reason the cake was squashed at the top.'

Cherry's eyes went wide. 'And the whole reason why you ended up finding this place… Ooh, so it's fate!'

'Ha ha. Very funny. Right, come on.'

Cherry nodded. 'Yep. Okay, let me show you what I've done in the kitchen.'

Emmy scooped up the fish and chip wrappers, shoved them into one packet, and dropped the lot into a black bin liner hanging on the back of one of the chairs. 'It has to look better than it did when I left you up there this morning.'

When Emmy walked into the kitchen, she shrieked. When she'd left her mum with the cleaning materials and the gigantic box of goodies her mum had been collecting for the kitchen makeover, she'd not held out much hope. She clapped her hands to her face. 'Mum! Oh my! It looks fantastic! Thank you.'

'I know, amazing, eh? There is one good thing about a kitchen just big enough to swing a cat in, and that is that it takes not long to clean and not long to makeover.' Cherry nodded, clearly exponentially pleased with herself. 'I need to go on a DIY show. Me and your dad would win hands down, even if I say so myself.'

'I can't believe it!' Emmy said as she stared at the tiny kitchen. The horrid tiled, black scribbly backsplash had been covered by sheets of gorgeous white shell-shaped, ever-so-pale green-blue peel-and-stick tiles. The long garish stainless steel handles were gone and replaced with lovely cup pulls. The old cork noticeboard on the wall was gone, the sash window sparkled, and sported a clean white linen blind. A tiny table and two café chairs were butted up to the window, the tongue and groove walls, which had been the same nicotine-cream as the rest of the flat, were now white, and there was a seagrass runner on the stripped floorboards.

Cherry pointed to the cupboards. 'How different do these look with the cup pulls? Your dad is good at some things,' she joked.

Emmy squinted at the green-blue splashback. 'I can't believe how good that looks.'

'I know. We'll see how it holds up when you actually use it. It was a bit of a sod to put on, but I got there in the end.'

On the worktop, gorgeous new appliances were positioned just so – a four-slice toaster, kettle, and coffee machine, all in matte Scandi white. At each end of the worktop, tiny lamps glowed. Emmy felt a tear escape from the corner of her right eye. 'I can't believe you've done this for me, Mum. It must have cost loads. All the appliances…'

'Don't be silly, darling,' Cherry said and gesticulated towards the gap in the units. 'I have a dishwasher coming for you tomorrow. There's no way you're washing dishes on top of everything else you'll be doing here.'

'What? Thank you.'

'And I couldn't resist.' Cherry lowered her voice. 'Don't tell your dad or Callum the real price. He thinks it was on offer, but I've ordered a Smeg fridge too, which should also be arriving tomorrow. It matches the tiles.'

'I can't believe it! This was meant to be a *budget* makeover.'

Cherry shook her head. 'Darling, when have you ever known me to stick to a budget? No daughter of mine is living in a hovel.'

Emmy laughed. 'No. I suppose not.'

'I'll get onto the sitting room as my next project, shall I? To tell you the truth, I've already started a mood board.'

Emmy hugged her mum. 'What would I do without you, Mum?'

'All part of the service, darling,' Cherry said as she filled the new kettle. 'Right, time for a cup of tea and then we'll be off. Things are looking up, Ems, things are looking up.'

'They are,' Emmy said as she looked around at the lovely kitchen. 'Thank you.'

Cherry chuckled. 'I wasn't talking about the kitchen either. I was talking about the man from Cornwall next door.'

18

Emmy felt as if someone had poured concrete into her legs. It was all very well accepting the double shifts at work, but actually doing them was long, tiring work where Emmy had to be happy and agreeable all the time. Not always an easy feat. She strode into the canteen on her break, ready to take the weight off her feet for a bit. Rachael, the canteen manager, was standing chatting to another colleague Emmy had known for years. Rachael beamed as Emmy walked up to the counter.

'Ears burning? We were just talking about you.'

'I hope it was all good. What have I done or not done now?' Emmy joked.

'Neither. I was just saying how happy my mum was with the Love Emmy x parcel. Thank you for that.'

'Ahh, good! It arrived safely. I meant to check the tracking notification.'

'She said it was beautifully packaged as usual,' Rachael gushed.

'She liked it?'

'She loved it. I'm so grateful. Thank you.'

'My new branding is doing well.' Emmy smiled. 'The feedback has been really good so far.'

'I had no clue what to get the woman who has everything. Who would have thought she'd love that locket so much? Your advice was right.'

Emmy nodded. 'They always seem to go down well. I've learnt over the years that people love a locket.'

Rachael smiled. 'Especially when they're presented and packaged by you.'

'Aww, thanks.'

'How's it all going with the business and the shop?'

Emmy puffed out her lips and blew out. 'The online shop is doing well. The rest of it is, how can I put it? Not quite what I was expecting. It's going to take ages. I'm accepting that.'

'Harder than you thought?' Rachael asked.

'Much harder. You live and learn,' Emmy acknowledged.

'So, what's the plan? What's next?'

Emmy looked around, flicking her eyes towards the rest of the canteen. 'I think I'm going to slow it down and add another day here. Though by the way my legs feel, I'm not sure they can take it.'

'Might be an idea. Give you a bit more time to think,' Racheal suggested.

'Yeah. I reckon so.'

'How are you finding it there on Darling Island?'

'It's lovely. Really lovely. Much better than I had hoped or expected. I was walking by the sea yesterday evening. Everyone seems friendly enough, too, apart from a few weird things about having to get permits for things, and the parking is a bit of a nightmare.'

'Do I detect a but?' Rachael asked with a chuckle.

'Not at all. Far from it. It's so lovely living by the sea. I mean, we work by the sea right here, but it's different actually being surrounded by it, if you see what I mean. It's very different to being at the port.'

'Totally agree. Since I moved down the road here, it's been part of my life. Before that, I used to drive in for forty minutes, and I could go all day without even seeing the water. What about the ferry? How are you finding that?'

'Not too bad, actually. It's not a bad way to commute, I guess. Overall, I'm loving it. I just need a bit of time to get my feet under the table and get the place sorted. So much for my spreadsheet and plans of having it all done quickly.'

'Ahh, that'll all come together in time. What can I get you?'

'Coffee, strong one, please.' Emmy paused and peered at the counter. 'I'm going to have to have a doughnut to get me through the rest of the day. I need it.'

'I'll bring it over. Sit yourself down and put your feet up for a bit.'

'Thanks, Rachael. You're an angel.'

Five or so hours later, Emmy not only felt as if concrete had been poured in her legs, it was now in her head too. Work problems swirled around as she waited for the gate to open on the Pride of Darling ferry. The man in charge tipped his hat, gesticulated for her to drive off and waved as she went past. Emmy felt a little sigh escape, glad that the day was over and hoping that Callum had followed her instructions to put the cottage pie in the oven. She felt her shoulders drop. Darling Island already felt like home.

As she pulled into the lane, it was full of cars, and she drove past the gate to an empty spot further down. After a decidedly dodgy reverse parking attempt, she sat in the car for a bit checking her phone. Just as she was thinking about getting out, as she leaned around the passenger seat to pick her bag up from the back footwell, she watched as the gate to Tom Carter's place opened. Twisting around and expecting to see him, she squinted at the sight of a very pretty woman with long dark hair closing the gate behind her. Emmy craned her neck and watched as the woman strolled to her car in a blur of gorgeousness. Tall, slim and perfectly turned out in a cream tight-fitting leather skirt, khaki rib knit top and designer crossbody bag slung across her middle. So pretty she seemed to float an inch above the ground. Emmy looked down at her work uniform and her support control tights. She sighed a little bit at the just visible splodge of jam from the doughnut on her jacket she'd sponged off with a paper napkin. She watched as the woman flicked her perfectly beach-waved dark hair over her shoulder, clicked the key for a flashy little car and got in. The woman then pulled the rearview mirror towards herself, checked her appearance, applied some lipstick and smiled at herself.

Emmy bundled her bag up, got out with her heavy legs, locked the car door and walked past. The woman smiled a huge big beam making her already pretty face a million times prettier. She was not only super attractive but, like everyone else on the island, friendly too. Annoying. Emmy noted the exquisitely clean, shiny car and its electric purring engine as the woman started it. As she fumbled with the gate and attempted the knack to open it, she sighed and shook her head. Her neighbour Tom's visitors were clearly as attractive as he was. As she made her way inside with her legs feeling like lead and her work uniform crumpled she laughed ironically to herself. As she dragged herself up the stairs she wondered who the woman was. Maybe a romantic friend of Tom's? She hoped not. She did know one thing for sure; she wasn't anywhere near in the same league.

19

Emmy had been working on her online shop since the crack of dawn. She wasn't going to complain that the social media ads she'd created on a whim had miraculously started to work and generate sales, but she *was* surprised. She couldn't actually quite believe it. A slow but sure trickle of sales was happening, and she was ecstatic about it. She might have a much longer road ahead of her with her actual commercial premises than she'd planned for in the rose-tinted version in her head, but her digital version was doing fairly well. Long may it last.

Her eyes, however, after staring at the computer for hours with shop updates and printing off labels, were seeing double, and her head was spinning. Popping the last butterfly necklace into her beautiful new packaging, and sticking a label on the front of the packet, she closed her laptop, stacked the pile of packages in her bag, and propped it by the front door. After a long week of three full days of double shifts at work, two days working on the walls in the yet-to-be shop, and staying up until all hours painting woodwork in the flat, she was not only exhausted but needed a break.

Looking out at the lovely, warm early evening sky and not having to pick up Callum because he was with Kevin, she decided a walk was in order. After a shower, a bit of makeup, jeans, a nice top, and a cardigan, and with the bag full of Love Emmy x orders over her shoulder, she set off for the post office. After depositing her padded envelopes in the box, she looked up and down the road, then down at the map on her phone, and plotted a route. She'd take a long walk around the back streets of Darling, end up at the bay and see where she went from there.

A few minutes later, she was away from the bustle of the main street and wandering through Darling, gazing at lovely white houses and pretty blue doors. She peered at well-tended gardens, looked over old picket fences, and lusted over hanging baskets. She'd need to up her gardening game if she was to happily live on Darling, that much was obvious. A chocolate box cottage with striped lawns stretching away and window boxes full of flowers made her stop and ponder for a minute or two. A long row of blue and white Darling houses edging its way in the direction of the hazy blue looked good enough to paint and put in a frame.

Emmy couldn't put her finger on it, but everything on Darling seemed to simply feel as if people cared. A man with two grandchildren by his side said hello as he passed, and a woman standing in her front garden with a watering can in her hand smiled. Emmy felt as if someone had dropped her into a place so lovely she wasn't quite sure if she was imagining things. As she continued her walk, turning down another road and heading further toward the sea, everywhere was rosy. Taking in deep breaths of Darling air, she hoped some of the potential of Darling would rub off on her and Love Emmy x. She gazed at a huge willow tree where a dog was fast asleep underneath and thought about The Old Ticket Office with its dust, the flat still rammed with her moving boxes, the outside area still very much having seen better days. Would she be able to turn it all around and be part of this gorgeous Darling coat of loveliness? She winced and hoped so. She could but try.

Strolling along a tree-lined road, Emmy loved it when walks were filled with pretty things, when grey winter days were long gone and there was hope in the air. Strolling towards the bay, she looked up at old chimneys, peered down at stepping stone paths and over at Darling Island residents wrapping up their days. As she got closer to the bay, she realised that it hadn't changed much at all from the days when she'd visited with Callum; the same rows of tall white houses where every so often one was painted in the Darling blue, bunting as far as the eye could see, the same hazy blue of the water and sky, the boats bobbing around in the harbour, the tiled aqua-blue pub on the far side.

Lost in a world of her own, she rolled her shoulders back ten times, then reverted and changed the rolling to the other way, took deep inhales of sea air, and ambled closer and closer to the bay. She sighed at the vision of a house with an old boat shed to its right. A sweeping narrow driveway led to a covered porch where a hammock and a couple of Adirondack chairs were positioned just so. The hazy blue of the water danced with shimmering light behind, and an old weather vane on top of the boat shed spun around in the breeze. Life on Darling looked really rather good.

Walking around the bay, Emmy sat on a bench people-watching for a bit and let her brain lose thoughts and all the things on her mind. Just as she was thinking about strolling back home, her stomach grumbled, and she realised she'd had nothing to eat all day. Lunch had passed in a blur of Love Emmy x orders, and she'd had nothing since a quick slice of marmalade on toast just before she'd seen Callum off to school.

Before she knew it, she was standing outside the pub, looking up at the gorgeous aqua-blue tiles. She perused the menu on the chalkboard outside, thought about the ready meal in the fridge, peered along at the fish and chip shop, and wondered whether she might pop into the pub and let someone else worry about the washing up. Deciding there was no time like the present, she pushed open the door, and the cosy, welcoming pub smell greeted her. For a minute or so, she stood looking at the noticeboard before she went in. A flyer for Darling's wicker basket collection took the top right corner, a notice from the Municipality of Darling announced a council meeting about upcoming Christmas celebration planning, and a small business card advertised the local taxi company. As she stepped through into the main bar, she suddenly wasn't quite as sure it was a good idea and was just about to head back home again when a woman spoke to her.

'Oh, hi. How are you getting on?'

Emmy had no clue who the woman was. She tried to hide it. 'Hi.'

'Evie. From the café,' the woman said in explanation.

Emmy realised the woman looked different with her hair down and without a Darlings apron on. 'Oh, sorry, yes. Miles away.'

'What are you up to?' Evie asked pleasantly, with what seemed like a genuine tone of interest in her voice.

Emmy indicated behind her. 'I had a load of things to drop at the post office, and then I found myself down here at the bay. I had a nice walk. I needed to clear my head, you know?'

'Ahh, lovely evening for a stroll.'

Emmy nodded and took in the bar behind Evie, packed full of locals. She was surrounded by happy people in little groups and tables full of couples. She suddenly felt very out of it, very alone, and *very* new. As her mind raced and she heard Evie say something about a charity event, she decided stopping in the pub on her lonesome was a bad idea. Billy No Mates didn't seem much fun from where she was standing. She took a small step back, and as if reading her mind, Evie raised her eyebrows. 'Come and join us if you like.'

'No, no. On second thoughts, I think I might head back home, actually.'

'We won't bite. We've just had an end-of-the-week staff catch-up and drink, but that's wrapped up now. The staff have gone, and I'm just sitting here having a chat and another quick one for the road. Come and have a natter.'

Emmy felt both ridiculously grateful and a little bit awkward in saying yes, but she found herself following along behind Evie. Why not? Moving to Darling was meant to include broadening her horizons and making new friends. There was only one way that was going to happen; if she made a bit of effort.

As Emmy approached the table, she took in the pub around her. It was packed with people, the sound of glasses clinking and people chatting. Again, as she had done a few minutes before, she felt very out of it and alone in the world. A whoosh of feeling like a complete fish out of water flooded through her bones as she stood by the table, where she suddenly realised a very handsome, burnished man with a huge grin was sitting with an inch left in the bottom of a pint glass. The muscly bronzed man stood up and held out his hand.

'Leo, how are ya?'

Emmy gulped, and her eyes widened. Unless she was seeing and or hearing things, there was an Australian surfing god right in front of her in a small pub on a little island in the middle of an English sea. The Australian was not too hard on the eyes, it had to be said. Emmy added a few very quick blinks to the gulp. To her horror, she heard herself spluttering. 'Hi.'

Evie pointed to Leo and then back to Emmy. 'This is Emmy from that shop that was for sale along from Holly's place.'

The Australian frowned, little creases arriving in the glowing skin between his eyes. 'Sorry, whereabouts?'

'You know, the old insurance office there,' Evie explained.

'Yeah, nah, right you are. Down our end of town. She'll be right,' Leo replied.

Emmy was momentarily at a loss for what to say as she took in Leo, who was wearing a thin jumper over a collared shirt, a signet ring on the little finger of his left hand, and was wafting some kind of expensive Southern Hemisphere cologne across the table. She coughed and felt very English and uptight. All she could say was, 'Yes.'

Evie saved her. 'What can I get you to drink?'

Leo made a move to get up. 'I'll get them.'

'No, no,' Evie shushed him. 'My turn.'

'Thanks. Just a small glass of white for me,' Emmy replied, forcing herself to take the kind offer and not insisting on paying as she was normally inclined to do.

Leo settled back down into his seat, seemingly completely unaware of how astonishingly attractive he was. It was as if he was the walking-talking, much more highbrow Hollywood version of someone on Home and Away. And how was he getting away with the bronzed, burnished skin? Emmy was having a hard time tearing her eyes away from the biceps.

'How ya going with it? Bit of a mess in there, right?'

'Not too bad,' Emmy replied as she fiddled with the edge of a beer mat.

'That's good.'

'It will be when it's up and running.'

'And what do you do for a living? Just the shop, is it?' Leo said, happily making conversation.

Emmy squidged up her lips, considering for a second. 'Well, I work at the port on the liners, but this move is a bit of a new adventure for me. What about you?'

Leo beamed, and he appeared to glow even more. 'For my sins. I'm a doctor.' His halo caught the light on top of his head.

Inside, Emmy squealed. *A doctor. Nice. Kill me now.* This Leo chap got better and better. He must be an actor or something, having a bit of a chuckle with her. An image of her lying in a hospital bed with Leo taking her pulse filled her mind. She shook her head quickly. 'Ahh, right.'

'Sounds impressive, right?' Leo drawled.

I should say so. I'll take two of you. Or four. Emmy found herself unable to speak much. 'Yep.'

'Yeah, nah, it's not. Long hours and a lot of paperwork, but I love it. I started off as a nurse.'

Emmy had to stop herself from outright swooning. *Goodness gracious me. Who are you?* It didn't get much better. She coughed. 'I see.'

Evie came back to the table with a glass of wine, a half pint, and what looked like a gin and tonic. She put the wine on the beer mat in front of Emmy. 'There you go.' She chuckled. 'What's our bronzed one from Down Under been telling you?'

Emmy couldn't have cared less what Leo was *actually* saying. She just quite liked basking in the glow of his presence and the halo perched on top of his head. 'He's been telling me about his job.'

Evie chuckled. 'He puts in his pound of flesh for the NHS.'

'I do that.'

Evie smiled. 'How are you getting on with renovating the shop?'

'Not too bad. I've had to apply for approval for a new sign and a floral window dressing to go out the front.'

Evie nodded. 'Ahh, yep, you have to apply for everything on Darling. You'll need to join the Chamber of Commerce. It opens many a business door. Ask me how I know.'

Emmy stopped herself from wrinkling her nose. She couldn't think of anything worse, but from the look on Evie's face, she knew what she was talking about. 'Right. How does one do that?'

'Someone like me who likes the look of you nominates you.' Evie laughed.

'Oh, okay.'

'I'll do it next week if you like. Then you just have to come along to a dinner and make sure everyone, well, you know, approves. There's a dinner coming up shortly. So if you want me to nominate you, I will.'

Emmy was a bit on the spot, but she decided she might as well say yes. 'Thanks. I'd be grateful for that.'

'Consider it done. I'll get Paul to second it, and you'll get an email.'

'Great, thanks.'

Leo leant forward and smiled. 'So speaking of the Chamber of Commerce, have you met your neighbour yet?'

Emmy frowned at the little bit of edge to Leo's voice. She presumed Leo was talking about Tom Carter. This was the second time she'd been asked if she'd met Tom, and she wasn't sure what he had to do with the Chamber of Commerce. She coughed. 'Sorry, who?'

'Tom,' Leo said straight-faced.

Emmy knew exactly who he was talking about, obviously. She pretended to consider for a second. 'Oh, yes, next door. Yep, I've bumped into him a couple of times.'

'What do ya think?'

Emmy didn't know what to say. She felt as if the question was loaded with all sorts. 'Nice.'

Leo laughed, and Evie joined in. 'Yeah, ha ha.'

'Sorry, am I missing something?'

Leo chuckled. 'No, no. Not at all.'

Just as he was about to say something, the door opened, and Tom Carter rushed in. Leo got up. 'Speak of the devil. Mate, you're late.'

Tom looked harassed. 'Sorry, I did message you.'

Leo held up his half pint. 'One for the road, mate. I'm on an early in the morning.' Leo flourished his hand towards Emmy. 'Hear you've met your neighbour already.'

Tom smiled quickly, his eyes brushing over Emmy. 'Hello, how are you?'

Emmy blinked furiously. She might have the god of all things Australian perched beside her, but he was left standing. The English one did it so *very* much better. Ahead in leaps and bounds. Leo faded into the distance as all Emmy could see for a ten-mile radius was Tom Carter with his piercing blue eyes and moody standoffish air. 'Good, thanks.' Emmy's heart was beating at a million miles an hour. She may, in fact, collapse.

'I see the skip is still there,' Tom noted brusquely.

Emmy forced a smile. 'Yes, it is. There's quite a bit to get rid of, and the carpet didn't take up as much room as we thought, so...'

Tom nodded, cutting her off. 'Right. No worries.'

Emmy's heart fluttered of its own accord. She swallowed and held the wrist of her left hand with the fingers of her right, digging her fingers into her skin. 'It shouldn't be too long.' Emmy could feel Leo watching the exchange with interest.

'Are you being nice to our newest resident?' Leo bantered.

Tom's gaze lingered on Emmy for a moment longer. Again he was direct. Emmy liked it very much. So, so much. 'Yep. So far.'

Emmy felt herself radiating heat. Was she, in fact, a nuclear reactor? It was as if she had a flashing cone on top of her head announcing to all and sundry that she fancied the pants off this mysterious Tom Carter. A call from the other side of the bar broke the moment. 'Oi, Tom! You planning on joining the rest of us sometime tonight?'

Tom smiled somewhat apologetically and nudged Leo. 'Duty calls. Sorry, mate. I didn't realise you were leaving early tonight.'

'No worries.' Leo smiled as Tom walked away.

Emmy felt as if her eyes were burning with red-hot lust as they trailed after Tom. What in the world was happening to her?

This Tom was OUTSTANDING. She'd thought he was quite nice when he'd fixed the gate. Quadruple that and then some.

Emmy felt as if she was in a bit of a daze. It wasn't as if she hadn't had her fair share of nice, handsome men since Kevin. There had been a few. But this feeling was different, and it was probably why said handsome men had never stayed the course. She'd never felt the way she was at that moment about anyone before. She felt as if someone had doused her in something, and her whole body was furiously fizzing. Tom Carter was a puzzle, and she was suddenly very interested in figuring him out.

Leo nudged her playfully, breaking her daze. 'Yeah, nah, Darling Island never lacks for intrigue.' He winked and raised his glass. 'To new adventures.'

'To new adventures,' Emmy echoed, her mind four hundred and fifty per cent on the man who was now standing by the bar on the far side of the room. She willed herself not to look again and gripped the stem of her glass like a vice. Emmy didn't want this adventure or whatever it was to ever end. The world inside the nuclear reactor was very nice.

20

Emmy hadn't even finished half her drink when Leo drained his glass and made moves to leave. Evie wasn't far behind him, and Emmy found herself alone at the table, swirling the second half of her wine in her glass. She watched as the room continued to buzz with life. Laughter rang out, glasses clinked, and the warm, inviting scent of pub food wafted through the air. She tried not to feel lonely and as if she was the only one in the place with no one to talk to. She wished Amy was with her, having a laugh.

She took one look at the clock above the bar and sighed. It was too late to even think about cooking, and she really didn't fancy another microwave meal. She tried to convince herself that was why she was happy to stay in the pub on her own just because she didn't want to cook. It wasn't the only reason. It might have been because there was a certain blue-eyed neighbour who had piqued her interest and was standing not too far away. She reckoned if she ordered another drink and some food, she might just bump into him again. Shame that.

Making up her mind that even without the delightful chance of bumping into Tom, she really couldn't be bothered to go home and cook and gathering resolve and her glass, she approached the bar and ordered a steak pie. Feeling a bit less conspicuous than she had sitting at the table, she took a seat on a barstool tucked right up at the end of the bar. It just so happened that the end of the bar was not far away from where Tom was standing, talking to a couple of friends.

Emmy sipped her wine, made out she was very interested in the screen of her phone and watched Tom from the corner of her eye. His demeanour, confidence, and odd air of mystery blew Emmy away. As if sensing her gaze, even though she was trying not to look at him, Tom's eyes flicked along the bar; he gave her a small nod and a bit of a smile. Emmy returned the nod and quickly looked back down at her phone. She chuckled to herself. What was she doing? She was well used to having dinner on her own; she'd done it enough times, especially now Callum was getting older, but this dinner for one was a tad more interesting than usual. It appeared that Emmy was indeed, as Leo had intimated, on a new adventure. An adventure that made her fizz. She was now nuclear. She could not and would not argue with that.

Just at the same moment as Emmy's pie arrived, Tom stepped over towards the bar to order some drinks. 'Looks nice,' he said, nodding to Emmy's plate.

'Yep, I couldn't face another ready meal. You know what it's like when you move.'

'All getting a bit much, is it?'

'Just a bit.' Emmy laughed.

Tom glanced at the pie, then back at Emmy, and inclined his chin towards the wine fridge. 'Drink?'

Emmy actually didn't fancy another wine, but there was no way on earth she was going to say no, though. She sounded just a little bit too enthusiastic. 'Love one! White wine, please.'

Tom leant on the bar. Emmy swooned. 'So, do you always eat alone in pubs?'

Emmy didn't really like that. *Not at all.* The nice fuzzy rug that had been underneath her feet, radiating pleasant things up her legs, was whipped away and quickly. Was this Tom taking the mickey out of her? She wasn't quite quick enough to shoot something witty back as something inside her deflated. 'If needs must.'

Tom read her vibes in a flash and looked instantly regretful. 'Sorry, I wasn't being rude.'

'It's fine.' It really wasn't fine. Emmy felt as if someone had punctured her on the side. Yep, her life was pretty much about eating in places on her own unless Amy, Callum or her mum and dad were around. Sad.

Tom took the glass of wine from the barman, stepped forward, and placed it in front of Emmy. 'There you go.'

'Thanks.'

Tom nodded, handed his card to the barman, and smiled. 'I'll let you eat in peace.'

Emmy took a sip from her wine and watched as Tom moved away, heading back to his group. He caught her eye and gave a small, apologetic smile before he was swallowed up by the banter going on around him. How to take the wind out of someone's sails. As Emmy sliced the pastry off the top of the pie, she fixed her eyes on her plate and felt a pang of something she couldn't quite define. Disappointment and stupidity. She shrugged it off, chastising herself. She barely knew the man, after all. Why did she even give a stuff what he thought? She turned her attention to her pie, but her mind kept wandering back to Tom and whether or not he had been a bit snarky, asking her if she was on her own. She wasn't sure. She was sure she felt like an idiot.

The pub was getting more and more packed, so at least as she ate, she was surrounded by people, and no one really took much notice. Emmy found herself glancing over towards Tom every now and then. She watched him so easy with his mates.

There was some pull about him that drew her gaze again and again, despite feeling deflated and alone. She'd long finished her meal and was nursing the last of her wine with her head down to her phone, reading an article about shopkeeping in the digital world, when she felt a tap on the bar in front of her. She looked up to see Tom with a smile on his face.

'Are you heading off home?' Tom asked.

Emmy looked around and glanced towards the door and assumed that Tom had thought she was driving and wanted to scrounge a lift. 'Sorry, I walked. Can't give you a lift,' she stated a bit shortly, shaking her head to the left and right.

'No, no. I'm offering *you* a lift.'

'Oh, right.' A chill ran down Emmy's spine, and she was completely thrown. She didn't know this man, and she was going to accept a lift and get in his car. All the sensible voices in her head, which normally warned her and kept her safe, kept quiet. 'Yes, okay. Thanks.'

'If you're sure. You seemed to be enjoying your alone time,' Tom added quickly.

Emmy felt pathetically happy that he'd noticed she was still sitting there. She really needed to get a grip on herself. She laughed, gesturing to the empty seat across from her. 'Believe me, I'm ready to go home. I've had enough of sitting here on my own.' As soon as the words were out of her mouth, she regretted them. Now she sounded like *such* a loser. Maybe she *was* a loser. She didn't see many other people in the pub sitting at the bar with a meal for one staring into their phones.

Tom hesitated for a moment, then pulled his car keys out of his pocket. 'Ready when you are.'

Emmy felt so awkward as she walked to Tom's car she didn't even recognise herself. Where was the woman who spent most of her working life talking to people and sorting out problems? She was so tongue-tied, she ended up sounding as if she'd left her brain at home. This neighbour of hers must think she was not just strange but also thick as chips, barely able to hold a conversation or string two coherent words together.

As she sat in the front seat and Tom reversed, he chatted. 'I met Callum the other night.'

Emmy nodded. 'Oh, right, did you?' She was both surprised and not. Callum had a habit of not telling her things. 'He didn't say.'

'Nice lad.'

Emmy felt as if she could have kissed the ground at that. She liked nothing better than people saying that Callum was a good kid. 'He's good most of the time,' she joked. 'As teenagers go.'

'He seemed pretty interested in watersports on the island.'

Emmy shook her head. Callum, the typical teenager that he was, hadn't said anything about anything to her. 'Right.'

'Yeah, if he fancies it, I can take him out.'

'Okay, thanks,' Emmy said. She'd rather Callum didn't go out on the water, but at sixteen, she was no longer always in charge. She'd learnt with Callum, though, that more often than not, things didn't happen anyway. 'I'll keep that in mind.'

As Tom drove across Darling Island, the conversation flowed easily. Tom's hands left the steering wheel to make a point, and Emmy was completely and utterly drawn in by him. It was strange. She was actually hanging on his every word. She found herself telling him about her job at the port, being in the rental trap, how she hoped that Darling Island would be the answer to all her prayers, and that the lifestyle would be beneficial for Callum. Tom listened, and Emmy couldn't quite work out what was going on inside as she heard herself rambling on and on.

As they drove down the back lane behind the shops, the glow from the dashboard flickered on Tom's face, and Emmy gulped as the same as in the pub she seemed to fizz. She was, in fact, a human nuclear bath bomb.

'Here we are,' Tom said. He joked, 'Just need to get past the skip.' He bumped the car up onto the verge, turned off the engine, and the air felt suddenly very clunky and awkward. Emmy sighed, not wanting any of it to end. She scrambled for the door handle.

'Thanks for the lift. Appreciated.'

'Anytime. It was a pleasure.'

Just as Emmy was about to open the door, in an instant, she turned. She wasn't sure what made her suddenly lean over, whether it was the wine or the conversation, Tom's aura or their chatting, but before she knew it, she was closing the distance between them. All of a sudden, she found herself kissing him – a quick, unexpected press of her lips against his. For a fleeting second, she felt a jolt of electricity. A split second after that, reality came crashing down, hitting her on the head with a mallet. She scream-swore in her head, pulled away suddenly, eyes wide in surprise at her own audacity. What on earth had she done? She flicked her head back and forth repeatedly. 'Sorry,' she stuttered, her face flaming red. 'I didn't mean to. That was, I don't know. Sorry.' So embarrassed she wanted to die.

Tom looked just as startled, his eyes wide in surprise. There was a tense moment, the air charged and awkward. 'No, I…' he began, rubbing the back of his neck. 'It's fine. I mean, I was just surprised. Look, I should, err...'

The tension between them palpable, Emmy forced herself to take a breath. Her heart was racing. 'Sorry. I'll go. Sorry about that. I don't know what came over me,' Emmy managed to say. She made a hasty exit, leaving Tom behind in the car. Despite the embarrassment, the kiss made her heart flutter wildly. Even amidst the awkwardness and her embarrassment, it was deliciously, excitingly nice.

Emmy legged it to the gate. Her fingers fumbled on the latch, she pushed it, and just as it had the time before, it refused to budge. She cursed everything and everyone. ***** my life.* An odd growl came out, and she swore again. 'Typical.'

Giving the gate an almighty shove with her right shoulder, it flew open, and she bounded in and almost fell on the path. She closed it behind her, and as quick as a flash, she made her way to the back door, a ball of regret settling in the pit of her stomach. Her heart was pounding, her mind racing. She stepped inside and let the door shut behind her with a thud. The Old Ticket Office seemed particularly silent and dark, with only a soft glow of the streetlights through the windows at the front. Nothing felt like home, and now she'd gone and kissed her neighbour on a whim. Grimacing, she slowly went upstairs, the evening whirring around her head; the casual banter at the pub, the unexpected lift, the conversation in the car, and the kiss. What even was that? An impulsive, ridiculous, pathetic, desperate kiss. The taste of Tom, though. Not bad. The smell. Nice, so nice. She could also see right in the front of her mind his startled expression. Yeah, not quite as nice.

What had she been thinking? She had acted on impulse, driven by something she couldn't even compute. Why had she done that? To have kissed him out of the blue. Emmy shook her head, trying to shake off the image forming in her mind. She had crossed a line, and there was no going back. Mortifying.

She went into the kitchen, let the tap run for a second, and then downed a glass of water. She poured herself another glass and took a long sip. It did nothing to quench the burning embarrassment. She wondered if she should call her sister. As if reading her mind, a text pinged from Amy.

Amy: *Yeah, Ems, I was on the phone with Mum earlier. It seems you forgot to tell me something.*

Emmy frowned, wondering what she'd forgotten to tell Amy. She squeezed her eyes shut, trying to recall if she had forgotten to remind Callum about babysitting her nieces.

Emmy: *???*

Amy: *Next door.*

Emmy took another gulp of her water, her mind going back

to Tom's expression. He had looked as shocked as she'd felt. What must he be thinking of her now? Would this incident make things awkward? Just a bit. She felt silly and sheepish. She'd never intended to kiss him. She literally knew not a single thing about him, really. The car chat had mostly been superficial.

Emmy: *I just kissed him.*

Amy: *wtaf!!!!!!!!!!!!!!!!!!*

Emmy: ****

Amy: *I'm calling you.*

Emmy sighed and watched as Amy's name went across the top of her phone screen. She answered as she walked up the stairs to the top room. Amy didn't let her speak.

'Sorry! What?'

'Oh, my god! I just leaned over and kissed him in the car. In the lane. I can't believe it. I am such a loser.'

'What? Mum was joking and calling someone Poldark.' Amy's voice was incredulous. 'Sorry, why? No, not why. How? How did you kiss him? Who even is he?'

Emmy sighed and swore. 'This isn't funny.'

'Wait. How don't I know about this?'

'I don't know. It's been manic here.'

'You forgot to tell me you were going on a date with someone?'

'I haven't been on a date.'

'What? Sorry.'

'He's the neighbour.'

'Yeah, Mum said.'

'It's…'

'You kissed your neighbour. What in the garden? In the street? What the heck, Ems!'

'I know.'

'You're going to need to start from the beginning.'

'There isn't much to tell. Apart from that I have the hots for my neighbour, who is devilishly handsome, and I am a sad, desperate individual with no life who lurches at random men who kindly offer me a lift.'

'When did he offer you a lift?'

'Tonight!'

'You got in a car with a stranger? Who are you? That wasn't clever.'

'Oh gosh. I know. I thought it at the time too, but I just found myself doing it.'

'So you kissed this man who looks like Poldark Mum said about. I'm lost.'

Emmy sighed again. 'I went to drop off Love Emmy x parcels. I went for a stroll. I ended up at the pub. I got a lift with Tom. I kissed him.'

'Wow! It takes a lot to render me speechless, Ems.'

Emmy didn't feel like anything warranted a wow. She felt so embarrassed, it was comical.

'So, who is this bloke? Mum said he looks like an actor on the telly.'

'He's from next door. I don't really know a lot more. Well, I do know he lives there alone, but that's about it. Plus, everyone here seems to know about him.'

'What, and he asked you to go for a drink?'

'No! As I said, I went on my own. He was there.'

'So you went to the pub on your own but came home with him?' Amy clarified.

'Yes. And he's the one who bumped into me with the cake when I first saw this place. Remember?'

'Oh my! It's fate. Blimey, Ems.'

'It is *not* fate. I don't know anything about him. He's a bit standoffish and rude. For all I know, he has a wife and four children somewhere, even though he said he lives here alone. I don't know. I'm monumentally embarrassed.'

'Yikes.'

'Precisely.'

'What was the kiss like?'

'Shut up!'

Amy burst out laughing. 'Sorry, this is funny. You, Emmy Bardot, the sensible one, kissed your new neighbour on a whim.'

'It's not. This is nowhere near funny. I'm so embarrassed. Who does that at my age?'

'I told you Darling Island was going to be full of new opportunities. Just hadn't foreseen you doing this. Oh my.'

Emmy suddenly clamped her hand over her mouth. 'This is really bad.'

'What do you mean?'

'I mean, what if it had been the other way around?'

'Right, I see.'

Emmy swore again.

'I think you're overthinking.'

'No surprise there. Plus, I'm realising I saw what is probably his very pretty girlfriend come out of there the other day. Blimming heck, this is not good.'

'It will be fine in the morning.'

'Don't remind me of that. I have to see him in the cold light of day.'

'Yep. Emmy Meets Tom P in the Lane. Coming to BBC1 at Christmas,' Amy joked.

'Shut up, Amy. I'm going.'

'Yeah. Bye. I'll call you tomorrow for an update. Love you.'

After the call with Amy, Emmy felt worse. Much, much worse. Her thoughts were muddled, and as she fussed around moving things from one side of the kitchen to the other, she decided to go outside with the hope that some fresh air might do something, anything to clear her head. She was way too wound up to go to bed. Some night air might possibly do her good. Hopefully.

As she slipped on a cardigan, padded downstairs and

through the back of the shop, she made her way out. Silently, she stepped down the path to the gate, and of course, this time, it opened as clean as a whistle. Stepping around the skip, she stood looking up at the sky. The lights were still on a few doors down. She quickly looked away, walked down the lane, took a left, and double-backed so she was on Darling Street. It was bathed in a silvery glow from the moonlight as she walked aimlessly along. As she strolled, her mind wandered back to earlier in the night. The exchange with Tom when she'd been sitting next to the Australian. The conversation when she'd been sitting at the bar, the blue eyes, the lift home. Everything had been perfectly okay until just before she'd got out of the car.

With The Old Ticket Office in sight, Emmy stopped at the tram shelter and sat staring ahead, her gaze fixated on the tram rail glinting under the streetlights. She would have to apologise properly for what happened. But the awkwardness made her wince. A tiny little bit of her thought maybe Tom hadn't minded the kiss and that he was okay with what happened. But the majority of her said that was wishful thinking.

As a tram went past, she realised that there was a real chill in the air, and with a sigh, she got up from the bench and started her walk back home. She was so lost in her thoughts that she almost didn't realise when she had reached her doorstep. Tucked in the corner was a small basket. She shook her head at the funny little Darling tradition. As she opened the door and stepped in, she smiled at the contents; a packet of fancy artisan pasta, a jar of handmade pickles and a box of water biscuits.

Welcome to Darling Island so very far from care.
Good luck and here's to trying new things.
Regards from all at Darling deli. Come in for a chat and say hello.

Walking back upstairs, she put the basket on the side in the kitchen, flicked the light on in the bathroom, dropped her clothes on the floor, and turned on the shower. Tonight had been eventful, draining, and embarrassingly unforgettable. Later on, as she got into bed, she replayed the night in her mind. There was one thing she knew for sure. Life on Darling Island was turning out to be a tad different than she had expected, and the note hadn't been wrong. She'd definitely tried new things.

21

The next day after an early start, dropping Callum at the ferry and spending the morning working on both the digital and real-life version of Love Emmy x, Emmy had walked to Darlings café, strolled in, and, as if she'd known what she was doing (she hadn't), ordered herself a lunch basket. Not that she'd known what a lunch basket consisted of, but she was willing to give it a go. After a long morning stuck mostly at the top of a ladder, either vacuuming up cobwebs, cringing in embarrassment about what she'd done in the lane or painting ceilings, she'd needed a break.

Now she was sitting by the bay on a bench in the sunshine, counting her lucky stars that the weather fairies had delivered a gorgeous day. The water glittered in front of her, boats bobbed around, and though she was still fairly concerned that her jewellery boutique dream was a lot more involved than she'd first thought, the sea air, the landscape, and the friendly locals, including the one she'd kissed, were making her begin to see that her decision might not have been a bad one. Every cloud has a silver lining and all that.

Her mind zoomed as she thought about friendly locals. She'd been more than friendly to one of them. She groaned repeatedly inside. What in the name of goodness had taken hold of her? It must have been the wine. She'd have to seriously apologise the next time she saw Tom. Or maybe she'd just leave it.

Trying not to think about it, she put the little white basket she'd taken from Darlings beside her on the bench and opened the gingham linen with interest. Inside, everything was tucked in beautifully in a similar fashion to the breakfast basket she'd had before. A little glass jar with a gingham lid held piccalilli, a sourdough roll was tucked in the side, a beeswax wrap held sliced radishes, a tiny insulated fabric packet had cheese and sliced sausage, and just in case that wasn't enough, there was also a hard-boiled egg. Nothing had been left to chance. Wedged in the side of the basket was a small knife, a pot of smoked sea salt, and a napkin. A label on a glass bottle told her blackberry cordial was inside. All of it aimed to please.

Emmy smiled to herself as she tucked in. She could get used to lunches like this. She could also get used to the strange traditions and the funny little island surrounded by the hazy blue sea. And so, as she sat there, she tried to really appreciate the scenery, the bobbing boats and the way the sky seemed so blue and so huge. It was a far cry from her lunch spot at work in the demountable staff canteen - that she knew for a fact. She forced herself not to obsess about the kiss and tried to tell herself that it was fine.

Flipping up the ceramic cap on the top of the blackberry cordial bottle, she read the handwritten label on the front telling her it was homemade on a nearby farm with love and that the berries had been picked from the hedgerows of Darling. She put the bottle to her lips, took a tentative little sip, then nodded to herself as the cordial hit her taste buds. It was so much better than a vending machine can of drink, it almost blew her mind. Evie at Darlings was a master of baskets and lunch.

Sitting there enjoying her quiet lunch for one with the crusty sourdough, cheese, and sausage, Emmy's mind wandered back to The Old Ticket Office. There was a part of her that still couldn't quite believe what she was doing. She actually had her own shop, a real physical space to work alongside her digital presence. The transition from a purely online side hustle venture to a brick-and-mortar shop had been quite the up-and-down journey already. She tried not to dwell too much on how intimidating it all was. She tried not to let imposter syndrome fill her mind and tell her that she couldn't do it. She must just tell herself that she could.

Peeling back the beeswax wrap, she picked up a slice of radish, wondered why it was covered in a thick layer of butter, sprinkled on some of the burgundy-red smoked sea salt, popped it in her mouth, and promptly went to heaven. How had Evie even done that? How could the humble radish taste so good? As she sat there polishing off the radishes and butter, she tried not to think about how much worse the shop had been than her romanticised version and attempted to remain buoyant on a cloud of positivity where she looked the finished version in the eye.

She squinted and saw the artificial flower installation enveloping the whole of the shopfront in full bloom, her collection of vintage jewellery alongside flickering lanterns and lovely lights. She thought about the beautiful vintage display case proudly showcasing her carefully curated collection. Even the floor tiles with 'Love Emmy x' inlaid seemed to shine in her imagination. Oh yes, the lovely rose-tinted version in her head looked so very good.

Emmy dusted sourdough crumbs off her lap and laughed. She'd been so naive and unprepared, but somehow that was also part of it all. It had not been a breeze, which was making her all the more determined. Her little dream was risky, with no guarantee of success, but it was evolving. Plus, it felt so very good to be in charge.

On top of everything else, now she'd made the move, she was so pleased and, dare she even think it, proud of herself. As Marcel, her old neighbour, had said, you had to take life by the scruff of the neck and have a go. It was about following a passion and fulfilling a promise she'd made to herself long ago when she'd been in the flat with Callum, and she'd decided that there was no way she was going to give up.

Emmy finished her lunch, carefully wrapping all the components of it back up in the napkin. She now got the whole Darling Island basket thing. How funny and delightful and lovely. It was almost as if she'd slipped back in time. The whole world seemed to be ranting on here, there, and everywhere about sustainability, aristocracy from their private jets liked to lecture about the real cost of jetting around on a plane, but a little island off the south coast was reusing bottles and jars, utilising beeswax wraps, going with the seasons, and contributing little to food miles or food waste. It was nice to be part of that.

As Emmy tucked the basket in her bag and made her way past the pub to the tram, the Darling scenery made her all the more happier that the little place was her new home. Things were not only looking up, she was on a roll. After waiting a few minutes, the tram rails hissed, a tram pulled up, and after showing her resident permit, she sat at the back, looking out the window with the wind in her hair. Life in this place really did seem rather good. She winced and screwed up her face. It was looking very good, but not the bit where she'd overstepped a mark and kissed her neighbour after a lift. Ouch.

Trying not to worry about what had happened, she hopped off at the shops, and The Old Ticket Office stared back at her from down the road. It wasn't looking too bad. She nodded to herself with a little bit more confidence that it was only a matter of time until it would be done.

Just as she was shuddering in embarrassment at what had happened in the lane, the same woman she'd seen leaving Tom's gate emerged from the building. Closing the door behind her, the woman pulled her perfectly blow-dried hair over her right shoulder and smoothed down her top. Emmy peered from behind her sunglasses taking her in. The woman was the kind of exquisitely turned out creature who instantly made you feel as if you needed a good scrub behind your ears. In wide-leg cream high-waisted trousers with a thick tan belt, tucked-in silky shirt, and designer tote bag held just so in the crook of her arm, Emmy sighed inside. She went cold as she realised it was the second time she'd seen this woman in the vicinity of Tom's place. He'd told her that he lived alone and he'd been alone every time she'd seen him, but who was this woman?

Arriving at the front door as the woman went past in a cloud of expensive perfume, Emmy promptly forgot about her as Emmy frowned at a small rectangular basket tucked up by the left-hand window to the shop. She smiled as she bent down and picked it up. Turning her key in the lock and pushing the door open with her foot, she pulled tissue paper off the basket and peeked inside – a fancy jar of lavender bath salts with matching hand cream. A small card was tucked in beside the jar.

Welcome to Darling. Pop by for a drink on us.
From all at Darling Sailing Club.

Emmy shook her head as she walked across the shop and up the steep stairs to the flat. The basket thing was *so* simple and *so* good. A little gesture of loveliness that somehow made you feel welcome. Trudging up the stairs with the basket in her arms, she stopped in her tracks as she got to the kitchen door. Everything suddenly didn't look quite as bad, thanks to the lack of mice, her family's hard work and her vision. Emmy nodded to herself. She'd gambled, but she wasn't like Kevin. Her betting was perhaps taking off. She could be wait and see.

22

It was a week or so later, and despite all Emmy's overthinking and fussing about what had happened in Tom's car, she'd not seen or heard anything at all from Tom. His car had not been in the lane, and she'd noticed, not that she'd gone out of her way to look, of course, that the lights at his place hadn't been on at all. She'd concluded by the lack of goings-on that he was away. As the days had gone by, she'd thankfully put the kiss to the back of her mind, got stuck into working on the shop, taken Callum back and forth to cricket and spent a few long tiring days doing double shifts at work.

Emmy opened her laptop and read through an email from the Darling council concerning the sign she was wanting to put out the front of the shop. Everything seemed to be very serious, and the list of dos and don'ts concerning commercial zoning on Darling was very long. The same went for parking permits and resident stickers, and then there were the exhaustive details regarding the Chamber of Commerce, which Emmy was hoping to join. As Evie had promised in the pub, she had nominated Emmy to become a member of the group, and it had been seconded by Paul the postman. She'd wondered at the time what small business Paul had but hadn't liked to ask. Emmy recalled how when she'd mentioned the sign and floral instalment to Evie and Leo that there had been a lot of sucking in of air and shaking of heads. The end conclusion being that Emmy should become a member of the Municipality of Darling Chamber of Commerce sooner rather than later.

Evie had put all of that into play, and now it was time for Emmy to attend what was clearly disguised as a panel interview by way of the Chamber of Commerce monthly dinner. Emmy had been invited and would be sitting at a table with members of the committee who would ask her various questions about various things. Emmy hadn't liked the sound of it at *all*. She'd never been one for groups and committees, and that hadn't changed on moving to Darling. Evie, though, had said that once you were in the Chamber, it was basically a meeting every now and then with a glass of wine and a lot of Darling specialities to eat. According to both Evie and Paul, once you'd got through the first round table committee event and were accepted, it was fine. Emmy had thought that she could put up with that. Now, though, she wasn't sure.

She'd spent ages deciding what to wear to the event at the town hall and dissecting every part of her appearance. When she'd lived in the cottage, all she had to worry about was making sure her work uniform was clean and ironed and which jeans she would wear at the weekend. Now she seemed to be thinking about clothes way too much. Just as she'd decided on a nice blouse and was putting a pair of her grandma's beautiful earrings in the shape of tiny shamrocks in her ears, her phone buzzed.

'Hi.'

'Hi, Ems. How was work?' Amy asked in a cheery voice.

'Fine. Usual problems with people. All part of the job in customer service. How are you? How's your week?'

'Good. Busy, happy and tired from my end.'

'Ahh, yep, I hear you,' Emmy agreed.

'What are you up to?'

'I'm getting ready for that panel thing I was telling you about.'

'Oh, I'd forgotten about that.'

'I've spent way too long trying to decide what to wear. Pathetic, really.'

'Is it *really* a panel?'

'Sounds like it to me. I have to sit with the committee members and pretend to be nice and likeable. So yes, totally a panel. Just that it's in disguise.'

'Wow, serious. So what are you wearing?'

'My black silky trousers with the side split and a nice top.'

'Sounds just right. What jewellery are we taking out for the occasion?' Amy joked

Emmy laughed. 'Small and insignificant to any onlooker but seriously significant to me.'

'I know, I know.' Amy chuckled. 'Grandma's shamrock earrings.'

'The very ones.'

'For good luck.'

'Yeah, from the sounds of the email and the very long list of things to look out for, I think I'm going to need them. You should see the list of do's and don'ts.'

'Surely it's just a formality, isn't it?'

'You'd think so, but Evie said that initially, they are quite serious about who they let in.'

'Really? Do you want to be part of it? You hate stuff like that.'

'Don't know. I do know I want that sign on the front of the shop and the floral instalment going around the top without any drama, hence why I am attending this evening. Apparently, being part of it opens a lot of doors.'

'Yeah. Just smile sweetly and say all the right things,' Amy advised.

'I know. I do that all day long at my job. I'm well-practised.'

'You are.'

'It seems community things are part of living here. I have that regatta to go to tomorrow too.'

'Oh yeah. That sounded lovely, though.'

'True. I don't know if I can be bothered, but I replied that I was going, so I guess I don't have a lot of choice.'

'It will be good to meet some locals.'

There was possibly only one local Emmy wanted to meet. 'Yep.'

As if reading her mind, Amy asked about Tom. 'What about Mister P next door? Anything on that?'

'No, thank goodness. I've not seen hide nor hair of him still, which I am taking as a huge plus. Maybe he's been giving me a wide berth. Who knows? I'm no longer quite as embarrassed. I'm just going to bury what happened, and hopefully, he will too. I might not bump into him again for weeks if I play my cards right.'

'Yeah, maybe it's a good thing. On thinking about it, you really don't need complications with someone who lives a couple of doors down.'

Emmy wasn't so sure. Any sort of complication with Tom could be nice. 'Exactly.'

Okay, look, I have to run. I'll message Callum. Speak to you later. Let me know how it goes with the business people of Darling.'

'Will do.'

Emmy arrived at the town hall by way of the tram and right away had a few wobbles about her outfit. The building was old, imposing, listed, and very impressive. She'd not even gone in, and she suddenly felt *very* underdressed. She stared up at a Victorian clock tower on the left, a green dome on the right, and an information plaque noting the place had been built in 1898. A fancy-looking sign in front of her told her that she was indeed in the 'Municipality of Darling.'

Inside, the building was quiet, and Emmy was enveloped by the smell of time and wood as she walked down a long, wide corridor, where oak panelling ran down either side. It seemed to get quieter as she made her way into the depths of the building, to the point where it crossed her mind that she'd got the wrong day. After following laminated signs for the Chamber of Commerce dinner down a labyrinth of corridors, she began to hear signs of life as she came to three huge windows looking out towards an enclosed garden. Further down on the left, a reception area was busy. Arriving at a small, empty registration desk, a dark-haired, very attractive woman with a broad smile and friendly eyes approached. Emmy realised it was the woman she'd seen in the lane coming out of Tom's place and when she'd hopped off the tram. The same perfume she'd smelt before hit her nose. As before, Emmy instantly felt grubby.

'Emmy Bardot?' The woman held her hand out, and Emmy took it gratefully. Suddenly she felt not just wrongly dressed but definitely ill-prepared. The woman's handshake was strong and businesslike, as was her attire.

'Nice to meet you. I'm Cara Dehavier. You should have received an email from me.' Emmy looked blank. Cara explained, 'With the questions.'

Emmy hadn't received any sort of email as far as she was concerned, but it was more than possible that she hadn't bothered to open it. She pretended she'd received it and planted a smile on her face. 'Oh yes, yep.'

'So you're well-prepared then?' Cara waved an exquisitely manicured hand energetically as Emmy noted the expensive solid diamond tennis bracelet on Cara's arm. She looked at Cara's left hand to see if there as a ring. Cara didn't wait for an answer. 'Excellent. That's good. The last one who came hadn't prepared at all and didn't get in.' Cara stopped and looked Emmy directly in the eyes, 'And we don't want that, do we?'

Emmy smoothed her top down and tightened her fingers around the handle of her handbag as she followed Cara. She didn't know what to say in response, so she just chuckled. She so wished she'd worn a smart jacket.

Cara studied Emmy for a moment after Cara held her security pass over a keypad and then heaved open a door. 'Just make sure you answer what you think they want to hear, and you'll be fine.' Cara beamed, 'Hopefully, you'll pass.'

Emmy wanted to roll her eyes. It all seemed very serious. It was like she was going to meet the King. She said a million thank yous that at least she decided to wear the nice blouse and not a t-shirt. The invitation nor Evie had belied the impressiveness of the building, and by the way Cara was conducting herself, this event was a big deal. As she continued trailing along behind Cara, she sort of wished she wasn't there. She was all for an easy life, and the more she was hearing from Cara about previous applicants not doing well at the table, the less it seemed this was easy. All she wanted to do was erect a Love Emmy x sign above the shop door and put up a few garlands of artificial flowers. Was that such a big deal on this little island? Did she really have to be part of a stupid, boring council group to facilitate that? It was all very exasperating. Cara was talking about things Emmy wasn't even sure she knew what they were. Emmy's brain felt as if it was spinning around with talk of planning permission and permits. Kylie had nothing on her.

A few minutes later, they arrived at an inner lobby area with two huge Chesterfield sofas, a gigantic chandelier, and panelled walls. Various people were milling around with drinks and chatting. She could see Evie in a little black dress and heels on the far side with a glass of wine in her hand. She recognised the woman from the tram, Shelly, who was wearing a floaty white dress. Paul the postman was in a suit. Emmy gulped and held onto her handbag strap for dear life. Cara, in her tight pencil dress with a zip up the back, led her up to a circle of people, including a short older woman in a fluffy pink jumper who was holding an iPad out in front of her at the same time as talking to two women. 'This is Emmy Bardot,' Cara said. 'For the questions.'

The woman in the pink jumper held out her hand. 'Xian. Nice to meet you. Ready?'

The other woman smiled. 'We're ready for you.'

A man in a slightly grubby-looking suit and bright red tie shook her hand. 'Ahh, The Old Ticket Office's new owner. Welcome. Hope you're prepared for us.'

Emmy smiled, nodded, and swallowed. It was like a combination of waiting to line up for a firing squad and auditioning for a local amateur dramatics society play. She made a strange sound in response to a question, fiddled with her pearl-hammered bangle and listened to the woman called Xian, who was telling her that it wouldn't be too hard.

Cara passed Emmy a glass of wine then turned as the door at the opposite end opened and a few more people filed in. 'Right. Okay. Finally, that's just about everyone here. Let me just introduce you to a few more people over here, and then we'll be ready to go in.'

A few minutes later, Emmy had been introduced to more members and gulped her wine down way too quickly. Then a set of doors opened, and she followed Cara into a bigger room where people were milling around, chatting and taking seats. Cara led the way shimmying in her sky-high heels in and out of tables until they were at what was clearly the most important table at the front. Cara flicked her eyes around, assessing whether everything was okay, and then pointed to a seat with a name badge displaying Emmy's name. Emmy pulled the chair out and noted a man with small reading glasses and thick gold mayoral chains over his suit opposite her, the woman in the pink jumper beside him, and the man in the grubby suit whose jacket was now on the back of his chair.

Emmy sat down, smiled, waited, and prepared herself to be perfectly lovely and employ her best customer service voice. How hard could this be? She took a sip of her wine and looked over as Cara waved at someone coming in the side door. And then she had to stop her eyebrows shooting to the top of her forehead and keep her chin from dropping to the floor. Because the person who had just come in needed no introduction to her. She definitely knew this person. She knew what he looked like and what he smelt like. What his lips were like. Right there in front of her was Tom Carter.

Emmy blinked so many times it made her a bit dizzy. Tom P Carter is in the Municipality of Darling Chamber of Commerce. He may have gone down in her estimation a touch. Or perhaps not. Cara beamed and sort of basked in the devilishly handsome Tom P Carter glow. Emmy was soaking up the glow too. It appeared that perhaps everyone was. Cara was preening in her lovely dress, and her voice now purred. She seemed to almost jig up and down beside Tom as she flourished her hand out. 'This is Emmy. She's been nominated, and so she's on this table for the night,' Cara said, her words loaded with Emmy knew not what.

Tom looked directly into Emmy's eyes and didn't miss a beat. 'Yes, we've met,' Tom replied.

Cara was now openly gushing and fluttering her expertly applied, perfectly curled lashes. 'I thought you might have done. I wasn't sure if you two had met yet. You didn't say.'

Tom cut Cara off. 'We have.'

'Right,' Cara cooed and then clapped her hands together. 'Excellent. So, you've read the emails regarding this evening?' Cara asked. 'I also left them for you by your desk.'

Tom was definitely abrupt. 'Not had a chance.'

'Never mind! No problem whatsoever. We all know how busy you are.' Cara breathed.

Emmy felt her cheeks go crimson as she remembered the kiss. How she had leant over in Tom's car. She wanted the white linen-covered table in front of her to swallow her up. Tom wasn't crimson but irritatingly unreadable. He was so handsome she wanted to jump on him, but clearly there was something going on between him and the ever-so-beautiful Cara. Emmy had never felt quite as insignificant. She sat rooted to the spot, gripping her wine glass so tight her hand hurt. Tom grazed Emmy's elbow as he went to sit down – a sort of cross between holding out his hand in introduction and something friendlier. 'Nice to see you again.'

Tom was so confident and sure of himself it touched on annoying. All Emmy could do was smell him in the car. Words seemed to be stuck to the roof of her mouth. 'Likewise.'

Tom turned to Cara. 'Sorry, I was running a bit late.'

Cara almost tripped over herself in her gushing. 'No worries at all! I know your day was manic.'

'Yes.'

Cara looked at Emmy and did an odd sort of squeaky laugh. 'Emmy here said she's well-prepared, so that's good.'

This must be some sort of a joke, Emmy said to herself. Maybe it was a test, and she should be laughing at how seriously everyone was taking themselves. Before Emmy had time to think, Cara hit the table with a gavel hammer, everyone stood up and then sat down again, and the table turned mostly silent. Emmy wasn't sure what to do. She wanted to laugh, but she kept her face straight. She felt herself look to her left and her right, and her teeth clamped together. The man with the chains cleared his throat. 'Doctor Kogan, here. Chairman.' His tone was clipped, definitely upper-class. Horrid little half-moon glasses were perched on the end of a bulbous yet pointed, greasy nose. The huge chain glinted in the lights from above. 'For the record.'

He looked over the top of his glasses. 'I take it Emmy is short for Emily. Is your name actually Emily? You like to be addressed as' – he paused for a second – 'Emmy?'

Emmy heard herself squeak. 'Yes, I mean, no.'

Doctor Kogan didn't smile or frown or raise his eyebrows or move an inch. His face and unwavering stare didn't change at all. He just bored his eyes right into Emmy's. He didn't even blink. 'Sorry, is that a yes or a no?'

Doctor Kogan reminded Emmy of one of the passengers at her check-in area. He'd pushed all her buttons at once. There was no way she was having him look at her as he was and she wasn't going to squeak again. She put on her best, most practised, exceedingly professional but affirmative work voice. 'It's a no, my name is not Emily. Emmy Bardot.'

'I see.' Doctor Kogan made no other movement apart from a very light flick of his left finger to move his glasses a millimetre up his nose. 'Right, Mrs Bardot.'

Emmy interrupted him as quick as a flash. 'No. I didn't note myself as Mrs on the form.' The whole table was silent. It felt as if everyone was watching her. They were.

Doctor Kogan's glasses slid again on the greasy, bulbous nose. 'And so you are...?'

Emmy employed her same professional voice. She didn't miss a beat. 'As I said, Emmy.'

Doctor Kogan wrote something down on the piece of paper in front of him and then looked directly up again. 'So, have you been involved with a Chamber of Commerce before?'

This time, Emmy didn't answer straight away because she was trying to decide whether or not it was a trick question. She decided that honesty was the best policy. 'No. I have not.'

That was written down on the piece of paper too. Emmy was beginning to question everything about her choice of moving to Darling Island. She felt as if she was in a sitcom, whereby everyone was about to get up and stop acting. This

Doctor Kogan man was seriously annoying, and no one was saying anything. 'And you've been involved in business by way of?' Doctor Kogan asked.

Cara, thankfully, butted in. 'Doctor Kogan, I did circulate all Emmy's details to all members of the committee.'

'Yes.'

Xian, the woman in the pink jumper, markedly differently dressed to everyone else, leant across the table. 'Love the business idea. I can't see how you can go wrong with that, especially if you have the digital side of it in place.'

Emmy wanted to kiss her. 'Thank you.'

'You'll do well on Darling,' Xian reassured. Emmy thought she was seeing things as Xian took out a small silver flask and glugged an amber-coloured liquid into her glass.

The man in the grubby suit addressed her. 'Any criminal convictions?'

Emmy went to make a joke and quickly stopped herself. 'No. Never.'

The man jotted her answer down, seemingly satisfied.

Tom nodded, and with a knowing look and glint in his eye, he also asked a question. 'How are you finding the residents?'

The image of sitting next to Tom in his car flashed in front of Emmy's mind. *Quite nice. So nice, in fact, that I kissed one of them.* She ordered herself to focus on the questions. *Be happy, informal, yet intelligent.* She commanded herself. 'They're lovely so far, yes.'

'Everyone has been welcoming, have they?' Tom asked.

Emmy squirmed in her seat and wrung her hands. 'Yes, yes.'

'And you've found yourself making, err, friends with the residents? We take that very seriously on Darling. Being friendly, that is. You've been friendly?'

Emmy was now positive that Tom was making her squirm on purpose. She'd done more than be friendly with him. It was as if a line of fire was running across the table between her and him. She felt, in fact, as if she was red-hot. Something nuclear was happening again, just as it had in the pub. She was positive that every single person around her could see right through her. There was no way she was going to pass this test.

'And how have you found parking, the permits and zones, etcetera? The lanes on Darling are always eventful,' Tom asked, his pen poised.

Emmy's heart was racing. The event in the lane front and centre in her mind. Her eyes flicked to Cara, who was sitting very close to Tom and looking at him admiringly. Emmy felt all sorts of stupid. Emmy wasn't sure how to prettily smirk, but Cara was pulling it off admirably. 'Okay, so far, thanks,' she replied, now convinced not only Tom but also Cara were laughing at her. So embarrassed and uncomfortable, she needed to get away for a sec and regroup. She pushed out her chair quickly as the bread started to circulate. 'Sorry, I just need to pop to the loo.'

A few minutes later, she'd been to the toilet and was standing peering into the mirror, taking deep breaths as she clung onto the side of the basin. Bright red, inappropriate lips looked back at her. Thank goodness for the shamrock earrings. Once she'd washed her hands, dabbed her face with a damp paper towel, and removed most of the lipstick, she was back in the lobby.

She'd successfully pulled herself together and felt slightly better. She'd just have to get through the dinner and try not to think about the fact that she'd kissed her neighbour, and now he was sitting in front of her with what might be his ludicrously attractive girlfriend by his side. As soon as she could, she'd make a quick exit and run. Just as she was getting to the door to the function room, she saw Tom coming the other way, heading away from the men's toilets. The same as in the room, she couldn't work out what he was thinking. It was as if just being around him tangled her up into a load of weird twisty knots where she had no idea what was what. The knots were strangely nice. He strode purposely towards her. 'Congratulations. Looks like you're in.'

Emmy screwed up her face. 'What?'

'You didn't let Doctor Kogan phase you. He's the test.'

'Are you serious?'

'Deadly.'

'What? He purposely asks questions people could possibly sue him over?'

Tom didn't miss a beat. 'Yep, and you didn't blink.'

Emmy stopped herself from launching into a lecture about how almost all the men she'd met through her job of Doctor Kogan's generation assumed all sorts of things about women like her. It irritated her no end. She decided against it. 'I see.'

She was now sort of jogging to keep up with Tom P Carter, her heels clip-clopping across the shiny floor. She frowned, wondering what to say. She wanted to address the kiss before anything got any more awkward than it already was. 'Err, yes, umm, look, right, about the other night.'

Tom looked around. 'Yep?'

'Sorry about that.'

'It's fine.'

'No, no. It's not. Especially with, well, you know, with…' She was about to say the fact that he was sitting there next to his girlfriend, but she felt too ashamed.

Tom cut her dead. Emmy couldn't decide if he was angry or amused or what. She did know she was finding him a trillion more times attractive than she had at the pub. She was a nuclear reactor. 'All good.'

Emmy didn't know what to say. Part of her wished he'd said it was amazing. He wasn't saying that at all. Nothing like it. He'd sort of just brushed it off. As if it was nothing. As if *she* was nothing. Emmy felt more foolish than she had when she'd been looking out the window into the lane. She went cold as her brain computed what was now absolutely blimming obvious; clearly, women threw themselves at Tom Carter all the time! Here he was with his beautiful Miss UK-style girlfriend having to deal with another woman fancying him.

She was just another one in an annoyingly long line of women who'd kissed him out of the blue. It was as clear as day to her. Tom Carter obviously had legions of women lusting after him in every walk of his life, and his new neighbour at The Old Ticket Office was no different. He was *so* used to being *so* attractive it pained him. He'd flicked her off as if she was a fly. Her brain couldn't quite percolate it all at once. She didn't know what to say and so said nothing as she followed him as he strode purposefully back towards the table. As Emmy Bardot sat back down and fumbled putting her napkin on her lap, she felt about one inch tall.

23

The next day Emmy was up bright and early, waiting for Callum to get home from Kevin's. He bounded through the door, dropping his cricket bag by the top of the stairs. 'Hi, Mum! How are you? I'm starving.'

'Good. You're always starving. How was cricket?'

'Boring, really.'

'Right,' Emmy replied. *Shame it cost me so much money in fees for you to be bored then. Marvellous.*

'I'm just going to have a shower. Have you had breakfast?'

'Yep. Have you?' Emmy knew Callum had probably had breakfast, but in his world, he was always hungry.

'I had cereal at Dad's, but that was ages ago.'

Emmy knew when a cooked breakfast was required. She could read Callum like a book. 'Want me to do you a fry-up?'

'Yes, please. Oh, I forgot to say about the regatta,' Callum shouted as he pushed open the bathroom door.

Emmy got up and poked her head around the door. 'Sorry?' she called into the hallway.

'Tom next door said about it.'

What the actual? Now Callum was casually mentioning Tom

next door. Emmy attempted to keep her voice breezy and nonchalant. 'When did you speak to him?'

'The other day. Ages ago.'

'Right.' Typical Callum, he'd not only spoken to Tom and not said anything to her about it, but he was now only telling her half-snippets. She would have to extricate things out of him by way of excruciatingly basic questions, where he would give her one-word answers.

'When the other day?'

'Dunno.'

'What did he say about the regatta?'

'He said it's good.'

'Good?'

'You can wander around and look at the boats, and there's like a community barbecue and stuff like that. For free.'

'Yes, I know. We got an official invite,' Emmy clarified. 'The postman said about it too.'

'Oh. Didn't think you'd fancy it,' Callum called out. He knew Emmy only too well. Normally it wouldn't have been her sort of thing, just like the Chamber of Commerce thing, but from the big deal that was made about the invite, she felt it was her civic duty to turn up. If she was going to run a business and fit in on the island, it looked like going to these events was part of it.

'No, but I sort of feel obliged to.'

'Yeah, well, it sounds quite good, according to Tom.'

Emmy shuddered at the thought of Tom at the Chamber of Commerce event, where he'd brushed her off as if she was an irritating little fly. She could see him sitting there with Cara, the pair of them so devilishly beautiful they existed on another plane. As she heard the shower go on, she walked into the kitchen, pulled out a frying pan, and turned on a gas ring. After dropping bacon in the pan, putting baked beans in a saucepan, flicking the kettle on, and cutting up bread for fried bread, she busied around making the breakfast and thought about the event and the Darling Inn night and cringed. She'd have to avoid Tom and Cara at the regatta like the plague. There was no way she was getting herself into that situation again.

With the breakfast ready, as she waited for Callum to get out of the shower, she stared around at the tiny kitchen and then walked around the flat and sighed. Tom P Carter was the last of her worries. It all seemed like so much work. Although the walls were now clean and prepped thanks to her dad, they still needed painting, and the old timber fireplace, now rubbed down, showed potential but wasn't great. Trying not to think about the Chamber of Commerce event, Tom, Cara or the regatta, she thought about her week ahead at work and her supposed plan for Love Emmy x. She shook her head as she walked along the hallway and stood staring into the room where her bed was. It was just as bad in there, although it was now clean and without any furry friends, so she had to count that as a bonus. She peered at the doors needing paint, the scuffed and marked skirting boards and the huge sash window looking out over towards the estuary. None of it pleasant, and all needing the makeover help of her mum Cherry. Everything at every turn emphasised to Emmy what a huge task she'd taken on and how naive she'd been. She'd thought she'd play being a shopkeeper whilst looking after Callum, going to work and trying to keep all the balls in the air. She chastised herself for her stupidity and for leaving her comfy little life in the rented cottage. For running around islands randomly kissing men. Reality had kicked into her idyllic dreams, and it did not feel at all nice.

As she stood there mulling over the flat, she thought about how straightforward her life had been in the cottage. She'd go to work, do her time, drive home, pay the bills, clean the house, keep Love Emmy x ticking over, and make sure Callum was okay, and that was more or less it. Weeks would turn into months, months into years, and she would rinse and repeat the whole thing over and over again, and that was her so-called life. Life had pottered along quite nicely without many problems at all. Now in the grotty flat, problems seemed to be swatting her in the face pretty much constantly. There were also other problems – ones with blue eyes and ever-so-nice broad shoulders who made her act strangely. And kiss them. She tried not to think about it, and just as she was back in the kitchen pouring the tea out, her phone pinged with a message from Kevin. *Not him as well. **** sake.*

Kevin: *Morning. Great few nights. Cricket was good. Have you spoken with Cal yet?*

Emmy: *No, he's in the shower. What's up?*

Kevin: *Nothing. I had an idea. I mentioned about us going away for the whole summer, not just the usual few weeks.*

Red flags started to wave for Emmy. When Kevin had an idea, it usually involved Emmy forking out for it. How was Kevin intending to pay for being away for the whole summer? She'd have one guess.

Emmy: *I see.*

Kevin: *I'll let Cal tell you about it. It would be good for my mental health too.*

Kevin added an emoji with sunglasses, and Emmy felt the muscles just above her jaw tighten as she gritted her teeth together in irritation. Blackmail vibes from the mental health mention. Another thing Kevin had become quite the master at doing. He would plant a seed in Callum's head to facilitate their father-son time, and Emmy would end up paying for it just to keep both of them happy. She tried to remind herself that Kevin was a good influence in Callum's life and that his relationship with Kevin was uppermost. Sometimes she wanted to do the complete opposite and tell Kevin to sling his hook. She decided she couldn't be bothered to say anything. It wasn't worth the ensuing onslaught of how Kevin had to live with his disorder every hour of the day and that she didn't understand that he was also often depressed.

Emmy: *OK.*

Kevin: *Also, what's happening tonight re the party?*

Emmy sighed and felt like throwing her phone across the room. Kevin knew exactly what was happening with the party Callum was going to because, as usual, she had sent Kevin the regular weekly detailed schedule of what was happening with school runs, after-school sports, cricket training, and anything else that might have come up. Callum had a party which was nearer to her mum and dad, so they were collecting Callum at the ferry, and he was staying at theirs for the night.

Kevin, though, where Callum was concerned, liked to constantly ask questions and reiterate what was going on even though it was written down in front of him in black and white. It seriously irritated Emmy, but she sucked it up nonetheless. She had realised many moons before that it was all part of Kevin's narrative of being a good dad. He asked constant questions to reiterate that he was involved, at the same time as shoving his gambling and lack of finances under the carpet. Then he threw into the mix that he saw himself as a struggling single parent whose ex-wife had been mean to him because she hadn't understood his addiction. It was his way of fooling himself that he'd done nothing wrong. He liked to tell himself and anyone else who would listen that he was in charge of Callum. Whereas it had always been Emmy who'd done the real nuts and bolts of the day-to-day grind of parenting. It had been that way since the day Callum had been born. Kevin just liked to kid himself that he was in the Super Dad league. Emmy sighed, didn't bother to reply, and slipped her phone into her pocket.

Callum came sloping into the kitchen with wet hair and smelling of shower gel. At just under 6ft, sometimes Emmy wondered if he was really hers. 'How was it at Dad's?'

'Yeah, good. Same as usual. Bit boring.'

'Did he drop you at school yesterday?'

'Yep.'

'Right.' Emmy paused while she dished up the fry-up and waited to see what Callum said about Kevin's idea. It didn't take long.

'He said about going down to the flat for the whole summer and doing loads of sport and stuff.'

Emmy tried to remain calm and smiled. She'd thought it would involve money, and it did. Kevin had the bright idea of taking Callum to Kevin's brother's place in the south of France, but Emmy would have to stump up the cash involved.

'Right. I thought you said last year it was boring.'

'Nah. Dad said we could go windsurfing and stuff like that now I'm sixteen. There are loads of activities I can do now. Jet bikes and all that. He was talking about getting a motorbike too.'

Emmy winced at the thought of how much jet bikes and windsurfing would cost. Plus, it was the first she'd heard about a motorbike. Shame Kevin could never stump up any funds for things like school uniform or cricket fees. She should have known it was coming. Kevin would get to spend the summer playing sports with Callum, and she would be expected to work so that she could pay for most of it. 'Right.'

As if Callum was reading her thoughts, he waved his hand. 'Don't worry. I'll ask Grandpa if he can give me money for the summer.'

'That's not the point, Cal. Grandma and Grandpa are not here to constantly give us money.'

Callum turned his head to the side for a moment in contemplation. 'Why not, though? They're loaded. Might as well take it.'

Emmy tutted. 'Please don't speak like that, Cal. It's not pleasant.'

'Right, okay, but it's true.'

Callum sat down, started to tuck into the breakfast and

changed the subject. 'So, what about going down to the bay this afternoon for the regatta, then?'

Emmy sipped her tea. 'I'm not sure. I've replied yes, but I'm sure it will be okay if you go on your own. I don't even know anyone who's going or anything.' *Apart from the fact I know the man next door that I kissed is going. There's also the fact that I'm pretty much thinking about him twenty-four seven. He might be there. So might his girlfriend. I do know that.*

Callum jerked his thumb and shoved a fork full of bacon into his mouth. 'You know next door, don't you? You said you'd spoken to him.'

Emmy gulped. She'd more than spoken to him. 'Yes, I know that, Callum, but that's all I know.'

'What do you need to know?' Callum asked with wide eyes as if it was the simplest question in the world.

Inside, Emmy chuckled to herself. *Oh, to be young.* She wanted to know everything about her neighbour, like every single detail. She coughed a little bit. 'Cal, you just never know. You have to be careful in life.'

'Don't be ridiculous, Mum.'

'I'm not sure about going.'

Callum rolled his eyes and huffed a bit. 'It's not a big drama.'

'Don't be rude, please, Callum.'

'How is that rude?'

'It is, and don't answer back, please.'

Callum did another little huff. 'Whatever.'

Emmy couldn't quite decide if she wanted to go to the regatta or not. She was still recovering from the Chamber of Commerce event. She did know that she'd need to get out of her old bed t-shirt and fleecy fairy pyjama bottoms with saggy knees. Something would need to happen to her hair too. 'Okay.' Emmy got up and rifled through a pile of papers on the worktop until she found the invite delivered via Paul. 'This is the invite to the main event.'

Callum read it and looked up. 'Sounds good. I wonder what the Darling sausage consists of?'

'Don't know, but it all sounds quite serious. According to the postman, the tickets are hard to come by.'

'Exactly, which is why Tom next door said to go.'

'Right.'

Callum scanned the invite. 'Food starts at 1 p.m.'

Emmy chuckled. 'You'll need filling up again by then.'

'I will,' Callum agreed as he put his knife and fork together and then drained his tea.

'We can go to the regatta, then I'll walk back here or get the tram and get changed. Grandma is picking me up at the ferry, and then I'm going to the party from there. Correct?'

'Yes. Grandpa will pick you up from the party, so you're not to be late. You need to text me on the hour.'

'Yep, I know. We're going to go look at phones in the morning too.'

Emmy shook her head. 'Have you conned Grandpa out of a new phone?'

Callum chuckled. 'Not yet.'

After Emmy had cleared up breakfast, she walked back into the bedroom, stripped off the fairy pyjamas, and went into the bathroom with her head absolutely brimming with thoughts of the day ahead. She didn't even know what to think. What would the regatta bring? Would she be able to interact with Tom normally after he'd seemed to dismiss her at the Chamber of Commerce event? She felt sick at the thought of seeing him with the gorgeous Cara. She'd been monumentally flicked off as if she was nothing. She shook her head, trying to get rid of her thoughts. She'd need to avoid Tom as her best bet. She wondered what he was thinking as she stepped into the shower.

So much for not thinking about him, all she could see was him as the water washed over her. She closed her eyes, leaning into the stream, splodging shampoo into her hands, and rubbing her head so hard as if it might rid her of her thoughts of him. It didn't work. She replayed her feelings in the pub when she'd been sitting with Leo and Evie, and he'd come in. She thought about how when she'd been sitting at the bar on her own, he'd looked gorgeous. She couldn't stop seeing his face, his blue eyes, and his dark hair. She wondered why no one had said anything about Cara. Her brain ran through reasons Cara might not have been in the pub.

Her thoughts then started to veer towards their awkward parting in the car. She'd kissed him, taken by a moment of attraction fuelled by nuclear power. But the immediate regret, the awkwardness that had ensued together with his attitude at the Chamber of Commerce, left a sour taste. Plus, now she realised there was possibly the girlfriend, Cara, thrown into the occasion. She was so wrong to have acted on impulse. It was going to be so embarrassing seeing him again.

With a sigh, Emmy realised it was futile to dwell on it, and she couldn't turn back the clock. Today was a new day, and she had a new life to facilitate. She needed to turn up at the regatta and get her feet under the table of the Darling community. More importantly, she needed to show that she was more than capable of moving past a moment of awkwardness. She watched as the water washed away the suds and decided she was over-thinking and making a mountain out of a molehill. People randomly kissed neighbours they knew nothing about all the time. Didn't they? Yep, she'd face the day head-on, whatever it consisted of, be it Tom Carter or stupid greasy bulbous nose doctors and generational misogyny. Nothing would throw her off her stride.

Feeling much more confident than she had when she'd got in the shower, Emmy found herself standing in front of rows of moving boxes in a whirlwind of indecision. 'What to wear from my vast wardrobe of fashion?' she joked as she haphazardly opened boxes. She rummaged around for her faithful little black wrap dress, but holding it up, she frowned. Too formal, too try-hard, too black. More suited to an evening dinner than a sunny community event.

Next, she pulled out high-waisted denim shorts and a white, ruffled blouse. On any other sunny day, she'd have reached for them without a second thought, but today, Emmy hesitated. Too casual? Too casual-day-off-going-to-the-beach. If the Chamber of Commerce event was anything to go by, Darling-ites took local occasions seriously. Doubt trickled in, and the outfit found its way back onto the top of the box. Pale floral floaty jumpsuit? Trendy, with wide legs and a waist tie. She tried it on – not unpleasant, but not right. Emmy chuckled to herself at the situation. Who was she trying to kid that the clothing crisis was anything to do with Darling-ites? It was totally to do with the possibility of seeing Tom P. *Who had a girlfriend.*

After rummaging around a bit more, she decided on a pale blue sundress. She slipped into the dress and looked at herself in the mirror. She'd put on a bit of weight after stress-eating her way through the move, but the cut hid loads of bad food choices. It hugged her waist just right and floated around at the bottom. Perfect for a sunny day at a community event. After blow-drying her hair and putting in a curl, she stood in the reflection of the mirror and nodded. Not too bad. She wondered what the regatta would bring.

24

Emmy strolled down towards the bay with a smile on her face. Was there much better than the south coast of England when the sun was out to play? She thought not. Sun rays shimmered off the water, and the bay buzzed with people out enjoying the weather. Emmy nodded to herself. The sundress was a good choice and just right for both the blue sky and the occasion. As she got closer, she realised that Darling Island, when it was putting on a show, didn't mess around. She'd thought the blue and white bunting had been profusive before. This took it to whole new levels. Everywhere she looked, bunting went back and forth, and little flags flapped in the sea breeze strung across the boats, between the buildings, and down the streets.

It wasn't just the bunting, though, or the sunshine that looked lovely; the roped-off ticketed area just along from the boats had stepped right out of a coastal postcard. When Emmy had read about the beer tent and the barbecue, she'd envisioned ugly blue market gazebos, perhaps the odd fold-up chair. That was so not part of the equation, it wasn't even funny. Beautiful round canvas tents strung with bunting and stripy blue and white deck chairs looked back at her. The smell of barbecue and sun lotion wafted in the air, and people with not a care in the world and ice-creams in their hands strolled by the sea.

Callum rubbed his hands together. 'Nice. It smells amazing.'

'You took the words right out of my mouth,' Emmy said at precisely the same time as her phone pinged with a message. She pulled her phone out of her dress pocket and read it. 'Oh, it's Grandma. She's realised she needs to pick you up at the ferry a bit earlier.'

Callum frowned. 'Okay.'

Emmy looked back towards the tram. 'You're going to have to pretty much eat and go, or I can take you later, I guess, but that will mean I have to drive back.' Emmy really didn't want to have to do that. She had the evening earmarked for painting the walls in the shop.

Callum looked at the time on his phone. 'It's fine. I'll just eat and go.'

'You sure?'

'Yeah. Otherwise, you'll spend ages getting back over here.'

Emmy nodded. The ferry and getting off the island had been one of her concerns about moving to Darling, and this was one of the occasions where it was proving to be a pain. She looked around at how beautiful it was, though; the hazy blue, the unspoilt scenery, the lovely people. Right in front of her was the payoff for having to get to the place by way of a floating bridge. 'Okay, well, you'd better get your skates on.'

As they arrived at the roped-off area, a man smiled, and Emmy held out the ticket. 'Ahh, yes, Emmy and Callum. Correct?'

'Yes,' Emmy confirmed.

'I was at the Chamber of Commerce last night,' the man noted with a smile.

'Ahh, right. I hope I performed well enough to be in?' Emmy

bantered even though Tom had said she'd passed the test she actually didn't know for sure.

The man didn't really laugh. 'Let's hope so.'

'I'm crossing my fingers,' Emmy joked, digging herself further into a hole.

'Yep, you need your fingers crossed.' The man appeared to be way more serious than necessary.

Emmy made a funny little sigh and then pointed to indicate that Callum was with her.

The man nodded and gesticulated to a tent on the left. 'Right. Darling sausage there. You'll want the Darling crab before it runs out. Good job you got here in time. With the sunshine coming out, the place is heaving. The food won't last long.'

'Thanks. I'll make sure I try the crab,' Emmy replied and walked in and watched as Callum said hello to a couple of lads and headed off towards the barbecue. As she was making for the beer tent, she saw Lucie from Darlings café. Lucie turned and raised her eyebrows in greeting. 'Hi, how are you?'

'Good, thanks.'

'The sun came out for us,' Lucie chirped. 'Isn't it just a beautiful day?'

'Yes. So nice!'

Lucie turned to the man on her left. 'This is George. George, Emmy.'

Emmy held her hand out. George wasn't ugly. Did this island breed handsome men? 'Nice to meet you. Emmy Bardot.'

'I hear you're turning The Old Ticket Office into something sparkly,' George joked.

'That's the plan, though it's going to take quite a bit longer than I thought,' Emmy said. 'I'll not be ready by Christmas at the rate I'm going.'

'Like most things in life,' George said with a slight flick of his eyes upwards.

'Yep!'

'You're getting used to our funny ways?' George asked.

Emmy chuckled. 'Slowly.'

'You experienced the joys of the Chamber of Commerce panel, didn't you?' Lucie laughed. 'Evie said she'd nominated you.'

'I did. She said it needed to be done if you have a business on the island.'

'Yep. I bet that was an eye-opener,' George stated.

'All about who you know.' Lucie laughed.

'Ha ha.' Emmy chuckled appropriately whilst thinking inside that she was beginning to see that on this strange little island, who you knew could make or break you.

George held his glass up. 'Drink?'

'Oh, I'm fine, I can get one,' Emmy said and flicked her eyes towards the beer tent.

'Don't be silly.' Lucie looked at George. 'I'll have another one of these, please.'

Emmy nodded towards Lucie's glass. 'Whatever Lucie's having would be lovely. Thanks, George.'

A few hours later, Emmy, helped by whatever it was that Lucie had been drinking, was having quite a nice time. Rather than enduring what she thought would happen – inconsequential small talk with Darling-ites and making an exit as soon as she could – she'd actually enjoyed herself. For the first time in a long time, she felt relaxed. The locally brewed Darling ale might have had something to do with it. She'd had a long talk with Lucie, who she'd assumed only worked in Darlings café, but it turned out had a thriving small business born from a love of sewing and crafts. Via Lucie, she'd chatted for ages with a man called Mr Cooke, who she'd realised she'd initially met on the tram. He'd informed her of all sorts, including, but not limited to, information on collecting stuff from the beach, the ins and outs of living on Darling, and how the floating bridge did a great job of keeping the specialness of Darling just that.

Sitting at a table outside basking in the sun with Lucie and her husband George, one conversation had led to another until Emmy realised that her hard, stressy sides were softened around the edges. She'd clicked with Lucie at the same time as feeling a little bit of girl/life envy. It seemed that Lucie had quite the existence; a lovely husband, a local job, a doing-well small business, and a group of friends she'd known since school who she went on holiday with and all sorts. Emmy could only wish for a smidgen of the same. As Emmy sat listening to Lucie, she felt as if she had her mum and dad, her sister, Callum, and not a lot else. There was a little teeny bit of a pity-party playing in the wings.

As Leo, the Australian, joined the group, Emmy decided that despite The Old Ticket Office clearly not going to be the easy ride she'd hoped and planned for it to be, Darling Island clearly had other attributes. Community being one of them. She was quite happy to find out more.

Leo, owner of bronzed biceps that required their own Darling resident permit, sat down next to Lucie. Said biceps were ever-so-close to Emmy's arm. 'How are ya?'

'Good, thanks,' Emmy replied and then indicated to the beer tent. 'I was only meant to be popping in for one of the famous sausages. I haven't even made it over there yet.'

'You'll be right.' Leo held up his plastic glass full of dark ale. 'This is a cracker. You don't need sausage if you have a few of these. They're like a meal supplement.' Leo winked.

Emmy chuckled. 'It appears I may have found a new drink to love.'

Leo pointed to Emmy's shoulder. 'Looking a bit pink there.'

He peered up at the sky and then back at her. 'The sun is stronger than you think in this spot.'

'Oh, am I?'

'You don't want to be getting sunstroke,' Leo joked.

'I don't think there's any chance of that.' Emmy laughed. 'We're not in the Med. Have you seen the temps over there and the fires? Crazy!'

'Ha, yes, I have. I know it's not that hot, but it's easily done. Anyway, how are things and how are you finding the commute?' Leo asked.

Emmy nodded. 'Not too bad, actually. I thought it might be horrendous, but it's fine. I leave at the crack of dawn, so the traffic isn't a problem.'

'Same here,' Leo agreed. 'That's one good thing about shift work. You work at the port, you said?'

'I do. In customer service. I negotiated so that I can do double shifts to save on the commute time and do the shop on the weekends. That was the plan, at least. I think it's going to be a good while until I open the doors of the shop at the rate I'm going, so I'll probably do more hours at work.'

Leo took a sip of his drink. 'I bet you've got some stories to tell working over the port there.'

Emmy chuckled. 'I do. I assume the same can be said for you at the hospital.'

'Oh yes. And that's the staff, not the patients,' Leo joked. 'So, how are the double shifts going?'

Emmy paused for a second. 'To be quite honest, so far, they're exhausting. I'm used to spending the whole day on my feet, but this takes it to whole new levels. I suppose I'll get used to it. Can't argue with a stable job these days, what with the state of the economy and everything. Work is work. A job is a job.'

'Yup. There is that.'

'And I'm very valued by my boss.'

'Excellent,' Leo said as he drained his glass. He held it up. 'My round. What are you having?'

Emmy went to say no. She'd not even made it to the bar herself, and she really should make a move. Wall painting was calling. Just as the words were coming out of her mouth, someone else joined the little group at the table. Someone whose gaggle of muscles and thick dark hair made Emmy draw in a small but well enough hidden gasp of air. Someone who was on his own, too. 'Yep, thank you. I'll have whatever you're having. A small one, though, please.'

Leo turned and smiled at Tom. 'The man himself! Gracing us with his presence. Good timing.'

Emmy swallowed and felt her eyelashes blinking over and over again. She also felt herself sit up straighter and push her left shoulder towards Tom P Carter, and her face seemed to move of its own accord, rearranging itself into something that was a cross between coy and embarrassingly weird.

Tom looked directly at Emmy, his face polite as if there was nothing really between them and certainly not a kiss in a car. 'I just bumped into Callum. Nice lad.'

Emmy felt ridiculously pleased for both the compliment about Callum and the attention. She suppressed a shiver as the smell of Tom in the car was front and centre of her mind. 'Thanks.' She lost herself for a bit in a scene where Tom was playing the lead role.

Suddenly, a voice cut into Emmy's daydream. 'You wanted the same, did you say?' Leo of the hard biceps clarified.

It took Emmy a second to zoom herself out of the car in the lane and back to the table outside the beer tent. She flicked her head quickly. 'Yep, thanks, yes, just a small one for me.'

Emmy watched as the hulk of Tom followed the burnished arms of the Australian. It was as if someone had dropped her onto the set of a funny little show, where she was sitting outside a delightful beer tent on a summer's day. She smiled as the woman she recognised from the Chamber of Commerce in the fluffy pink jumper shuffled over to the group, plonked herself down next to George, and started to chat. She was then joined by another woman who Emmy vaguely recognised as the woman who had sold her the cake in the bakery. There were clearly two degrees of separation between everyone on this island. She'd have to be very careful about what she said. Or who she kissed.

Leo put her drink down and sat back down beside her, and Tom pulled up a chair and wedged it between Leo and the woman from the Chamber of Commerce event, who was today wearing a jumper bordering on a scary shade of shimmery purple. Emmy remembered the woman's name was Xian. 'So, how are you finding everything?' Xian asked.

'Good, thanks.'

'Have you had lots of baskets delivered?'

'I have, yes, thanks.'

'It's a lovely custom, isn't it?'

'Yes, it definitely is. I have lots of nice bits and bobs.'

'I bet you thought it a bit strange at first?'

Emmy nodded.

'How have you found everyone further down that end of Darling Street?'

One of them is particularly nice. Shame it appears he has a love interest and or girlfriend. 'Good. It's not a bad spot to end up.'

'Any run-ins with any of the neighbours?' Xian joked and laughed.

Emmy stole a tiny flick of her eyes toward Tom. As before, she couldn't really read his face. She spluttered, 'Err, no, not as yet.' *If only you knew.*

Leo butted in. 'I hear ya had a bit of drama in the lane.' He winked with a very knowing look on his face.

Emmy went ice cold, as if someone had shoved her in a walk-in freezer for a few minutes. Tom had clearly told his

Australian friend what had happened in the car. She tried to hide a full-body cringe and plastered one of her customer service masks on her face. Her brain scrambled to think of a witty quick-fire response, but it was like a snail and didn't know which way to play it. She didn't know what Leo knew or what he was actually referring to, but it appeared that he knew what had happened with Tom in the car. 'Did you?' was all she could come up with.

Leo didn't provide any further embellishment of his question. 'Yeah.'

'Sorry.' Emmy wrinkled her nose and shook her head. 'Not sure what you mean.' She employed one of the strategies she used at work, which she had learnt from her boss, Judy – reiteration. 'Drama in the lane?'

'The skip delivery,' Leo stated.

Emmy looked blank and again repeated what Leo had said back to him. 'The skip?'

'Wasn't it a bit touch and go whether or not it was going to fit down the lane there? It's quite narrow.'

So Leo wasn't talking about the kiss at all. Emmy felt as if someone had pierced a tiny little hole in the side of her hip. Tension and embarrassment whooshed out of the hole, and she felt her body ever-so-slightly deflate. She let herself look at Tom, lifted her chin just a touch, and widened her eyes a tiny amount, hoping that he would grasp her silent thank you that Leo wasn't talking about the kiss. She scrambled quickly to keep the conversation on the skip. 'Ahh, yes, yes, it was close.'

'How is the shop?' Xian asked.

'It's good, but it's going to be a lot slower than I thought,' Emmy replied, very grateful to get the conversation anywhere but the lane.

George then chatted across the table to Leo, and the conversation thankfully moved away from both Emmy and the lane. As the local brew continued to fuzz Emmy's edges, she sat in a bit of a happy daze with the late afternoon sun beating down on her. A text from Callum told her he was on his way to the party, and any notion of spending the evening tending to shop walls was long gone. By the time George and Lucie had called it a day and Leo had just left, the early evening had rolled around. Emmy suddenly realised that while sitting on the chair, she was fine, but her head was spinning a little bit. Tucked up in a sun trap in probably the warmest spot on Darling Island, she suddenly felt faint. The air felt hot and sticky and almost as if she couldn't breathe. She'd forgotten to put on sun lotion, and as Leo had noticed hours earlier, she could feel her shoulders starting to smart.

'You alright, Emmy?' Tom asked.

'Yeah, I'm fine,' Emmy replied, not wanting to make a fuss. She pushed out her chair. 'I'm just going to pop to the loo, and then I'll head off home.'

'Right you are.'

Emmy stood up, and as she was attempting to remove her bag from the back of the chair, everything seemed to spin. The sounds around her started to blur, and her legs felt wobbly as she reached out to steady herself.

'Whoa, hold on there!' A hand grabbed her arm, and she found herself looking into Tom's concerned face.

'You don't look good,' Tom said, gripping her arm tightly.

'I'm fine,' Emmy insisted, grateful that she hadn't landed on the floor.

'You're not fine.'

'No, no, all good. Just a bit stuffy. I must have had too much sun.'

Tom touched Emmy's shoulder. 'You're red-hot.'

'No, I'm alright, honestly,' Emmy protested weakly, but her legs seemed to give away under her, and she clung onto Tom's arm for dear life and then proceeded to plonk herself back on the chair.

'Where's Leo when you need him?' Tom said under his breath, looking at Emmy with concern.

'I'm fine.'

'Stay there. I'll get you a glass of water,' Tom said.

Emmy watched as Tom made for the bar and, two seconds later, was back at the table with a glass of water. Xian was now sitting next to her. Emmy gulped back the water and went to stand up again. 'Thanks, all good. I'll get going. I just need to get out of the sun. I didn't realise quite how warm it was.'

Xian clapped her hand on Emmy's arm. 'Don't be daft. You're not fine by the look of you.'

'Just need to get out of the sun,' Emmy repeated with a weak smile and flapped her hands in front of her face in a pathetic attempt to cool herself down.

Tom stood up and gently pulled Emmy to her feet. 'Let's get you home.'

The trip home was a blur, and Emmy felt as if the whole world was spinning as she sat in the front seat of Tom's car. The car seemed to float along the narrow roads, and Emmy felt detached from everything. She barely registered the lane when Tom parked the car and helped her out. As she felt the solid ground of the lane under her feet, she attempted to appear fine. It didn't work, and she stumbled towards the bonnet. Before she knew what was happening, Tom had scooped her up, kicked the gate open with his foot, and sped down the path as if he was holding a shopping bag, not a fully-grown woman with a spot of sunstroke.

'It'll be cooler upstairs,' Tom said, his voice sounding far away as Emmy felt herself being carried up the stairs to the flat.

'It's a bit of a mess up here,' Emmy heard herself mumble. It felt strange to be carried up the stairs in her own house, but at that stage, as her head spun, despite it being Tom, she didn't care less. She just wanted her head to stop doing what it was doing.

A few minutes later, she was sitting on the sofa, staring at the mountain of moving boxes in front of her. Tom appeared with a glass of water. 'Here, sip this slowly,' he instructed, and then pushed up the old sash window to let in a whoosh of cool air.

'Have you got any fans?'

Emmy shook her head.

'I'll be back.'

Emmy felt the cool water slide down her throat, already making her feel better. She touched the back of her right hand to her forehead and felt red-hot skin. She realised her error – she'd sat drinking the local brew in the corner in the sun, getting hotter and hotter until her body overheated. She stretched her left shoulder forward and gasped at the colour of her skin. She'd been baked. A few minutes later, Tom was back with a fan in each hand. He plugged one in on either side of her, and she let her head fall back on the sofa, looking up at Tom. She was about to thank him when a yawn interrupted her.

Tom chuckled, shaking his head. 'You really don't look great. How are you feeling now?'

'A bit better. I just needed to get out of that hot corner.'

'Want me to wait here while you go and have a cold shower or something? It might cool you down.'

Somewhere inside, underneath the burning heat radiating out of her skin, Emmy saw the irony of the situation. The man she'd been daydreaming about was standing by her sofa, asking her if she would like to take a cold shower. She didn't even have the energy to think about a funny, sassy response. 'I'm fine.'

Tom turned his lips upside down. 'Fair enough.'

Emmy's head was pounding, and her shoulders felt as if flames were flickering on top of them. Despite the whirring of the fans, a hot, prickly sensation stung under her skin, and her bones felt as if someone had put them in an oven. Moving her shoulder made her wince, and it felt as if her skin had shrunk, pulling tight across her shoulders, restricting her movements. She looked at her other shoulder, where the skin was a vibrant, angry red.

Tom winced. 'Yeah, that's not looking good.'

Emmy squeezed her eyes together, berating herself for both not putting on sunscreen and sitting in the sun all afternoon long. 'No.'

'How's your head?'

'Pounding.'

'Go and have a quick shower to cool you down, and then I'll be off,' Tom instructed.

The state of Emmy's head told her to do as he said. He helped her up, and still feeling wobbly, she made it to the bathroom. Once the door was shut, she leaned her forehead against the mirror and closed her eyes. Stupid and embarrassing. Not only had she kissed the man, she'd now acted like a child and had come home from an afternoon out with raging sunburn. Dropping her clothes on the floor, she turned the shower to cold and stood under it for a full five minutes, feeling the cold water leech the heat out of her skin. After fathoming the energy to wash, she got out, dried off, and yanked her dressing gown from the back of the door, wincing as the fabric touched her shoulders. She stared in the mirror at her nose resembling Rudolph's and the tops of her cheekbones, which were not just red but bordering on a deep burgundy.

She did, though, feel much better after the cold shower had done its thing – her legs had stopped wobbling, and her head wasn't pounding anywhere near as hard. 'Sorry about that,' she said as she walked back into the sitting room. 'I should have known better.'

'Easily done,' Tom acknowledged. He jerked his thumb towards the kitchen. 'I put the kettle on and put some toast in.'

'Oh, right, okay, thanks.'

'You didn't have anything to eat, correct?'

Emmy felt embarrassed. 'Nope.'

'Might be a good idea to have a cup of tea and sleep it off.'

'Yes. Thank you. I feel like an idiot.'

Emmy smiled as he walked out and could hear Tom in the kitchen, making the toast and pouring the tea. The sound of the tea being made and the comforting smell of toast were oddly calming. Emmy wobbled into the kitchen and sat at the kitchen table. She took sips of the tea and smiled.

'Here you go,' Tom said, putting a plate of toast down in front of her. He watched her with concern in his eyes.

Emmy nibbled at the toast, her roasting hot head throbbing behind her eyes. The act of chewing made it feel worse. She felt quite *pathetic*. She would have roasted Callum for getting severe sunburn; she'd lectured him about putting on sunscreen for cricket enough times. Now here she was, the person with all the signs of sunstroke.

'There we go. You're looking a bit better now,' Tom said, watching her carefully. Emmy wondered how he could tell that; as far as she was concerned, she still felt like she'd been fried in a pan.

Tom didn't rush to leave. Instead, he stayed until she'd finished her toast and tea. He then cleared away the dishes, as Emmy felt a trillion times better after the toast, and her heart did an odd flip in her chest.

'Right then,' Tom finally said, standing at the doorway. 'You get some sleep and don't worry about that sunburn. It'll be better by morning. What's your number?'

'What?'

'In case you need anything quickly. You've not got anyone on the island, I hear.'

Emmy blankly said her number, and her phone promptly rang. Emmy nodded, the gesture making her head throb. 'Thank you, but I'll be fine. Just a little bit too much sun.'

With a nod, Tom slipped his phone into his pocket and left,

leaving Emmy alone in the quiet flat. She felt an odd pang of disappointment as the door shut behind him, but another part of her sighed with relief that he was gone. She needed to go to bed. With a sigh, she unplugged the fans, lugged them to her bedroom, faced them in the direction of the bed, and turned them on.

She fell into bed, the cool sheets feeling soft on her burning skin and her eyelids already heavy. Once her head had hit the pillow, everything seemed to blur into a haze. Her mind went over the unexpected turn of the day. An unexpected turn she'd have to think about tomorrow. Despite her throbbing headache and the stinging sunburn, Emmy found herself smiling. Tom was indeed a conundrum; grumpy and mysterious and also quite kind. She checked to make sure her phone was on in case Callum was in trouble, and the last thing she heard before sleep was the rumble of a tram somewhere outside. As she drifted off, she wondered about the next time she would come across Tom and hoped that it might be under far less embarrassing circumstances. She wouldn't mind another carry up the stairs, though. That had been quite nice.

The next morning, the first thing Emmy did was wince. The second thing she did was check her phone that there wasn't a message from or about Callum. The third thing she did was recall being carried up the stairs by Tom. That wasn't a bad way to wake up. She gingerly pushed herself up, every move causing a prickling sensation across her shoulders. Her skin was not feeling at all pleasant, but overall she felt better after a good night's sleep. Everything, though, remained tender to the touch as she padded over to the full-length mirror to inspect the damage. Her shoulders were still angry, and the redness seemed now to have taken on a deeper hue. She grimaced at her reflection and cursed herself for forgetting the sunscreen. Such a stupid rookie thing to do.

Trudging to the bathroom at the same time as repeatedly tutting, she turned on the shower, wincing at the thought of the water hitting her sore skin. She gingerly stepped in and let out a small gasp as the lukewarm water hit her burnt shoulders.

After showering, Emmy made her way downstairs to the kitchen, dressed in clean, comfy relaxing clothes, a gigantic hairband pulling her hair off her face and a scrunchie tying it in a bun on top of her head. Her stomach grumbled as she got to the kettle, and she remembered she'd not had much to eat the day before. She also recalled how she'd sat in a daze at the table shovelling in toast, with burning shoulders, Rudolph nose, and pounding head.

Making a bacon sandwich, she replied to a message from her mum that Callum had gone into town to look at phones with his grandpa, and was going to stay so that they could go night fishing. Emmy didn't really see the attraction of fishing, but she was well aware of its therapeutic mind-positive benefits, and as long as Callum was happy and out of trouble, it more than suited her. As she drank her tea, she smiled to herself as she remembered Tom's attempts at taking care of her. It was quite sweet. She remembered how he'd swept her up into his arms, carrying her upstairs as if she weighed nothing. That image sent a flutter through her stomach. Tom Carter was doing things to her she didn't know what to think. She shook her head as Cara flitted into her mind. If Cara was Tom's girlfriend where had she been the day before?

Shuffling around in the flat, she sat down on the sofa with her mug of tea in hand, further contemplating the events of the previous day. Sunshine streamed through the window, reminding her of the afternoon and the not-so-great aftermath. Or maybe it had been great. She wasn't going to complain about being rescued and carried up the stairs by someone who made her feel all sorts of things in all sorts of places. She sighed, sipping on her tea, her mind filled with thoughts of Tom. As she gazed out of the window, she couldn't help but look forward to the day, despite the sunburn and embarrassment. She had the feeling things were about to get a lot more interesting.

25

After dabbing calamine lotion on her shoulders, Emmy made a milky but strong cup of coffee, then dragged her way up the steep stairs to the top room and strolled over to the window at the back. Squinting into the lane, she could see no sign of Tom's car. Shame. As she stood lost in thought, a picture of him carrying her up the path was front and centre of her mind. She stood thinking about it and then admonished herself. What was she doing? There was no way he would be thinking the same thing about her. She didn't know much about him, but from the knowing looks and a few things that she'd heard, he clearly had quite the reputation. She imagined him with a string of beautiful women falling at his feet, the gorgeous Cara being one of them. As if he would look twice at a customer service agent who lived with mice, had a teenage son, a Rudolph nose, wore support tights to get herself through the day and had not a lot going on in her life. She nodded to herself. She had to put a stop to thinking about this man and get on with what she was meant to be doing; getting the shop ready.

Heading back down to top up her tea and grabbing a couple

of Rich Teas, Emmy trundled down the stairs to the shop. As she stood dipping the biscuits in her tea, she assessed what had to be done. The now-exposed old ticket counter had a lot of potential, it just needed a good clean and polish. The walls, now undercoated courtesy of her dad, were ready for a couple of coats of paint, and the windows needed to be cleaned. She made her way to the small paint spray machine her dad had carefully instructed her on how to use. Picking up the leaflet in the box, she read dubiously how it was ideal for painting a typical fence panel in less than two minutes. Her dad had used it for the primer without any problems. That's not to say it would work for her.

Twenty minutes later, the old floorboards and the ticket counter were covered in layers of dust sheets, the windows were taped up, and Emmy was in control of the sprayer. Just as she'd watched her dad and he'd instructed her, it was quite easy and quite therapeutic. With a mask on her face and a disposable suit over her clothes, she worked from left to right around the room. As the white paint went on top of the primer, Emmy very slowly began to see light at the end of the tunnel. It was as if the room, once the holder of all things insurance, was awakening. It shook off boring old insurance details and the remnants of nicotine yellow paint, and got itself ready for its next life where it would be the space for sparkly, pretty things. For the first time since Emmy had taken possession of the building, with each horizontal spray of the paint, she actually began to see that maybe her initial vision could work.

After balancing precariously on the top of a ladder and trying not to think what health and safety at work would think of her setup, she stood back and admired the room. All of a sudden, it gave her hope. The white paint bounced light all over the place, the deep tones of the wood lost before under melamine casing were at the fore, and the high ceilings gave an air of old-fashioned luxury.

As she finished tidying up, she video-called Amy to show her her progress. Amy appeared on the screen and made a funny face. 'Blimey! What in the name of goodness happened to your face?' Amy exclaimed.

Emmy had forgotten all about the sunburn on her face. 'Oh god, does it look that bad?'

'Bad? Your nose is the colour of a postbox, and your cheeks look like you had an argument with a cheap blusher. What in the world? I take it you enjoyed the regatta.'

Emmy chuckled and squinted at the screen. Her nose was very red, and it did now have the odd speckle of white paint on it. 'I did, actually. Though yes, I was in the sun too long.'

Amy got closer to the screen. 'What's that voice?'

Emmy flapped her left hand a bit. 'Nothing. I was just going to show you the room after the paint. Hang on, let me flip the camera.' Emmy panned around the room, and as Amy oohed and aahed, she herself, too, was surprised at how well it had come up.

'Good job. Dad said that spray thingy was good.'

'I had visions of most of the paint being on me, but it was super easy,' Emmy said as she flipped the camera back around.

'So, how long until you think the shop will be open?'

'Goodness knows.' Emmy rolled her eyes. 'All those spread-sheets and plans were pointless. At this rate, I'll be lucky if I'm ready for Christmas.'

'Maybe that's the goal?'

'Yeah, but Evie and that Xian from the bakery said the visitor traffic on Darling is huge in peak summer. I don't know, the online stuff is keeping it ticking over at the moment, and the ads are working. I'm just going to do what I can. Thank good-ness for Grandma's money.'

'Yeah, she'd be so proud of you.'

Emmy wasn't so sure about that. She was very grateful that her grandma's money had meant she could try out her dream, even if, at that precise moment, the dream wasn't quite as straightforward as she thought it was going to be. 'Thanks.'

'Anyway, don't think I was going to forget about what happened yesterday.'

'What?'

Amy shrugged and lifted her eyebrows. 'Ems, you are the queen of telling Callum and all of us about the dangers of the sun, and here you are with sunburn. You force Callum to wear sunblock for cricket when it's raining. Plus, your voice is weird. I'm not buying it. What happened?'

Emmy kept her gaze averted. 'Nothing. I just forgot to take sunscreen with me.'

'And what, you were in the sun all afternoon?' The disbelief in Amy's voice was palpable, her mouth dropping open in an exaggerated gasp.

'Yep,' Emmy affirmed with a chuckle.

'I know that face! Don't try and pull the wool over my eyes.' Amy pointed an accusing finger. 'What are you not telling me?'

'Ha ha.' Emmy shook her head.

'Did something happen with Tom P?'

Emmy sighed and pretended to make light of it. 'I got a touch of sunstroke.' She raised her hands and shrugged her shoulders. 'There's nothing to tell.'

'And?' Amy leaned in closer, her eyes sparkling with anticipation.

'And he, well, he brought me home. Again,' Emmy admitted.

'He?'

'Tom from next door.'

'Ooh! What else?' Amy asked with excitement.

'Nothing.' Emmy's response was quick. Too quick.

'Nothing at all?' Amy said, crossing her arms in mock indignation.

'Nup.' Emmy popped the 'p' and didn't say anything else.

'No kiss?' The question hung in the air.

'No!'

'Tell me all of it. From like how he gave you a lift home again,' Amy asked, leaning back in her seat, an eager look on her face.

'It's quite embarrassing, really. I just sat in the corner, getting hotter and hotter and drinking the local ale,' Emmy admitted, cringing at the memory.

'Yikes. Not a good combo.'

'Until I felt like my head was going to combust.' Emmy placed a hand on her forehead as if the memory brought back the sensation.

'And then?'

'He offered to take me home,' Emmy heard herself speaking in a strange, soft, almost dreamy voice.

'The second time in what, like a week or so?' Amy's eyebrows shot up, an incredulous grin on her face.

'I feel like an idiot.'

'So there was definitely no kiss?' Amy prodded.

'I'd have told you! He did carry me up the path, though.' Emmy's cheeks flamed at the memory.

'What? Oh my god!' Amy shrieked, her hands flailing dramatically.

'I know. It was quite nice.' Emmy giggled. 'However, I am trying not to think about it too much.'

'Yeah, course you're not. This is epic. Not only do you have a dark, mysterious man next door, he actually carried you up the stairs,' Amy gushed.

'Yeah, as if I was as light as a feather. I mean, you have to laugh.' Emmy shrugged.

'Wow, you were actually rescued! A damsel in distress.'

'Don't be ridiculous! I do not subscribe to that narrative.'

'I know, but, well, you know. So what's next?' Amy asked eagerly, with her head tilted to one side.

'Nothing. It's ridiculous. I know nothing about him. I'm

taking a wide berth,' Emmy stated, shaking her head in resignation.

'No, you are not!' Amy protested. 'Why ever would you do that?'

'Yes, I am. I'm not going there,' Emmy declared.

'Come on!' Amy protested.

'I think there might be a girlfriend.'

'What? What do you mean? That's the first I've heard of it.'

Emmy sighed. 'There was this woman in the lane getting into her car. I didn't really think much about it. Then she was outside on the pavement the other day.'

'I thought you said he said he lives alone.'

'Yeah, he did say that.'

'Well, there you are then.'

'She was all over him at the Chamber of Commerce thing too.'

'Oh, she was there. What with him?'

'I'm not sure.'

'Surely she would have been with him at the pub or the regatta if she was with him.'

'Yeah, I know. I thought that.'

'Hmm.'

'But why would she be around here?'

'Dunno.'

'Anyway. Nope. It's just not happening,' Emmy said firmly. 'Honestly, just leave it, Amy, and certainly don't let Mum get wind of it. You know what she's like. We'll never hear the end of it, which is ridiculous because there's nothing there anyway.'

Amy shook her head. 'Okay, if you say so. But we'll wait and see. I have one of my feelings. I reckon you and Tom P were meant to be. That's how you got on that island in the first place. It's fate. He bumped into you and the cake, and now he's carrying you up stairs and all sorts.'

'Pah! There's no such thing as meant to be.'

'Let's wait and see. Anyway, I have my painting clothes ready, the children are all sorted, and I'll be with you mid-afternoon for a couple of hours to help out. We'll discuss this more then.'

'Great. See you later.'

After clearing up and deciding she needed to get away from paint and moving boxes and before Amy arrived, Emmy stripped off, dabbed more calamine on her shoulders, and changed out of her plastic painting overalls. Deciding to leave her Belisha beacon nose to its natural self, she put a sun hat on her head and slipped on huge sunglasses. Making her way back along Darling Street, she headed for Darlings. On arrival, Darlings was heaving. Just as she was about to turn around and give up on the possibility of a table, Evie waved from the doorway. 'One spot in the corner if you want it.'

Emmy nodded gratefully and walked in. Evie turned around and chuckled. 'Get a bit of sun, did you yesterday?'

'Just a bit.'

'I've heard.'

Emmy cringed a little bit. Hopefully, the Darling grapevine hadn't also heard that she'd been carried up the stairs to her flat. She joked, 'Yeah, I must have warned my son a million times about the dangers of the sun, and then I go and get a spot of sunstroke. Untrue!'

'Yep. It's easily done down there by the water,' Evie noted.

'I guess so. I'll say it was the water reflection, the sunshine, and nothing to do with the ale.'

'Ha ha! Too funny.'

'I'm fine apart from this,' Emmy said, pointing to her burnt nose and sitting down.

'Oh, looks painful.'

'Not too bad. My shoulders know about it, though.'

'Coffee? Basket?'

'Please.' Emmy nodded. Ridiculously happy that Evie was including her in the Darlings ritual of coffee and a basket. A few minutes later, a coffee in a bowl arrived with a basket beside it. Emmy's phone buzzed as she started to undo the knot on the gingham linen cloth in the basket.

'Hey. How have you got on with everything?' her mum asked.

'Good. The walls are now white. Thank goodness for Dad and his gadgets.'

'I know.' Cherry laughed. 'If there's one thing your dad knows about, it's gadgets.'

'How's Cal?'

'Fine. They're out looking for phones.'

'I told Callum he's not on to get Dad to con him out of another new phone.'

'Oh, leave them to it, Ems. Honestly. It's fine.'

'Okay, if you say so, but Callum has to learn the value of money. I really don't want him just getting things whenever he wants them. There's nothing worse than a spoilt teenager.'

Cherry swiftly changed the subject. 'He's fine. What else has been happening?'

Emmy knew by the sound of her mum's voice that she'd spoken to Amy and probably knew about the sunstroke and Tom. 'Not much.'

'How was the regatta yesterday?'

Now, Emmy was certain Amy had spoken to Cherry. 'Good.'

'Was it hot?'

'Yeah, I got a bit of sunburn.'

'Ouch. That's not like you! You're always telling us about the dangers of the sun. Did you stay long, then? Callum said he left you at a table talking to someone from Australia. I thought he must have got that wrong, but he then started talking about some Australian cricket thing, I don't know. Was there an Australian there?'

'No, he didn't get it wrong, and yes, his name is Leo.'

'Ooh. Hmm. Nice.'

'And yes, he is very handsome and no, I don't fancy him,' Emmy clarified.

'I wasn't saying that.' Cherry chuckled.

But I do very much fancy the other man who was at the table. 'It was a nice afternoon, but I did get quite, umm, hot.'

'Right.'

Emmy decided to get it out in the open that Tom had brought her home. 'Yeah, the neighbour gave me a lift, so that was good.' She didn't say she'd totally swooned as he'd carried her up the stairs.

'What neighbour?'

Emmy knew by the sound of her mum's voice that she knew exactly who the neighbour was. 'Mum.'

'You mean the one who knocked on the gate?'

'Yup.'

'Ooh!'

'It's nothing.'

'Did you say he was married or anything?'

'No, I didn't.'

'What, no you didn't say, or no he isn't?'

'No I didn't say.' Emmy laughed inside as she played the whole thing down.

Cherry sighed. 'Well. I wouldn't say no to a lift from a neighbour like that.'

'Mum!'

'Sorry. Right, well darling, if you're not going to tell me any juicy information, I'm going to go.'

'There's nothing to tell!'

'See you then, darling.'

'Yep. See you.'

Emmy smiled to herself. Her mum wasn't the only one who wished there was more juicy information to tell.

26

Emmy strolled through the back streets away from Darlings café with a bit of a spring in her step. Something about the regatta, despite the sunstroke, the lovely weather, and the coffee shop, had made her feel good about the gigantic leap she'd made to move to Darling Island.

As she walked along, she sucked up all the Darling feels; lovely old coastal buildings higgledy-piggledy squashed together along the street, blue half doors right on the pavement, pots full of herbs, odd little skew-whiff portholes here and there. White brickwork with window frames in the Darling aqua-blue, dormers poking out of wonky roofs. Lovely, quaint, old places woven into the cobblestone streets. She meandered along the narrow pavement as it twisted and turned here and there around clusters of gorgeous old houses and stopped for a sec to ponder whitewashed walls speckled with moss and weathered by the sea air. Every crevice of Darling seemed as if somehow it was smiling at her and welcoming at the same time. She smiled back. There was no way she was going to argue with that.

Cheery window boxes sat on windowsills, houses stacked

snuggly on top of each other in the sunshine, and the occasional black old-fashioned signpost pointed the way to the church and the village hall. There was no doubt about it, as Emmy wandered in and out, she found herself charmed by Darling Island. As she gaped at little alleyways leading off here and there and stopped to read a sign to a secret passage down to the sea, she took in a deep breath and recalled what she'd seen on the sign on the ferry when she'd been collecting the cake; Darling Island was so very far from care. She wasn't quite that far from care yet, but it certainly felt as if Darling was working its magic on her. She smiled at an elderly couple sitting in their front garden sipping mugs of tea, a chubby cat basked lazily in a sun-drenched window, and front gardens vibrant with flowers loving the sun. Emmy nodded at all of it; Darling Island, it seemed, was the gift that kept on giving. Long may it last.

Before she knew it, Emmy was approaching Darling Street. She could hear the clang and hum of the tram tracks, and as she got to the tram shelter, a tram arrived. She hopped on and smiled at Shelly, the conductor.

'Hi, Emmy! How are you?'

Emmy was really pleased to be recognised. It made her fuzzy inside. 'Hey.'

'Looks like you enjoyed the regatta! Get a bit of sun, did you?'

Emmy laughed and touched her nose. 'I did. I won't be doing that again in a hurry.'

'Easily done! And how did you find the Chamber of Commerce peeps?' Shelly asked as she yanked the rope on the bell in the middle of the carriage and wiggled it from left and right.

'Yep, fine. I think,' Emmy said and screwed up her face as if to say she didn't think it was fine.

'Yeah, a funny lot, but worth being in it,' Shelly acknowledged.

'So I've been told.'

'You want to put a sign up on the shop, don't you?'

Emmy nodded. 'Yes, and a flower garland around the top, over the window. That needs to be approved too.'

Shelly laughed and joked, 'Everything on Darling has to be approved. You have to apply to leave the island and to breathe around here.'

'Sounds like it.'

'All joking aside, how are you getting on?'

Emmy stopped for a second and considered. 'Actually, I'm loving it.' She frowned and squinted. 'I have to say that I definitely had wobbles and a few regrets when I first got my feet under the table and saw the state of the place, and then...' She trailed off for a second. 'I don't know. Like, for example, I've just walked around, and everything is so pretty. And this seems a bit weird, but it feels like I'm being welcomed or something. Everyone is really friendly, or am I imagining it?'

Shelly tutted and laughed. 'That means Darling likes you. The old saying about Lady Darling not letting you go.'

'Right.' Emmy felt mildly alarmed that what Shelly was saying was actually true. She shook her head quickly, not one for superstitions.

Shelly tapped the back of the seat. 'Don't worry about it. You'll get used to it. Trust me. Now you're here, you'll never leave. You've been captured by Darling.'

Emmy smiled as the tram trundled away from the stop. Actually, she quite liked the sound of that, indeed. Getting off the tram, Emmy was responding to a text from Callum, as she approached the front of the shop. Just by the door was a wicker basket with a small potted plant inside. Alongside it sat a white cardboard box with a ribbon. Pulling off the ribbon, Emmy smiled at the contents, a neat little stack of mini cinnamon buns just like the ones that had been on the top of Callum's cake. She read the card.

Welcome to Darling. So very far from care.
Sorry our basket is a bit late. From all at the bakery.

Just as she was fiddling with her key in the lock, someone approached. She turned around to see Tom, looking a tad rushed but with a smile on his face.

'Hi. How are you feeling? I'm just on my way to the ferry.'

'I'm good,' Emmy stuttered a little bit, embarrassed at what had happened the night before and still feeling sheepish about the whole situation. 'Thanks ever so much for last night.'

'No worries,' Tom reassured her.

'Sorry, I, umm... I feel like a bit of a numpty,' Emmy confessed, the rest of her face turning as red as her sunburnt nose and cheeks. And she'd said numpty. Where in the world had that come from? Her face flushed even further.

'Not at all. It's easily done,' Tom said casually.

Emmy felt awkward and embarrassed. 'I seem to have been saying sorry to you a lot, and I've only been here five minutes. Sorry. Oops, there it is again.'

'It's fine,' Tom said with a strange sort of smile on his face.

Emmy squirmed. *Oh god, I amuse him!* She then went cold as she remembered her bright red nose. *Or he pities me! Crikey, it's both! He's so used to women falling at his feet he's put me in the boat with those he feels sorry for. He and that Cara must have laughed their bottoms off at me.* 'Okay, well, thanks for yesterday.'

'Anytime.'

Tom ran his hand through his hair. 'Look, I'm going to something at Darlings tonight. Fancy tagging along? Might be a good way to meet a few more of the locals. Darlings puts on special events for residents only every now and then.'

Emmy nearly collapsed on the step in a heap of gratitude. Another part of her quickly reminded herself that she should stop this thing, whatever it was, with this man from next door. He was obviously just doing the Darling friendly thing just as

Shelly on the tram had. He clearly had a thing going with Cara whoever, De-Have-a-Bum or something. He was simply fulfilling his civic duty to the new person in town. And the way she was feeling inside, it was only going to end up in trouble. She couldn't quite bring herself to say no, though, instead she sort of just fluffed. Should she ask him about Cara first? 'Oh, umm.'

'Sorry. Of course, you're probably busy.'

Busy watching literal paint dry in my exciting life, Emmy thought. She held up her phone and found herself wiggling it in front of him weirdly. 'Just got a text from Callum. He's not here this evening, actually.'

'Right, so you're not busy?' Tom asked, not breaking eye contact. 'Or you are?'

As if. The voice inside commanded her to tell him she was busy at the same time as it told her to stop openly leering at the bright eyes, the broad shoulders, and the aura. 'Not busy, nooooo.' Emmy heard her voice all strange and squeaky and shrill. 'No, no, not doing anything at all.'

'Well, if you fancy it. Look, I've got to rush. No pressure. I'll text you later. If you fancy it, come along or whatever.'

Emmy nodded as if she would consider it later. She was already at Darlings in her mind, sitting with a drink and wondering if her life could get any better. Tom's arm brushed against hers as he strode away. It felt like someone had plugged her into a battery. The Duracell bunny had nothing on her insides.

27

A while later, Emmy was upstairs in the flat when she heard Amy come through the gate. Just after that, Amy had given her a peck on the cheek and laughed when she saw Emmy's sunburn.

'Blimey, it's even worse in real life! You must have been sitting there for hours to get burnt that bad in this country,' Amy noted.

Emmy thought about how at the regatta, outside the beer tent, she'd stayed glued to the spot just to keep herself in the vicinity of Tom. She winced. 'I did.'

'You're lucky you didn't end up in A&E.'

'I know.'

'But you did get carried up the garden path by a dashing neighbour.' Amy laughed. 'So there is that.'

'Yep.'

Amy's eyes widened. 'Ooh, has something else happened since I spoke to you this morning?'

'Errm, not really.'

'Not really?'

'I mean, yes. Sort of.'

'What?'

Emmy gestured towards the window. 'He just popped in on his way to the ferry to see if I was okay.'

'Ooh, I am loving this story.' Amy giggled. 'It's getting better by the minute.'

'It's nothing.'

'And?'

'And, well, he asked me if I wanted to go along to Darlings tonight.'

'Oh, my goodness! Ems, you have a date with Tom P!'

'No! It's not a date.'

'Sounds like a date to me.' Amy giggled.

'No, it wasn't like that. It was... I don't know, casual.'

'Casual? What?'

'I think he pities me.'

'Don't be ridiculous! Tell me exactly what happened.'

'Alright.' Emmy sighed, resigning herself to the inquisition. 'So, I was just about to unlock the front door when Tom walked along on his way to the ferry. He asked how I was feeling after the sunburn debacle.'

Amy's eyes twinkled. 'And?'

'He just asked how I was.' Emmy felt her cheeks flush slightly as she recalled the interaction.

'Hold on, right, so he came out of his way just to see how you were? That's not a neighbourly concern, that's something more.'

Emmy rolled her eyes. 'Don't start reading into things, Amy. It wasn't out of his way. The ferry is that way,' Emmy said, pointing down to the street. 'He just feels sorry for me.'

'So, then what happened?'

'Then he mentioned something happening at Darlings tonight. Said it might be a good opportunity for me to meet more people on the island.' Emmy twirled a strand of her hair nervously, recalling how casually Tom had extended the invitation. 'Yeah, thinking about it, he was definitely just being neighbourly.'

'I don't think so! Come on, he asked you out, surely?' Amy's eyebrows arched upwards in question.

'No, it wasn't like that. He didn't *formally* ask me out. It was more like a casual suggestion. I suppose he thought I might be feeling a bit lonely.' Emmy dismissed Amy's hopeful look with a wave of her hand. 'Yes, that's it.'

'You do realise that's still a form of asking out, right? You seem to have lost all sense where this bloke is concerned. Ems, he's totally asked you out.'

Emmy huffed. 'Maybe in your perfect world. In mine, it was just a neighbour being friendly. He hasn't asked me out. It's just a pop-over to Darlings with a local. He even said it would mean that I would get to know people. He's just doing the right thing. Everyone here is the same.'

Amy shook her head. 'No. I stand by my point – it's a date. A casual one, but a date nonetheless.'

'You're daft. It's not. Anyway, regardless of what you think, it's a nice chance to get to know the locals, so I said yes. That's all there is to it.'

Amy laughed. 'This is gold. Ems trying to pretend it's about getting to know the locals. Yeah, right. Too funny.'

'It is!'

Amy did a little jig and fist-pumped. 'It *is* a date. You must prepare to be wined and dined. This is a wax your inner thigh occasion.'

Emmy smiled, feeling a little flutter of excitement at the idea but pretended she didn't care. 'Honestly. If you'd been there when he'd asked you'd realise. It's nothing.'

'Where's Cal?'

'He's not here.'

Amy threw her hands up. 'See, the stars are aligning. Like I said, this whole thing is fate. You won't even have Callum here. Ooh, what will occur?'

Emmy laughed. 'There is nothing unusual about Callum not being here.'

'Ahh, but there's something in the air, Ems. I know it, I can smell it, I can feel it. I can see it.'

'Don't be ridiculous. There so is not. Also, what about the divine Cara?'

'You must have read that wrong. He wouldn't blatantly ask you out to a local place if he has a girlfriend. Plus, she's never with him.'

'True,' Emmy mused.

A few hours later, Emmy and Amy had made significant progress with the sitting room. The small sofa Emmy had brought with her from the cottage was covered in plastic, Bob's spray-painting device had been hauled up the steep stairs, and the walls were now less nicotine and more a lovely shade of fresh, clean white. Amy touched the walls. 'Well, they haven't taken long to dry either. Wow, it looks different.'

Emmy nodded, then grimaced as she looked into the corner where she'd seen the little black figure darting towards the skirting board. 'That was where I had my first encounter with the mice.'

'Anything since?'

'No, not a sausage. I haven't seen anything, and nor has Cal.'

'That was money well spent then.'

'Yep.'

Amy ran her finger along the now white mantelpiece. 'This is gorgeous. Real old-fashioned workmanship.'

'Yeah. In the future, when I actually have some time, I might strip it back to the natural wood.'

'That would look nice.'

Emmy slipped her phone out of her pocket and navigated to Marketplace. She tapped on a saved post. 'Ooh, it's still for sale by the looks of this.' She turned her phone around to Amy to show her the sofa she'd seen for sale by someone called Jane. 'What do you think?'

Amy enlarged the picture and then nodded. 'Looks perfect. Have you messaged?'

'Not yet. I thought it would be gone by the time this place was ready,' Emmy replied and started to type out a message. 'Fingers crossed.'

Two seconds later, a message came in. 'Yes, it's still available. Ooh, that's good.'

'Seems like your luck's turning around.'

Emmy chuckled. 'Don't jinx it.'

They looked around the room, and Emmy felt a spark of excitement about the transformation of the place. From a grotty, abandoned flat over an insurance office, she was bringing it back to life. Her life and her route out of a life of paying someone else's mortgage.

Another message came in about the sofa: *Come and have a look if you like.*

Emmy whooped as she showed Amy the message.

'If I like it, I'll need a way to pick it up.'

Amy shook her head. 'Hmm. Cross that bridge when we come to it.'

Emmy quickly typed out a response, arranging to go and look at the sofa the following day. The sitting room was really coming together. Now, with the promise of the sofa, things were looking up.

'Now all we have to worry about is what to wear to Darlings tonight,' Amy said, changing gears and winking. 'All the decisions, ha ha.'

Emmy groaned, a flush creeping up her face. 'Right, that's another challenge. Anyway, he hasn't even messaged me yet. He might have changed his mind.'

'He won't, trust me on this.'

'I'll make a cup of tea,' Emmy said, and ten minutes later, they were sitting amidst paint cans and dust sheets. Perched on makeshift seats, they cradled mugs of tea.

'Right,' Amy started. 'So, what are you going to wear for your "not-a-date" with Tom?' She made air quotes with her free hand.

'It isn't a date!' Emmy protested. 'And why should it matter what I wear? It's all about what's in here,' Emmy said, tapping the side of her temple. 'I'm not so shallow that I have to worry about how I look.'

Amy rolled her eyes dramatically, gesturing with her mug as she spoke. 'Pah! Oh, come off it, Ems. You've been grinning like a Cheshire cat since he asked you out. And, trust me, what you wear *always* matters.'

Emmy groaned. 'You're not helping, Ames. This is stressful enough without worrying about that.' She pointed to her nose. 'Plus, I have to take this out for a spin.'

'Lol, it needs a warning. Seriously, Ems. What are you thinking of wearing on your not-a-date date? You need my input on this.'

Emmy sighed, putting her mug down on an upturned paint bucket. 'No idea. I'm not used to having this question in my life. I don't know... something casual, but nice. Not too dressy…'

Amy tapped her fingers on her mug. 'Your white linen dress could work. It's easy, comfortable, and looks lovely on you. And now you, ahem, have a bit of colour. Might as well make the most of the good weather, too.'

Emmy nodded, chewing on her lower lip. 'That could work. Maybe with those blue sandals I bought last summer? If I can find them, they're still in a box somewhere.'

'Perfect.'

Emmy smiled and sipped her tea. 'And, just to be clear, it's not a date.'

Amy laughed, shaking her head as she stood. 'Sure, Ems, whatever you say.'

As they moved on to cleaning up the remnants of their afternoon, Emmy's mind was filled with a blend of nerves, excitement, and anxiety. Despite her insistence that she was not going on a date, she couldn't shake off the butterflies that seemed to have taken permanent residence in her stomach. Her phone pinged in her pocket; she dusted off her hands on her paint-splattered jeans and peered down. A rush of anticipation ran through her veins as she computed a notification from an unfamiliar number.

Tom: *Hey, just checking to see if you'd still like to join me at Darlings tonight. No pressure at all, but it'd be great to have you there so you can meet a few people.*

Emmy stared at the text for a moment, her heart pounding in her chest. It was simple enough. She didn't need to start obsessing and overthinking. But her 'not-a-date' with Tom made her want to happy dance around the newly painted room.

Emmy: *Yep, great. Love to. What time?*

Tom: *About 6.45 p.m., if that's good?*

Emmy: *OK. See you then.*

Emmy rubbed her hands together. She didn't really care what it was, but she did know that she was excited. Whether it was just a casual thing or, dare she say it, a date, she was going to jolly well enjoy it. Getting out and meeting new people was one of the reasons she'd moved to Darling Island. She'd just look at it as a part of that. Simple.

28

After Amy had gone home and Emmy had finished with the last few bits of clear-up, a nap was looking very attractive, but she had a lot of preparation to do. Trying to ignore the tired old bathroom, she ran a bubble bath, slapped a conditioning treatment on her hair, and stepped in. Laying back, she let the day slip away and allowed her mind to wander. She wondered whether she should have just shut Tom down and said no. Here she was, thinking all sorts, when he was undoubtedly just being friendly. Plus, she still didn't know quite who Cara was. Tom probably felt a bit of pity for the singleton who'd moved into a grotty old flat above a shop. She knew it was pointless to overthink it, but she couldn't help herself. She could still feel the way her heart had leapt when she'd received Tom's message. As she mused the evening, she was suddenly second-guessing herself. What would she even talk about? There was little to nothing interesting about her at all. She'd worked at the port for years, brought up Callum, got Love Emmy x going and not done a lot else. Her life was boring. *She* was boring. Just blame Kevin.

Rinsing her hair, she then scrubbed her hands with a nail

brush to get rid of the paint, stepped out of the bath, wrapped herself in a towel, and felt a ripple of something weird inside. She was going to Darlings with Tom for the night. Wahoo. The thought of it filled her with some sort of swirly anticipation. Plus something else. She raised her eyebrows and shook her head when she realised what it was. Lust. Fancy the pants off lust. As simple and as straightforward as that. Lust was right there in the bathroom with her in all its glory. It had been conspicuous by its absence in her life, and now it was back with a big old bang. Emmy hadn't seen nor heard from it for a very, very long time. She barely recognised it at all.

After putting on her underwear, Emmy spent a few moments in front of the mirror. She wasn't quite over the moon at what looked back. She attempted to be kind to herself, but time and life stared back; saggy bits here and there, all sorts of things no longer quite as pert, and things in places that had taken on a life of their own. Bright red shoulders and matching nose. There was, though, a bit of a glow from her lovely soak in the bath, and her hair smelt good from the conditioner. She contorted her face into a strange shape, pulled the skin back over her cheeks, and blinked rapidly. Was this the sort of woman someone like dashing Tom P Carter would take out for dinner? She shook her head. Who in the world was she kidding? No, it was not. She was just the neighbour down the road. The one with the boring life.

Hey ho. She'd just go along and see what happened. In for a penny, in for a pound, her mum would say. She brushed her damp hair and applied layers of foundation over her nose, attempted and failed at a smoky eye, took a packet of fake eyelashes out of the bottom of her toiletries bag, opened them, changed her mind, and fluffed blusher over her cheeks.

Putting on the white dress Amy had suggested, Emmy stood in front of the mirror and gave herself an encouraging smile. Not too bad. She'd scrubbed up okay. She nodded in an attempt at confidence. She was going to enjoy her time at Darlings, whether it turned out to be a casual neighbourly thing or what. She would go with the flow and see what the night would bring.

Just as she'd been to the loo for the hundredth time, added another layer of foundation on her nose, and investigated her armpits, she heard the knocker on the shop go downstairs. With her heart thumping wildly in her chest, she grabbed her bag and jacket, ran down the stairs, made her way through the shop, and reached for the doorknob. Taking a deep, calming breath, she reminded herself just to be natural and opened the door.

Tom looked stupidly handsome in chinos and a blue casual button-down shirt. As she breezed out the door and stepped closer, she got a whiff of his aftershave – fresh and masculine and a bit musky. Very, very, exceedingly nice. Rich. Expensive. All the things. She felt the feeling she'd experienced in the bathroom hit her like a tonne of bricks. Every one of her senses felt as if they were tingling. Emmy Bardot was, in fact, lightheaded. It was not unwelcome.

'Hi,' Tom said.

Emmy gulped, wondering if Tom could somehow see or hear her racing heart. Whether he was in possession of the knowledge that she was actually a nuclear bomb. She looked at his eyes, feeling a blush creeping up her cheeks. 'Evening.'

'How are you?'

'Good,' she replied as she closed the door behind her, took another calming breath and told herself to get a grip. As they stepped out into the fading daylight, Darling Island was doing its thing. It seemed to be wearing a magic of its own as the late sun, low on the horizon, painted the whole sky in a warm hue of deep amber, pink and gold. The whole of Darling Street was bathed in the pinky glow, and Emmy gasped as they started to walk down the street. 'Wow. It's stunning this evening.'

'Ahh, yes, when Darling puts on a show, you know about it.'

Tom looked up at the sky and nodded. 'Wonder if we'll get fog in the early hours? Doesn't look like it.'

Emmy had no idea. She did know she'd never seen a sky quite as stunning. She also knew she was having trouble breathing, walking, speaking, and concentrating.

Tom, however, didn't seem bothered and chatted as if he didn't have a care in the world. As they walked side by side, their shoulders brushing occasionally, Emmy felt a thrill run through her body. This was so very good. So, so, so good. As they strolled nearer and nearer to Darlings, the sunset only got better as it did things to the scenery; old wooden fences took on a pink hue, white brickwork and aqua-blue window frames glowed, and the evening air was laced with the scent of flowers and sea salt.

Emmy loved not only Darling and its sunset, but also was utterly revelling in being with Tom. There was an ease about him, as if he wasn't bothered about anything. A sort of natural charm that wasn't forced or rehearsed with a bit of gruffness thrown in for good measure. He just seemed all-around genuine and all-around handsome to boot. All of it continued to make her heart pound.

As they approached Darlings café, the sky blazed with the pinks, oranges, and yellows of the sunset, and Emmy gasped at the sight of the café. She'd been there that morning and thought how lovely it was, but in the glow of the fading light, it was almost magical. The squat white shopfront was now bathed in twinkling fairy lights draped haphazardly over the front. The quaint 'Darlings' sign glimmered under the old-fashioned lights that bracketed the bow-fronted door. A row of bicycles wedged tightly into the rack to the left of the shop glinted against the orange sky. To the right of the door, an old doormat rested on the half step, worn and faded. A few tiny café tables and chairs were set up outside, each holding small glass jars with tealight candles on gingham tablecloths, and lanterns swung from the parasols above.

Emmy felt spellbound as she peered up at the whitewashed exterior of Darlings layered in hues of gold and pink. The twinkling fairy lights blinked beside climbing flowers. Emmy turned to Tom. 'It's so pretty, isn't it?'

'Yup. It really is putting on a show tonight,' Tom agreed.

Emmy peeked in the window as they got to the door; tiny tealights flickered inside glass jars on the tables, and the whole place was full of people. The magic of it all seeped into her as Tom held the door open; the overhead bell just audible over the jazz playing inside, lanterns hung from the roof, hundreds of tealights were propped in between bowls on the floor to ceiling shelves flickering off every surface, and pots of plants and flowers seemed to dance in the ambient light. The scent of cooking and wine, the gentle hum of conversation, and standing beside Tom made Emmy feel giddy.

Emmy glanced at Tom, watching as he spoke to a young waitress as if he knew her. The light from the candles flickered across his face, making her heart race. With the soft lights, the ambience, and the company, she had the feeling that the evening at Darlings was going to be quite special. It was so lovely she felt as if someone had dropped her slap bang in the middle of a dream.

In a haze of loveliness, she followed Tom to a small bistro table nestled near the window. As she sat down, she caught a glimpse of Evie, the owner, and took a moment to savour it all – the warmth, the music, the soft lighting, and especially the company. Oh how good was the company. Looking around, she suddenly felt as if she'd started a new life. She was here, on Darling, in a lovely café, with a man who seemed nice. It was quite the departure from the life she'd left behind, and as she heard herself say yes to a glass of bubbles, she couldn't help but think that perhaps this was exactly where she was supposed to be. Kevin and his gambling, the horrible flat, struggling and feeling as if she was never going to recover felt far, far away.

As Emmy and Tom settled into their table, Lucie, who Emmy had met at the regatta barbecue, bustled over. In her Darlings uniform of navy-blue apron over a white top, she looked the part and smiled broadly. If Lucie was surprised to see Emmy with Tom, she didn't show it. 'Hi. Emmy, it's lovely to see you again.' Lucie turned towards the windows. 'What a stunner of an evening, eh?'

Emmy smiled in recognition. 'Good to see you. Yes, it was a lovely walk here.' Emmy flicked her hand around the café. 'This all looks amazing too.'

'Yep, we like a tealight or two,' Lucie joked.

'It's packed in here.'

Lucie laughed, her eyes sparkling. 'Oh, yes. When Darlings opens in the evenings, we know about it. We're run off our feet.' Her gaze flitted over to Tom. 'Hi, Tom. As dashing as ever, I see,' she teased in a friendly, joking tone.

Tom responded with a laugh. 'Likewise.'

Lucie turned back to Emmy, her hands planted on her hips. 'And you. Love that dress.'

'Thanks.' Emmy felt herself blush, and she let out a little laugh.

Tom continued, 'Where's George this evening? A sunset sail on the boat?'

Lucie shook her head with wide eyes. 'He's been roped in in the kitchen. George is chief washer-upper for the night. We laughed about it. He's been slicing onions all afternoon and putting up lights.'

'Blimey. You lot conned him into that, did you?'

'Needs must, Tom. Like everyone else around here and the whole country, it seems we're tight on staff. Right, best get on.'

As Lucie walked away, Emmy and Tom chatted, and the hustle and bustle of Darlings ebbed and flowed around them.

With a few sips of her bubbles and the atmosphere, Emmy started to relax as the clinking of cutlery, the chatter of conversations, and the aroma of food surrounded them. Despite her reservations and nerves, and what she'd seen of Tom's grumpy side in the lane, the conversation flowed naturally. They talked about the café, the island, the people, Callum, Emmy's job, and how she'd ended up on Darling.

Emmy found herself wrapped up in it all as she sat under the glow of the lights. She sighed as a basket of garlic bread arrived on the table. The evening had only just started, but she already didn't want it to end. For Emmy Bardot, life was feeling really rather good.

29

Emmy had felt as if she had been lost in a delightful dream for most of the night in Darlings. The dream-like quality extended right through the amazing food, the desert, the wine, and just about everything else. Especially the man sitting opposite her. Though, to be quite honest, he was more than dreamy; he was borderline supernatural.

Not only was it the company that was blowing Emmy's mind – Darlings and Evie knew how to put on an evening. As the night had worn on, the atmosphere had got better and better, and up by the counter where the shelves overloaded with coffee bowls and tealights reached from floor to ceiling, tables were squashed together, chairs were moved, and a makeshift dance floor emerged. Emmy had gladly accepted an Irish coffee and sipped contentedly, surrounded by lovely music, and surveyed the makeshift dance floor that had sprung up not far away. She watched as the dresses twirled and swirled, an elderly couple dazzled, and a young pair in the middle giggled their way through attempted dance steps.

All of it was lovely: the impromptu dancing, the low hum of

conversation, the clinking of glasses, and the flickering lighting. A magical atmosphere in a magical place. Emmy beamed, her eyes sparkling, leant across the table and flicked her eyes around the room. 'I didn't expect this. What an evening.'

Tom nodded. 'It's lovely. This night has turned out really nice – starting with the sunset.'

Emmy's heart fluttered as Tom laughed, put his glass down and held out his hand. 'C'mon. Is dancing one of your skills? I'm useless, but I'll have a go.'

Emmy giggled as she got up, and as both of them squeezed between tables, Tom led her to the cleared area near the serving counter, and she couldn't believe what she was doing. The night had started off dreamily, and it was looking like it was ending that way too. She soaked in the music, the warmth of Tom's hand on her back, and she giggled as they swayed next to the old couple who looked like they'd just walked off *Strictly*. She tried not to read too much into it all, but the dance floor, the music, the café, everything seemed to blur into the background as she danced with Tom. It was like she, Emmy Bardot, was the only person in the world.

As she stared and swayed, lost in a world of her own at the flickering tea lights tucked in between the coffee bowls, Emmy suddenly felt a touch overwhelmed. The previous months before the move had been fraught, tense, and busy. Now she was standing in a lovely place, dancing with a man who made her feel things she hadn't for a long time. It felt as if all her old stress and worry had floated off out the door into the distance. She never wanted to see it again.

Once they were back at their table, Emmy was reluctant for the night to end but couldn't stop herself from stifling a yawn. As Darlings slowly emptied and Tom paid the bill, she gathered her bag, went to the loo, and came back to him standing by the door.

'Ready? Let's go,' Tom said, and they both stepped out into the street.

Emmy strolled along beside Tom with a thrill running through her veins as the cool night air hit her face. They strolled through Darling, their steps slow and leisurely, with the sounds of the night all around them; distant waves, rustling trees, and the occasional hoot of an owl.

Tom chuckled. 'How about a midnight walk on the beach? Fancy it?'

How about it's a yes from me? Emmy blinked at him, surprised. A midnight walk on the beach was not what she'd expected. She was starting to feel tired, but there was no way she was going to say no. *A walk on the beach on this not-a-date civic duty date? Could the night get any better? Well, there was something that could have made it an incy-wincy bit better.* She put an end to the thought right away. 'I think that sounds lovely.'

They changed course instead of turning towards The Old Ticket Office and ambled the other way to the beach. Once they got to the bay, it seemed as if the whole world had gone to bed. The beach, under the glow of the moon, added to the ethereal feel that had enveloped Emmy since she'd first stepped out of the shop door onto Darling Street hours before.

As they strolled along, Emmy was lost in the moment; the nervousness that had started with her when Amy had been talking about what to wear was long gone. It had melted away in Darlings with the tealights and the bubbles. As she looked up at the stars with the cool sand under her feet, she chuckled. 'Well, this is a turn-up for the books. What a beautiful night.' It all felt surreal, like a daydream that happened to somebody else.

'It is. I've enjoyed it,' Tom said. 'It's been really nice.'

'Yep, me too. Thanks for inviting me.'

'I thought it would be the neighbourly thing to do.'

And there it was. The neighbourly word. Slap. *Oh, right, okay.*

Emmy felt her heart sink at that but decided to stay in the moment as they walked back up to the road and started to stroll along Darling Street, chatting about the various businesses lining either side of the road. As they reached Emmy's place, the glow from the light above the door illuminated the area. Everything was serene, silent, the street deserted and quiet around them. Emmy looked up at the shop, then turned her gaze towards Tom.

'Looks like we're the only ones still awake on Darling,' Tom whispered, peering down the street. 'Even the trams are quiet tonight.'

As Emmy got her keys out, Tom reached out, gently brushing Emmy's arm. The touch sent a surge of electricity through her, and she caught her breath. She looked into his eyes as he stepped forward, and then before she really knew what he was doing, Tom had tilted Emmy's chin upwards, and the world seemed to slow as he leaned in. The moment stretched, butterflies danced, and the ground seemed to pull away from underneath her. Boy, was it fab.

Emmy's heart pounded in her chest as she returned Tom's kiss, and she put her hands on his back. She felt his arm wrap around her waist, pulling her closer. The taste of him, the scent of him, the warmth of his body against hers. All of it intoxicating. The rest of the world faded away as Emmy lost herself in everything Tom.

Finally, she pulled away, and Emmy didn't really know what to do next. Stepping back, she smiled as Tom squeezed her hand, and she fumbled with her keys, and for a brief moment, she thought about inviting him in. 'Err, thanks, Tom.'

'Thanks. See you.'

As she slowly made her way up, Emmy replayed the events of the night in her mind. She remembered how she'd felt before it had begun when she was in the bath, a mixture of nerves and anticipation. Now the only thing she felt was divine. She was sitting on a little shelf above her life, looking down, wondering how everything was quite so lovely.

In the sanctuary of her flat, Emmy kicked off her shoes and let out a contented sigh. The evening had way exceeded her expectations – the sunset, Darlings, the food, the beach. Tom. She shook her head in a bit of a daze as she put her bag on the side and slipped out her phone. It was as if she could still feel Tom, and she kicked herself for being sensible, not inviting him in and throwing him onto her bed.

After filling the kettle, she stood in the kitchen and messaged Amy.

Emmy: *U still up?*

A message fired back as quickly as a flash.

Amy: *How was it? xx*

Emmy: *Good.*

Amy: *Where are you?*

Emmy: *I just got home.*

Amy: *Ooh.*

Emmy: *It was really nice.*

Amy: *So, can we now call it a date???*

Emmy laughed and sent a laughing emoji.

Emmy: *Not sure.*

Amy: *How did it end?*

Emmy: *On the doorstep.*

Amy: *You're a comedian.*

Emmy: *KISS!!!!!!!!!!! Another one!*

Amy: *Excellent work. This was defo a date.*

Amy sent a fist pump emoji.

Amy: *This is epic. I'll phone you in the morning for a full debrief. Love u Ems x*

Emmy: *Love you. xxx*

Emmy moved to the bathroom, flipping on the light and

chuckling to herself about her earlier preparation, which now felt a million moons away. It seemed it had served her well.

As she scooped cleanser out of a tub, massaged it over her skin, and began to wipe it off with a muslin cloth, she peered in the mirror. The woman staring back was not only glowing but sparkling ludicrously. She actually smiled at herself, and when the smile crinkled the little wrinkles at the side of her eyes and lifted her heart, she realised that she hadn't smiled properly just for herself for a long time. Yes, she'd smiled at, about, and with Callum, ditto Amy and her girls. She'd smiled and loved her mum and dad to bits. But since Kevin had started gambling, and it had rocked her to her core, the real Emmy smile that was for her hadn't been there at all. It had got lost somehow in the flashing lights of a fruit machine and a whack of reality on the back of her head. Now it was back. It looked so nice. As she wiped the cleanser underneath her eyes, she continued just to smile and look and beam and stare. Emmy Bardot's smile was back. It felt so very good to make its acquaintance.

Turning on the tap, she let the water cascade over her hands and watched as it spiralled down the plughole. She then squeezed a different cleanser from a tube onto her cheek, massaged until there was a creamy lather, repeated the whole process, and realised that the smile was still there. It was all very odd, but it was almost as if the evening had washed away the remnants of her old self. New Emmy had arrived and joined her in the room. New Emmy was in possession of a winning smile.

Picking up her toothbrush, she began to brush her teeth, stood with her back turned to the mirror, leant on the sink, and let her mind wander deliciously back to Tom. She thought about how his eyes had twinkled under the street light, how the two of them had just seemed to click, how her heart had fluttered on the dance floor. How she was a nuclear reactor.

Rinsing her mouth, she splashed water on her face, patted it dry, and looked at herself in the mirror again. New Emmy was still there. New Emmy looked back. She might have had a red nose, but she had a new smile too. Emmy raised her eyebrows. The evening had changed something in her. A door had been opened that had been closed for a long time. As she padded back to her room, deliciously tired, she couldn't quite wait to wake up the next day and see if the smile was still there.

30

The next day, Emmy swung in wild abandon from feeling like the cat who'd got the cream, to superbly happy and gleeful, to wondering what in the world she was playing at. The plan on moving to Darling Island had included maybe meeting a few new people, attempting to be part of a community, and perhaps joining a book club or something. It had not detailed going on a not-a-date with her neighbour, flinging herself at him and kissing him, not once but twice in a short amount of time. Nor had it included being rescued and carried up the garden path by said neighbour. All of that was taking integrating into the Darling Island community a bit too far.

With that in mind, rather than sitting with love hearts in place of her pupils and openly swooning out the window in Tom's direction, she took the more sensible, boring route; got her head down and got on with jobs, and pretended she didn't care about any of it at all. After spending hours working on the shop, she'd taken a break with the biscuit tin and a pot of tea, and was sitting by the window watching various Darling-ites stroll past and trams whizzing back and forth.

As she sat there, she checked her phone for the millionth

time to be met with nothing. No phone call or message from Tom. Not even a sniff of a message. Absolute zilch. As the hours ticked by with nothing from Tom, she started to feel a little bit of stupidity and a whole lot of angst. Here she was, waiting with bated breath, anxiously hoping for some form of communication, but by Tom's lack of engagement, it was clear that he was thinking nothing of the sort. The dreaminess of the previous night didn't now feel quite as ethereal. Maybe indeed, she had dreamt the whole thing. Shouldn't he have messaged right away? She knew he had her number. Did she need to call him or something? She really had no idea how to go about the situation whatsoever.

The hullabaloo high of what had happened slowly began to wane as the day wore on. It was all very well getting into something with her neighbour, but now in the cold light of day, having heard zilch from him, she was back to thinking that the whole thing was one of her more stupid ideas. A little voice was telling her to wrap it all up and leave it well alone. The other voice was remembering how she'd felt when he'd kissed her. Of that, she wanted more.

As she comfort ate her way down the biscuit tin, she convinced herself that so what if he hadn't called or messaged? That was the way of the modern dating world. Who even cared? Yadda yadda. Take it, leave it, and have a little bit of fun. People did it all the time. All the time. Too easy. No dramas. She must not stray into overthinking territory; she would instead just chill. She could do that. Sure thing. Easy-peasy, right?

Mulling it over, she shuddered. It wasn't easy at all. She didn't care less about the way it was done in the modern digi dating world. And also she didn't really want a bit of fun. What even was that? Who, really, just wanted fun? Fun had been so absent in her life she couldn't even really remember how it felt. The more she analysed the whole thing, the more she realised that dashing Tom P Carter, however, was doing just that. It all made sense if she really looked at it; rescuing her at the barbecue, giving her a lift, then asking her to the Darlings thing; all of it just a bit of inconsequential fluff with the woman a few doors down. Nothing serious. Nothing even meant in it or by it. Maybe he did it all the time; little dalliances with various women. Her one day, Cara the next.

She snatched her phone up as it rang with a video call from Amy. She tapped the screen and propped her phone on the windowsill.

'Hey! How is it on *Love Island* today?' Amy joked with a huge beam on her face.

Emmy let out a massive sigh and scrunched up her face. 'I don't know.'

'Oh! What? I was expecting you to be, I don't know what, but not this.'

'Ames, what am I doing?'

'Don't be ridiculous! What do you mean?'

Emmy picked at the biscuit crumbs on her jeans. 'I mean, I don't know. What if it's all just a game to him?' She squirmed. 'What if I've made a complete fool of myself? I bet people are saying that. Now I think about it, a few people intimated stuff about him. What if he has Cara on the go and now me, and he thinks this is all funny?'

Amy seemed taken aback. 'You're overthinking this. Why would he do that? He wouldn't have Cara and then take you to Darlings. No way. Did you ask him about it?'

'No, I just didn't get the opportunity. It didn't come up.'

'Why would he take you there if he was seeing her?'

'Good question. But what if…' Emmy started, but Amy cut her off.

'Don't even start on the "what ifs," Em,' Amy said firmly. 'We all know where they end up. You need to trust yourself, trust your feelings. If Tom wasn't interested, he wouldn't have spent time with you, wouldn't have kissed you.'

Emmy sat there in silence, pondering Amy's words. She stared blankly at the trams whizzing past the window, her mind spinning. 'I clearly have trust issues.'

'You're just a bit scared. Kevin hasn't helped with that. Just blame Kevin.'

'Yeah.'

'Totally normal,' Amy said. 'Totally.'

Emmy swallowed, her throat dry. 'You're right.'

'It's not like you haven't had relationships since Kevin. Where is this coming from?'

Emmy knew exactly where it was coming from – it was different with Tom, which was scaring the heebie-jeebies out of her. There was no way she was going to trust someone again, love someone again, to have them pull the rug out from under her as Kevin had done. She pretended she didn't know. 'No idea.'

'Just go with the flow,' Amy reassured her. 'You deserve a bit of fun and happiness. Right?'

'Okay. Yeah, right. I did try to tell myself that earlier. Cripes, I'm all over the show.'

'You'll be fine. Look, I'll speak to you later. Let me know if there are any further developments.'

'Will do.'

Emmy let out a long sigh, staring at her reflection on the screen. She needed to chill a bit. Amy was right. She didn't want to be stuck in a loop of doubts and 'what ifs'. She wouldn't get anywhere if she didn't take a few chances. After all, that was how she'd ended up on Darling in the first place. She tried to think about what Grandma Emily would say. But Grandma Emily was stubbornly quiet.

Gathering the biscuit tin and her mug, she went back up to the flat, and then as she made her way up to the top room, she decided that she would do just as Amy said. She wouldn't read too much into it all, she would simply play it by ear and see what happened. At the end of the day, what did she really have to lose?

Keeping hold of that thought, she stood with her hands on her hips and looked around the top room. In her initial plan, it had been on the bottom of the list of jobs in The Old Ticket Office, but because of the delay in getting approval for the sign and the floral installation, and because she had decided to take the shop renovation and opening a lot more slowly, the top room had moved up the list. She'd decided to turn it into her bedroom with zero budget, the spray painter from her dad, a sander, and a whole lot of elbow grease. Now it was halfway there.

Emmy had spent hours on her hands and knees with a belt sander, following Bob's instructions to 'go over it quickly.' She'd laughed wryly at that after spending most of a morning with Callum's help, bent with her back in two, sanding for all she was worth. After that, she'd spent another half day, also on her hands and knees, but without the help of Callum pasting on a dark wood stain which had promised a 'colonial feel' and had ended up everywhere, not just on the floorboards.

In between all that, the sprayer had yet again done its job well, and the walls were now the same white as the ones in the shop. The huge window at the front and the matching one looking out over the back were painted and clean, the room was ready to be foofed and holding its breath for Emmy to move in. She couldn't wait to wake up in the mornings to the view.

She strode over the floor in her socks, remembering how her back had felt the night she'd stained the boards. Now it seemed worth much more than a bit of backache. The no-budget room had scrubbed up well. She smiled at the little collection of boxes and decorative things gathered by Cherry, her mum; a huge seagrass rug, a lovely bed frame (put together by Callum and Bob) and a new mattress, curtains, bedside tables, and two lamps. Cherry hadn't been strangled by the same budget restrictions as the rest of the room and had gone to town a bit on nice things. Emmy couldn't have been more grateful if she'd tried.

Emmy started to pull the plastic packaging from the rug and rolled it out on top of the dark stained floor. It juxtaposed beautifully against the old timber and gave the room some depth. Then, heaving with all her might, she dragged the bed frame on top of the rug and started to yank the protective covering from the new mattress. Once the mattress was on the frame, the bedside tables went next to it, and she spent the next half an hour furiously cleaning the windows until there was not a smear or speck of dust in sight.

She then dragged the stepladder up the stairs, opened four packets of white linen blackout curtains and placed them on the double layer curtain poles over the matchstick blinds her dad had put up on a flying visit a few days before. Already exhausted, she was running out of steam when she stood back and squinted at the room. When she'd looked at it with Dan the estate agent, it had been sad, dusty, and stale. Added to that, when she'd moved in, there had been evidence of little furry things in the walls. Now, it was lovely. The dark stained timber looked like it had cost a bomb rather than the price of a bucket load of elbow grease and a tin of stain. The freshly painted walls with the picture rail at the top bounced light around like a dream. Dressed with the double layer curtains, the windows now framed the distant view of the estuary, and the huge bed invited sleep like never before.

The same smile from the night before, the smile of the new Emmy, touched the corners of her mouth and eyes. The room really was nothing short of gorgeous. She clapped her hands together, not really believing that it was hers. So far from the crummy little single bed she'd slept in in the flat and the small bed in the cottage.

An hour later, shattered but determined to get the job done and forcing herself not to think about her neighbour, Emmy had put clean ironed sheets on the bed, the lamps from Cherry were on the bedside tables, and her pyjamas were tucked up under the pillows, ready for her to fall into bed later that day.

Emmy walked into the tiny strange little bathroom at the other end of the room; a boxed-in clad bath, a pedestal sink, a funny little window butting up to the floor looking out over the old rooftops of Darling Street, a toilet squashed in with barely room to sit down and do a wee. Emmy pursed her lips together and stood for ages looking at the timber-clad room. She wondered who had lived in it right at the top of the house. By the looks of the tide mark on the bath and the state of the toilet pan, whoever it was hadn't liked cleaning too much.

Emmy recalled what Dan had said about the top room and how he'd said if the building were a house, it would have been worth a fortune. She remembered how he'd pointed out the value of turning the room into a bedroom. She'd taken that and run with it, and couldn't quite believe it had turned out as well as it had. She nodded and told herself to give one more huge push on the bathroom, and she'd have not only a large bedroom with a view but an ensuite too. Life goals. She raised her head to the ceiling and spoke out loud. 'Thank you, Grandma Emily. Thank you, thank you, thank you.'

An hour later, Emmy had scrubbed the toilet pan with bleach on a toothbrush and could entertain the idea of going to the toilet or, indeed, entering the bathroom without getting a staph infection. She'd removed the old-fashioned goose head shower and descaled it to within an inch of its life, and the strange waist-high sash window was wedged open with a brick.

Fresh sea air rushed around the place, and Emmy couldn't wrap her head around the fact she actually owned what she was looking at. Her mind raced back to the flat she'd lived in with Callum. The bathroom there had been so small she'd had to sit on the loo with her knees touching her chin, and because there hadn't been a window, it had been permanently damp and permanently grim. The bathroom in the cottage had actually been quite nice, but this place was all hers. Totally hers, not even hers to share with Callum or anyone else who happened to be in the flat, namely a man with a name beginning with 'T'. Her very own loo, sink, and bath. Gold.

Thanks to a lot of saving, hard work, and Grandma Emily, Emmy had a pale pink bathroom with a huge old-fashioned shower head, taps that turned the wrong way, and a funny little window. All of it a tad in need of love. All of it to call her own. Just as she was pouring bleach into the toilet pan, her phone pinged. Hoo blimming ray.

Tom: *Had a great time last night. Perhaps do it again maybe. Tom*

Emmy plonked herself down on the side of the bath. She reread the message, wondered what to make of it, pondered what to reply, and read it three more times. Perhaps do it again. Huh? What did that mean? Maybe? Perhaps?

She felt her heart sink. She wasn't sure what it meant, she *was* sure she'd been hoping for a different message. So it was just a little something to him. A bit of dinner, a bit of a stroll on the beach, a bit of chatting, a bit of a kiss. Something he might do again sometime in the future. The taste left in Emmy's mouth was not good. She didn't like it at all.

Emmy shook her head. Oh no. No. No, no, no, no, no. She wasn't having that. Tom P could go and get stuffed. She wasn't having him 'maybe' doing it again sometime. No. Slamming out of the bathroom, she stood staring at her new bed for ages. She wasn't having someone like this Tom bloke thinking he might like to pick her up and take her out again, maybe sometime in the future. Balls to that. Shiny ones.

She contemplated what to reply and took her phone out of her pocket. She considered telling him to poke his dinner. And his walk on the beach stargazing, for that matter. She considered all sorts. But eventually, she decided that, yes, it had been great, and she'd leave it where it was, thank you very much.

There would be no 'perhaps' as far as she was concerned. And she wouldn't be having a 'maybe' in her court either. That might be good enough for the Caras of the world but not for Emmy Bardot. Stabbing out the reply as if her life depended on it, she grimaced.

Emmy: *I enjoyed the night too.*

Emmy then spent another hour trying to utilise the therapeutic benefits of painting anti-mould primer to the cladding in the bathroom. It did not work to calm her jagged edges one iota. She attempted to forget about the text and not to analyse it. She told herself that she would view the whole situation as a taster of trying new things that wouldn't be going any further. She grimaced at how Tom had said maybe and shook her head. Her heart could not deal with the Tom Carters of the world messing her around, that she knew without a doubt. She so couldn't be doing with all that. Maybe? Perhaps? No, no and no again.

31

There had been no further communication on either side. Emmy hadn't heard anything else from Tom since her reply, and there was no way in the world she was going to message him again. There may have been rather a lot of thinking about things that had happened on doorsteps. Not that she'd had much time for contemplating her love life, or lack thereof, as the next few days had passed quickly in a whirl of work and life. Since the text, Emmy had spent three long double shift days at the port dealing with problems including but not limited to stolen passports, lost children, and a suspected heart attack in the check-in area.

She'd driven home towards Darling Island, inched her car onto the ferry, and couldn't wait to get home to her new bed. As she watched the island get closer and closer as the ferry crossed the water, her mind flicked back to the evening in Darlings with Tom. She pondered how dreamy it had been; the setting, the company, the walk along the beach and back down Darling Street as if they'd been the only two people awake on the planet. She thought about how that hadn't quite felt as nice when the subsequent text had come in. She shook her head. As Amy had said, if she hadn't gone, she wouldn't have known. It still didn't feel very nice. She attempted and mostly failed at keeping self-loathing at bay.

Just after she'd pulled off the ferry and was waiting to turn down into the lane behind The Old Ticket Office to park her car, she saw Tom approaching. In fitness gear and clearly on his way home from a run, he held his hand up, smiled, and pulled the earphones from his ears so they dangled around his neck. Emmy couldn't pretend that she hadn't seen him, so she rolled down the window, not really sure what to do. She *was* sure, however, that he looked as if he'd just walked out of a costume trailer on a BBC production. She felt her heart absolutely pounding as Tom leant on the window of her car. Her body was reincarnated as a nuclear reactor.

'Hi.' Emmy smiled, attempting to look friendly though she felt far, far, far from it. She was in worst-case scenario territory. She'd let herself take a chance, and it had gone horribly wrong. She was *pitied* by a neighbour. A neighbour who had done his civic duty taking her out to dinner and kissed her for a bit of fun.

'Hey! How have you been?' Tom pointed down the lane. 'I haven't seen you around.'

*No *****. 'No. I've been at work on long shifts,' Emmy replied. She was suddenly mortifyingly embarrassed. She'd had fantasies about this man who clearly was not thinking anywhere near the same things about her. The things she'd done in the fantasies had not been for the faint of heart. She felt as if he could see inside her head. She felt stupid and small, oh so small, clumsy, and pathetic. She didn't really know what to say. It was if her mind was fumbling and clawing at words for something to say. 'How have you been?'

'Good, really good. Busy!'

Yeah, too busy to message your silly neighbour. 'Right, yes, I bet. Me too.'

'How was the traffic today?' Tom asked, inclining his head in the direction of the ferry.

Emmy fiddled with the steering wheel, wishing she hadn't seen Tom. All she could think about was kissing him, and he was asking her about her commute. Really? He was making stupid inconsequential small talk with her. Another little tick in his civic duty box. She didn't give a hoot about the traffic. He was so casual and nonchalant about what, to her, was a very big deal that he was talking about trivial stuff. She wanted to lean out the window and wring his neck.

'Fine.' Emmy nodded as she checked her rearview mirror to make sure a car wasn't coming up behind her. 'Okay, well, I need to get home. I have to go back out again later and collect Callum from cricket. Nice to see you.'

Tom ran his fingers through his hair. 'Yep. Right. Okay. See you later.'

Emmy flushed with disappointment. So he definitely wasn't going to mention what had happened or ask her to go out again or anything, and there was no way *she* was going to do it. So this was it. She looked in the mirror again as Tom put his hand on her arm. 'Yeah, thanks for before. I had a nice time.'

Emmy felt her cheeks burning. 'Yes, you said in your message. I'm glad you enjoyed yourself.'

'We might have to do it again at some point.'

Emmy was irritated with herself for being pleased at the same time as being annoyed with him – who did he think he was that he could dangle a 'might' in her face? Balls to that. 'Mmm.'

'Good fun… I, err, wondered.'

Emmy was not happy. She interrupted him, nearly jumping down his throat, reiterating what he had said but adding a sarcastic edge to it. 'Fun?' Lilting the end into a question.

Tom picked up on Emmy's tone. 'Sorry, are you okay?'

Emmy went to say yes and then shook her head. 'Umm, yeah, no, actually, I'm so not okay with that.'

Tom's eyes went as wide as saucers. 'What?'

'Sorry, not sorry, Tom, oh no, Tom, not sorry at all. Nope. I'm not up for a bit of fun, as you call it.' Emmy's hands gripped the steering wheel tight, her knuckles white. She didn't quite know what she had expected him to say, but this wasn't it. A pit of disappointment whirled in her stomach mixed with fury at his casual up-himself attitude. 'I'm not…' she began, swallowing against the sudden lump in her throat. 'I'm not up for fun.'

Tom frowned and looked confused. 'Right.'

Emmy was on a roll. 'While we're at it, I'll give you a bit of neighbourly advice, shall I? Yes, I will. Oh yes. I think you need a bit of advice from someone in the real world. Don't ask people out to dinner and then kiss them and well, no…' She shook her head, very rattled. 'Do you know what, Tom Carter?' She leant forward on the windowsill and pointed her finger. '*You* are not very nice if this is how you treat people. Not. Nice. At. All.'

Tom blinked at her, clearly taken aback. 'Emmy, I—'

'Save it,' Emmy cut him off dead and, to her absolute horror, felt a prick at the corner of her eyes. She was getting teary over this. Ridiculous. What even was this?

'I didn't mean to imply…' Tom started, but Emmy shook her head, cutting him off again.

'You didn't mean to imply what, eh? Eh? What? I want to hear this.' Emmy was surprised at the level of aggressiveness in her voice, but at this stage she couldn't care less. Tom had both upset her and filled her with fury at the same time. 'Come on. What did you mean to imply then, eh? Mr I'm-such-a-nice-neighbour, eh?'

Tom went to reply, and Emmy interrupted him again. 'Actually, I think it's best if we don't discuss this,' she managed to say, her voice shaky. 'Look, let's just leave it.'

Tom nodded and didn't speak for a second. Emmy willed

herself not to cry as the seconds felt like hours, and she fumbled to put the car into gear. Tom put his hand back on her arm. He swore. 'I didn't mean it like that. I think there's been a massive misunderstanding here.'

'Oh really? Yeah, of course there has. How did you mean it, then?' Emmy asked as the words 'bit of fun' echoed in her mind.

'I didn't mean it like that, Emmy,' Tom said, his voice strained. 'You've got the wrong end of the stick. Blimey!'

'Don't tell me, yeah, yeah, yeah, I got the wrong end of the stick about Cara too. Think I was born yesterday, Tom? No. Fresh off the boat, am I? I hope Cara gets wind of this.'

'Cara?'

'Yes, now you're pretending as if you don't know. You take the biscuit, you really do! Cara De-Have-a-Bum or whatever her perfect surname is. Unbelievable. Unbelievable and nasty.' Emmy couldn't believe her own voice. She was on fire.

Tom shook his head. 'Cara rents an office in my building…' He looked confused. 'I really am not sure what you're on about. What are you talking about?'

Emmy side-eyed as she tried to compute what Tom had just said.

'You didn't let me finish. I don't know what you're thinking about Cara, but what I was trying to say before was... I wondered if we could go out again, like on a proper date. Because the other night was more than just a "bit of fun" for me. Look, I'm going to be away for the next few days, but I'll text you. If you want to that is.' Tom frowned. 'Sorry if there's been a bit of a mix up here.' He winced, 'Maybe you don't want to?'

Emmy was caught off guard; she'd expected it to go the other way. She wasn't sure what to think or say or do. She'd been way over the top. Cara rented an office from him. She slipped down a bit in her seat, blinked furiously and scrambled for words. 'Okay. Oh, right, okay. Umm, oh, I do.'

Tom smiled. 'At least we're on the same page on that then. I think. Is Callum at home tonight?'

'Yes, I'm going to pick him up later. I came back to get the dinner sorted and stuff.'

'Okay, we'll leave it for tonight then. Look, I'll message you.'

Emmy's words tumbled out at a hundred miles an hour. 'Right. Great. Okay. Yes. Thanks, Tom. Thanks. Yes, you do that. Message me.'

32

A couple of hours or so later, Emmy had crossed back over on the bridge, picked up Callum and was again back on the ferry going home. As she'd taken a phone call from Judy, from work, about the man with the suspected heart attack who now also had a missing bag, and Callum had told her about a cricket match he'd forgotten about, her mind underneath was mostly on Tom. All she could think about was how he'd looked when he'd realised she'd taken what he'd said completely the wrong way. She went over her words again and again whilst pretending to listen to Callum telling her about a bowler in another team, who'd done something amazing and broken a record in a fast bowl. She really could not have cared about anything less than cricket balls and how fast they travelled through the air. She still didn't even understand the rules of the game. A group of people throwing a hard ball at each other and three sticks while others stood around observing? Each to their own.

As Callum stopped talking and started looking at his phone, she got out of the car and went and stood by the railing. She leaned over and looked down, captivated by the blue and white livery of the Pride of Darling ferry as it slipped down into the water. Tom continued to be front and centre of her mind. *I am going out with Tom P Carter. I am going out with Tom P Carter.*

A few seconds later, Evie from Darlings was standing by her side.

'Oh, hi, how are you? I didn't see you when we got on,' Emmy said.

'I just made it in time. I was standing over the back there.'

'How are you?'

'Good. I've had the day off today, and I've been up to town on the train. It's nice to get off the island every now and then.'

'Lovely. Did you have a nice time?'

'Yes. My calves are certainly feeling it, though. I've done sixteen thousand steps! How about you? What have you been up to?'

Emmy jerked her thumb towards the car and lowered her voice a bit. 'The joys of the cricket run and after-school sport.'

Evie laughed. 'I hear you.'

'And I've had full days at work, so I'm also feeling it.'

'How's the shop? Are you doing okay with that?'

'Slow but sure. I'm getting there.'

'Good to hear. It takes a lot of time and effort to set up a business.'

'Yep, I'm finding that out. By the way, thanks for the event the other night. It was amazing. I felt as if I was in a dream with all those candles and the music. The food was outstanding too,' Emmy gushed.

'Aww, thanks. We work hard for those events. I am so lucky to have Lucie and good staff around me. It's so hard to get staff these days.'

'Yep, they were working their socks off.'

'I see you were in good company.' Evie chuckled.

Emmy felt her cheeks flush. 'I was.'

'How was that? Tom, I mean. Not being nosy.' Evie flicked her eyes. 'Actually, that's not true, I'm being totally nosy.'

Emmy laughed, but she wasn't sure how much to say. She wanted to jump up and down and say that she was going to go out with Tom again. She didn't want to count her chickens, though, and she certainly wasn't going to advertise anything on the Darling ferry. 'Very nice.'

'I must say, you two did look quite the picture together. You know, Tom is not usually the type to bring someone to our events. You must have made quite an impression,' Evie noted with quite a serious tone to her voice.

Again, Emmy didn't know quite what to think, and so played her cards close to her chest. 'Right.'

'Just between you and me, I'm rooting for you. Everyone here has been trying to set Tom up for years, but he's never shown any interest long-term, really. That is until now.'

The plot thickened. 'Oh, okay, right.'

'His actions spoke volumes that night.' Evie started laughing and swung her arm around the ferry. 'You were the talk of the town. You know what this place is like.'

Emmy didn't really, but she was beginning to learn. She blushed. 'Oh, it's nothing.'

'Trust me. It's something.'

Emmy couldn't resist asking a few questions. 'Sorry, so why have you been trying to set him up? What's wrong with him?'

'Nothing at all! He's told you about Sarah, right?'

Emmy nodded. Tom had briefly mentioned his ex, Sarah, when they'd chatted, but she didn't know the ins and outs of it.

Evie screwed up her nose. 'Yeah, that didn't end too well.'

Emmy wanted to pick Evie up and shake every little bit of information out of her. Instead, she pretended to be mildly interested, but she couldn't stop herself from asking more. She attempted to sound nonchalant. 'Oh, what happened? I didn't get the full story. We talked about so many different things.'

'Tom's ex, Sarah, received an unexpected job opportunity overseas. You know, like a dream come true, and she couldn't pass it up. She didn't want to do a long-distance relationship, and so she just upped sticks and left. Like one day she was here, the next day she was gone. They lived in the other house on the other side there.'

'Yeah, he did say he had a house over there,' Emmy replied. Tom hadn't gone into that much detail, though.

'It was all very hasty. And then, well, don't say it came from me but turns out the, err, the job offer was a bit of an excuse.' Evie screwed her face up painfully. 'Sarah actually took up with one of Tom's friends from uni. It had been going on for ages, apparently. The thing is, she didn't tell him, and he found out on social media. He then went off the rails a bit. Like he's had more girlfriends than hot dinners, and there is no way he ever brings anyone to Darlings events.'

'Right.' Emmy swallowed.

'And then there was what happened with the sunstroke.'

Emmy shook her head in bewilderment. How did Evie know about that? She screwed up her nose. 'Sorry?'

'He totally took you home and sorted you out.' Evie screwed up her face into a frown. 'Tom would never have done that for, well, for anyone else.'

'Oh, right. It was just a lift as far as I was concerned.'

'Ha! Yeah, no. So you're pretty special by all accounts,' Evie joked.

Emmy nodded. She hadn't seen that coming, but she'd take it. Was she special? Maybe actually, she'd run with that. New Emmy was in the house, and yes, she was special. Also as she listened to Evie continue, she thought that she wasn't going to stand there and let anyone somehow intimate in a back-handed sort of way that she should feel lucky that Tom may or not have an interest in her. No, Emmy was going to carry on as she had started in the car earlier on that day when Tom had been running. The rest of this would be on her terms. Tom P Carter was the lucky one because she, from now on, just as Evie had pointed out, was very, very special indeed. And she wasn't going to let anyone forget it.

33

Tom's message had asked Emmy if she wanted to go out. Emmy had replied in the affirmative. The date had arrived, and it had started with him knocking on the front door of the shop. It proceeded to a stroll around the bay and ended up in the Chinese restaurant China Darling a few doors down from The Old Ticket Office. Emmy had never been to a restaurant like it. When Tom had held open the door and she'd stepped in, she'd gasped at how pretty the place was. Silk umbrellas strung with tiny gold lights hung from the ceiling, a woman in a pale blue silk high-collared jacket had welcomed them, and they'd walked in under a multitude of fabric flower lanterns with blue tassels and sat down to beautiful blue and gold china gracing the tables. Emmy's night had been nothing short of wonderful. Over a Chinese banquet where the food had been amazing, she and Tom had chatted and put the world to rights. On the stroll home through thick fog along Darling Street, Tom had taken Emmy's hand in his, and she'd gone up to his flat for a coffee. It wasn't just coffee drinking that had taken place.

It was the next day after the date, and reality hit when Emmy woke up to her alarm going off. She was back to her actual life rather than her Tom P Carter life with a bang and the alarm trilling to tell her to get out of bed for cricket. Wondering if, in fact, the night before had been an illusion, she'd padded to the shower, pulled on her clothes and made tea with a head full of what had happened the night before. After making sure Callum's cricket gear was intact, getting him out of bed, and feeding him, they'd taken the ferry and driven to Callum's cricket match, all in a bit of a daze. Emmy was just setting up her fold-up chair, rug, flask of tea and picnic basket when her phone buzzed from Amy.

'Hello, just calling to discuss and dissect the date of the century.' Amy joked. 'How was it?'

'Date of the century? I'm not sure about that, but it was definitely... something.'

'Ooh, come on! Tell me it was amazing! I'm the boring, needy one here who needs to hear what a fun, exciting night you had.'

'It was pretty special,' Emmy admitted.

Amy squealed, 'Ooh, spill the details. Where did you go?'

Emmy glanced around, making sure no one was within earshot. 'We went for a walk around the bay. Then the fog started to roll in as we walked back to the Chinese restaurant. You might have seen the restaurant - it's just down the road?'

'Yeah, I looked in the window the other day when I couldn't park in the lane, and I ended up down that side road. It looked really nice in there.'

'It was stunning. Honestly, I've never been to a Chinese restaurant like it. There were silk umbrellas and flower lanterns everywhere.' Emmy sighed. 'So nice. You'd love it.'

'Sounds dreamy. How was the food?'

'Out of this world! We had the banquet, and every dish was so delicious. It just kept on coming in little Darling-esque bowls one after the other. We have to go with Mum and Dad. You know how much Dad loves food like that.'

'We must. Anyway, that's not why I'm calling. How was the delectable Tom P?'

'Yeah, good.' Emmy felt herself reddening.

'Just good?'

'I don't know, just nice. Easy. Comfy. We chatted and laughed. It felt so, I dunno, like we've known each other forever.'

'You sound mushy.'

Emmy hesitated for a moment. 'I really like him.'

'But?'

'I just feel like I'm going to mess it up somehow, Ames.'

'Oh, don't be silly! You deserve this, and nothing is going to happen.' Amy reassured her.

Emmy smiled gratefully. 'I guess I'm just not used to this. It feels like a whirlwind, and I don't want to get my hopes up. You know?'

'I get it. It's okay to be cautious. Just blame Kevin. You deserve to be happy, though, Ems. You really do.'

Emmy didn't feel as if she did. That was for other people. 'Yeah.'

'Take things one step at a time.'

Emmy nodded. 'You're right. I just don't want to mess things up or misinterpret anything. I think I've done enough of that already.'

'Don't overthink it, just go with the flow,' Amy advised. 'Didn't I tell you that before? Look how the Cara thing turned out.'

'True.'

'You totally overthought that, and she rents an office from him. Do not overthink.'

Emmy chuckled. It was easy for Amy not to overthink things in her perfect world. In Emmy's world, things were never quite as straightforward. She cringed as she felt that things always went wrong where she was concerned. 'Ah, there's that wise "go with the flow" advice you always give me.'

'It's true. When has it not worked out?'

Emmy shook her head at Amy. She felt as if nothing had ever really worked out for her. She could start with her marriage and go from there, but she didn't. 'Hmm.'

'So, when are you seeing him again?'

'When Cal is at Kev's. We're going to the cinema.'

'Who asked who?' Amy asked.

'He asked me.'

'Good. Yep. Love that.'

'And Friday,' Emmy said with a laugh knowing Amy would jump on it.

'Ooh! Serious! Where are you going on Friday?'

'Just to his for a takeaway because I mentioned Callum will be at Ben's.'

'Will there be a sleepover?' Amy joked with a squeal.

'Shut up, Ames.'

'Sounds like he's smitten. That's like three dates in one week.'

Emmy blushed. 'I hope he's smitten, Ames, because I can't stop thinking about him. It's ridiculous.'

'Run with it.'

'You know what? I'm going to...'

'I'm just so happy for you. The move has gone well, and now this.'

'Thank you.'

'Thank goodness you bumped into him that day.'

After the conversation had finished, Emmy sat watching Callum play cricket and relived the night before in her head. As the match dragged on, and the more she thought about Tom, she realised that she was just going to have to stop worrying that she would mess things up and get on with it. As she was pondering what would happen next, a text appeared from Tom on her phone as if he'd heard her thoughts. Her heart skipped a beat, and the nuclear reactor started up as she read the message.

Tom: *Hey, how's cricket?*

Emmy: *Good. It's a lovely day which helps.*

Tom: *I had a great time last night.*

Emmy: *Me too. Thanks. The food was great.*

Tom: *I wasn't talking about the food.*

Emmy blushed.

Emmy: *Lol.*

Tom: *So I don't get the wrong end of the stick: We're going to the cinema and having takeaway here Friday??? Just sorting my movements for the week.*

Emmy: *Yes, if that all still suits?*

Tom: *Absolutely x Can't wait. xxx*

Emmy's heart first fluttered and then fist-pumped at the message ending with kisses. It seemed as if this was a thing. It also seemed as if she wasn't going to mess it up. As she watched the cricket match going on in front of her, her mind wandered to first bumping into Tom and how it had somehow turned into her dating him. She couldn't quite believe it, and she couldn't wait to see him again.

Lost in a world of her own, she realised that she'd never felt the things she was feeling. It was as if the move to Darling Island had started something beautiful blossoming in her life. As she turned her Grandma Emily's ring over and over on her finger, she felt grateful for the unexpected turn her life had taken all because of the money she'd received via the will. That had started a domino of events, and since the day she'd collected the birthday cake, there had been all sorts of twists and turns, a fair whack of stress and a whole lot of unknown. The shop wasn't anywhere near ready to open, money was tight, and she had a lot on her plate, but now it felt as if it had all been meant to be. Best thing about it? Tom was part of it all.

34

It was a few months or so since the week when Emmy had been out to dinner, to the cinema and to Tom's for a take-away. There had been many dates since and now Emmy had driven over to Amy's to drop Callum off and then was going away with Tom for Saturday night. Emmy Bardot was going on a grown-up sleepover. Finally. Hoo-blooming-ray. She still couldn't believe that firstly, she was actually now going out with Tom properly, and secondly, that she was going away with him to a hotel. Not any old hotel either. The sort of hotel she'd only been able to dream about. The sort of hotel that other people went to.

She parked the car outside Amy's and looked up at the house expectantly, got out of the car and called over to Callum as he lugged his huge cricket bag out of the boot. 'So, Dad is picking you up from here in the morning and taking you to cricket. I'll text him to remind him later on. You know what he's like, he might be a bit late.'

'Yeah, thanks.'

The front door opened, and Amy beamed. 'Hey, Cal. Thanks for babysitting.'

'No worries,' Callum replied as he lugged his cricket bag into the hallway.

Amy kissed Emmy on the cheek and whispered in her ear. 'All set?'

'Yep. I can't believe I'm doing this. I hope Cal doesn't need me for anything.'

'He'll be fine. You're going. You don't need to worry about anything.'

They traipsed into a quiet house. Emmy frowned. 'Where is everyone?'

'They've gone to the park, so I've got a bit of peace. Cup of tea before you go back?'

'Love one,' Emmy said as she followed Amy to the kitchen.

Callum called out from the spare room down the corridor. 'Yes, please.'

'Sandwich?' Amy called back.

'Yes. Thank you. I'm starving.'

'Thought as much.' Amy smiled as she yanked a loaf of bread out of the bread bin. 'He eats me out of house and home when he's here. Where does he put it all? I suppose he's six foot. There is a lot of him now.'

'Tell me about it. He's not starving, either. He's literally just eaten.'

'But he's a very good babysitter.' Amy laughed. 'So we'll give him that. I don't just pay him with money. I pay him in food.'

'He could be a lot worse,' Emmy said with a smile.

Amy lowered her voice to a whisper. 'Does he know about you-know-who yet?'

Emmy shook her head. 'Nope. He doesn't know any more than that Tom has been around a bit, and we've been out for a few drinks. I'm not sure what he thinks.'

Amy leaned in closer and whispered. 'It's getting serious between you two, Ems. I've never seen you like this.'

Emmy blushed. 'I know. It's going really well.'

'I have never known you to go out as much,' Amy noted.

'Tell me about it. I've never had the opportunity. I'm like a new woman. I've been out for more meals and dates and outings since I moved to Darling than I have in the past ten years. I feel like I've been given a new lease of life. So much for the double shifts and shop making me tired. It's been the opposite where my social life is concerned.'

'You have. I love it.'

'It just feels amazing.'

'He seems very into you, too,' Amy whispered. 'It's so romantic.'

'You reckon? I feel like it's the other way around.'

'Come on. He's taking wining and dining very seriously if he's not that into you.'

Emmy giggled. 'It's since that day when I saw him in the street after the post-date text. That was me with my assertive hat on. I think I frightened him into dating me. I actually scared myself a bit that day. Ha ha.'

'He's scared to put a foot wrong after that.'

'It works for me,' Emmy said dreamily.

You're totally officially a thing now by the looks of how this is going.'

'I suppose we are. It feels weird, though. You know? I don't want to jinx it.'

'You're going away for the night with him,' Amy said with her eyebrows very high and very wide. 'That's serious.'

Emmy swore. 'Don't say it like that. I feel bad that Cal doesn't know. I just don't want to jump into anything too quickly.'

'Hilarious! You cannot seriously think that you haven't gone into this head first! That's precisely what you've done. Too late now. You've jumped.'

'Ahh. Don't say that! Not only have I jumped, I've got it bad. I did a dive from one of those high diving boards, not just a jump. I'm actually an Olympic-level diver at this,' Emmy joked.

'You don't need to tell me,' Amy said, shaking her head. 'I can see it with my own two eyes. If you're diving in the Olympics, I'm a professional spectator.'

'Can you really see it? Is it that apparent?'

'Ha! Oh, yes. Mum knows, too, though I know you've only told her half the story. She's been asking me all sorts of loaded questions. It's written all over your face, Ems.'

'God, is it really that obvious?'

'Yep. I have never, and I mean ever, seen you like this. The only thing like it was when you had Cal. I'll never forget walking into that hospital and the look on your face.' Amy nodded as if confirming something to herself. 'Yes, that's totally what it is. It's just like that.'

'Aww. I fell in love with Cal in a split second.'

'Exactly my point!'

'Oh, blimey. Yep. When you say it like that.' Emmy nodded as realisation dawned. 'So that means…'

'You're in love with Tom P. Ha!'

'It feels different with him. But I'm also scared, you know? I don't want to mess this up like I mess everything up.'

'You do not mess everything up! Blame it on Kevin.' Amy laughed, falling back on their old in-joke.

'Poor Kevin. He gets the blame for everything in my life.'

'Good. Sorry, not sorry.'

'Anyway yeah, so I really like him, and so I just have to trust him, right? It is what it is.'

'Just be yourself and go with the flow. If it's meant to be, it will work out. Simple.'

Emmy smiled. Everything was simple in Amy's life. Simple and perfect. It wasn't quite as black and white in Emmy's world because it hadn't been simple. At all. Unlike Amy, who everything always seemed to work out for, Emmy felt as if she was always waiting for something to go wrong. A lot of the time, things did go wrong. She felt as if she was constantly peeping around an imaginary corner, waiting to see what problem would come up for her next. Amy just didn't have that in her life. No problems and horrible corners to peek around for Amy. 'I'll just take it one step at a time and see where it goes. Right?'

'Right,' Amy said, passing over a mug of tea. 'And don't forget I have your back.'

Emmy kept her voice low and pointed to the door. 'Which is why I'm not telling anyone anything yet. We'll never hear the end of it once Mum gets hold of it. I want to make sure I'm sure when I tell Callum.'

'Can we ever really be sure about anything in life?'

'I guess not.'

Amy sipped her tea thoughtfully and whispered. 'He probs knows anyway.'

Emmy shook her head emphatically. 'No. He doesn't.'

'Kids get wind of everything. Trust me.'

Right at that second, Callum emerged from the spare room, strolled into the kitchen, picked up the cup of tea by the kettle, and grabbed the sandwich Amy had made him. 'Who gets wind of everything?'

'Nothing,' Amy said, brushing it off as quick as a flash. 'We were just talking about how with social media, things go viral really quickly.'

'Yep,' Emmy added. 'Everyone gets wind of things quickly on their socials.'

'Right.' Callum raised the mug in the direction of Amy. 'Thanks, Aunty Amy.' He then stepped into the conservatory and headed out towards the back garden.

Amy shook her head, 'He totally knows. I'm sure of it.'

'I don't think so. He doesn't.'

'The look on his face, Ems.'

'I hope not. Anyway, if he does, too late now.'

'I wonder what Kevin is going to say?' Amy pondered.

'I'll cross that bridge when I come to it. Quite frankly, it's none of his business whatsoever. Not only that, I don't care.'

'I just worry. The depression and everything. Not wanting to burst your bubble.'

Emmy nodded. Since she'd left and Kevin's gambling addiction had continued to ebb and flow, he'd also suffered from depression. He'd been okay for quite some time, but it was always in the shadows. 'I've thought about that.'

'Nope, you can't let him dictate more than he already has in your life. He made his bed,' Amy stated firmly.

Emmy chuckled. 'Oh yes, he did. I, on the other hand, have a new bed, and what's happening in it is very good indeed.'

Amy swore. 'Flipping heck, Ems. Who even are you?'

As Emmy drove back to Darling, she mulled over her conversation with Amy and wondered if Callum did know what was going on with her and Tom. It wasn't as if she'd hidden it from Callum totally, and she definitely hadn't outright lied, but she had avoided things and left things out. Lying by omission was a very fitting description of what she'd done. She'd spent a lot of time with Tom when Callum had been at Kevin's, his best friend Ben's, or with her mum and dad purposely so it wouldn't be an issue. She'd seen Tom when Callum wasn't around and avoided telling Callum too much at all.

She shook her head as she pulled her car onto the floating bridge, put the brake on, and moved from thinking about Callum to thinking about herself. Life had a funny way of working things out. Here she was in her own home and about to embark on a Saturday night away with a man who hadn't been in her future at all. Now, she was not only falling for said man, but there was possibly a premise of a future with him too.

Twenty or so minutes later, she'd arrived back home and had her previously packed overnight bag over her arm, Grandma Emily's ruby earrings in her ears, and she was unbolting the back gate. As the gate stuck on her first pull, she laughed to herself as she remembered when she'd first moved in, and Tom had seen her at the gate, swearing repeatedly, trying to make it budge. Now she knew the knack to get the gate open as well as learning many other things since moving to Darling. Mostly, above making herself familiar with the ins and outs of spray painters and renovating an old shop, she'd learnt to welcome Emmy back into her life. Post Gambling Habit Emmy and Mum Emmy had been in the foreground of her life for many years, but now here on Darling with a hopeful future, a somewhat stable financial situation, and Callum growing up, she felt able to breathe, able to let Emmy from before back in. She loved how it was making her feel.

As she got to Tom's car in the lane, she also thought about the first morning on Darling when she'd had the terrible night with the mice, and things had not turned out to be quite as good as she'd thought. She'd hot-footed it out the door with her hands full, dropped her bag, and been furious at Tom for blocking in her car. Her mind flitted back to Tom, then, in the lane. He'd been quite unfriendly and standoffish. Really cranky about parking and permits. Emmy smiled to herself. These days she was on the receiving end of a very different Tom P.

She heard him walking down the path, and he opened the gate. He beamed. 'Hello gorgeous, how are you? What are you looking so pleased with yourself about?'

'Oh, nothing. I was just thinking...' Emmy shook her head. 'Nothing.'

Tom put his bag down and kissed her on the cheek.

Emmy chuckled. 'You're not allowed to kiss me in public.'

'Oh, yeah, right, sorry.'

Emmy inclined her head along to her gate and her car. 'Remember when you were cranky about my car? I was thinking about that.'

Tom crumpled up his face. 'No. I wasn't cranky. I was forthright.'

'Yes, you were!'

'What? When you were crawling around on the ground peering under cars?'

Emmy laughed. 'Yeah. You'd blocked me in.'

'Also not correct. You had plenty of room.'

'You thought I was illegally parked and not a resident.' Emmy laughed. 'And you were really cranky. Plus, you were so serious about it too.'

Tom chuckled. 'You think that was cranky?'

'Blimey, you're a bit scary.'

'I think you win on scariness.' Tom raised his eyebrows. 'When you got the wrong end of the stick before we went on the first date.' He put his head to the side. 'Technically, that wasn't our first date. That was the Darlings evening.'

Emmy giggled. 'You don't want that girl in the car to make another appearance?'

'God no. You were evil.' Tom laughed.

'Well, you'd better play your cards right then.'

'I do like a hard woman,' Tom bantered.

'Lucky you got one. Just make sure you don't mess with her. If you do anything bad, she will make your life around here a living hell.' Emmy sounded very jovial and quick on the outside, but on the inside, she was swooning because it seemed by the way Tom was talking, just as Amy had said, that Tom P Carter was very much intending on hanging around in her world.

'Ready?' Tom asked as he opened the boot.

'I'm so ready. I can't believe we're sneaking off for a night away.'

'I can, and I'm really looking forward to it. No work, no stress, just you and me, baby.' Tom smiled.

'Yep, I looked at the pictures. It's Insta-swoony.'

Tom closed the boot. 'All we need to do now is get off this island without anyone seeing us. Or we'll never live it down and Callum will definitely find out by way of the school slash ferry grapevine.'

'You really think we're not going to be the talk of the town once we get on the ferry, and then no one sees us all weekend?'

'Good point.'

'A video of us taken from the ferry's CCTV will be on Facebook. Darling Island neighbours sneak off together for a Saturday night away.' Emmy hooted.

'Just hope Callum doesn't get wind of it.'

Emmy sighed. 'I know. I just want to wait to tell him until I feel the time is right.'

Tom went to say something and then didn't, and Emmy sat back and let herself get comfy in the front of his car. Tom was now mentioning telling Callum as if they were both acknowledging that this was a thing. It was all getting very serious. She smiled to herself as she thought about how excited she'd been when she was getting ready for the night away. She'd packed pretty underwear, bought a new dress, and was ready for a lovely time. She, Emmy Bardot, was going away for the night with someone who cared about her. As Tom drove down the lane on the way to the ferry, she flicked through the Instagram squares of the hotel. It looked really, really nice and really, really expensive. She couldn't quite believe that someone was treating her to nice things. It was almost as if she'd somehow got it wrong, and it was all going to turn out to be a joke. Something horrible was going to be around the corner.

An hour or so later, they arrived at the hotel, greeted by a beautiful country house drowning in ivy and an old branded wheelbarrow parked just so by the front door. Emmy read from the hotel website as Tom slowly drove the car up the sweeping drive.

Berty's Place hotels are a collection of boutique hotels known for their beautiful rural locations, charming interiors, and exquisite dining experiences. Each place is nestled in a country setting and offers a unique and relaxed atmosphere to take in the simple beauty of England at every turn. Get ready to delve deep down into long walks down narrow lanes, sweet sits by lakes, and take picnics down to the sea. Berty's Place hotels are serious about sustainability, use of local produce, and mostly just promise to deliver you very good food and very good service at every turn.

'Sounds amazing,' Emmy said. 'Looks it, too.'

As Emmy and Tom pulled up, Emmy shook her head over and over again. Lush greenery spilt from gigantic pots against ivy-covered walls by a huge front door at the entrance. Oversized terracotta planters filled with flowers and shrubs were dotted around the small car park, and gravel crunched underneath the tyres.

As they stepped out of the car and gathered the bags, Emmy's eyes widened as she took in the old house. 'Wow. It's stunning!'

Tom smiled, pleased with her reaction. 'Looks good. Hopefully, it's just as nice inside.'

The reception area didn't let down; rustic wooden beams lined the ceiling, and soft, vintage leather armchairs and plush sofas adorned the corners. Huge vases of freshly cut flowers were propped here and there, and an inglenook fireplace sat right in the centre of panelled walls.

A friendly receptionist greeted, 'Hello. Welcome to Berty's. Lovely to have you with us this weekend.'

Emmy gazed around, listening with half an ear as Tom checked in.

'We have you down for a suite in the main house,' the receptionist said. 'It's lovely and quiet over that side.'

'It's so beautiful here.' Emmy swooned.

The receptionist smiled, clearly accustomed to such reactions from first-time guests. 'If there's anything you need during your stay, we'll be happy to help, but you'll hopefully find we've covered everything. If not, give us a bell.'

After completing the check-in process, Tom and Emmy were handed the keys to their room. Walking in, Emmy didn't know where to look first; a large, plush bed adorned with a collection of peacock blue plump pillows, a writing desk by the window, and a clawfoot bathtub in the middle of the bathroom. Piles and piles of soft fluffy towels, copper taps, and old-fashioned heated towel rails. An old fireplace, an overstuffed sofa, candlesticks, and side tables loaded with lamps.

Emmy fell back on the bed, landing in the middle of the pillows. 'I've died and gone to heaven. Thank you! This is so good.'

After a long walk, an even longer, very deep bath, and the best afternoon tea Emmy had probably ever had, she'd put on the nice underwear, the pretty new dress, and heels. She fastened one of her favourite necklaces, with a tiny print of Callum's newborn feet pressed into the gold charm, around her neck and slipped on one of her grandma's rings. Everything about Emmy Bardot felt just right. It had been a long time coming.

On the way down to dinner, Tom took Emmy's hand. 'You look absolutely gorgeous.'

Emmy smiled. 'Thank you.' For once, she actually felt gorgeous. It felt so nice to be dressed up, so nice to be out with someone handsome, so nice to be treated well.

After winding through the old house with her chin on the floor at the decor, she sat down in the lovely old dining room, picked up the menu, read through. and raised her eyebrows. 'This looks incredible. Yeah, I don't think we should have had lunch. How many courses? Is this like a set menu or something?' She grimaced. 'It's going to be really expensive.'

'I didn't expect it to be like this. It's part of the room rate I went for.' Tom nodded in agreement. 'No way we'll get through this after that lunch and the afternoon tea.'

'You'll be carrying me up to bed.' Emmy giggled. 'In fact, you might need to wheel me up.'

'I thought I'd do that anyway. You know, continue as I mean to go on. Seeing as I carried you up the path before,' Tom joked. 'Do you have a habit of needing to be rescued?'

Emmy laughed as she remembered feeling as if her head was going to explode from the sun when Tom carried her from his car to her flat. 'Yeah, quite different circumstances.'

'I'm hoping it doesn't quite end the same way tonight. No cold showers and fans.'

'What were you hoping would happen?' Emmy bantered.

'Nothing at all. All I need is you.'

'Are you sucking up to me, Tom?'

'I am. One hundred per cent.'

Emmy giggled. 'It's working.' She loved the banter between them. She loved even more the anticipation. She'd first realised what it was in the bathroom when she'd been getting ready to go to the Darlings event with Tom. It didn't look as if it was going to cease anytime soon. She wanted to bottle it and keep the feeling forever.

By the time they'd had so much food both of them were stuffed, they moved into the bar where huge Chesterfield sofas were gathered around a fireplace. A couple of women were sitting in the corner with steaming drinks, and a young couple looked lost in chat at one end of the sofas. A waiter approached, Emmy accepted an Amaretto and, a few minutes later, sat sipping on it as Tom chatted. 'This is so nice. What a find. We'll have to come here again.'

'It is.' Emmy leant forward. 'Do you know I haven't stayed in a hotel like this since I had Callum? It feels so good to be away. So good. I can't even tell you.'

'Glad to hear it,' Tom said with a smile.

'You are also good, Tom P.' Emmy giggled, realising that she was going to say the nickname she had for him and stopping herself.

'What?'

'Oh, nothing.'

'You were saying how good I am. Yes, feel free to continue on that topic,' Tom joked.

'So good. Do you know what?'

'What?'

'Come to think about it. I have actually never done *anything* like this.'

'Like what?'

'Like get taken off to the country for, a well, a, you know, a weekend of fun.'

'Is that what this is? I'm pleased you've filled me in on that.'

'Yup.' Emmy laughed.

Tom raised his eyebrows and nodded. 'I'm so glad I bumped into you in the street that day.'

Emmy hiccupped and collapsed laughing, 'Ditto. I didn't think that at the time, though. I was cursing you. You nearly ruined a sixteenth birthday party.'

'True.'

'But you bumping into me more or less changed the trajectory of my life. Wow. That's huge when you think about it like that.'

'Depends which way you spin it.'

'I like that way,' Emmy said. 'If I hadn't bumped into you, I'd be still in the cottage without the shop and, well, yes, all the rest of it, too.'

'Here's to lots more weekends like this,' Tom said, raising his glass.

Emmy basked in the moment, the company, and herself. Especially herself. And oh how she adored feeling so special. 'Oh yes, Tom. I will definitely drink to that. Give me all the weekends with you at all the country house hotels.'

35

Emmy spread hummus onto each of the six sourdough rolls in front of her, added grated cheddar in huge mounds, a thick layer of avocado, slices of tomato, and ground pepper and salt over the top. Wrapping them in greaseproof paper, she tucked them into a cool bag along with boiled eggs, crisps, a large tub of tuna and pasta salad, which was her dad Bob's favourite, and a homemade apple pie.

She called out to the sitting room. 'Okay, Cal, your pack-up is done. I'm putting it in the top of the fridge. Don't forget it when you leave.'

Callum managed to heave himself up and drag himself away from the PlayStation. 'Thanks, Mum.'

'Grandpa is on his way to the ferry, so you need to get going soon.'

'Yeah, he just messaged me.'

'Do you want me to take you down to the ferry?'

'No. Don't worry. I'll get the tram. Thanks.'

'Make sure you text me later,' Emmy instructed.

'I'm only watching snooker with Grandpa.'

'I don't care what you're doing. You always need to message me so that I know you're okay.'

Callum nodded and huffed a little bit. 'Where is Grandma again?'

'In Cornwall with her golf ladies.'

'Oh yeah.'

'Hence, why I've done that packed lunch for you two to take fishing in the morning. I did tell you all this.'

'Yeah, sorry. I forgot she was going away. Thanks for doing that. You didn't have to. Grandpa and I could have made sandwiches.'

Emmy didn't say anything. She'd known full well that without Cherry in situ, the likelihood of Callum and Bob arriving at fishing with nothing more than a packet of crisps was very high, so she'd packed them a bag of stuff. She was more than grateful for the way her mum and dad had always been involved with looking after Callum; the least she could do was prepare a bag full of food. 'All good.'

'What are you doing?' Callum asked.

Emmy had told Callum at least three times she was going to the Chamber of Commerce Summer Picnic, but it seemed to go in one ear and out the other. 'The picnic.'

'Oh, yeah. Where was that again?'

Emmy had also told Callum the picnic's location repeatedly. 'Over in the gardens of Darlington House.'

'Nice. Are you going with Tom?'

Emmy swallowed. She'd also told Callum this but ever so casually. Callum's direct question made her feel quite uneasy. Callum still didn't know the full score. 'I'm meeting him there. He's been to the city.'

'Oh yeah, you said.'

'I'm going to start running the bath, so you'd better get going. Don't even think about putting that PlayStation back on,'

Emmy said and leaned up to kiss Callum. 'Text me when you get to the other side and you're with Grandpa.'

'Will do.'

Emmy had heard from Callum, had a long soak in the bath, and was ready for the Chamber of Commerce Summer Picnic. Ever since she'd received the email that she'd not only been accepted as a member but invited to one of its most prestigious events, it had been on her mind. She'd thought about what she was going to wear, what it would be like to be going with Tom, and once she'd realised that Callum was going to stay with her dad overnight because Cherry was away, where she would end up afterwards.

She looked in the mirror just before she made her way out. The dress was en pointe along with her jewellery; a silky floral dress with bell sleeves and a necklace from one of her suppliers with hundreds of tiny gold love hearts all the way around. She'd scooped her hair up into a soft updo, and her espadrilles wore a huge satin bow at the ankle. Even though she might be blowing her own trumpet, Emmy Bardot was looking good. After checking the windows were shut, she sent a text to her dad to make sure everything was okay, popped the requisite picnic rug as per the instructions on the email under her arm, picked up her basket with a chilled bottle of champagne in it, and locked the front door.

After hopping on the tram, Emmy checked her phone, where a message from Tom told her he was running late because of traffic. She sat on the timber seats staring out the window as Darling passed by. The little place was beginning to really feel like home, the landmarks now starting to feel familiar; the old church, the strip of shops with the butchers, the pretty café covered in wisteria. As the tram took a different line away from the line to the sea and towards the other side of the island, she was lost in a world of her own, not really a care in the world.

About fifteen minutes later, she'd just disembarked and was half wishing that she'd stayed at home and waited for Tom as couples, families, and people in little groups ambled along on their way to the gardens. She checked her phone again for a message, and just as she was popping it back in her bag, she bumped into Lucie, George, Leo, and Shelly from the tram.

'Evening. How are ya?' Leo, burnished biceps intact, asked.

'Good, thanks. How are you?'

'Right up there with fantastic at the moment,' Leo replied.

Shelly smiled. 'Hi, Emmy. I hear you've been initiated into the Chamber.'

'I have indeed.'

'Half your luck.' Leo laughed. 'I'm not in it, but I get a side door to events because I have friends in high places on this island. It's all about who you know.'

Emmy smiled. 'I'm beginning to realise that.'

'Tom's been stuck in traffic, right?' Leo stated. 'He messaged the group WhatsApp.'

Emmy loved how it was a given that she was with Tom. It seemed it wasn't only Amy who was taking their relationship as a thing. She didn't miss a beat. 'Yes. He's going to whizz home for a shower and see us here.'

Shelly opened a lid on a wicker basket and pulled out a bottle. 'Pre-picnic tipple, anyone?'

'Ooh, what are you travelling with?'

'Mr Cooke's homemade special.'

Lucie smiled. 'Gosh, last time I had that, I was under the table.'

'Yep,' Shelly said as she dished little bottles out. She widened her eyes as she passed one over to Emmy. 'You only get one if you promise me you eat and don't sit in the sun. We don't want anyone having to be rescued and carried up the garden path.'

Emmy giggled. 'I'll be careful.'

Emmy fell into step beside Shelly and they chatted about the trams and the shop. 'How are the renovations going?'

'Well. I've taken delivery of a few things and I've got the ball rolling on the sign and the flower installation. It seems to have moved a bit faster now I've been accepted into the Chamber. Overall though, I've decided to just take it one step at a time. It was a lot to take on and I was trying to run before I could walk.'

'That would make sense. I can't wait to see the flower installation. Just the spot for it there.'

'What I hadn't expected was my website sales growing,' Emmy added. 'I got a mention on a TikTok video which was a bit bizarre and it's been coming in thick and fast from there.'

'Wow. Sounds good.'

'I'm not complaining.'

Shelly took a sip from the bottle. 'What about you and your neighbour? How's that going?'

Emmy didn't know what to say. She was still half pretending that she was playing it by ear. She so wasn't. 'Yeah, it's good.'

'Bit of an item, you two now? It's been a while.' Shelly lilted her sentence into a question.

Emmy shook her head quickly left and right. 'Sort of.'

Shelly cackled. 'Sorry, I'm a right old sticky beak, aren't I?'

'No, no, it's fine.'

'It's just that it's good to see it, if you ask me.'

'Good to see it?'

'Yeah, Tom. With you.'

'Right. Thanks'

Shelly lowered her voice. 'All that rigmarole with that Sarah.' Shelly turned her face into a downward smile and then wrinkled her nose. 'Never liked her myself. Never. You know when you just know about someone? Yeah, dodgy as. I wasn't surprised in the slightest when her supposed job overseas turned out to be something else. Nasty bit of work. You live and learn.'

'Oh, okay.'

'And wasn't I right? Oh yes, I was,' Shelly said, seemingly very pleased with herself.

'Hmm,' Emmy said, nodding, not wanting to say too much but loving the information.

'Nice if you're on the right side of him,' Shelly noted. 'As long as you don't park in his lane.'

Emmy giggled. 'He is nice.'

'Nice and, from what I've seen, smitten – you lucky duck.'

Emmy wanted to hug both herself and Shelly. She also wanted to remind Shelly that Tom was the lucky one. She couldn't be bothered. 'Thanks, Shelly.'

Just as they were getting closer to the gardens, a deep trumpet-like blast sounded. Shelly nodded, 'Yeah, I knew it was coming. We're going to be in for a foggy one tonight.'

'At least there's no rain forecast.'

'Nope. Not a drop is on the cards,' Shelly said as she looked up at the sky. 'But we'll be walking home in the fog by the looks of it.'

As they got closer to the gardens, Emmy raised her eyebrows as they approached the house. The instructions for the event had said to bring a picnic rug and drinks. Emmy had packed a bottle of champagne into a picnic basket and a rug under her arm. The email hadn't said that the house and gardens would be gorgeous. Flickering gold lights covered the whole of the house. All the way down sloping grass verges, groups were settled with picnic baskets. Dome-shaped canvas tents drowning in the blue and white Darling bunting were perched here and there. In a bandstand just to the right of the house, a band was playing music.

Leo squinted down at his phone. 'Coastguard's section.'

Shelly nodded. 'Yep. Over on the right there.'

Emmy had seen the same on her ticket but hadn't thought much of it. She realised that it was probably similar to the parking zones. 'Oh. I thought I would be in Ticket Office.' She held out her phone to Shelly and Leo.

Shelly shook her head. 'No, not for this. You're with Tom.'

Emmy raised her eyebrows not really sure how that explained it. As far as she knew, both her and Tom's permits on their cars were in the Ticket Office zone. 'Right.'

Leo nudged her. 'Yeah, nah, I don't get it either. A quick tip from me: don't even think about trying to work it out.'

Emmy chuckled. 'I'm getting used to Darling's ways.'

'Trust me, there are many more things for you to discover,' Shelly joked.

'Like the Darling sausage,' Leo added. 'Have you had one yet?'

'I have.'

'As long as you know that whatever you do, you don't ask for the recipe.'

'I've been warned. Who makes them?'

'DJ Meats on Darling Street there. Secret recipe from years and years ago. It's tightly held like the property on this island.' Leo laughed at his own joke.

After going through the gate and wandering through picnic blankets, they found their way to the correct section where stripy blue and white director's chairs were gathered in a semi-circle around a large patch of grass where a few people were already sitting. A fairy light-lit beer tent sat just off to the right, and the sound from the bandstand trickled over the evening air.

Nearly an hour later, Emmy had enjoyed a few drinks and cheese boards had made an appearance. She was thoroughly enjoying herself as she sat there chatting away without a care in the world. Just as she was beginning to wonder about Tom, she saw him picking his way through the people. He waved at her and smiled. Once he was in the zone, he kissed her on the cheek, shook hands with Leo and George, and sat down.

'Sorry I'm so late. I really underestimated that journey. Have you been okay?'

'Yep. I've been fine.'

'You look beautiful.'

Emmy was getting used to Tom's compliments. She loved how Tom made her feel. Inside she was swooning. 'Thank you.'

Tom looked around as Emmy passed him a drink. 'This never disappoints. The fog is rolling in, though.'

'Yeah, we heard the foghorn go off as we got here.'

'It's going to be thick tonight.'

'Sort of romantic, really.'

The evening had got lovelier as it had gone on, and Emmy moved from the director's chairs to the blanket and back again with all sorts of drinks and all sorts of foods. A light show mesmerised the front of the house as it slowly became topped by a layer of fog, and the bandstand music tinkled away into the thick night air.

With Tom's hand on her arm, Emmy gazed down at the house and almost purred in pleasure – she was having that nice a time. All of a sudden and taking her completely unawares, she felt quite overcome with emotion as she took in everything around her. Since the day when Tom had helped her with the gate, she felt as if she'd been on a journey. In that journey, she'd been carried up paths, wined and dined, brought breakfast in bed, treated in hotels, and been to lovely evenings in Darlings. It was as if Tom had charged into her life and she'd not quite looked up for air. She took in a long delicious breath and savoured the moment. It was nothing short of amazing.

As the music played, her mind zoomed through the years

from when she'd first had Callum. She remembered cradling him in her arms, a tiny bundle of the sweetest things. She remembered how she'd tumbled head over heels in love with Callum, and here she was in the most different of circumstances feeling a similar thing now. She laced her fingers over and over again with the weight of Tom's hand on her arm. She couldn't get her head around the fact that just as Amy had said about the look on her face when she'd had Callum, she'd gone and fallen in love. Most unexpectedly, most deliciously.

She thought about bumping into Tom all those months before and the squashed cake. Had the whole thing been meant to be? Was there someone up there twiddling the knobs on her life? Had that person thought that perhaps it was time for Emmy's life to take a good turn? No more looking around corners waiting for things to go wrong. She realised that since the gambling that had walked into her life by way of Kevin, she'd been scared to do anything in life. But here she was no longer frightened. Somehow, strangely, weirdly, oddly, with Tom, she felt something she'd never felt before. Not just love or romantic notions or rose-tinted glasses or diving from diving boards. As she sat in the Darling air, she realised precisely what had happened since she'd moved to Darling Island. Emmy Bardot felt two glorious, wonderful things; happy and safe.

36

The next day, Emmy had woken up a few doors down from her flat. She looked over to the other side of the bed to see crumpled sheets and the curtains blowing in the breeze. She could hear a tram stopping outside and the twittering of morning birds. She sighed about the night before. Wrapped in Tom's jacket, they'd strolled home slowly through the fog. After checking with her dad and Callum, she'd walked along the lane with Tom, totally bypassing The Old Ticket Office and going through the gate a few doors down to his. They'd sat in the garden drinking hot chocolate and chatting long into the night.

Padding down the stairs, she found Tom sitting on the sofa. He jumped up and went to pour her a cup of tea. As she sat down, her phone pinged from Amy.

Amy: *How was the picnic?*

Emmy: *Good. I'm at Tom's.*

Amy: *Ooh. I take it the night went well then?????*

Emmy: *Yep. I had a really wonderful time.*

Amy: *I'm so happy for you Ems. xxx*

Emmy: *Thx.*

Amy: *Did Dad message you?*

Emmy: *Yeah, they've gone fishing.*

Amy: *Yep, they popped in on the way there.*

Emmy: *Did they remember the pack-up?*

Amy: *Yes. Look, I think you're going to have to tell Callum. I feel awkward.*

Emmy: *Yeah, I realised that last night.*

Amy: *Good, that's settled then. So, this is really official now. Exciting.*

Emmy: *Yes, it really is xxx*

Amy: *Love you, Ems. Soooooooo happy about all this.*

Emmy: *Thx. Love you more xxxxxxxxxxxxx*

Tom passed her a mug of tea. 'Who are you texting?'

'Just my sister.'

'We need to meet properly.'

'You do.'

'I've already met your mum and dad,' Tom joked, referring to the morning when he'd poked his head in the gate when Emmy had just moved in.

'I think you'll need to raise your game,' Emmy fired back. 'You were quite short then.'

'So, I *am* getting to meet them properly then?'

'I'll consider it,' Emmy said as she sipped her tea and threw in the word Tom had used in his text to her that had riled her so much. 'Maybe.'

Tom burst out laughing. 'And what about Callum?'

'What about Callum?'

Tom scrunched his face up. 'Look, it's not my place, but well...' He stopped mid-sentence and paused for a second. 'It's all getting...'

Emmy nodded, not sure where the conversation was going. She went a bit cold. Was the messing-up bit on the way? What was Tom going to say? She felt as if she was peeking around another of the corners of her life where things went wrong. He was going to say that it was all getting too serious. *Here we go again.* Just blame Kevin.

Just as she'd been starting to feel good about things too. Just a few hours before, she'd felt happy, content. She'd even dared to think she was safe. Silly, silly, silly. Now she felt the opposite, as if she wasn't just peeking around a corner but she'd tumbled towards it and banged into the side. Boom. She gripped the handle of the mug so hard her knuckles imprinted into the side. She heard Tom continue to speak but had no idea what he was saying as her mind swirled, and it felt as if the sofa had fallen away underneath her. She felt a poke in her arm. 'Emmy?'

Emmy blinked and released the grip on the mug handle. 'Sorry.'

'Emmy? Are you okay?'

'I'm fine.'

'As I was saying.'

'Sorry.' Emmy squeezed her eyes shut and shook her head in tiny movements trying to get rid of the spinning in her head. 'I didn't hear you. Away with the fairies for a second,' she said, trying to make light of it.

Tom put his hand on her leg and inched further along the sofa. 'It's all getting quite serious and going fast between us.'

Emmy wanted to slap Tom as the safety fell away. She couldn't even speak. Barely able to nod.

'And...' Tom screwed his face up. 'I'm thinking that if I love you, I don't want to be sneaking around left, right, and centre. It doesn't really seem right. I know you've got to be careful with Callum and everything. I knew what I was getting into from the start.'

Emmy closed her eyes again. 'What?' She couldn't really work out what Tom had just said. 'Sorry?'

'Emmy. I love you.'

Bang.

'Oh, right, okay. Right. Sorry. Do you?' Emmy's voice was incredulous. She repeated, 'Do you? Really?'

Tom laughed. 'I take it you weren't expecting that.' He swore.

Emmy didn't know what to think. She blinked over and over again. 'Err.'

'I was going to say that because of what's happened and because I love you, well, I thought that it really is time to tell Callum. But as I said, it's not my place. I know he's your first priority.'

Emmy just stared at Tom's mouth.

'Emmy? What are you thinking?' Tom swore again. 'I've totally messed this up. I thought you…'

Emmy shook her head and squinted. 'Sorry. You love me?'

Tom nodded. 'I do.'

At the same time as Emmy's face broke into a beaming smile, a tear pricked at the corner of her right eye. 'I guess we'd better tell Cal then because I feel the same way too.'

'Maybe or totally?' Tom joked as he put his arm around her.

Emmy nodded. 'Totally. One hundred per cent.'

Order the next part in Emmy's story at Amazon.

Secrets at The Old Ticket Office Darling Island

Emmy Bardot is going rather well. She's feeling all the Darling Island feels and doing all the things. Life really is quite good. As she settles down into The Old Ticket Office with her son Callum, she begins to thrive; in the pace of island life, in her small business and in her new relationship. Moving to Darling Island was one of her better ideas, and as Darling works its magic, she is absolutely loving her new start in so many parts of her existence.

Life, though, decides it might like to throw a little curveball Emmy's way just to, you know, spice things up a bit. When one day on a train Emmy sees something she wasn't expecting, her world is tipped upside down. When it lands back on the ground lets just say it's not that pretty...

As Emmy navigates what in the world she is going to do, we watch on from the sidelines and wonder what secrets she is going to keep.

The second book in romance author Polly Babbington's Old Ticket Office contemporary romance trilogy. Get ready to swoon as you fall deep down into Polly's world and Darling Island speaks to your soul. You will utterly love it.

SECRETS AT THE OLD TICKET OFFICE DARLING ISLAND

READ MORE BY POLLY BABBINGTON

(Reading Order available at PollyBabbington.com)

The Old Ticket Office Darling Island
  Secrets at The Old Ticket Office Darling Island

Spring in the Pretty Beach Hills
  Summer in the Pretty Beach Hills

The Pretty Beach Thing
  The Pretty Beach Way
  The Pretty Beach Life

Something About Darling Island
  Just About Darling Island
  All About Christmas on Darling Island

The Coastguard's House Darling Island
  Summer on Darling Island
  Bliss on Darling Island

READ MORE BY POLLY BABBINGTON

The Boat House Pretty Beach
- Summer Weddings at Pretty Beach
- Winter at Pretty Beach

A Pretty Beach Christmas
- A Pretty Beach Dream
- A Pretty Beach Wish

Secret Evenings in Pretty Beach
- Secret Places in Pretty Beach
- Secret Days in Pretty Beach

Lovely Little Things in Pretty Beach
- Beautiful Little Things in Pretty Beach
- Darling Little Things

The Old Sugar Wharf Pretty Beach
- Love at the Old Sugar Wharf Pretty Beach
- Snow Days at the Old Sugar Wharf Pretty Beach

Pretty Beach Posies
- Pretty Beach Blooms
- Pretty Beach Petals

OH SO POLLY

Words, quilts, tea and old houses...

My words began many moons ago in a corner of England, in a tiny bedroom in an even tinier little house. There was a very distinct lack of scribbling, but rather beautifully formed writing and many, many lists recorded in pretty fabric-covered note-books stacked up under a bed.

A few years went by, babies were born, university joined, white dresses worn, a lovely fluffy little dog, tears rolled down cheeks, house moves were made, big fat smiles up to ears, a trillion cups of tea, a decanter or six full of pink gin, many a long walk. All those little things called life neatly logged in those beautiful little books tucked up neatly under the bed.

And then, as the babies toddled off to school, as if by magic, along came an opportunity and the little stories flew out of the books, found themselves a home online, where they've been growing sweetly ever since.

I write all my books from start to finish tucked up in our lovely old Edwardian house by the sea. Surrounded by pretty bits and bobs, whimsical fabrics, umpteen stacks of books, a plethora of lovely old things, gingham linen, great big fat white sofas, and a big old helping of nostalgia. There I spend my days spinning stories and drinking rather a lot of tea.

From the days of the floral notebooks, and an old cottage locked away from my small children in a minuscule study logging onto the world wide web, I've now moved house and those stories have evolved and also found a new home.

There is now an itty-bitty team of gorgeous gals who help me with my graphics and editing. They scheme and plan from their laptops, in far-flung corners of the land, to get those words from those notebooks onto the page, creating the magic of a Polly Bee book.

I really hope you enjoy getting lost in my world.

Love

Polly x

AUTHOR

Polly Babbington

In a little white Summer House at the back of the garden, under the shade of a huge old tree, Polly Babbington creates romantic feel-good stories, including The PRETTY BEACH series.

Polly went to college in the Garden of England and her writing career began by creating articles for magazines and publishing books online.

Polly loves to read in the cool of lazing in a hammock under an old fruit tree on a summertime morning or cosying up in the winter under a quilt by the fire.

She lives in delightful countryside near the sea, in a sweet little village complete with a gorgeous old cricket pitch, village green with a few lovely old pubs and writes cosy romance books about women whose life you sometimes wished was yours.

Follow Polly on Instagram, Facebook and TikTok @PollyBabbingtonWrites

PollyBabbington.com

Want more on Polly's world? Subscribe to Babbington Letters